Wild
HEART

The Hearts of Sawyers Bend
Book Six

IVY LAYNE

GINGER QUILL PRESS, LLC

Wild Heart

Copyright © 2024 by Ivy Layne

All rights reserved.

No part of this book may be reproduced in any form or by any electronic or mechanical means, including information storage and retrieval systems, without permission in writing from the author. The only exception is a reviewer, who may quote short excerpts in a review.

This book is a work of fiction. Names, characters, places, and incidents either are products of the author's imagination or are used fictitiously. Any resemblance to actual persons, living or dead, events, or locales is entirely coincidental.

Editing by:
Samamntha Skal, samanthaskal.com
Julia Ganis, juliaedits.com
Olivia Zugay, blacksheepdigitalva.com

Find out more about the author and upcoming books online at www.ivylayne.com

Also by Ivy Layne

Don't Miss Out on New Releases, Exclusive Giveaways, and More!!

Join Ivy's Readers Group @ ivylayne.com/readers

THE HEARTS OF SAWYERS BEND

Stolen Heart

Sweet Heart

Scheming Heart

Rebel Heart

Wicked Heart

Wild Heart

Broken Heart

THE UNTANGLED SERIES

Unraveled

Undone

Uncovered

THE WINTERS SAGA

The Billionaire's Secret Heart (Novella)

The Billionaire's Secret Love (Novella)

The Billionaire's Pet

The Billionaire's Promise

The Rebel Billionaire

The Billionaire's Secret Kiss (Novella)

The Billionaire's Angel

Engaging the Billionaire

Compromising the Billionaire

The Counterfeit Billionaire

THE BILLIONAIRE CLUB

The Wedding Rescue

The Courtship Maneuver

The Temptation Trap

Chapter One
HAWK

Standing in the doorway of the gatehouse, my home on the estate, I drank my coffee, watching the mist curl around the Manor, rays of weak late winter sun gilding the roof. Heartstone Manor was three stories of warm, gray granite, designed a century ago to mimic the English country estate William Sawyer's bride had left behind.

Dawn was my favorite time at Heartstone Manor. Winter or summer, the mornings were misty, the damp air clinging to the edges of the great stone house, the sun barely cresting the vast forest surrounding the Sawyer estate.

At times like this, Heartstone Manor didn't feel like a real place. More like a movie set, where I wasn't an actor, but an extra, watching the beautiful people live their lives. In the back of my mind, I expected a voice to yell *Cut* and a crew to melt out of the scenery. The guy who'd been holding the roses at the perfect angle to catch the light. The set dresser who'd arranged the ivy draped over the windowsill just so.

It never happened. As hard as it was to believe, Heartstone Manor was a real place with real people living inside. It was a home, its inhabitants mostly normal human beings, living mostly normal lives.

Maybe that was why it looked so much like a movie set—it was a place out of time, on the wrong continent. Now, the day barely begun, the sight of it should have filled me with peace.

Kind of. There *was* all that murder and mayhem. The reason I was here in the first place. Knowing everything that had happened there over the past year, the tranquil image didn't fool me. There was danger everywhere, and it was my job to keep it at bay.

Finishing my last drop of coffee, I left the mug on the gatehouse steps and headed out, planning to loop around to the woods on the east side of the Manor, then past the cottage, crossing behind the pool house and formal gardens to the west side of the Manor and the forest there.

A year ago, Prentice Sawyer, the billionaire patriarch of the Sawyer family, had been found sitting at his desk, a bullet hole in his forehead. His son, Ford, the presumed heir to the Sawyer fortune, pled guilty to Prentice's murder. No one had seen that coming.

In a second twist, Prentice's will left everything to Griffen, the son he'd exiled fifteen years before, and the man I considered my brother in every way but blood. Unfortunately for Griffen, the *everything* Prentice had left him included the target on his father's back. Griffen hadn't been home long before someone tried to kill him, too.

Griffen and I had met during our first days in the army and been together through Ranger school, then later at Sinclair Security, where we joined another of our Ranger buddies in the private sector. When Prentice's will forced Griffen back to the home he hated, with an unknown killer gunning for him, I'd been there.

I owed Griffen. While he'd stayed in the Rangers, I'd accepted an invitation to join a team that operated outside the normal boundaries. Off the books. In the dark. I'd been reeling from the loss of my parents in a freak accident, and a change of scenery felt like the only way to shake off my grief. How wrong I'd been.

I should have stayed with the Rangers, with Griffen and Evers Sinclair and work I was good at. I should have stayed in the light. Instead, I'd jumped ship for my new team and sank straight to dark depths I'd never imagined. Before that, I thought I had understood right and wrong, good and evil. I hadn't understood how loyalty and lies could twist the world until up was down, and I was pulling the trigger on the innocent as easily as on the guilty.

By the time I dragged myself out of the dark, I was only half human. I knew I could never do enough good to atone for the crimes I committed under orders I should have questioned. I showed up one night on Evers Sinclair's doorstep, and he let me in. Evers and his brothers gave me a job. Griffen gave me a place to live. They gave me time to find myself again. Without them, I would have slipped into the darkness completely. I owed them everything.

No one wanted Griffen to leave Sinclair Security for the wilds of western North Carolina. But even without the threat of murder, I would have come to Sawyers Bend. Griffen needed family at his back. Not the family that had exiled him all those years ago. His real family. His chosen family.

Putting a guy like me in charge of security was a little like bringing a rocket launcher to a knife fight, but I didn't mind. I slept better here, surrounded by thousands of acres of forest. And I wasn't going to let anyone touch Griffen or his family. Sometimes you needed the dark to protect the light.

I always ended my rounds on the west side. Ever since I'd discovered her sleeping under the trees instead of safe inside the Manor. Late last night, I'd watched her as she'd snuck out again, stealing across the lawn in silence and disappearing into the dark woods. I'd bet she was still there, sleeping peacefully, under the illusion of a safety that didn't exist.

I shouldn't care. It was her life. Not my problem. I'd reported the situation to Griffen, and he'd told me to let her be. That should be enough.

But I found I couldn't drop it. Couldn't let it be.

It was March, for fuck's sake. Too cold to sleep outside when she had a perfectly good bedroom in the Manor. I told myself for the millionth time that it wasn't my problem.

I told myself that a lot where she was concerned. *Not my problem*. And she wasn't.

I was going to check on her anyway. I couldn't seem to help myself. Not when it came to her.

I headed to the woods on the east side of the Manor at a slow jog. As I found my rhythm, I texted the team watching the cameras from our base in the lower level of the Manor.

> Anything to report?

> No, boss. Quiet night.

> Doing my rounds. I'll stop by after.

Everything was quiet in the east side woods, the cameras and the perimeter system operating perfectly. As we did every day, I signaled in front of each camera, receiving an acknowledgment from the team at our base. Finished with the cameras, I moved into position and texted my team again.

> Triggering zone one

I deliberately stepped through the almost invisible laser that created the first zone of the perimeter alarm.

> Trigger received

I wasn't expecting anything else. We had the woods wired every way we could. No one was getting anywhere near the Manor if I could help it. We'd had more than enough trouble with people who were allowed on the property. I didn't need anyone sneaking up on us.

Between me, my team, and Griffen, we'd reverse-engineered every approach to the Manor. We had a strategy established for every conceivable scenario. Considering our combined backgrounds, that was a lot of scenarios. So far, no one had gotten in. Not since the beginning and that first attempt on Griffen.

We'd still had plenty of trouble. After we added the cameras and perimeter alarm, whoever was after the Sawyers shifted their attention to the Inn at Sawyers Bend. Sabotage. A knife attack meant for Griffen's brother Royal. Then another murder: Vanessa, the fiancée Ford had stolen from Griffen, then married and divorced. She'd sworn she knew who Prentice's real killer was. Maybe she had, but we'd never know. Whoever was behind all of this had gotten to Vanessa first.

Garden-variety theft had interrupted our string of murder and attempted murder: a cousin who thought room and board entitled him to walk off with Sawyer heirlooms. After we took care of the stealing, we swung back to murder, this time courtesy of Parker Sawyer's now-deceased husband, convinced he could win back his mother's love if he murdered Parker. Crazy bastard. Shooting him hadn't been a hardship, especially after he almost killed Parker, her sister, and one of my best guys.

The last real excitement we'd had was when Savannah's estranged mother-in-law had tried to kidnap her son, Nicky, just before Christmas. Savannah was the housekeeper of Heartstone Manor and practically kept the place running single-handedly. After a chase across half the state, her mother-in-law was in court-mandated psychiatric treatment, and Nicky was doing fine. I'd thought we might have an issue when Griffen got the headmaster of Nicky's school fired for letting Nicky get kidnapped, but he'd left the state without causing any more trouble. Things had been quiet since.

Finished with the east side of the Manor, I followed the edge of the forest, skirting the back of Savannah's cottage. The front door opened, and Finn Sawyer stepped out, stopping to lock the deadbolt behind him before heading to the Manor to start breakfast. He was running late.

Finn had taken me by surprise. At first, I thought he was using Savannah. In my world, staff and family didn't mix. You never fuck the client. Griffen was the closest thing I had to a brother, but that didn't make me a Sawyer. And Savannah might have grown up in Heartstone Manor, but that didn't make Savannah a Sawyer either. No, Finn had done that when he'd married her on Valentine's Day, just over a month ago, and the look on his face as she walked down the aisle finally convinced me he loved her.

Finn disappeared into the side door of the Manor. I circled around behind the pool house and the barren gardens to check the cameras and perimeter alarm on the south side of the Manor. Everything was functioning normally.

It made my skin itchy. We hadn't had a stretch of quiet this long since I'd been here. Three months since Nicky had been kidnapped, and other than two weddings, life had been calm.

Okay, not exactly calm. We'd gotten word that Ford had survived an assassination attempt in prison. But that could just be Ford pissing people off. I'd gotten the impression that while he was better liked than Prentice had been, he wasn't everyone's favorite Sawyer. Ford's lawyer was convinced his siblings poking into Prentice's murder had made Ford a target. Maybe. Either way, I was convinced that whatever was causing trouble for Ford would spill over onto the rest of his family. If not today, then eventually.

I wouldn't—couldn't—let the quiet make me soft. If I'd learned anything in my former career, it was patience. How to stay sharp through hours, days, and months of monotony. Never lose your edge. Never let the boredom blur your focus. That was how people got killed. I'd lost enough. I wasn't going to lose anyone else.

The west side of the Manor was as quiet as the rest, the woods as still as they ever were. I went through the routine with the cameras and perimeter alarm. All operating as usual.

I didn't see her on my rounds. She knew where the cameras were. I didn't like that she'd chosen to build her nest where we couldn't see her. Couldn't keep her safe. The whole thing made me a little crazy.

It shouldn't. Quinn Sawyer was part of the job. A client. She was nothing to me. In the year since we'd met, we'd had fewer than a handful of conversations. She was Griffen's sister. Another reason I owed her my best.

My best was ice cold. Detached. Clinical.

Not annoyed, frustrated, and ready to bite her head off.

I'd seen her the night before. I'd been walking the perimeter, as I did on the nights my dreams chased away sleep. Quinn had crept out the side door of the Manor not long after eleven, a backpack slung over her shoulder. I didn't know why she snuck out to sleep in the woods. It was a bizarre thing to do, especially for an heiress with a castle to sleep in. But she did it, almost every night, regardless of the weather.

The first time I saw her gliding across the dark grass, lit only by the moon, I hadn't stopped her. I'd followed.

She'd disappeared into the trees at the edge of the woods, and I'd almost lost her. She was alert, her head turning at the slightest sound, as surefooted as if it was full daylight. I had to be careful and quiet, two things I was very good at. Still, I almost missed her hiding spot.

I'd watched from the cover of a rhododendron bush as Quinn pulled a camping hammock from her backpack. She gave it a brisk shake before hooking it between two straps already secured to the trees. An insulated under-quilt came next, followed by a sleeping bag that looked like it was rated for subzero temperatures and a rainfly to keep her dry from the damp that would come in the night.

She had the whole thing set up in less than three minutes. She climbed in. I heard the whirr of the zipper on her sleeping bag, the rustle of fabric as she got comfortable, and that was it. Snug as a bug in a rug, as my mom used to say.

I'd been mystified. I still was. We'd never spoken about it. I hadn't spoken to Quinn about much of anything. She was family. I was security. The distinction was important with everyone but Griffen. My job was to keep them safe, not be friends with them, but Quinn was something different.

Quinn was—

I didn't know. All these months later, I was still trying to figure out what it was about Quinn Sawyer.

She didn't sleep in the woods every night, but she was there more than she wasn't. In the coldest bite of winter. In the heat of August. Didn't matter. On the nights when I couldn't sleep, I walked the grounds and checked on Quinn. There had been times, too many of them, when I'd sat at the base of a nearby oak and dozed, my ear cocked for anything that might come too close to the sleeping Quinn.

Nothing ever did. The animals moved past her as if she was neither threat nor prey. To them, she was a part of the forest. I'd seen deer cropping at the undergrowth feet away from her hammock. Fox playing in the clearing. She was like Snow White without the creepy dwarves. I understood the woods and loved the wild. It was part of why I'd been so willing to come here. But I knew the wild wasn't forgiving. And Quinn was defenseless.

So, I kept watch.

My feet brought me toward her clearing, a path I knew better than any other on the estate. It was early, the sun barely cresting the mountains. This time of year, Quinn's guide business was mostly closed down. She wouldn't be up with the dawn, preparing to guide kayakers down the river or hikers into the mountains. Like the wild creature she was, she'd be curled in her nest, fast asleep.

It was a few minutes' walk before I saw the dark arc

of her hammock against the slowly growing light. No rainfly. Mist wound around the base of the trees.

It was quiet. Too quiet.

I froze and watched. Another shape resolved, moving behind her hammock, a dark blur in the foggy trees.

My hand went to the weapon at my hip as I crouched and moved faster, closing the distance between me and the sleeping Quinn. The shape in the woods moved at a steady pace, splitting into three shapes, one hulking, the other two far smaller, all three dark blobs in the trees.

Goddamned mist. As pretty as it was, it fucked my visibility. I was too close to call the base and see if they had anything on the cameras. Man or beast, it would hear me at this range.

I reached the hammock. Risking a second to glance inside, I caught the barest glimpse of dark hair, the curve of a pale cheek, the rest hidden by the sleeping bag. Still asleep. Good. I didn't have time for explanations.

The dark shapes in the trees drew steadily closer. Moving in front of the hammock, I raised my weapon as they came into focus. A sow and two cubs. Black bears. The female was large for her breed. I'd guess close to two hundred pounds. The cubs were tiny in comparison, which made mama bear very, very dangerous.

In mid-March, this might be the cubs' first foray outside their den. I'd seen bears in these mountains before. Everyone who lived here spotted a bear eventually, and I spent a lot of time in the woods. The black bears here weren't aggressive. If you gave them space, they'd give it back as long as you were smart about food and didn't get close to a mama with her newborn cubs.

I'd just broken rule number two.

Fuck. I'd never seen a bear so close to Quinn's hiding place. And this one kept coming. Ambling, not charging, but way too close. Why?

Quinn wouldn't have food. My heart jerked at the thought. Surely, she'd know better. Of course, she did. She ran a guide service, for fuck's sake. The online reviews of her business were glowing. That wouldn't happen if she was getting tourists mauled because she didn't know how to handle living in bear country.

The sow ambled a few feet closer, finally turning her head to study me. I wasn't fooled. Her sharp nose had already picked me up. The cubs passed her, circling around to wander behind me, far too close to Quinn. The sow wagged her head, lurching forward. On instinct, my gun arm came up, aimed at the sow. At this range, I could get a headshot, but I put odds on the bear's thick skull deflecting the bullet. Especially if she charged.

I didn't love the idea of killing a mama bear either, but I would if I had to.

"What the hell are you doing?" a voice behind me hissed. The bear's gaze shifted to my left. I couldn't risk turning and taking my eyes off the sow.

"Be quiet," I hissed back. My gut turned to ice as the sow looked past me at Quinn's hammock. *Fuck.*

I shot a quick look back, my heart thundering in my chest. Quinn was sitting up, her cheeks pink and puffy with sleep, dark silky hair sliding all over the place, her blue eyes bright and alert as they fixed on the mama bear.

"Get fucking down, Quinn."

"No," she murmured. "I don't have anything she

wants." In the quiet morning air, her soft voice was musical. Mesmerizing.

The sow seemed to agree. She watched Quinn, her gaze only straying to check on her cubs rolling in the scrub beneath the hammock.

"I don't have any food, mama. You're just curious, aren't you?" she asked the bear. "Just taking your babies out for a stroll."

"Quinn," I growled. "Shut the fuck up and get down."

"Hawk," she said, the soothing music gone from her voice. "Put that gun away and scare her off. Don't tell me you don't know how to scare off a curious bear."

I let out an annoyed grunt, my gaze moving back to the sow. She was right; I did know how to scare off a bear. I'd done it before when I'd run into a brown bear while fishing in Montana. Sliding my gun back into its holster, I waved my arms to make myself look as big as I could.

"Get out of here! Go! Get the fuck away!" Ignoring my instincts to run, to shoot her, to do anything but get closer, I stepped forward and roared louder. "Get the fuck out of here! Go! Go! Go! Get lost!"

The bear turned, backing up a hesitant step before her eyes shifted to the right. Her cubs had wandered to the far side of the hammock, no longer cut off from their mother. With an ursine shrug, the sow ambled away, collecting her cubs and disappearing slowly into what remained of dawn's mist.

"Were you going to shoot her in the eye with that thing?" Quinn asked, sounding amused and not the least bit scared. "Is your aim that good?"

"Yes," I grunted, too annoyed to bother lying. At that range, I could have shot her in the eye. Unless she'd charged.

Quinn sat cross-legged in her hammock, her long underwear rumpled, her eyes sparkling.

"Why aren't you scared?" I demanded, my gut still churning at how close she'd come to being a bear snack.

Quinn shrugged. "She didn't want to hurt me. She was just out for a morning walk with her cubs."

"Quinn, there was a fucking oversized sow less than ten feet from you. Her cubs were playing right underneath you. Do you not understand how dangerous that was? You're wrapped up in that hammock like a fucking human burrito. It's still winter. They're hungry. How can you be so reckless?"

She shrugged again, sending my heart rate through the roof. I was going to kill her. Or have a stroke.

"Quinn," I tried again. "It's not safe to sleep out here."

She shook her head. "I'm safer out here than I am in the Manor."

"It's safer than it used to be," I said, knowing she had a point. There'd been a murder and more than a few attempted murders inside the Manor. Animal attacks? Zero. "There were bear cubs right under your hammock," I reminded her.

"I know." She grinned, lighting up the forest. "Isn't it cool?"

"No!" I shouted back. I heard myself and snapped my mouth shut.

It was only Quinn who did this to me. Quinn with

her pixie body and her bright eyes. She looked delicate. Fragile. The first time I saw her, I wanted to protect her. Ironic, because of all the people living in Heartstone Manor, Griffen aside, Quinn needed protection the least.

She knew the woods like the back of her hand. She was fit and strong. She could hike for hours. She knew how to shoot. She knew how to use a knife. The knife was for fileting the fish she caught, not combat, but it was wickedly sharp, and she held it like it had been made for her. I'd seen all of this with my own eyes.

I knew Quinn wasn't weak. She wasn't stupid. She wasn't careless. And here I was, roaring at her like she was the bear I was trying to scare off.

Fuck.

She made things misfire in my brain.

That bear in Montana? I'd faced him down with icy calm, waving my arms and yelling just as I had with the mama bear. The one in Montana had been bigger, a male brown bear who'd wanted our trout for his dinner. I hadn't bothered with my weapon, charging at him when he'd come for us, as calm as when I'd been making coffee that morning in camp.

With Quinn in the picture, all that icy calm had burned away. She fucked with my head. I'd seen the bear, seen Quinn sleeping, and let fear take the driver's seat.

When was the last time that had happened?

I knew the answer. The last time I'd let fear make my decisions, I'd fallen into the darkness. I'd destroyed too much. More than I could live with.

I had to hold on to the ice. The control.

I had to stay far away from Quinn Sawyer.

I was here to keep her safe. To keep her alive. Letting her get any further under my skin would only put her in danger. I couldn't allow that.

Quinn Sawyer wasn't for me. I wasn't the kind of man who could have a woman like her. The things I'd done could never be redeemed. Ever.

I wouldn't lose another woman I cared about. Not again. And not this one.

Without another word, I walked away, ignoring Quinn's grunt of annoyance. *Good.* If she was annoyed, she'd stay away from me. I didn't need the temptation.

If I did nothing else in my life, I was going to keep Quinn Sawyer safe.

Especially from me.

Chapter Two
QUINN

The necklace burned a hole in my pocket. I kept my hands on the steering wheel the entire ride into town, resisting the urge to slip my hand into my jacket pocket and run my thumb over the rippled surface of the pendant. Right up until I reached Harvey's office, I was going back and forth in my head.

Should I stop? Should I say something? What if it was nothing? The necklace in my jacket pocket was probably nothing. Jewelry wasn't my thing. I'd take good hiking gear over a diamond any day, but even if it was solid gold, it wasn't worth much. A delicate gold chain with a pendant shaped like an oak leaf, not much bigger than a fifty-cent piece, it was well made, I was guessing by a local craftsperson, but it wasn't valuable.

The value wasn't in the gold; it was in the artistry. It was a beautiful piece, but it wasn't the jewelry itself that had me spinning in circles. It was where I'd found it—wedged behind the bed in my father's hunting cabin, a place where no woman was allowed.

For most of my life, the hunting cabin had been more myth than reality, children forbidden along with women.

And for most of my life, I thought my father actually used it for hunting. I hadn't realized I was still that naive, but there you go. Years ago, I'd discovered it on one of my hikes, sneaking up to peer through dusty windows and see what was inside.

When I'd looked through the windows as a kid, the answer to what was inside had been—not much. A square folding table with half-rusted metal legs and two equally decrepit folding chairs. When I'd mentioned the place to our groundskeeper, who'd been at Heartstone since before my birth, he'd made me promise never to go there. "That's your father's place. Not for young girls," he'd said gruffly, giving my shoulder a firm squeeze. "Don't wander that way again."

Another child might have disobeyed, drawn purely by it being forbidden. Not me. I'd already learned not to attract my father's attention. He had no time for an awkward, skinny girl with eyes that were too big. "She's creepy," he'd said once to my mother when he'd thought I was asleep. "With those bug eyes and bony legs. And she's too quiet. She never talks."

My mother had pulled him away, saying, "Quinn talks when she has something to say. And when she grows into her eyes, she's going to be a knockout."

I didn't know if my mother was right about my eyes. When I looked in the mirror, I saw my father's eyes. Sawyer eyes. I thought my father hated sharing them with me. After my mother died, it seemed like he hated everything about me.

I hadn't dared to go inside the cabin until a few months after my father's death when I had hiked out there and poked around. Even with him gone, the place remained forbidden in my mind, but I wanted to see what kind of shape it was in. Prentice was gone, and it didn't make sense to let the place fall to ruin. I didn't know what I was expecting to find. I guess the same thing I'd seen all those years ago when I'd pressed my face to the window and peeked inside.

Not exactly. In the years since, my father had redecorated. Big time. Hunting cabins like this were common in the area and usually pretty basic. A place to sleep and eat, maybe enjoy the companionship of some buddies after a long day of lying on the cold ground waiting for whatever animal was in season to wander into their line of sight. From the outside, the cabin was the same. Stacked logs with graying mortar between, a stacked stone chimney on one end. On the inside, though, he'd turned it from a sparse hunting cabin to a gentleman's retreat.

I couldn't imagine how he'd managed to get all this stuff up here. Helicopter? Ridiculous, but still the most likely answer. There weren't any roads nearby or trails wide enough to bring in the deep leather armchairs or the matching sofa facing them. There was a new woodstove and, most bizarre, running water.

A beautiful wood table and matching chairs replaced the folding table of years past. In the small bedroom, I found a queen-sized brass bed, stripped bare, the mattress lightly dusty but relatively new. Had my father sent cleaning staff out here? I couldn't imagine him making the bed himself. Not Prentice Sawyer.

On that first visit, I hadn't done more than look around. It still felt very much like my father's place. No matter how many times I reminded myself that he wasn't going to storm through the door demanding to know what I was doing there, I still felt like a criminal for being there at all.

When I told Griffen what I'd found, he thought it over and asked, "Do you want it for yourself? You spend more time in the woods than the rest of us combined."

"Not to live in full-time," I'd said, after considering the idea. "It's too far from the house or any road to use every day, but I wouldn't mind keeping an eye on it, maybe staying out there now and then, if that's okay."

In the months since, I'd gone to the cabin at least once a week, just checking on the place. I dusted and cleaned, and remade the bed with sheets and blankets I'd bought myself. I'd stocked it with canned goods and did maintenance on the water system, staying overnight when I could get away for a day or two, slowly building the idea in my head of a winter campout. I'd done it before, in a four-season tent pitched deep in the mountains. There was nothing like the quiet of winter solitude in the mountains. But as much as I loved sleeping in my tent, I didn't hate the idea of living in luxury that far away from civilization. I could base out of the cabin and really explore that part of the forest in a way I hadn't dared to when my father was alive.

On my last visit before my planned trip, I'd decided to rearrange the bedroom, moving the bed to face the double window and the view of the woods. On my own, I'd shifted the furniture with painstaking slowness, an inch at a time. And when I'd dragged the heavy bed away from the wall, there it had been, the gleam of gold catching the light.

It hadn't belonged to my mother. I was sure about that. She'd died when I was eight, but I remembered well that she never wore necklaces. Too many little hands tugging on them, she used to say. And from what I remembered, the gold oak leaf wasn't her style. When she wore jewelry, it was understated, with a touch of sparkle. Despite living in the center of thousands of acres of forest, my mother hadn't been an outdoorswoman.

Whoever the woman was that my father had fixed up the cabin for, definitely had been. I hiked for a living, and my best time to the cabin was forty-five minutes. I couldn't picture my father convincing one of his usual socialites to trade their heels for a pair of hiking boots and trek over an hour into the woods just for the privilege of fucking him.

So, who was it? Who was this mystery woman?

Maybe the simple gold oak leaf held the answer.

I parked in front of the familiar Victorian Harvey had converted for his office, finally giving in to the urge to pull the necklace from my pocket. My father had slept with a lot of women before, during, and after his marriages. Why would the one who'd owned this necklace be important? None of the others had been.

But someone had murdered Prentice, and we had no idea who. My brother Ford was in prison for the crime, but he'd been set up. The only clue we had pointed to the mysterious woman—maybe the woman whose necklace I held in my hand—Prentice had been planning to make the next Mrs. Sawyer. No one knew who she was. Prentice had never brought her to Heartstone Manor or been seen with her publicly. Blackmail letters and boxes of baby gear we'd unearthed in the Manor suggested the future Mrs. Sawyer had been pregnant, and there was someone out there who would be very, very angry to find out about Prentice's plans to marry her.

Now Prentice was dead, and there was no sign of the mysterious fiancée or their child. I rubbed my thumb across the rippled surface of the gold oak leaf. What if this was hers? If we could figure out who the woman had been, would it point us to whoever had killed our father?

I didn't give a shit about justice for Prentice. He'd been a miserable human being. A terrible father and an equally horrible husband. The world was a better place without him in it. I wanted justice for Ford. My older brother wasn't perfect. He'd made more than his share of mistakes, but he'd saved me, over and over again.

I didn't want to open this can of worms. I could have brought the necklace to Griffen, but my brother had enough on his plate. I thought about bringing it to Ford, but I'd promised him I wouldn't visit him in jail again. He'd looked so broken when he'd asked me to leave and stay away. As much as it killed me, I couldn't bring myself to put that look on his face again, so I'd kept my promise. I had a feeling this necklace wasn't a good enough reason to break it.

That left me with Harvey.

I got out of my car, sliding the necklace back into my

pocket. Harvey had been our family lawyer for as long as I could remember. More than that, he was a family friend. He'd been there for all of us our entire lives, most recently through the insanity of our father's will.

Harvey tried to stop him, but Prentice Sawyer got what Prentice Sawyer wanted. He'd set up trust funds for us, but if we wanted them, we had to live in Heartstone Manor for five years. There was more, but the rest mostly applied to Griffen. As far as I was concerned, only one thing mattered: if I didn't do as Prentice demanded, I not only lost access to the money he'd left me—money I didn't even want—I was banned from Sawyer property.

To my great regret, that included my guide business. Ford had been working on selling me the business so I could get out from under my father's thumb. He'd been close, but Prentice had died without signing the papers. One more betrayal in a lifetime filled with them. And my business, the one I'd built hike by hike since I'd been in college, remained Sawyer property. If I didn't play along, I'd lose everything that mattered to me.

Climbing the steps of the Victorian, I opened the front door, lifting a hand to wave at Harvey's receptionist.

"Hi, Quinn," she said with a smile. "Is anything wrong?"

I knew what she meant. I didn't usually show up at Harvey's office. I'd only been here once since the reading of the will. Shaking my head, I said, "Everything's fine. I just had a question for Harvey, and I thought I'd stop in and see if he was free. Does he have a minute?"

"He doesn't have a client for another hour. Just give a knock on the door and then go in."

Harvey's door wasn't closed all the way. From inside, I caught the tap of fingers on a keyboard. I rapped on the thick wood, pushing it open with each knock. Harvey's eyes lit when he saw me, his round cheeks plumping as he smiled. I'd hated my father for most of my life, but Harvey always got a hug. Growing up, he'd been one of the few adults I'd trusted unconditionally.

Closing his laptop, he pushed back from his desk and came around to greet me, folding me in strong arms. "Quinn, what a nice surprise. Is everything all right?"

"Everything's great," I said, giving him a squeeze back. "I'm about to head off on my vacation."

"Hiking into the forest with a tent and sleeping bag again?" Harvey leaned back, shaking his head. "Quinn, it always makes me nervous thinking of you alone out there."

I couldn't help laughing. I was far safer in the woods and among the wild animals than around humans. I'd seen enough of what humans could do to each other. "I know what I'm doing."

"I know you do, sweetheart," he said, shaking his head and stepping back with an affectionate squeeze of my arm. "But you have to understand, in my head, you're still six years old and heading off to kindergarten. The idea of you out there in the woods—" He cocked his head to the side, studying me. "You know there's weather coming in."

I nodded. "It's not going to be that bad," I said. "And I'm going to base out of the hunting cabin. I have it stocked up. Plenty of food, water, and firewood. The roof is tight, so no leaks. I'll be fine. And even if it does snow, it's not going to last long. It never does this time of year."

"True," Harvey said, an affectionate smile on his face. "I know you can handle it. Everyone I send your way for a hike or a fishing trip comes back raving. I'm just overprotective, I guess."

"That's all right," I said, smiling up at him. "We like you that way. Anyway, this is weird, but when I was setting up the cabin for my trip, I moved the bed, and I found this."

I pulled the necklace out of my pocket, arranging it on my palm so Harvey could see the gold oak leaf pendant on the delicate chain.

"Interesting," he said slowly, reaching out his hand, his eyes lighting with curiosity. "May I?" I pushed my palm toward Harvey, and he lifted the necklace, holding it up to the light. "I don't think I've seen this before."

"I know you and Griffen did an inventory of the family jewelry," I said, "and I didn't know if something like this might be missing. If it was a Sawyer piece. Or maybe—" I shifted, suddenly uncomfortable.

Harvey caught my meaning. "I don't recognize it from the family collection," he said. "I would guess it was left there. Maybe by a guest of your father's."

I shifted again, shoving my hands in the back pocket of my jeans. "That was my guess, too," I said, staring at the pendant in Harvey's hand. "It doesn't look old enough to be part of the Sawyer collection. Can we track its owner?" I asked, suddenly feeling foolish. This was a wild goose chase. How was a random necklace going to help? "I, uh, thought maybe it belongs to the woman

Prentice was involved with. The one we haven't been able to identify."

Harvey raised an eyebrow, and my cheeks flushed pink, but he nodded. Maybe I wasn't a complete idiot.

He turned it over again in his hand, studying the back. "I think I can see an artist's inscription, but I'm not sure. Do you mind leaving this with me? I can take a closer look, see if I can track down where it came from."

"Sure," I said, relieved to have the thing off my hands. I'd found it and brought it to an authority figure. Now, I could move on.

"You'll be out at the cabin all week?" he asked.

I nodded. "I'm leaving this afternoon. I was thinking, when I'm not out hiking, I could search the cabin and see if I find anything else."

Harvey stared down at the necklace in his hand and nodded slowly. "That's not a bad idea. I'll see what I can find while you're gone."

"Thanks, Harvey." I leaned in and gave him another hug.

"Anytime," he said, squeezing me back. "Take care of yourself, Quinn. Keep an eye on the weather."

"I will. I promise." I waved as I strolled out of his office, a weight sliding off my shoulders. That was the second to last thing I had to do before my vacation officially started.

Jumping back in the car, I headed to the Craftsman bungalow on the edge of town that served as home base for my guide business. I'd already put up the sign in the window declaring Sawyer Outdoor Adventures to be officially closed for the next week.

It was the perfect time of year to take a break. Too cold and often too wet for tourists to want to hike. Trout season had just opened, but I'd be back on the river soon enough. The dedicated anglers didn't need a guide to find the best spots, and the tourists who were my bread and butter didn't start booking trips until late March. By May, I'd be wearing my waders several times a week. But for now, Sawyers Bend was quiet, and I was playing hooky.

Before Prentice died and his will came into play, I had always left Sawyers Bend for an annual break. River rafting in Costa Rica. Rock climbing in New Mexico. Surfing in Baja. Now, with the will restricting my movements, I'd stay on Sawyer land. According to Harvey, as long as I was on the Sawyer estate, it counted as being home. I sent silent thanks to William Sawyer, who'd tied the land to the Manor in such a way that it could never be severed. Not that my father or his father would have given up a single acre. Sawyers believed in holding on to what they had.

Unlocking the front door to the bungalow, I flipped on the lights. The front of the building was a gear shop. Nothing major; there were too many big outdoor stores in the area for me to compete profitably on gear sales. I carried everything my guests usually forgot, like sunscreen and bug spray, along with a few high-end goodies tourists loved—hand-tied flies and custom-made hiking staffs. Behind the gear shop was a long maple counter that served as a front desk of sorts.

Usually, my younger sister Sterling sat there, perched on a stool, with a sunny smile for our clients as she checked them in or rang them up. She'd taken over organizing phone and online reservations, and lately she'd been working on revamping my website. It was funny—I'd given Sterling the job more as a soft place to land than because I needed the help. Nursing a broken heart, she'd quit her job, saying she wanted something quiet. It didn't get much quieter than my place. We had brief spurts of mayhem as we organized groups for a hike or fishing trip, but once the guests and I were out the door, Sawyer Outdoor Adventures was filled with peace and quiet, interrupted only by the occasional phone call.

I'd figured Sterling would take some of the less fun administrative tasks off my hands, and she'd have me at her back as she got on her feet again. I hadn't expected her to work as hard as she did. The place had never been more organized, and she was full of ideas for improvements. I'd been content with chugging along as a one-woman show, but Sterling had me making plans along with her. A new website. An upgraded reservation system. More cross-promotion with the inn. I was on board for all of it. After my vacation.

All the way in the back of the bungalow, I passed my small office and pushed open the door to the room that used to be my bedroom. Before my father's will, I'd lived here, sleeping on the twin bed still in the corner, currently covered in plastic bins filled with supplies and gear for the shop. Now that the will had forced me back into the Manor, I'd reluctantly converted this room into storage. It hurt too much to keep it as it was, a reminder that I'd had to leave the haven I'd built for myself, had to return to the place I hated most for five long years.

I'd be back, I promised myself. Four more years, and I

could get rid of all the boxes and bins and reclaim my room. Or maybe there was money in those trust funds, and I could buy myself a place of my own. Griffen had already promised that as soon as the terms of the will allowed him to transfer Sawyer Enterprises property, he was signing Sawyer Outdoor Adventures over to me. If there was even a little cash in my trust, I could add it to the money I'd saved to buy the business from my father and have enough for a place of my own. Then, I'd never have to spend another night at Heartstone Manor.

A tug of pure longing pulled at my heart as I stared down at my little bed. Life had been so much simpler when I'd been living here. I could pretend my father and Heartstone Manor didn't exist. For a while, I'd been at peace. Living in the bungalow was almost as good as being in the woods.

I needed my week away. A week when I didn't have to go inside Heartstone Manor, didn't have to face the house I loved and hated and feared, the echoes of my childhood everywhere. My father was dead, yet he haunted me every time I stepped over the threshold.

I needed a break. From the Manor. From my family. And maybe especially from Hawk Bristol.

I smirked to myself, remembering the furious expression on his face that morning as he'd scared off the mama bear. I'd never admit it to him, but I'd been a little nervous at how close she'd come, especially with her babies tumbling around under my hammock. I'd told Hawk the truth—I didn't have anything she was interested in. I knew about black bears. I knew these woods and the animals in them. I didn't use scented products.

Even the fabric softener on my clothes was unscented. I didn't bring food to the hammock or anything that smelled like food, especially not this time of year.

But still...she was a big animal, and I'd seen what bears did to people and other animals who got in between them and their babies. Black bears were normally shy, avoiding people and keeping to themselves, but all bets were off when their cubs were involved, and I'd had two right underneath me. He'd called me *a human fucking burrito*. I laughed to myself, now that he wasn't around to hear.

From the day he'd arrived at Heartstone Manor, Hawk Bristol had tugged at me. I'd never known anyone like him. I'd been around plenty of men who could command attention. Men who understood how to acquire and wield power. I'd grown up among men like that. Hawk was as commanding as any of them, but he was different. Hawk's mission was to protect those under his charge, and he took that mission to heart.

I'd watched him after he came to Heartstone, not sure I believed his loyalty to Griffen. He had the run of the house. He was armed. At first, on the nights I spent in the house because the weather was too awful for my hammock, I slept with a chair jammed under the door handle. I was an adult now, and no one was getting through that door unless I let them in. Not ever again.

Though I'd felt his eyes on me, more than once, lingering, considering, Hawk never tried my door. Of course, he didn't. All these months later, I understood how off base I'd been. Hawk would die before he'd let any member of Griffen's family come to harm. He would never be the one to bring that harm himself. Once I'd realized that, I'd watched him even closer, trying to figure out what made Hawk Bristol tick.

I didn't have an answer. I wasn't even close.

Hawk Bristol was locked up tight. Nobody broke through his shell. I remembered the way he'd lost his cool over the mama bear and her cubs because they were a perceived threat. To me.

No one got to Hawk Bristol. Except, apparently, me.

And I had a week to decide what I was going to do about that.

Chapter Three
QUINN

A few hours later, I set out for my long-awaited week away from everything. I shot a glance at the heavy gray sky hanging over skeletal tree branches. The news reports had been spot-on. Weather was moving in. The air teased my cold nose, damp with a hint of something fresh and clean. I knew that scent—the promise of snow.

We didn't get snow often in these mountains anymore. Not like when I was a child. Back then, we had a few good snowstorms every year, canceling school and leaving the forest blanketed in white. The snow rarely lasted long, except in the most shaded parts of the woods, but I loved the quiet, loved the way trails of animal footprints would appear, one by one—tiny divots from the chipmunks and the squirrels, the bigger tracks of the deer.

A flake drifted down through the branches, white and tiny. I stopped and looked up at the heavy gray sky above the trees. More flakes fell to dust the cold ground.

That wasn't a good sign. A big, fat snowflake usually meant low accumulation. Tiny flakes meant we were in for some real snow.

I kept walking. I wasn't turning back. I'd been looking forward to this too much. For the first time in a year, I was leaving Heartstone Manor behind. Despite the foreboding weather, I felt lighter with every step, the woods surrounding me, protecting me from the Manor. I needed this break. I needed to get away. Not from my family, but from Heartstone.

When I first heard the terms of my father's will, I'd been shocked to learn he'd left us anything at all, especially his daughters. And then that codicil, Prentice's final *fuck you* to his children. I didn't want his money, but if I wanted to keep my business, I had to live in that fucking house for five long years. I'd fled Heartstone for college when I was seventeen. Ford made sure Prentice didn't notice that I never again slept another night under Heartstone's roof. Not until Prentice was dead.

Since I'd been back, I spent almost every night in my hammock under the trees. The few times there'd been heavy rain or strong winds, and Griffen had asked me to stay in the house, I'd acquiesced but barely slept, the memories sneaking back in the dark to keep me awake.

I knew there was no one living in Heartstone Manor who would hurt me. Not now. Not under Griffen's watch. Not with Hawk there to keep us safe. I knew no one would hurt me, but my subconscious wasn't buying it. The terrified girl inside me didn't believe. My hammock was safe. The Manor was filled with secret nightmares.

I picked up my pace, step by step, putting distance between me and the Manor. There was a hush in the woods as I moved deeper into the trees. The quiet pressed in on me, the falling snow a layer of insulation, muffling everything. No birdsong. No crackle of leaves as squirrels raced around the forest floor. Even the rising wind was nearly silent.

It was the snow. Of course, it was the snow. We hadn't had weather like this for most of the winter. There'd been a flurry or two, and school had been delayed once or twice for freezing rain, but not much more than that. The newscasters had been talking about this storm hitting hard farther north. Maybe they'd been off, and we were going to get more than we bargained for.

I gave a mental shrug. I could handle this. The snow was coming down faster with every minute, but visibility was good, and my footing was solid on the trail. Even at this relaxed pace, the cabin was less than an hour's hike. Once I was there, I could wait out any weather the North Carolina mountains could throw at me. If I'd been in Maine or Montana, I might have taken a different approach, but here? I'd be fine.

I shifted my pack, squinting into the branches above to gauge the falling snow. Was it coming faster, or had the wind picked up? Either way, I wasn't turning back. I took a deep, icy breath, the cold air freezing the inside of my nose, my eyes watering.

Something tickled between my shoulder blades, and I looked behind me.

Nothing but my tracks in the snow. The woods were still and silent. I was alone. I turned back to the trail and forced myself to keep moving despite the lingering sense of being watched. It was the snow throwing me off. I thought of the mama bear from this morning. No, I wasn't prey to her, especially with this pack making me look twice my size. And she'd already had her wander in the woods this morning. With this snow and the temperature dropping, she'd be tucked up tight in her den with her cubs.

In theory, there were plenty of things in these woods that could hurt me, but this close to the Manor and town, it seemed unlikely. We didn't have any major predators in these mountains. People said there were still cougars out there, but the only ones I'd ever seen were at the nature center in Asheville. Every once in a while, somebody posted a picture on social media, swearing it was of a cougar hanging out on their back porch. But the pictures always turned out to be faked or taken in California.

There was nothing here big enough to cause me harm, I reminded myself, resisting the urge to stop and look behind me. I was just tweaked by the bears from this morning. Those cubs had been cute but way too close.

My hand drifted to my pack where I'd stored my nine-millimeter. I'd packed it more out of habit than anything else. I knew my way around these woods, and I wasn't worried about bears or other wildlife. Or other humans. The people who hiked these woods were ninety-nine percent nature lovers like me. Still, it paid to be cautious. When I was alone in the forest, I carried the gun, just in case.

It wasn't a big deal. My father had taught all of us to handle a gun when we were kids. I tried to go to the range every few months to keep my skills sharp. I'd only used the gun a few times. Once to scare off a fellow hiker who thought he could take advantage of our isolation to get what he wanted. With him, all I'd had to do was pull the gun and aim it at his balls. We hadn't been that far from the trailhead. I'd held the gun on him until we got back to the parking lot, and I could call West, our police chief. The second time, I'd used it to fire a warning shot at a black bear that had wandered too close. That time, the blast of the bullet had been enough to scare off the bear.

In all the years I'd been disappearing into these woods, I'd only used the gun those two times. I packed it anyway. There were more than bears in these woods. We had coyotes, bobcats, and foxes. Of the three, the coyotes were the most likely to cross my path now that the fox and bobcat populations had been winnowed down by humans. Nothing would be out hunting in this weather, especially not for something as big as a human.

There was nothing out here to worry about except the weather.

I slowed when I reached the spot where the trail split into three narrower trails. The one on the far left circled back to the Manor. The one on the right dropped down the hillside. If I followed it far enough, I'd end up at the Inn at Sawyers Bend. I stayed on the center trail, the one that led to the cabin. Squinting at the sky as I walked, I watched the snow fall, the clouds above dark against the trees.

This part of the trail to the cabin could be hard to navigate on a good day. With the light dimmed by the clouds and falling snow, only someone who knew the way would be able to find it. Not a problem for me. I could walk this trail blindfolded. So why did something feel off?

Turning, I looked behind me, surprised to see all but my closest tracks already covered by snow. I wasn't turning around, despite the weather and the itch between my shoulder blades. I scanned the silent woods. Nothing moved. Not a squirrel. Not a bird. Nothing.

Shaking my head, I unzipped the side pouches on the right side of my pack and pulled out the nine-millimeter and a compact holster I could clip into my waistband. The gun on my hip didn't help, mostly because I couldn't figure out what had me so spooked. The snow? The quiet?

I resettled my pack back on my shoulders, scanned the woods yet again, and forced myself to move forward. It was either that or turn back, and turning back was not an option. All I could think about was the cabin—the firewood I'd carefully stocked up over the last few weeks, the hot cocoa packets in the cupboard, along with powdered milk, soup, and tins of beef stew. I'd even brought out fresh eggs and a half gallon of ice cream a few days before.

This was a vacation, after all, and I planned to make the most of it. If it kept snowing like this, tomorrow the woods would be a gorgeous fairyland, sparkling in the sunshine that always came after a winter storm.

I wanted the fairyland, and it was only a short hike away. Setting one foot in front of the other, I kept my eyes on the trail. I knew where I was, but visibility wasn't great in the snow. I'd been around long enough to know that even the experienced could get into trouble in the woods if they got careless. Step by step, I noted landmarks and kept moving, the itch between my shoulder blades ever-present, driving me forward.

I tried to shake off my unease. I couldn't help stopping and turning to look behind me again. Nothing. My footsteps filling in from the rapidly falling snow, winter-bare trees, and glimpses of gray clouds above. Nothing else. I stood there for too long, fighting a war in my head.

Something's off.

Go home.

Now.

If I went home and the snow kept coming down like this, it was unlikely I'd be able to make it back to the cabin before my vacation days ran out. If I didn't go now, I couldn't go at all. I had hikes and fishing trips booked after my return, and I wouldn't cancel and ruin my clients' vacations just because mine had been ruined.

And it would only be ruined if I was a wuss and went home because of a little snow and a case of the creeps. There was nothing out here.

Right hand floating over the gun at my hip, I turned back to the trail, gauging my distance from the cabin. If I kept a good pace, it couldn't be more than twenty minutes from here. *If* I kept a good pace. I kept my ears pricked and my eyes sharp, scanning the woods.

Nothing. Always nothing. Not a bird, not a squirrel, not a chipmunk. Nothing bigger than a deer. No threats. No bear, no coyote, no fox, no bobcat, no cougar. Nothing. And still, the sense of invisible eyes drilling into that exact spot.

I watched. I listened.

And still, I never saw it coming.

A blur of white barreled out from behind a tree, flying into my shoulder and knocking me to the rocky ground, tearing off my pack as I fell. I went down hard, my hip landing on a sharp rock, pain flashing up my spine and down my leg, stealing my breath, the back of my head bouncing off the cold earth.

Panic set in. I was pinned to the ground. Everything was gray and white. My eyes focused. The body on top of me was human, not animal. Male, based on the size and weight. He was clothed head to toe in gray and white camo, a matching balaclava covering his face. In the dim light under the trees, I caught a flash of dark eyes. No one I recognized. No one I knew.

I wasn't thinking, my fear flooding from me in an explosion of sound. "Get off me! Get off me!"

Hard fingers encircled my left wrist, dragging it down, pushing me to my side, and pulling my hand behind my back. He was trying to restrain me. Why? What did he want?

It didn't matter. I couldn't let him tie me up. I couldn't let him take me. I wouldn't.

I went wild, kicking, screaming, yanking on my wrist as hard as I could. His grip didn't budge. I swung my right fist, hitting nothing but hard muscle through his cold weather gear. I'd been to enough self-defense classes to know that if he got my hands secured, I was screwed. Rocking my shoulders and twisting my body, I tried to dislodge my attacker, remembering the weapon at my hip far too late.

I managed to get my hand down my side, yanking my

gun free of the holster with a rough jerk. There was a split second of utter stillness from the body on top of me. He moved so fast I couldn't track him, his arm flashing down, setting fire to my arm with one strike. My fingers went numb, the gun slipping to fall into the snow. From my wrist to my shoulder, pain burned up the nerves of my right arm. I screamed again, the sound sharp and desperate, cut off by my sob as I tried to breathe through the agony.

Rough hands rolled me over, my face shoved into the wet snow, filling my mouth and nose. I dragged in air, choking and coughing through the snow. Rocking my shoulders, I pulled at my hands. He pinned me easily, feeling like he weighed a thousand pounds. I managed to twist my hips, tilting us just enough to the side to knock him off-balance. Just a little, but the ground on this side of the trail dipped toward a ravine. A little off-balance was enough. Struggling, we rolled toward the ravine.

Chapter Four

QUINN

For the briefest of seconds, I was free, except for his grip on my left wrist. I struggled to my feet, lunging, trying to use my body weight and momentum to yank my arm free. Pain shot through my left shoulder as he hauled back on my wrist, dragging me forward. I lost my footing, falling, my ankle turning under me. Agony flashed up my leg. I gasped in a breath, letting out another scream of rage and pain.

I caught a brief glimpse of those dark eyes. Cold. Determined. Then I was flipped facedown, my nose shoved into the snow again. A knee jammed into my lower back, driving the air from my lungs. Hitching, wheezing screams scraped at my ears. Me. That was me, trying to scream and whimpering instead.

Hot, furious tears blurred my eyes. My right ankle was numb. He hauled my left arm up. My right moved to join it, my fingers still tingling from whatever he'd done to make me drop my gun. A sob caught in my throat.

I wasn't going to be able to get away. And whoever

this was, whatever he wanted, it was going to be bad. There was nothing else it could be. I curled my fingers into fists, trying to make my wrists as big as possible. Maybe I'd be able to get out of whatever restraints he put on.

I didn't know what else to do. I just knew I couldn't let him take me. I couldn't let this happen. I'd have to keep fighting.

Even as the thought crossed my mind, I realized I was fucked. I went limp, thinking, thinking, thinking. My racing mind couldn't find a way out. How could I stop him? I was strong and smart. And still bound by the physics of being a small-framed woman pinned beneath a man who was probably twice my weight, and most of it muscle.

All these years, the woods had been my sanctuary. And now this man, whoever he was, wanted to take that.

Something cold wrapped around my wrists, the edges digging into my skin. Long, strong fingers pulled down my jaw and shoved fabric into my mouth. I tried to spit it out, to shake my head, screaming against the fabric.

And then he was gone, his weight torn from my back.

I scrambled to my knees, spitting out the fabric in my mouth, watching as two bodies rolled across the snowy trail, one in white and gray, the other in a familiar faded green and khaki camo. Hawk or one of his team. My attacker's grayish-white camo blended into the light layer of snow on the forest floor as they grappled. I caught a glimpse of dark hair. Hawk. It was Hawk. I registered the gun in his hand, and my brain cleared.

I was just sitting here, out in the open. My hands

were bound but I could move. I couldn't help Hawk with my attacker, but I could get myself out of his way. I tried to stand, my only thought to get away from the two men. My right foot crumpled beneath me, pain spiking through my ankle and up my leg.

Fuck. *Fuck*. I tried again, slowly, falling back to my knees as the first hint of pressure sent hot pain flaring through my ankle. I didn't think it was broken. Maybe a sprain, but either way, I couldn't walk on it. *Fuck*. Hands and knees would be faster, but my fucking hands were behind my back. I tugged at them, but whatever bound my wrists was tight, with no give.

I glanced back to Hawk and my attacker. Hawk almost had the other man in a bind, his arm close to a lock on his neck, when the man twisted himself free, drawing out a knife. My gut lurched. I wanted to help Hawk. I couldn't leave him. What if—

No. I had a fucked-up ankle, and my hands were restrained behind my back. I couldn't help Hawk. I was only going to distract him. I needed to get away from both of them, and I needed to do it now. My pack was too far away. I couldn't see my gun anywhere. I was low on choices, and I needed to move. The best place to hide was down. To my right, the ravine beckoned. It was steep, but not too steep. I hoped.

Tucking my chin down as tightly as I could, I curled into a ball and rolled, squeezing my eyes closed as I went. Growing up in the country, I'd rolled down a hillside more than a few times. On the right hillside, it was a hell of a good ride, everything whirling and turning and spinning until I came to a halt in summer-warmed grass, laughing and giggling. This was not the same thing.

I rolled, picking up speed, smacking into trees, bumping over rocks until I came to an abrupt halt wedged under a fallen pine. The good news was I'd be very hard to see from above. The bad news? There was no fucking way I was getting back up the side of the ravine. And if Hawk didn't take care of my attacker, it was going to be tricky to get my hands free.

Without my pack, without a weapon, and wedged under a tree, there wasn't much I could do to improve my situation. I tried anyway. Using my bound hands and left foot for leverage, I got myself into a seated position. Shifting my weight forward, I shoved my bound hands down, trying to get them under my butt to pull them through to the front. I'd done it before, in self-defense training, but my wrists were bound too tightly and my winter parka was too thick. On top of that, every jostle of my ankle was agony. *Fuck.*

A shot echoed through the woods, and my heart lurched painfully in my chest. Hawk.

Hawk. Fuck. Oh, please. Please.

A few feet away, I spotted a rock half buried in the snowy hillside, with a corner that might be sharp enough to cut through whatever was around my wrists. I was pretty sure he'd used a zip tie. Those could go either way. The cheap ones from the hardware store broke pretty easily. I'd learned that the hard way fastening gear. The pricier zip ties, especially the kind that had wires running through the plastic, were a different story. I had a knife in my pack, but my pack was back on the trail. On the trail with Hawk.

Please, please let him have pulled the trigger. An image of him bleeding out in the snow flashed through my mind. *No.*

I braced my good foot in the snow and shoved, wiggling backward until I reached the rock with the sharp edge. Lining my wrists up with the edge of the rock, I started moving them back and forth, not sure if I was doing any fucking good. I had to try. I didn't have a better plan. I had to get my hands free. If that shot had hit Hawk, I'd—

What? What did I think I was going to do? If he'd shot Hawk, the man in the white camo would be on me before I could do anything.

I'd have to—

A dark shape popped up over the ridge, sharp eyes finding mine. *Hawk.*

A wave of relief hit me. He seemed to be in one piece as he carefully descended the side of the ravine. When he got close enough, he said, "Quinn, are you okay?"

I nodded, then shook my head. "Mostly bumps and bruises. I can't get my hands free. And I hurt my ankle." My head spun, and words tumbled out. "Who was that? What—? What the fuck happened? Why—? Did you shoot him?"

Hawk shook his head. "I need to get you secured, then track him down. Let me focus, Quinn."

The man in the white camo had gotten away. I snapped my mouth shut. I could ask questions later. For now, our immediate safety was more important. "I lost my pack," I said quietly. "I had a gun. He knocked it out of my hands."

"Understood." Pulling a knife from his boot. Hawk flipped out the blade, and my hands were free a moment later. "Wait," he said sharply as I started to stand.

He checked me from head to toe, his hands moving efficiently, probing for injury. I winced a few times as he touched newly forming bruises, but nothing was bad until he got to my right ankle.

"Sprained or broken?" he asked.

"Sprained, I think." Hawk's hand hovered over my foot. "I don't think we should take this boot off," I said. "Not until we're at the cabin." I glanced up the ravine. "If I can get there," I added. Even if I could make it to the top, there was still the rest of the trail, which only grew rougher the closer we got to the hunting cabin.

I shivered, my adrenaline spiking.

It was too far to go back to the Manor. The snow was coming down in heavy curtains, the flakes small and dense. Fucking hell. How had this gone to shit so fast?

Hawk gave a long look to my right foot, tightly laced in my waterproof hiking boot. He nodded and moved to my right side, slinging an arm around my back and pulling me upright until my weight settled on my left leg.

"Don't put any weight on that right foot," he said, glancing at the ravine wall. "You're going to have to—"

"Crawl." I finished for him. "Yeah, I figured. At least my hands are free."

Hawk scanned the woods surrounding us. "I need to make sure he's gone."

"Did you shoot him?" I asked.

Hawk's eyes slid to the side, and I thought I caught a shade of embarrassment. "I think I grazed him. Your cabin is close."

I nodded in the affirmative.

"Stocked up? Food? Firewood?"

I nodded again. "Yes to all of it."

"We'll head there. Temperature's dropping. I need to get you inside. You can handle getting up that hill?" he asked, worried eyes flicking from my face to the hill I'd rolled down only minutes before.

Could I handle it? I guessed I was going to find out. Not like I had a choice. I nodded. "I've got it. Go do what you need to do. I'll get myself back up there."

Hawk gave another of those short, sharp nods in return. "Good thinking, getting out of his line of sight in the ravine. Gutsy move."

A warm glow filled my chest at his succinct praise.

"I'll get you as far as I can," he said, tightening his arm around my back and taking most of my weight, stepping forward slowly enough to let me hop along with him. He was like granite. I knew he wouldn't fall. Wouldn't drop me. Wouldn't slip.

There weren't many people in my life I could say that about. I was glad one of them was here.

A few steps farther, the incline was too steep. I tipped forward, catching myself on the hill with my hands.

"Okay?" Hawk asked.

"I'm good." Now that they were untied, my hands were fine. Proving it, I inched up the hill, watching in envy as Hawk climbed up in seconds and disappeared into the trees. Getting back up the hill was no less painful than rolling down had been, the terrain not exactly soft under my knee and palms, snow soaking into my pants, leaching away my precious body heat. I used my right knee as much as I could, but the second anything touched my right foot, hot pain surged, my ankle pulsing in the tight boot.

Fucking ankle. God damn it.

I continued my slow progress, reminding myself I was trained to survive in the fucking wilderness, in all kinds of weather. I'd been caught in a snowstorm on Mt. Washington. I'd hiked Mt. Fuji without oxygen. I could do this. I was freezing and wet, and everything hurt, but I could do this.

I was halfway up the side of the ravine when I heard the crunch of boots in the snow and looked up to see Hawk. He got down beside me, the incline still too steep to walk upright. "Come on, I've got you."

Hawk's arm came around my back, pulling me into his side, taking enough of my weight that I could move faster than on my own. It was still awkward and slow, both of us on our hands and knees, me trying to hold back grunts of pain every time I moved my right knee and my foot dragged over the ground. Every bump of a rock or a twig was another nauseating roll of pain.

Fuck, fuck, fuck, I chanted in my head. My ankle didn't feel broken. I'd broken my foot before, and I'd sprained that ankle before. I knew that throb, knew it was a sprain. But it didn't stop it from hurting like a motherfucker.

At the top, I rose up on my knees, trying to figure out

the next step. I couldn't walk. If I got out my hiking poles, maybe I could use them as a crutch? My pack leaned against a tree beside the trail.

"I found your weapon," Hawk said. "I put it in your pack."

"Did you find him?" I asked, feeling a little woozy. Hadn't I asked that before? Had he answered? Fuck. The cold and my ankle had my head spinning. I had to get to the cabin and get warm.

From the way Hawk was looking at me, he'd come to the same assessment. He shook his head. "I definitely winged him. Tracked blood back to where the trail split. He headed back toward the inn. I got a message out to my team. They're on high alert in case he goes to the Manor. I told them we're waiting out the weather at the cabin." With a meaningful look at the sky, Hawk crossed to my pack and hefted it to one shoulder. "Let's get this on you."

I shook my head. "I can't carry it. I have hiking poles. If you can carry the pack, I can use them as a crutch."

Hawk shook his head and held out the pack.

"What do you think he—?" I started to ask.

Hawk shook his head. "Questions later. Put on that pack. You're going to climb on my back, and I'm going to get us to the cabin."

I stared at him, eyes wide, uncomprehending. "You can't carry me and the pack. I'm too heavy. We can leave the pack here and come back for it."

Hawk snorted a laugh. "You're not too heavy."

The pack was a good thirty pounds. I was small but not a featherweight. And the footing on the trail was uncertain, especially in the snow. Hawk couldn't carry me.

"Put the pack on," Hawk said patiently. "I'm carrying you to the cabin. We don't have time for you to limp your way there."

"What if you—"

"I'll be fine. Put the pack on." Hawk sighed as I just stood there. "I tracked him back to the trail that leads to the inn, but that doesn't mean he took it. He's injured, but he's mobile, and he didn't get what he wanted, whatever that was. The Manor is covered. We're exposed, and he may be coming back. The weather might help us out, but not while we're out here. We need to get to the cabin. I'm not leaving your gear. It won't be safe to come back for it. Get your pack on so we can get moving."

His implacable tone and clear logic broke through my paralysis. With a nod, I held out my arms, helping him slide the pack on my back. As soon as I had it clipped in and secured, Hawk crouched in front of me, giving me his back. I hesitated, not sure how to climb on. The last time I rode piggyback, I was nine years old.

"Quinn," Hawk growled. "Stop thinking and get on my fucking back so we can get moving."

"Okay." Feeling suddenly awkward and suddenly shy, I leaned over him, plastering myself to his back. Gripping his shoulders with my hands and his hips with my knees, I climbed on. Strong fingers hooked behind my thighs, holding me in place as he rose to his feet.

I was still settling as he began to walk, moving briskly despite the snow. Winding my arms around his shoulders, I held on, soaking in his body heat, his back so warm and solid. My front was warm, but the rest of me was cold and wet, bruised and aching. My ankle throbbed. And despite all of that, the firm grip of his hands on my thighs sent heat spiraling through me.

I told myself I was being ridiculous. This was not the time. I'd been attacked by someone who had clearly planned to kidnap me and do— I didn't know what. I wasn't thinking about it. We were in the middle of a freak snowstorm that was just supposed to be flurries, and I'd fucked up my ankle. We were running out of time to get to the cabin. Hawk was carrying way too much weight for the uncertain footing, especially as fast as he was walking. This was not the time to get turned on by the tall, muscled body I was currently wrapped around. But it wasn't just the body. It was Hawk.

With a sigh, I relaxed against him, resting my cheek against the back of his head. He smelled of spice and sweat and the crisp scent of the snowy woods.

For the first time since that tickle between my shoulder blades, I felt safe.

Even though I knew that in our current predicament, I was anything but.

Chapter Five
QUINN

Visibility was so bad the cabin appeared as if out of nowhere, a dark shape coming into focus through sheets of snow. For the first time, I wondered how Hawk knew the path to the cabin so well. And right after that thought hit, the follow-up struck me: Why had he been on the trail to the cabin in the first place?

I shot a glance at the inches of snow already on the ground, and I knew I'd have time to ask my questions. For now, we weren't going anywhere except inside the cabin.

"Door unlocked?" Hawk asked, his voice low.

"The key's in my pack," I said. "If you put me down, I'll get it."

A grunt. My weight shifted, and Hawk set me on my feet so gently my injured ankle barely twinged. As I was finding my balance, my pack lifted away from my back. I looked up to see it swinging from Hawk's hand.

"Where?" he asked.

"Top pocket," I said. "On a key ring."

Hawk found it and pulled it out, the key dangling in front of him, a little pewter hedgehog hanging from the other end.

"Cute hedgehog." Hawk turned to unlock the cabin door, wiggling the key in the cold lock.

I didn't know why I cared that he thought my key ring was cute. But just like when he'd complimented my escape down the ravine, my chest glowed with warmth. I'd been obsessed with hedgehogs when I was younger; something about their spiky bodies and adorably friendly faces calling to me. I'd always thought I'd own one someday, but it had never happened, and for good reason.

Hedgehogs, it turned out, were not low-maintenance pets. And pets were for people who had a home. A stable life. At the moment, I couldn't bring myself to sleep indoors. Not exactly the responsible adult I pretended to be. Maybe when this thing with the will was over, and I could leave Heartstone Manor for good, I'd consider a pet. A hedgehog. And a dog. I'd always wanted a dog to take hiking, but Prentice hated them, forbidding dogs and cats not just in the Manor but on all Sawyer property, including my guide business.

Despite my throbbing ankle, freezing wet pants, the weather, and everything else that had gone wrong, I smiled. Prentice was gone. His days of manipulating me were done. I still had the will to deal with, but that was a remnant. A ghost. Soon enough, the terms of the will would expire, and I'd finally be free. I just had to be patient. And not get kidnapped or freeze to death in the meantime.

I tried to hop after Hawk, following him into the

cabin. His arm came out, blocking and steadying me at the same time.

"Wait." Leaving me leaning against the doorway, Hawk disappeared into the cabin. He was back less than a minute later. "It's clear. Let's go."

His arm came around my waist, taking the weight from my right side, helping me step-hop into the cabin. We made our way between the sofa and the woodstove to the table and chairs beside the small kitchen.

Hawk hooked a chair with one foot and pulled it out, lowering me to sit. He sat on a second chair and lifted my right leg, balancing my foot on his thigh. I was a block of ice, my wet pants clinging to my skin in the winter-cold cabin. So cold, yet still a rush of heat hit my cheeks as Hawk cradled my foot with such care, carefully picking at the frozen laces.

He lifted his head, his serious eyes meeting mine in apology. "We need to get this boot off. It's too cold in here. You need dry clothes, and I need to get back out there and do another check of the woods before the sun goes down."

I glanced out the window and saw only clouds of white swirling against the glass. It was darker than I'd realized. I'd been so focused on getting to the cabin I'd forgotten the passing time. Sunset wasn't for a few hours, but with the cloud cover and the snow, it would be too dark to see anything long before the sun was officially down.

I wasn't planning to freeze to death now that we were inside. "How long do you need out there?"

Hawk's hands stilled on my laces and he looked up. "At least thirty minutes."

"Then wait on the boot. Go now. I can get the fire started and—"

"No. You're colder than you realize. You need to get out of these wet clothes, and we need to wrap that ankle. I want to pack it in snow to stop the swelling."

I shivered at the thought of snow touching my skin, but he was right. I'd been cold like this once before when I'd hit rapids in a kayak and tipped into a river chilled by snowmelt. Just like then, my head was fuzzy, my limbs heavy with fatigue. I wasn't thinking clearly, inching closer to hypothermia with each second I sat here in wet clothes.

"Fine. Help me get over to the woodstove, and I'll get the fire going. There's a first aid kit under the sink in the kitchen. There should be an elastic bandage in there. I might even have an ice pack."

Hawk was silent for a moment. Then I was in his arms as he picked me up, the heat of his body reminding me how cold I was. I wanted to stop, to burrow into him, inhale his scent of spice and snow, and just stay there, safe and warm. A second later my cold, wet butt hit the even colder cabin floor right in front of the stove. At some point, probably when he redid the cabin, Prentice had added a slate surround to the woodstove. Great for fire safety, but it was like ice against my wet hiking pants.

Everything would be toasty as soon as I got this fire going. Grateful I'd thought to cut plenty of firewood before my vacation, I arranged a fire starter, kindling, and logs. A flick of my lighter, and we were in business. I liked knowing I could start a fire with flint and steel if I had to. Sometimes I preferred it. Like in the summer, when I wasn't on the verge of freezing to death. I watched the fire flare to life in seconds and felt more spoiled than if I'd been draped in diamonds and fur.

Heat blazed over my face, my skin prickling, reminding me that I was dangerously cold and needed to get into dry clothes. With another glance at the flames, I checked that the starter and kindling weren't going to burn out before the logs caught. So far, so good.

Looking up, I saw Hawk, a bandage in one hand and a plastic bag in the other. "Stay there," he said, nudging the pack beside me. "Find some dry clothes while I get this boot off."

I pulled the pack closer and unclipped the top, digging past several waterproof, stuff sacks filled with supplies before I got to the one holding my clothes. I hadn't packed much. Clean underwear, socks, and silk long underwear filled one sack. From another, I pulled out a fleece sweatshirt with a hood. It was too big but cozy as hell, especially with the hood.

I'd managed to ignore the twinges from my ankle as Hawk worked on the laces, but his first tug to remove the boot itself sent a bolt of agony straight to my brain. I sucked in a sharp breath, gritting my teeth against the whimper that wanted to come out.

"Hang in there, Quinn." Hawk's voice was low and rough, as if it hurt him to hurt me.

But I must've been reading him wrong. In all the time I'd known him, he'd never given me any sign he cared. "I'm okay," I managed to say. "Just pull it off."

"Patience," he countered, tugging the laces looser and pulling the side of the boot wide. Blood rushed into my ankle, igniting the nerves, and I fell back to the cold floor, trying to breathe through the pain.

"I'm okay," I breathed. "It's okay."

We both knew I was lying, but the boot had to come off. One more tug, another gasp from me, and the boot dropped to the floor. Hawk's fingers wrapped around the swollen flesh of my ankle with a light touch, probing, testing. I winced. The pressure of his fingers throbbed, but it wasn't the sharp stab of a break. I could handle a sprain. I healed quickly, usually. If I was careful, it would probably be much better tomorrow. Fingers crossed. I wasn't going to let a sprained ankle ruin my vacation.

What about a rogue kidnapper in the woods? a little voice asked in the back of my head. I ignored it. I wasn't thinking about the crazy man in the woods. Not yet.

"I want to pack snow around your ankle," Hawk said, interrupting my thoughts. "Before I wrap it, we need to get you into dry clothes."

We? Had he said we?

It wasn't that I had a problem with Hawk seeing me naked. The thought had crossed my mind more than once. Okay, it had crossed my mind a lot. Daily. But not like this. I hadn't looked in a mirror since we got here, but I could feel my face. My icy, dripping nose was probably bright red. My hair was wet from the snow, strands falling from my braid.

In my wildest dreams, I'd imagined seducing our silent, strong security chief, maybe stripping down to black lace underwear until his eyes popped out of his head. Never, in all my lustful dreams, had I been freezing, injured, nose running, and hair a tangled mess.

I let out a sigh. He was right. The fire was growing, putting out stronger and stronger waves of heat. Soon, it would be time to add another log. Even with that, I was freezing, my damp clothes leaching my body heat despite the fire.

"Turn around and I'll change," I said, knowing there was no way I could get myself into the bedroom and behind a closed door.

Hawk stood, turning his back on me. "Let me know if you need any help."

"Yeah," I said, forcing the mental picture of his hands on my bare skin out of my head so I could focus. I could dress myself, even with a bum ankle. Right?

Chapter Six

QUINN

Except, I couldn't. I did fine with the top half. I tossed my wet parka behind me, hoping it landed somewhere near the front door and the hooks meant for hanging outerwear. Next came my long-sleeved T-shirt and bra, both damp with sweat. I wished being topless in Hawk's presence was more exciting, but I was so cold that all I wanted was to put on dry clothes. I gave a discreet sniff to my armpit. I'd worked up a good sweat hauling my ass up the side of the ravine. Fortunately, my deodorant was holding up. I pulled the black silk long underwear top over my head without a problem. The fleece came next, falling around me like a blanket.

Leaning back, I worked on the snap of my hiking pants. From the waist down, I was soaking wet, the snap frozen, the fabric clinging to my skin. I had winter hiking pants, insulated and waterproof. Too bad they were stowed in the pack beside me. It hadn't been that cold when I'd left, and the snow hadn't been forecast to fall until later. Since I hadn't been planning to roll around on the ground, I'd worn lighter hiking pants that morning. Great for a walk in the woods in cool weather. Not ideal for rolling around in the snow.

My numb fingers slipped off the snap. *Fuck.* I had to lie down all the way to get enough leverage to pull it open, but the floor behind me was wet from my parka.

"Quinn?"

How did he know? I hadn't made a sound.

"The snap on my pants is stuck," I admitted, "And if I lean all the way back to get to it, I'll get wet again."

"Hang on." Hawk moved to kneel beside me. "Try not to put any weight on your foot."

Like that was going to happen. I nodded in agreement.

Hawk looped an arm around my back and hauled me up. The second my weight settled on my left foot, his hands went to my waistband. Warm breath puffed on the side of my neck. I caught a glimpse of Hawk's eyes, locked on his hands at my waist, all his focus on that snap. With a jerk, he ripped it free, the snap popping loose and the zipper tearing all the way down, exposing my plain gray undies.

A flush hit my cheeks, the only part of me that was actually warm. Why couldn't I have been wearing something sexy? Something lacy or a thong. Anything but my boring, gray, quick-dry underwear. Perfect for hand-washing on a hiking trip and a complete dud for seduction. Not that I was seducing anyone in my current situation. But still, this was not the way I'd imagined Hawk first seeing me in my underwear.

And worse, the undies had to go, too. They were as wet as the hiking pants. And though they dried quickly, that was on a line, not on my damp, clammy skin.

Sucking in a deep breath, I braced myself. Hawk had to get me settled so he could do what he needed to do outside before it got dark. We didn't have time for me to make this complicated. I was sure Hawk had seen plenty of women's bodies. Most of those bodies were likely a lot more impressive than mine. Hawk wasn't a flirt. He didn't have to be. With his rugged looks and that body, I'd bet he had women fighting to let him take off their undies. Much sexier undies than mine.

Ugh. Time to get over myself. I shifted, trying to get my cold fingers under the waistband of my now unsnapped pants. The fabric resisted, snagging on my damp skin. I shoved, rocking back against Hawk, instinctively leaning into my right ankle. I gasped at the sudden throb of pain.

Hawk's hands closed over my arms. "Stay still. Hang on to me, and I'll get them."

I squeezed my eyes shut, leaning back into Hawk, dizzy with embarrassment and arousal as he hooked his fingers in the waistband of my pants and shoved them down, taking my panties with them. I tried to focus on keeping my balance, tried not to think about Hawk leaning down to shove the pants to my feet, his soft, damp hair brushing my naked hip.

I sucked in a breath, desperate to pretend I wasn't so aware of him. Inch by inch, he pushed my wet clothes down my legs.

"I'm not looking," he said, his breath grazing my bare hip, sending heat everywhere.

"I know," I whispered, the faint sound all I could manage. I believed he wasn't looking. He was Hawk. He wouldn't lie to me. Not about this.

"Lift your right foot. I'll be careful."

He eased the wet, tangled fabric over my swollen foot. The scruff of his jaw brushed the side of my leg, short-circuiting my brain.

"Fuck," he murmured as we both saw our next problem. He couldn't get my wet clothes off my left leg when I couldn't stand on my right foot. "Hang on."

He stood, lifting me, my wet pants tangled on my left foot, dragging on the floor behind us. Hawk sat on the edge of the leather sofa, settling me beside him. Handing me the dry underwear and long underwear bottoms I'd taken from my pack, he leaned down to tug the wet clothes off my left foot, his head determinedly turned away from my half-naked body.

"Did your father airlift in all this furniture?" he asked.

"That's my guess," I said, leaning down to hook the undies and long underwear over my feet, biting my lip to stay silent as my right ankle protested. "Overkill, but I'm not complaining."

"At least he went for comfortable."

I agreed but didn't say so. I had my underwear and the waistband of the long underwear to my knees, but that was as far as I could go without standing up. *Crap.*

My voice squeaked and broke as I asked, "Can you...?"

"I've got you," Hawk said, his words clipped. "Stand up on your left foot and lean on me. I won't—"

"I know you won't," I choked out, suffocating in embarrassment.

I braced on his shoulder, and in one smooth pull he had my clothes on.

"Sit here. I'll wrap your ankle before I go take a look around outside."

I sat, staring into the lively flames behind the glass door of the woodstove. I could finally feel the tendrils of warmth heating the cabin. Now that my wet clothes were off, the silk long underwear and fleece could do their job, leveraging my own body heat to keep me warm. I shivered, partly from the cold but mostly from Hawk's hand, curving around my right foot.

"Lie back. I'm going to wrap this." I nodded. "It's going to hurt."

I nodded again. "It's okay. Do what you have to do." I knew he didn't want to hurt me. He didn't have a choice. He hesitated, his fingers a warm weight on my skin. "Hawk, it's okay. It'll hurt less later if you wrap it now. Just go for it. Don't worry about me."

The look he shot me told me that was an idiotic statement, and I hid a smile. I shouldn't like that he worried about me. Not as much as I did. Something inside me loved it, soaked up every bit of care he tossed my way. Maybe it was just that I'd been terrified and then almost froze to death. It was a survival reaction. That was all. I was grateful. And I had a crush on him. Appreciating him and wanting to see him naked didn't mean I needed him to care about me.

All of that rolled around in my head. I ignored my complicated feelings in favor of the question that had been bothering me since we got to the cabin.

"Why were you there?" I asked, hissing in a breath a second later as he began wrapping my ankle. The compression of the bandage sent nauseating pain rolling through me.

"Why was I where?" he asked, head bent, eyes glued to my foot.

"On the trail to the cabin. Did you know?"

"That someone was going to jump you on the trail?" he asked.

I nodded, my teeth clenching as he tightened the bandage, wrapping it around my ankle.

Hawk shook his head. "I was looking for you, but the timing was luck. I was down in the surveillance room, and they had the radio on the weather service. The storm shifted, and the snow is going to be a lot worse than we thought."

I nodded, not surprised. "How much are we going to get?"

"When I left, they were saying it could be a foot. Maybe eighteen inches. At this point, they're just guessing."

"Did they say how long it would be coming down?" I asked, wondering if I was going to get my forest fairyland the next day. It couldn't still be snowing tomorrow. Could it? Neither of us could hike back down to the Manor with this much snow on the ground—the trail was narrow and rocky. Not exactly dangerous, but definitely treacherous in places when it wasn't covered with a foot and a half of snow. With snow on it, it was impassable. We'd have to wait until it melted.

Hawk shrugged one shoulder in a short jerk that told me he'd worked out the same logic I had—that we weren't going anywhere anytime soon. I saw he was almost finished with the bandage. Now that he was on the second layer, it didn't hurt as much.

"Do we have enough food?" he asked.

"There's plenty," I assured him. "Not anything up to the standards of Finn's creations, but we won't starve, even if we're stuck here for a week."

Now that the pain had lessened, my brain went immediately to what two people stuck in a cabin for a week could get up to. I blushed, but if Hawk saw it, he didn't react.

Hawk nodded, using the little metal clamps that came with the bandage to secure the end. Lifting my foot, he stood, setting my wrapped ankle on a pillow. He grabbed the blanket draped over the back of the sofa and laid it over me. Digging in his pocket, he pulled out a packet containing a single dose of ibuprofen that I recognized from the first aid kit where he'd found the bandage. I had more in my pack, but this would do for now.

My fingers fumbled to tear it open. I was still so fucking cold. I wasn't going to die of hypothermia, not now, but it was still slowing me down. Hawk plucked the packet from my hands, trading it for the bottle of water he must have pulled from the side of my pack. A second later, the two blue tablets dropped into my palm.

"I'll be back in a minute." He snagged the plastic bag he'd had earlier and went outside, returning with the full bag, tied shut.

Setting it on top of my foot, he pressed gently, molding the snow-filled bag around my ankle. Cold seeped through the bandage.

"Don't move," he ordered, turning to add another log to the fire. "I want to scout the woods around the cabin. I'll be back in thirty minutes or less. I'm locking the door behind me. I'll knock three times when I get back so you know it's me." He dragged my pack to the side of the sofa, digging in a side pocket to retrieve my gun and handing it to me.

His implication was clear. I didn't ask what I should do if he didn't return in thirty minutes because I knew what his answer would be. If he didn't return, it meant he was dead, and I'd have to defend myself as best I could.

"Go," I said. "I'll stay put. I promise."

Hawk grunted at that, his eyes landing on me for less than a second. He'd barely looked at me since he'd pulled off my clothes. Had I embarrassed him? Repulsed him? No. I was no bombshell, but I wasn't gross. Maybe he was just annoyed at the situation. Or freaked out. Hopefully, I'd have time to figure it out later.

"Be careful," I said, knowing it was dumb. Hawk knew what he was doing out there. Probably better than I did. Definitely, when it came to scouting for the nutjob who'd attacked me.

Hawk didn't respond to my concern, focused on lighting the kerosene lantern I had on the kitchen table. When he was done, and a golden glow illuminated the kitchen area, he said, "Keep your weapon close. I wouldn't leave if I didn't think it was safe, but—"

"I know. I've got it." I set the gun on the top of the pack beside me. "Go, before it gets too dark."

With a nod, he left, locking the door behind him.

Chapter Seven

QUINN

Silence fell in the cabin, the occasional crackle of the fire muffled by the glass doors of the woodstove. The air was finally warming up, and beneath the thick wool blanket I wasn't toasty, but no longer freezing. Shivers racked me, my body doing its best to warm up. My eyes flicked to the door. Hawk was out there. Alone. Hunting for the man who'd tried to... what, kidnap me? What was he going to do with me? Maybe he was going to kill me, but he wanted me tied up first so he could—

What if he took Hawk by surprise? What if he shot him? What if he—

I forced myself to draw in a long breath on a count of six. I held it, counting to four before I exhaled on another count of six. This wasn't an avalanche, a flood, a sinking boat, or an animal attack. I'd taken every wilderness survival class I could, and not one of them covered scary kidnappers in the woods. I carried my gun and knew how to use it, but when I needed it, I never got the chance.

Remembering the way he'd hit my wrist, making my hand go numb as I dropped my gun, I shivered.

I counted to four, then started again with a six-count inhale. And again, until the panic cleared from my head.

Hawk knew what he was doing. If he thought he needed to scout around the cabin, I wasn't going to stop him. The only helpful thing I could do was calm the fuck down. Hysteria was not going to help anybody. A clear head was the most important asset in a crisis.

I counted in another slow breath, thinking of Hawk. His controlled expression, his dark eyes always alert, taking in every detail around him. At first, I'd thought he was missing a personality. Then I'd seen it. His sly sense of humor so dry it was easy to miss. The way he grinned at Griffen when he thought no one else was looking. He was professional to the core when it came to the rest of us, but with Griffen, he was different. Relaxed. Or as relaxed as a man like Hawk ever got.

After our encounter this morning with the mama bear, I'd had a fantasy of Hawk in the early morning, this time without the mama bear and cubs. I'd pull him into my hammock and finally get my hands under his snug T-shirt. After years of seeing men as a take-it-or-leave-it kind of deal, Hawk sent my hormones straight to a simmer.

And now he'd seen me wet and bedraggled, nose running, crying from the pain of a stupid twisted ankle. I sighed. That was not the plan. To tell the truth, I didn't have a plan. I'd never intentionally seduced a man before, and I'd never been involved with anyone as intimidating as Hawk.

I glanced at my watch. It was closing in on thirty minutes. Why wasn't he back yet? What if—

No.

Breathe and relax, I ordered myself. *He'll be back. Nothing is going to happen to Hawk. He'll come back and we'll be alone in this cabin until the weather clears.* Alone with Hawk. The possibilities made my head spin.

I liked sex. It was fun, most of the time. I wasn't desperate without it, but it had been a while. Maybe that was why Hawk had gotten so deep under my skin. I rolled my eyes at my excuses. It wasn't a lack of sex, it was Hawk. He was compelling. Magnetic. I'd wanted him since he set foot in Heartstone Manor. There didn't need to be a why. He was Hawk. That was enough.

Three quick taps and the scratch of metal on metal sounded at the door. The key turned in the lock. Hawk opened the door, snow swirling in behind him.

"Did you see any sign of him out there?" I asked.

Hawk shook his head, stopping to hang his wet jacket on the hook by the door. He pulled his boots off, knocked them together, and placed them in the boot tray beneath the jacket hooks. Silently, he padded across the floor in his socks and retrieved my jacket and boots, putting them away next to his.

"Thanks," I said, my lips curving at his nod.

I wasn't obsessively neat, but I was careful with my gear. I kept my things organized, and I couldn't stand cleaning up after other people. It looked like that wouldn't be a problem with Hawk.

"Is the snow slowing down any?" I asked.

Hawk stood beside the woodstove, soaking in the

heat. "Not slowing down. It's hard to say since it's getting dark, but it looked like it's coming down harder. As soon as it stops, we can head back."

"What? I'm not heading back," I said.

"Quinn, someone tried to kill you. You can't stay out here by yourself." Hawk glared at me, his chin jutting out. Obstinate.

I could be obstinate, too. "I can stay wherever I want. And don't try to tell me the Manor is safer."

"It is safer, and you know it."

I raised an eyebrow, thinking of the previous attacks inside the Manor while I'd been safe outside in my hammock.

Hawk shook his head. "It was never about you before. Now it is."

"It's not—"

"Why?" Hawk interrupted. "Why did he come after you? Who is he?"

"I have no clue," I said, startled by the idea that I might know anything about the stranger in the woods. I hadn't taken the time to think about it, but I realized that from the start I'd assumed it was random. That whoever he was, he'd seen an opportunity in a lone woman in the woods. Why would anyone come after me specifically?

Crossing to the sofa, Hawk pulled the bag of melted snow off my foot, carrying it to the sink. Leaving the bag to drain, he came back to the sofa, sitting on the arm.

"Are you sure you don't know him?" Hawk asked, his voice deadly serious. Before I could answer, he ran a finger along the bottom of my toes, the flesh tingling with heat under his light touch. "You feel that?" he asked.

I nodded. "It's not broken."

His eyes lifted to mine. "You're sure?"

I shrugged again. "As sure as I can be. I've broken bones before. This feels like a gnarly sprain. It hurts, but everything's in working order." I wiggled my toes, bracing for the flash of pain. "It's good. See?"

Hawk nodded and stood, moving to the armchair set at an angle to the sofa. I wanted him to stay, to sit on the sofa and pull my legs into his lap. But this was Hawk, and right now he was all business.

"You're sure you didn't recognize him?" Hawk asked again.

I shook my head but made myself think back to the look I'd gotten at his eyes. The rest of his face had been hidden by his camo balaclava. "I don't think so. I only saw his eyes clearly, and I didn't recognize them."

"Did he say anything?"

"No. Not a word." And wasn't that weird? I hadn't had a chance to think about it until now.

"You have no idea what he wanted?" Hawk asked, his eyes taking in every nuance of my expression.

I made myself think before I answered. I wanted to say that I didn't know. And I didn't, but I could guess. "I think he wanted to take me somewhere. Kidnap me."

Hawk's head tilted to the side as he absorbed that information. "What makes you think kidnapping?"

"He was focused on getting the zip tie on my hands. If he wanted to kill me, he had that knife. He could have just slit my throat. He probably had a gun. He could have shot me before I saw him." Option number two had to be addressed, as much as I didn't want to. "And he could have been getting my hands out of the way so he could—" My words cut off. I didn't want to say it. "But he didn't touch me that way. I don't think he wanted that."

Hawk nodded, not pushing further. I didn't want to think about what could have happened. I wasn't sure the man in the woods hadn't planned to kill me, eventually. But his hands on my body had been efficient. Clinical. He never lingered, never grabbed my breasts or anything else, even once my hands were tied. He'd had me pinned. He could have done anything he wanted.

"I don't know where he wanted to take me or what he planned when he got me there," I said. "But I'm glad I didn't find out. I'm pretty sure you saved my life."

Hawk didn't say a word.

"Thank you," I said, inwardly squirming under his heavy gaze.

More silence.

Finally, Hawk said, "What if he was taking you here?"

Icy shock washed through me. It made a sickening kind of sense. The cabin was the closest place to hide out, and no one else was headed this way. If the weather hadn't changed, if Hawk hadn't decided to come after me, I would have been alone, with no way to contact the Manor if I needed help.

But what would he want with me? Unless this wasn't about me, but about who I was related to? What if he wanted to kidnap me to get something from my family... and when he'd failed, he'd gone after them directly?

"Can you reach your team at the Manor? Did he go

there after you shot him? Is my family okay?" I asked, suddenly afraid.

"I checked in while I was scouting the woods. The sat phone's signal is spotty but good enough for texts. Everything is quiet at the Manor. We considered a rescue, but they can't get to us on foot with the snow this thick, and with the wind, coming in by air is too dangerous. I told them we'd sit tight and head back as soon as the snow clears enough to see where we're going."

Reality slammed into me. In this weather, I'd be forced to sleep in the Manor. And it wasn't just the weather. Someone had tried to kidnap me. Kidnapping was the best-case scenario. His plan probably hadn't included my survival.

Griffen had been cool about me sleeping in my hammock, but that had been before. Now? There was no way. I hadn't missed how protective he was since he'd come home. He'd let me sleep in the woods because he understood I needed it. But if my life was on the line, he'd lock me in my bedroom if he had to. Despair flooded my heart. Before it could settle in, I pushed it away. *Later*. I'd think about it later.

Hawk must have agreed. We could fight this battle when the snow let up. For now, the storm made leaving an impossibility. "How safe are we here?" I asked.

"Safe enough as long as the weather stays like this. After it clears?" Hawk shook his head. "Depends. Not safe enough."

I chose not to say anything to that. We were safe for now. That was good enough for me.

"And you don't know why?" Hawk asked. It took me

a second to realize he was asking about the man in the woods.

Automatically, I shook my head. "Why would anybody try to hurt me?" I was the lowest profile Sawyer. I didn't have any enemies. I didn't do anything to piss people off. I took people fishing and hiking. I was friendly and nice and helpful when I could be. I shook my head again. "I don't have any idea—"

And then this morning clicked into focus.

"I— This morning—"

"What? What happened this morning?" Hawk demanded, leaning forward.

"I— I went to see Harvey about—" My words stuttered as my brain flew through the conversation with Harvey and the reason I'd been there, pieces coming together in my head. "I went to see Harvey about a necklace I found in the cabin. This cabin."

I looked around the main room.

"This isn't what this place looked like when I was a kid," I explained. "It used to be a regular hunting cabin. There was a basic woodstove and a basin in the kitchen instead of a sink. Some folding chairs and a card table. When I was a kid, I would sneak over and look through the windows. There were rough bunks in the bedroom. Four of them. Gun racks everywhere."

Hawk nodded. I figured he'd seen a hunting cabin or two.

"When I came back after Prentice died," I said, "he'd turned it into this."

Together we looked around, taking in the leather

armchairs and couches. The solid table and chairs. The sink in the kitchen.

"The woodstove is new and much nicer than the one that was here before. There's a real bathroom with a composting toilet and a propane water heater. He even put in running water from a stream nearby. And a queen-sized bed."

At that, Hawk fully got my meaning. "Prentice was meeting somebody out here. A woman."

"That's my guess. He sure as hell wasn't out here hunting. Griffen said I could do whatever I wanted with the place, and I was gradually cleaning things out, bringing my stuff in. Last week I moved the bed. Prentice had it facing a mirror." I rolled my eyes. "I moved it to face the window so I could look out at the woods. When I did, I found a necklace. A gold oak leaf on a chain."

"You're sure it wasn't your mother's?" Hawk asked.

"I can't be positive, but I don't think so. She wasn't into the outdoors, and she liked pretty, sparkly things. I can't see her wearing a leaf as jewelry." It disturbed me a little to know that my father's lover and I shared the same taste in jewelry. Considering how much he'd hated me, it felt odd that he'd chosen a woman who was anything like his most despised daughter.

"So you brought it to Harvey?" Hawk pressed.

"He and Griffen went through the family jewelry collection after we all came home," I explained. "I thought if the necklace was part of that, he'd know. Or there might be matching pieces. I didn't know what else to do with it. We've been looking for the woman Vanessa mentioned in those blackmail letters. Maybe the same woman who bought all those baby things Savannah and Finn found in the attic. And I thought, I don't know, maybe Harvey..."

I trailed off, and Hawk asked, "Who was there when you went to Harvey's office?"

"Just his receptionist. She saw me come in. Harvey might have mentioned why I was there, though I doubt it."

"Just the receptionist and Harvey? That was it?"

I nodded.

"We don't know who Harvey talked to," Hawk said. "He was going to try to find out where the necklace came from?"

"That was the idea," I said slowly, understanding what Hawk was getting at. "He could have called anyone. Do you think that's what this was about? The necklace?"

Hawk shook his head. "We don't know, and as long as we're stuck here, there isn't much we can do to figure it out." He stood. "Are you hungry?"

I started to shake my head. I was warm, finally. And thirsty. And starving. "I could use some food. I have a good dinner for tonight."

Hawk raised an eyebrow.

"New York strips from the butcher in town. There are mushrooms and an onion. And butter."

"You brought steak?" Hawk asked. "Where?"

"In the front pocket of my pack. I picked it up this morning. The rest of the stuff is on the shelf in the kitchen. There's a propane stove and a cast-iron pan hanging on the wall. I brought two steaks, so there's enough for both of us."

Hawk unzipped the front pocket of my pack and pulled out the package wrapped in brown paper stamped with the logo of the local butcher shop. "What else did you bring up here?" he asked, crossing to the kitchen.

"I stocked it with canned and freeze-dried food a while ago, but this week, I brought up the butter and eggs. There's powdered milk and cocoa. Under the counter, there's a dual-zone cooler hooked up to propane. I don't usually use it, but I turned it on yesterday when I brought up the ice cream."

"You bring steak and ice cream camping?" Hawk asked, finding the cutting board and the veggies I'd stocked. He seasoned the steak with the bottle of salt and herbs on the shelf and went to work slicing the onion.

"Not usually," I admitted, "but this was supposed to be my vacation." I glanced down the sofa at my bandaged ankle. "I've been injured on trips before, but never on the first day. Not even that. On the hike in." I let out an exasperated sigh. "I won't get another break for months."

"At least you're alive," Hawk said.

"Good point," I said. I was all about counting my blessings. I'd almost been murdered, and I wasn't going to be exploring the mountain until my ankle healed. But I was alive and warm.

And I was snowed in with Hawk Bristol.

At that moment, being stranded with Hawk felt like a hell of a blessing. I thought about the way Hawk had lost his cool that morning when the bear cubs got too close. The way he couldn't look at me after he'd helped me change. Maybe I didn't repulse him. Maybe he was as aware of me as I was of him.

There was only one way to find out.

Chapter Eight

HAWK

It had been a while since I cooked myself dinner. Even longer since I'd cooked for a woman. Not that Quinn was a woman. Not like that. This wasn't a date.

I couldn't believe I had to remind myself this wasn't a date.

Quinn was my closest friend's little sister. And she'd just been attacked, for fuck's sake. She was a client. A patient, I added, thinking of her ankle. Not a woman.

Steak sizzled in the cast-iron pan, the cabin fragrant with caramelizing onions and mushrooms sautéed in butter. My stomach growled. I was no cordon bleu chef like Finn, but I could handle steak in a cast-iron pan, and Quinn was probably as hungry as I was. Hungrier, even, given the adrenaline surge she was coming down from. I knew what that was like.

I'd been attacked, and I'd been the attacker, and I knew being attacked was far worse. At least when you were the person doing the attacking you knew what to expect, knew when the hits would come. Quinn had been out for a hike on a pretty winter day, and boom. Some asshole had come out of nowhere and taken her down. I had to force myself to stop thinking about it, or the picture in my head would drive me crazy. Who the fuck had dared to touch her?

Giving in to the urge, I glanced over my shoulder at the slight figure bundled up on the couch, her injured ankle elevated, the wool blanket pulled up to her shoulders, her eyes fixed on the flickering firelight in the woodstove.

She looked at peace. Relaxed. Happy to be in the cabin, despite the circumstances. I didn't know what to make of a woman whose fondest dream was a vacation in an off-the-grid cabin. Alone. I couldn't fault her taste. This little place was as close to heaven as we came on earth. We were surrounded by some of the most beautiful forests I'd seen, with all the creature comforts I'd want and nothing I didn't.

She'd come here for solitude. Instead, she got attacked, injured, and now she was stuck with me.

I couldn't give her what she wanted. I couldn't leave her to her solitude. Not just because of the weather. Whoever had jumped her was still out there, potentially plotting their next chance to get at her. Not knowing their motive made me uneasy. More than just uneasy. Fucking scared shitless.

You didn't stalk someone with zip ties when you planned to return them in one piece. And this was Quinn. She needed me to watch over her, as much as she thought she didn't. Quinn Sawyer might be a pint-sized badass, but whoever wanted to hurt her would come back. I was sure of it.

Even as that dark thought swirled, I was glad I had my back to her so I could hide my grin as I remembered the way she'd hauled her ass up the side of that ravine, digging her fingers into the damp earth, ignoring the cold, the pain in her ankle, just doing what had to be done. I didn't know why I found that hot, but I did.

And that was the reason I shouldn't be here. Not just that I was interrupting her solitude and her vacation. I needed to get the hell out of here because when it came to Quinn Sawyer, I couldn't keep my head in the game. She destroyed my focus, and I couldn't seem to remember that she was Griffen's baby sister. She was a Sawyer, and I was very much not.

Quinn was not for me. I wasn't sure any woman was. All the shit I'd done, the blood on my hands, the ugliness that lived in my head— I couldn't picture a woman who deserved to be saddled with me.

But if there was, it wasn't Quinn. She deserved so much better than an ex-soldier steeped in darkness. In regret. She deserved a man who came to her clean, who could give her a family and children. None of that was me.

The fact that I wanted her didn't matter. It was wrong. It was all fucking wrong. And still, I wanted her. What I should be doing was leaving. But not only was that impossible because of the weather, she needed me to keep her safe.

To distract myself, I turned the steaks, my mouth watering at the crust on the done side. We were warm, dry, and we were going to have a hell of a dinner. Pretty good, given the state of things when we got here.

From the couch, I heard, "That smells fantastic. I swear I could eat a horse."

"I bet," I said. "Not the easy hike you were expecting."

"Yeah, that's the understatement of the century," Quinn said, then lapsed back into silence.

And I remembered. I shouldn't. But I did.

Inching down her wet clothes, my cheek against her hip, her skin like silk. She'd been cold as ice but so soft, smelling of snow and woman. It had taken everything I had not to look. Not to touch. Not to turn my head and bury my face between her legs. I never would have thought one small woman could push me so close to the edge of my control without even trying. But no woman had been Quinn.

I'd never been one for taking what wasn't mine, and Quinn was not mine. She wasn't, and she never would be.

"This is almost done," I said, trying to shake myself out of my circling thoughts.

"There are plates on the shelf to the left of the sink," Quinn said, "and silverware in the holder beside it. I don't have steak knives, but we can use the one you cut the onion with."

I nodded. "Drinks?"

Quinn sat up a little. I hated her wince as she moved her ankle, hated her being in pain.

"I'll stick with water for now. After dinner, I think I'll

have some of that bourbon I found stashed in a cupboard when I cleaned the place up."

"Good stuff?" I asked.

"Very good," she said. "I didn't agree with my father on much, but he had good taste in bourbon."

"I don't know many women who drink bourbon," I said as I plated the steak, piling onions and mushrooms on the side of each one and carrying them to the table.

Quinn pushed off the wool blanket and levered herself to sit on the edge of the couch, lowering her feet carefully to the floor. "I never used to like it," she said. "I always stuck to mixed drinks or beer. But a few years ago, a friend dragged me to a bourbon tasting, and I was surprised to find I love it."

I had a sudden flash of Quinn sitting in front of the fire, sipping bourbon, my arm around her. I blinked it away. *Not for me. Never for me.*

I snagged her water bottle off the floor and set it on the table beside her plate before coming back to her side. "Are you ready?" I asked. She nodded, and I leaned down, sliding an arm around her torso.

I tried not to think about how she felt in my arms.

"Three, two, one," I counted. On *one* we stood, Quinn leaning her weight into me. Together we made our way to the table, me walking and Quinn hopping.

"It should be a lot better tomorrow," she said as she lowered into her chair, letting me push it in. I came around to her right side, pulling out another chair.

"Rest it on this," I said, leaning down to lift her foot to the seat of the chair. "Okay?"

Quinn nodded through gritted teeth. By the time I was in my seat, she had her breath back.

As I sat, she smiled that bright smile that always got to me. There was something so alive about Quinn. Her blue eyes, the way she'd grin, vitality spilling out of her. She was a flame, her warmth drawing me in, pulling me closer and closer until I lost myself in her fire and ended up burned to a cinder.

Or I burned her. Badly. Because that was what would happen. I knew it, even if she didn't.

"It'll be a lot better tomorrow," she repeated. Picking up one of the knives I'd found in the kitchen, she cut into the steak. She stabbed a piece on her fork and held it up, declaring, "Perfect."

It looked perfect, pink in the center, tender and juicy. I took a bite and chewed. Pretty fucking good and exactly what I needed after the past few hours. Quinn finished chewing and swallowed, then flashed another bright grin my way.

"How do you know it'll be better tomorrow?" I asked, thinking I should keep my eyes on my plate and off her face.

"I've sprained it before," she said. "Always the fucking right ankle too."

"Is it weak?" I asked, knowing that repeated strains could leave the ligaments prone to future injury.

Quinn shrugged. "Not really. Not so I notice it, but it always seems to be the one I come down on wrong when shit happens. Usually, it doesn't take long to get back into shape." Her smile faded away, eyes dropping to her plate.

"It's not going to heal in time for me to do any real hiking while I'm here. Even resting it while the snow lasts won't be good enough. I'll be able to hobble soon, but not much more than that."

"Not if you want it to heal right," I added.

She nodded in agreement and let out a sigh. "I wish I'd shot him before he got my gun away from me."

"For trying to kidnap you or for ruining your vacation?" I asked, and there was that grin again. It shot straight to my heart. That smile was the best reward for cracking a joke. Not everybody got my sense of humor, but Quinn did.

"Both," she answered. "But at this point, maybe more for ruining my vacation."

"The snow isn't helping," I said.

Quinn shrugged. "Yeah, but once it stops snowing, and the sun comes out, it'll be beautiful out there, like a sparkling fairyland. So I can forgive the snow. The asshole who jumped me, tried to kidnap me and made me fuck up my ankle—he can rot in hell."

"Maybe we'll get the chance to put him there," I said. I immediately regretted my words when Quinn paled.

"You think he's going to try again?"

Without a doubt, I thought. Out loud, I said, "At this point, we don't know. We don't know why he was here, what he wanted, or why he went after you."

"The necklace—" Quinn started to say, and I shook my head.

"It could be about the necklace, or it could be something else. We don't know enough to make assumptions.

Assumptions won't keep you safe. As soon as this snow ends and we have visibility, we're headed back."

And there it was. Mutiny.

Chapter Nine
HAWK

Quinn set her jaw, and her eyes went hard. "I'm not going back."

"Are you suicidal?" I had to ask.

"No," she said, no give in her expression. "But I refuse to live in fear."

Our eyes locked. I tried to wait her out, but she held my gaze in silence. Her jaw didn't unclench. Her eyes didn't soften. She wasn't going to give in.

I should have known. I understood the sentiment exactly. But that didn't mean she was right.

I glanced out the window at the snow still falling in the fading light and decided to embrace reality myself. "There's no point arguing about it now," I said. "The snow is forecast to last until tomorrow morning. We'll figure out what to do when it stops."

"Fine," Quinn agreed, the temper draining out of her face.

She cut another piece of steak. I did the same.

Hers was half gone when she said, "This is really

good. Do you know how to cook or is this all you can make?"

I shrugged. I wasn't sure I wanted to talk. No good could come of talking about myself to Quinn, but what was I going to do, refuse to answer? I imagined seeing her face fall when I rejected her. She was just trying to be nice. I could pretend to be nice for an hour or two. "I wouldn't say I know how to cook," I said slowly. "Not like Finn."

Quinn snorted a laugh. "Nobody knows how to cook like Finn."

"True," I agreed. We were just talking about food. It wasn't a big deal. "I can make steak. I grill a mean burger. I know how to bake a potato. Meatloaf. I like broccoli, so I can make that. But that's about it."

"What's your favorite thing to cook?" she asked.

"Probably steak," I said. "Second would be spaghetti and meatballs, though I usually buy the meatballs frozen. What about you? You grew up with a cook. Do you know how to feed yourself?"

Quinn's laugh was like sunshine. She shook her head. "Not well," she admitted. "Camp food? Absolutely. I can cook over a fire like you wouldn't believe. Cowboy chili, coffee, burgers. Hot dogs and sausages. I can do a lot with a fire and a Dutch oven, but I'm lost in a regular kitchen. When I went to college, there was a food hall, and I had a meal plan, so I didn't cook there. And then after, Ford helped me set up Sawyer Outdoor Adventures, and I moved in there." A wistful smile spread across her face. "I love that place. There's a small bedroom in the back, along with a bathroom and a tiny kitchen. I use most of the space for the business, so I never tried to expand it. There's not really enough room to do much cooking. I like to eat, but cooking isn't really my thing."

"How did you get into guiding?" I asked, curious. I told myself I didn't need to know. I didn't need to, but I wanted to. I wanted to know anything she was willing to tell me about herself. Especially how Quinn Sawyer, a member of one of the wealthiest, most influential families in the country, ended up running a guide business. "You're not exactly following in the family footsteps of turning millions into billions."

Quinn's smile was serene and joyful. "I love the woods," she said. "Always, as long as I can remember, I was running off and hiding in the woods. Used to drive my mother crazy when I was little. I'd disappear, and they'd find me under the trees, watching the birds and squirrels. I always felt more at home in the woods than I did inside."

She chased an onion around her plate with her fork, her eyes distant.

"The old groundskeeper was an outdoorsman. He was like me, never more at home than when he was outside, the wind on his cheeks. I annoyed him, always asking questions about the trees and the plants."

I could picture that bright smile on a child's face, her infectious enthusiasm. She'd gotten me, a man known for monosyllabic answers, talking about my favorite foods. I had no doubt she'd charmed the old groundskeeper just as easily.

"I didn't want a garden," she said. "I just wanted to know about the outdoors. And then I found out that he loved to camp and hunt and fish and hike. And he taught me things. What plants I could eat, and what to stay away from. How to find or make a shelter. How to fish. How to leave the woods the way I found them. Later, I talked Prentice into sending me to summer camp, and I learned more. Kayaking and canoeing. I got to camp for real. Prentice didn't like having me around, so he was more than happy to pay to get rid of me. At least in the summer. When I was a teenager, I tried to get him to send me to one of those outdoorsy boarding schools, but Sawyers go to Laurel Country Day."

"Except for Finn," I said, trying to make her smile. I hated the look in her eyes when she talked about her father. All the life faded, leaving her dull and lost. Not like my Quinn.

I was rewarded with a quirk to the side of her mouth. Not exactly a smile, but I'd take it. "I wish I'd thought to set the principal's office on fire," she said, "but I never had the balls. Too scared of my father." Her eyes dropped and she looked away.

There was pain there. Not simply the pain of a neglected child. This was more. Deeper. Ugly. I wanted to ask. I didn't. I had my own ugliness buried inside, ugliness I'd never show someone as bright and lovely as Quinn. And I couldn't ask for hers if I wasn't willing to show her mine.

Fuck. This was why I didn't talk to people. Too complicated. I didn't want to know Quinn's pain…

And that was a lie. I wanted to know everything about Quinn. I wouldn't ask. But maybe I could make her feel a little better.

"From what I've heard," I said, "almost everyone was afraid of your father."

Quinn lifted her chin and nodded, stabbing at a mushroom still left on her plate. "Well, that's true. He was a real asshole. Anyway, I didn't know what I wanted to do with my life after college. After I graduated, Ford took me on a two-week kayaking trip out West. A few days into the trip, I was watching the guide organize us, showing us what to do and keeping all the gear together, and I realized that I could do that. I wanted to do it, to plan trips and show people everything I love about the outdoors. Ford thought it was a great idea. He helped me figure it out."

"What did he do to help you?" I asked, curious to see another side to Ford Sawyer. As Griffen's friend, I knew Ford as the brother who'd betrayed Griffen and stolen his life. In my mind, Ford was a villain, full stop. Clearly, that wasn't who Ford was to Quinn.

"He ran interference with Prentice to fund the business, for one thing," she said. "And he paid for all of the training courses I needed out of his own pocket. It would have taken me years to pull it off without him."

"You really love it," I said, though I didn't need to ask. It was written all over her.

She shot me that quick grin again. "I do. I didn't think there was anything that was better than being out in the wild, but showing it to other people, seeing them fall in love with it is amazing. So many people come to this part of the country to appreciate all the beauty we have here. It's a privilege to get to show them what it's really like."

Quinn straightened in her seat, taking a sip of water.

"I had a client last spring. He was a fly fisherman and dragged his wife and their two kids along with him to Sawyers Bend. They didn't want to come here. They were voting for Orlando and the parks. But man, his wife caught a rainbow trout, and the smile on her face–" Quinn glowed at the memory. "Then the kids got into it, and by the end, I had a family of fishermen. It was so cool. It doesn't always happen like that. Sometimes people hate it. Sometimes they complain. Sometimes they think they know what they're doing better than I do. Sometimes they do, and that's really cool, too. There's always more to learn."

She sat back and crossed her arms over her chest, the side of her mouth curling in a smirk.

"Sometimes the dudes try to mansplain fishing or hiking. That's always fun."

I snorted, picturing that exactly. "What do you do with them?" I asked, already knowing Quinn didn't take shit from anyone.

"It depends," she said. "It doesn't pay to fight with clients. And depending on where we are and who it is, it's not always a good idea to piss a guy off. I'm not exactly six-four or a black belt, you know?"

My gut went cold at the picture her careless words painted.

"I do have a speck of charm," she said. "I drag it out in those situations. And if the guy is being a total jackass, I just let him do what he wants. I had one guy last year who was absolutely convinced he could fly-fish with worms. Told me that was how his daddy did it, and that was how he did it. No woman was going to tell him different, and no amount of convincing could change his mind." She snorted a laugh and rolled her eyes. "Idiot."

"He catch anything?" I asked, wondering at her patience with that level of stupidity.

She laughed. "Not a damn thing. He got jack shit, and the rest of us had a great day. He stormed out and didn't show up the next day, which was fine with me. I had his money. Too late for refunds." She let out a sigh. "I do hope he finally bought some flies, though."

Looking down at her empty plate, I asked, "Are you done?"

"Oh, yeah. That was so good. Thank you."

"Any time," I said, meaning it more than I should. Despite the circumstances, I couldn't remember a time when I'd enjoyed a simple meal with a woman more. *Dammit.*

I carried our plates to the sink, staring out the window into a wall of swirling white. Was it snowing harder? Was that even possible? No, it was just getting dark, making the snow look thick, impenetrable, and unending.

I had to get the fuck out of here.

Self-control had never been a problem of mine. Never. So why now? Why her? Why Quinn, with her bright smiles and soft skin? *Fuck.* Why couldn't I keep my shit together?

"Where's that bourbon?" I asked, knowing alcohol was the last thing I needed.

"Lower right cabinet," Quinn said. "I don't really have glasses. Those camping mugs up there on the shelf should do the job."

I snagged the bottle of bourbon, a stout, rounded vessel of thick beveled glass with a distinctive horse and rider cork. Blanton's. This was the good stuff. I grabbed two of the blue-speckled enamel mugs and brought them to the table, pouring for both of us, Quinn's serving more generous than mine. The last thing I needed was too much alcohol in my system. My judgment was impaired enough with Quinn in the same room.

She took a sip and swallowed, letting out a sigh of contentment. "Thanks for rescuing me," she said quietly.

I nodded and didn't answer. I couldn't put words to the complicated twist of emotions in my chest. Bone-deep terror that someone had tried to hurt her. What would have happened if I hadn't been following to tell her the weather? What if— *No.* I shut it off. What-ifs weren't any good to anyone.

I wanted to promise I'd never let anything happen to her, that I'd protect her always.

I couldn't make that promise for so many reasons. For one thing, I shouldn't be close enough to her to keep that promise. And for another, I couldn't protect anyone forever. What was I going to do, follow her everywhere?

"We'll find him," I said, hoping I wasn't lying.

She just nodded and took another sip of the bourbon. "It hasn't snowed like this since I was a kid," she said. "The winter I was thirteen, we got almost two feet, and it stayed cold for over a week. It took ages to get somebody to plow the driveway, and we were all stuck in the house. My father was on a business trip and couldn't get home. It was just us kids and the staff who got stranded with us.

That week was the most fun I remember from growing up there."

I felt the smile lift the side of my mouth. I had my own memories of snow days and sledding, my mother waiting with hot cocoa and a hug. My childhood was long gone, but while it lasted it had been great. Quinn's best memory was a storm like this one, of being trapped with her siblings. I knew without asking that it hadn't been her siblings or the snow that made the memory good. It had been the absence of her father.

My life had gone to shit after my parents died, but while I'd had them, they'd been the best. People liked to think money could solve any problem, but I wouldn't trade the small house I'd grown up in, my thrift store sneakers, and store-brand cocoa for Quinn's childhood. Not for all the millions she might one day inherit. I'd ruined my own life with bad decisions, but while my parents lived, I'd had love, which was a hell of a lot more than Quinn had.

Chapter Ten

HAWK

Quinn let out a jaw-cracking yawn, shaking me out of my thoughts.

"It's too early for yawning," she said.

"Not given the day you've had. Sleep will help that ankle."

"I know." She yawned again.

"Ready for bed?" I asked.

"I don't want to be, but I think I am." She tossed back the last of the bourbon. "Can you help me to the bathroom?" I moved to help her stand, but she shook her head. "Would you grab that blue stuff sack I pulled out of my pack?"

"Yeah, sure." I grabbed the stuff sack, feeling the contents roll around as I lifted it. Toiletries, probably. I slid my arm around her waist and helped her up. We did the walk/hop thing to get her from the table to the bathroom.

"I've got it from here," she said, hopping into the small room and closing the door behind her.

I turned to survey the cabin. The table was clear. Nothing needed cleaning but the dishes we'd eaten on and the cast-iron pan. The water lines to the sink were shut off this time of year, but Quinn had left several full water jugs beside the sink. I had the dishes done and dried in a few minutes.

The fire had the cabin cozy and warm, and there was enough wood stacked beside the stove to keep it going well into the next morning. That brought me to the couch. It had been a perfect fit for Quinn. It was big enough for two adults to sit side by side without being on top of each other, but it was not long enough for me to sleep on. I glanced at the floor. Not a carpet in sight. Despite the woodstove, it was too cold to sleep on the floor. The couch would have to do. I'd slept in less comfortable places.

I carried Quinn's pack and stuff sacks into the bedroom, putting the sacks back in the pack and leaning it against the side of the bed where Quinn could reach it easily. Her water bottle I placed on the bedside table, switching on the battery-powered lantern she'd put there, casting a warm glow over the room.

She'd said she moved the bed so it faced the window. During the day, it was probably a nice view of the woods. Tonight, it was a yawning hole of darkness. No blinds, no curtains to keep out the cold because this was a hunting cabin and not a fucking house.

And whoever her attacker was, he was still out there. Probably out of the woods completely, if he had any brains at all, but I still didn't like the idea that anyone could see in.

But she had blankets piled on the bed. A feather comforter and two brightly colored fleece blankets. I went back into the kitchen and headed straight for the toolbox I'd seen earlier. A few small nails and a hammer were all I needed to hang one of the fleece blankets over the window. Security and added insulation. I liked a good two-birds-with-one-stone situation.

I fluffed the blankets remaining on the bed, rolling one into a tube she could elevate her ankle on. She'd be warm enough, especially with the fire going.

The door to the bathroom opened and Quinn hopped out. I met her in the hall, sliding my arm around her waist to get her weight off her right ankle for the short trip to her bed. The scent of Quinn—clean and warm—hit my nose, and I resisted the urge to breathe her in.

She looked from me to the bed and over my shoulder to the couch in front of the fire. "You can have the other side of the bed. The couch is too short for you."

"I'm good," I said.

"Hawk. Seriously?" Her eyes flared wide as she gave me an exaggerated head-to-toe scan, then looked at the couch again and shook her head. "Don't be ridiculous."

"I'm good," I repeated, trying to infuse my voice with resolve. I could only say no to her so many times. But no—that wasn't true. There wasn't a limit. I'd keep saying no until the end of time because I had to. For her.

"Hawk, come on," Quinn said. "I can keep my hands to myself. I promise."

An image of her hands on me burst into my brain, and I had to take a beat to push it back out.

"Sleep tight," I said, leaving her sitting on the side of the bed, watching me with curious eyes. I didn't look back.

I tried not to listen as she slid into the bed. It had to hurt. I knew the weight of heavy blankets like that on a twisted ankle wasn't comfortable. She didn't make a peep. Didn't complain. Not that I expected her to. I'd learned Quinn was tough as nails.

I turned off the lanterns in the main room as soon as she turned off the lantern by the bed, and settled into the couch, half sitting up, knees bent. I pulled the blanket over me. With the fire so close, the wool blanket would be plenty. I wouldn't have any trouble falling asleep. Despite the early hour, Quinn wasn't the only one who was tired. It had been a hell of a day.

Finding Quinn pinned underneath the man who'd jumped her, fighting him, getting her to safety—all of it was enough to leave me tired once the adrenaline drained away. On top of that, the good meal and excellent bourbon should have had me half asleep already. I would have been if not for the fucking couch.

I slid down farther, propping my feet up on the opposite armrest and adjusting the pillow under my head. Maybe this would work. My neck wasn't cranked in a weird position anymore. I stared into the fire and tried not to think. About the man in the woods. About Quinn. About anything.

Didn't work. My brain flip-flopped between Quinn and her attacker. The way he'd handled things bothered me. The zip ties. Those zip ties didn't come from the hardware store. They were meaty, designed for holding weight. Or for restraining people. And she'd said he'd been focused on restraining her.

What had he planned to do? Where was he going to take her? Once he got her there, what was he going to do with her?

She'd implied he hadn't touched her sexually. Maybe he wasn't after rape. I didn't like that assault was on the table at all. Not where anyone was concerned, but especially not when it came to Quinn. She was fierce but small.

No, not Quinn. Her face melted into faces from the past. I'd seen firsthand the horror of what happened to women in war. I wouldn't let that happen to Quinn.

I tried rolling to my side, pulling my knees up, then stretching out my top leg, letting it hang off the side. Like every other position I'd tried, that wasn't much better after a minute or two. If I could shut up my brain, I could fall asleep in any position, but my brain wasn't taking orders.

"Hawk," Quinn called out from the bedroom. "I can hear you out there tossing and turning. That couch is like five feet long. I swear I'll stay on my side of the bed—"

"Shut it," I called back, curling up to a half-sitting position.

Maybe I'd just keep watch all night and take a nap in the morning when Quinn was out of bed. But who would watch over Quinn then? And what if something happened? What if—

"I'll sleep on the couch," she said, "if you're too scared

to share with me. You can take the bed, and I'll sleep on the couch."

"Too close to the door," I said immediately. There was a window in the bedroom, but the door was the easiest way into the cabin. I wasn't putting Quinn closest to the most likely entry point.

"Fine, be a stubborn jackass," Quinn said. "If you won't come in here, I'm sleeping on the floor in front of the fire."

I sat up. "Don't get out of the bed," I ordered. God, she was muleheaded. And in this, I had to admit she was right. I was being a jackass.

We had a perfectly good bed that was big enough for both of us. We were both adults. I hadn't looked when I'd stripped her clothes off. Hadn't touched more than I had to. I could keep my hands to myself. And despite the images that flooded my brain every time she said she would keep her hands to herself, so could she.

"All right," I said, my mouth moving before my brain was on board. This was a bad idea. Maybe. But her sleeping on the floor with her sprained ankle, so close to the door, was a nonstarter. She wouldn't get any rest and she'd be vulnerable. I abandoned the couch easily once the decision was made.

The bedroom was colder than the main room.

"You warm enough under there?" I asked, taking in her slight form buried under the heavy blankets.

"Toasty," she answered, waving her arm at the empty side of the bed. "See, there's a whole half just for you. I won't cross over the middle. I promise."

I looked down at my waterproof hiking pants in the

almost full darkness of the bedroom. They were warm and dry, but they weren't clean.

Reading my mind. Quinn said, "I'm already asleep. I can't see a thing. Do what you need to do so you can get some rest."

I nodded, mostly to myself, since I doubted she could see me in the dark. My boxer briefs covered me well enough, along with the T-shirt I wore under my fleece. I slid into the empty side of the bed, painfully aware of Quinn so close. Before I could catch a glimpse of her tucked in beside me, I turned on my side, giving her my back, and pulled up the covers, prepared to wait out the insomnia that would come from having Quinn inches away. The bed was far more comfortable than the couch, but I wouldn't fall asleep. There was no way.

I woke hours later, lying on my back, Quinn curled on her side, her forehead pressed to my shoulder, the only place we touched. Her arms were wrapped around her pillow, her face at peace. She'd inched to the middle of the bed, probably looking for body heat as the temperature dropped in the cabin. The light flickering from the main room was so dim it almost wasn't there.

Moving silently, I slid out of the bed. After a stop in the small bathroom, I fed the fire with enough logs to keep it going till morning. The sheets were still warm when I slid back in. The bed was a cozy cocoon, the white sheets almost bright in the darkness. I pulled the covers up, my shoulder nudging Quinn's forehead.

She let out a sigh and relaxed, her dark hair shining against the white pillowcase, her lashes thick half-moons against her cheeks. There was nothing about her that wasn't perfect. In the deepest part of me, I knew I could have lain there for the rest of my life with Quinn beside me. Close enough to touch. Close enough to keep. Close enough to pretend she was mine. Just for now. Just for this moment. I could pretend she was mine.

Hours later, my eyelids cracked to see a dim glow at the edges of the blanket I'd hung over the window. An unwelcome twist of relief bloomed in my chest. That fight we had scheduled about going back to the Manor wasn't going to happen yet. The snow was still falling, and I had an excuse to stay here with Quinn.

Awareness filtered in, and my eyes opened all the way. I was stuck here with Quinn, who was no longer on her side of the bed. Quinn, who was draped across my chest, her breasts soft against me, her breath warm through my T-shirt, one smooth thigh insinuated between my legs, her hip pressing into my very erect cock.

Quinn. I wanted to stay exactly where I was. Forever.

That was the last thing I could do. Mentally, I rescheduled that fight. The second the snow stopped, we were getting out of here. We had to. If we didn't, I was going to make a mistake I couldn't take back.

Chapter Eleven
QUINN

I came awake slowly, too comfortable to be yanked out of sleep. The light peeking around the edges of the blanket covering the window had the clarity of daytime but was dim enough to tell me it was overcast and probably still snowing. Relief spread through me. I didn't want to leave the cabin yet.

Despite the trip here. Despite my sprained ankle. Even though someone had tried to kidnap and probably kill me, I didn't want to leave. Maybe that made me crazy. I didn't care.

I'd had a great night. Dinner with Hawk had featured in my fantasies for a while. In reality, it had lived up to—no, surpassed—my hopes. He wasn't chatty. Of course not. He was Hawk. He was never going to be chatty. That was okay, though, because I could go either way. Sometimes I liked to talk. Sometimes I loved the quiet. Talking to Hawk had been weirdly comfortable, considering we hadn't exchanged more than a few words in the past year. I could have sat and talked to him all night.

I blinked at the light, finally registering why I was so comfortable. It wasn't the feather duvet and fleece blankets. It was that my mattress was a long body, hard with muscle, warm, and smelling of spice and Hawk. Somehow I'd inched halfway across the bed, ending up mostly on top of him, my thigh snuggled between his, my hip squarely on top of a very impressive erection. Was that for me? I wanted to think so. I really wanted to think so. If it was for me, I might get my hands on it one of these days. But he was human, and that wonderfully thick cock could just be a morning thing. Nothing to do with me at all.

And how had I gotten all the way over here? I gave a mental eye roll. Had I really thought I wouldn't? I should have known I'd gravitate to Hawk in sleep, just like I wanted to when I was awake.

I didn't move. I was too warm, too blissfully comfortable, and exactly where I wanted to be. The second Hawk woke, he'd be gone. He wouldn't like this at all. Or, based on the hard length pressing into my hip, he liked it way too much. Which was exactly the reason he'd want to get the hell away the second he realized I was on top of him.

I stayed where I was, savoring the feel of him beneath me, the solid rhythm of his heartbeat under my ear. I felt it the second he woke up, his shoulders tightening, the sharp intake of breath just beyond my ear. Any second now, he'd disappear. Mentally, I braced, keeping my body relaxed, my breath even.

He shifted beneath me, and a gentle weight came down on the top of my head. His hand stroked my hair in a slow sweep. Once. Again. His fingers combed through the strands at the base of my neck, lingering, the tips warm on my skin before they moved away. Hawk drew in a long breath, letting it out in a shaky sigh. His hand lifted, the backs of his fingers stroking the side of my cheek, moving down to gather my hair, combing his fingers through the strands, every tug against my scalp setting off fireworks in my brain. I was in heaven.

Unexpected tears pricked my eyes. We'd started out with me lying on top of him, but now it was something more. His hand on my hair felt like... I didn't know what. I couldn't remember the last time anyone had touched me like this. With care. With longing. With reverence. I didn't know what to do. I'd dreamed about kissing him, touching him, Hawk touching me. I hadn't dared to dream of anything like this.

I hadn't known I wanted it. How much I needed it. Especially from Hawk.

With a jerk, he yanked his arm back, his body suddenly stiff. A second later, I was facedown on warm sheets, the blankets settling over me. I didn't know he could move that fast. A door closed with a sharp click. He'd fled to the bathroom. I stayed where I was, curious what his next move would be.

When he was done in the bathroom, would he come back into the bedroom? Or was he going to double down on the disappearing act?

I didn't have to wait long for my answer. The bathroom door opened. My eyes closed to slits, I watched him stride past the doorway into the kitchen, his jaw hard. I couldn't say I was surprised. Not by his flight. But before, the way he held me, stroked my hair—I would have given everything for another minute of that. And while it didn't tell me for sure if that erection was about me, now I knew he wasn't as indifferent to me as he pretended to be.

I heard him move into the kitchen, then the click of a lighter, the clank of metal. Coffee? I could only hope.

I lay in bed and thought over my next move. If any other man had run after spending the night with me, I might have been offended. Not with Hawk. The only reason he wanted to get away from me was because he didn't want to get away from me. I understood that much.

I'd heard about Hawk dressing down Finn for daring to get involved with Savannah. I knew in Hawk's mind there was family, and there was staff, and that line should not be crossed. And on top of that, I was Griffen's little sister. A guy like Hawk would see that as an automatic no-go. But I also knew there was something between us. It wasn't just me. He felt it too. Lifting my hand, I touched my cheek, still feeling Hawk stroke the backs of his fingers there.

He felt it too.

I could admit I had a crush. Since the moment I saw him, I thought Hawk was smoking hot in that rugged *I can get shit done and know what I'm doing* kind of way that always got to me. And he was smart. Really smart. I liked his sly sense of humor, the deadpan way he dropped comments most people missed with that glint of laughter in his eyes.

Yeah, I had more than just a crush on Hawk Bristol. He didn't treat me like he did my sisters. He never yelled at them, for one thing. A few days ago, I would have said I had no shot with him. But now I thought I had a chance. A slim chance. Very slim, given how firmly Hawk had put me on the other side of that line he refused to cross.

Still, I had a chance. I just wasn't sure what I was going to do about it. Not yet.

I rose up on my elbows, turning to look at the glow of light around the blanket Hawk had tacked up. The snow had bought me some time. A window of opportunity. But with every inch those clouds moved, my window closed a little more. Soon the snow would end, the trail would be passable, and my chance would be gone.

Yeah, there was a creepy bad guy out there, armed with zip ties and a knife. Probably much more than just a knife. I should be the one desperate to get out of here. It wasn't that I wasn't taking it seriously. It just didn't feel real. Not here in this cozy cabin, my face snuggled into a pillow that smelled of Hawk.

The pillow under my cheek felt real. Hawk felt real. My sprained ankle felt real.

Not the bad guy in the woods.

I'd worry about him when the snow stopped. Until that happened, no one was going anywhere.

I sat up, wincing just a little as the covers dragged at the toes of my right foot. Not the nauseating pain of the day before, but it wasn't nothing. I sat on the side of the bed, shifting to put weight on my left foot. Then a little on my right. A stabbing throb, but not agony. Improvement. I'd take it.

Another day of rest, ibuprofen, and ice, and it would be even better tomorrow. I wouldn't be walking for another few days, but I wouldn't be incapacitated for weeks. As much as I wanted to push my healing so I could enjoy my vacation, I had clients booked in a week, and I needed a functional ankle to do my job.

Like the bad guy in the woods, that was a problem for later. I started to stand, then realized my pack was on the other side of the bed. I flopped back and rolled to the opposite side of the mattress. The scent of coffee filled the small cabin. If there was coffee, I'd figure out a way to get my ass to the kitchen.

I hauled my pack up from where it leaned against the side of the bed and dug around for the stuff sacks with my clothes. I pulled out clean underwear, stretchy yoga pants, and a tank top I could wear under my fleece. Assuming I'd be here alone, I hadn't packed much. I had plenty of clean underwear and socks, but I'd planned to wear tank tops or T-shirts all week, so that was all I had.

Keeping my clothes in one hand, I stood, trying out a single hopping step. That same stabbing throb from before. I was sure my ankle wasn't broken, but it definitely needed rest—without weight—for as long as I could stand it. Walking was not happening.

I sighed, mentally recalculating. I had a set of collapsible trekking poles strapped to the side of my pack. I didn't use them often, but given that the weather was supposed to shift, I'd thought they might come in handy.

I wouldn't be doing any hiking, but I could probably use one as a crutch. It wasn't ideal, but it was better than crawling. Putting my clothes down, I expanded both poles and rolled my clothes into a ball that I shoved under my left arm. Holding my clothes to my side, I put weight on both poles and tried the same hopping step maneuver with the aid of the trekking poles. I didn't get far. But at least I wasn't completely immobile.

The second I took another hopping step, Hawk was there, his eyes narrowed, face twisted in a dark scowl. "What are you doing?" he barked.

Chapter Twelve

QUINN

"Going to the bathroom," I said, raising an eyebrow.

"You're not ready to walk on it yet. Why didn't you call me?" He plucked the trekking poles out of my hands before I could think to stop him. Taking my bundle of clothes from under my arm, he wrapped his arm around my waist, shifting my weight to him. As we step-hopped to the bathroom, he said, "You can cause long-term damage if you overuse it before it's healed."

The medical warning was textbook and something I knew well. Why the hell hadn't I just called for him?

"I wasn't going for a hike, just to the bathroom," I said, any irritation at being called out completely eclipsed by the fact that he had me pressed tight to his side, practically carrying me the short distance across the hall.

Then it hit me. I hadn't asked him for help because I wasn't used to asking anyone for help, and I had zero game. A smarter woman would have used any excuse to get exactly where I was, tucked into Hawk's side, as close as we could get with our clothes on. Sometimes it didn't pay to be so independent.

"I'll ask for help next time," I promised.

Hawk gave a low grunt that I took for agreement. Who was I to argue if he wanted to carry me everywhere? I should take it while I could get it.

Nothing here was going to last, not even my bum ankle. As soon as Hawk got me back to Heartstone and safety, he was going to run as far and fast as he could. But that was later. For now, I leaned into Hawk's side, the pressure of his body against mine making me wish the bathroom was a mile away.

Hawk deposited me at the door. "Wait here when you're done, and I'll come get you."

"Yes, sir," I said with a jaunty salute.

He shook his head with another grunt and shoved my bundle of clothes at me.

Pivoting on my left foot, I braced myself on the bathroom counter and hopped inside. The bathroom was luxurious for a remote hunting cabin, but it was tiny. Even with my bum ankle, it would be easy to navigate.

I'd never been so grateful for a composting toilet. With all the camping I'd done, I was used to making do, but between the cold, the snow, and my twisted ankle, I was very glad I didn't have to brave the outdoors to go to the bathroom. The pitcher of water beside the sink was cold as I washed my hands but far warmer than it would have been if I'd left the pipes turned on. The running water Prentice had installed came straight from the mountain stream nearby. It was wonderfully refreshing in the summer but ice-cold in winter and spring. I'd drained the pipes and shut them off at the first freeze in the fall, leaving us with the plastic bottles I'd filled with rainwater over the past few weeks.

I was glad I'd packed enough wet wipes to come close to approximating a shower. It wasn't the same, nothing was, but filling the water tank with snow and turning on the propane water heater would take ages and waste propane we might need if the storm lasted longer than expected. Not worth it when I had a brand-new pack of wipes in my bag.

I'd left my toiletries bag on the shelf beneath the mirror last night. It didn't take long to brush my teeth and clean my face. I looked a lot better than I guessed I had the night before. No runny, red nose and pale face. A solid night of sleep worked wonders. A good thing since I didn't have any makeup unless moisturizer and lip balm counted. I pulled a brush through my straight hair, thought about braiding it, and decided to leave it loose.

I wasn't pretty like my sisters. I didn't mind. I had gorgeous sisters. Parker with her cool, moonlit perfection. Sterling with her golden hair and bombshell body. Avery, taller than the rest of us, her dark hair and eyes magnetic.

I was just Quinn. I wasn't ugly, but I wasn't anything special. Only my eyes, my bright blue Sawyer eyes, were special. And I had good hair. It wouldn't hold a curl but it stayed neatly in a braid, and when I wore it down, it fell into a sleek, dark curtain that always made me smile.

My eyes and my hair were my best features. Body-wise, I was athletic and on the small side. I'd worked hard for every muscle, and I liked the way they made my arms and legs look both sleek and strong, but it was a functional body, not a sexy one. And I didn't have much in the boob department. There was a little curve to my hips, but I was no Sterling. My face was okay. I looked good when I had a tan. My freckles were kind of cute, but there was nothing striking about me.

That was okay. I worked a job where what I knew and what I could do were a lot more important than what I looked like. I could live with being admired for my skills and not my face. Anyway, in my sisters I'd seen the downside of being gorgeous. It wasn't always great to be the prettiest girl in the room. Being pretty made you a target. That was the last thing I wanted. I'd had enough of that kind of attention to last a lifetime.

I smoothed on some lip balm and moisturizer, my version of everyday makeup, and opened the bathroom door. I'd barely tossed my dirty clothes across the hall when Hawk was there, taking the trekking poles in one hand and slinging his other arm around my waist.

"I've got you. The less weight you put on that ankle, the faster it'll heal. You go back to work next week, don't you?"

"I do," I said, though after standing in the bathroom for a few minutes, I was beginning to doubt I'd be in shape to take my clients anywhere I couldn't manage on crutches.

I liked that Hawk knew my schedule. I liked that he cared. Liked that our minds had been on the same track. And I had to admit, *like* was too tepid a word for how I felt about all of that. Thinking about all I had in common with Hawk Bristol was asking for trouble. Or a broken heart.

I didn't care.

All I had to do was think about the last time I'd worried about a broken heart. Years before, I'd danced around the man I liked. He'd danced around me. When we finally got up the nerve to admit there was something there and plan a date, he went on a kayaking trip and hadn't made it home.

We'd wasted our chance messing around, thinking we had all the time in the world to figure it out. After he was gone, I decided I'd rather risk heartbreak than not go after what I wanted. And here was Hawk, probably destined to break my heart. He was not a man looking for a relationship. *You can't win if you don't get in the game, right?*

I thought of Hawk stroking my hair when he'd woken and discovered me on top of him. Hawk didn't want to admit it, but he felt something for me. I was more than just Griffen's little sister. More than part of his job. I just had to figure out how much more.

Hawk helped me to the table and put a steaming mug of coffee in front of me. "Milk?" he asked.

"A splash, please. It's in the cooler."

He nodded. "I saw it. I got out the eggs. Do you want breakfast? I was going to make scrambled eggs with cheese."

"That sounds perfect," I said.

"Bacon?" he asked with a raised eyebrow.

"I never turn down bacon." I sat at the table sipping my coffee. Excellent coffee, another point in Hawk's favor. The fire in the woodstove crackled and popped, the cabin cozily warm. He must have added more logs as soon as he got up. I watched him at the counter, efficient and competent, whisking the eggs while bacon sizzled in the cast-iron pan.

"Everything is quiet at the big house," he said, his back to me, his eyes on the bacon.

He must have radioed down to them while I was in the bathroom. I had to admit, even with my independent nature, having Hawk here looking out for me felt good. "Whoever went after me in the woods hasn't shown up at the Manor?"

"Not so far. Cameras are all operational. I'm going to add them along the trail to the cabin."

I made a face. I hated that idea. I liked technology in nature when it came to things like the composting toilet. But cameras in the trees? All that hard metal and plastic hidden in the leaves? No.

"Quinn," he started, and I shook my head.

"I don't like it, but you're right. I come out here a lot, usually by myself." I drew in a long breath and let it out in a rush. I wasn't sorry my father was dead, but I hated everything that had come after. Ford being in prison. These stupid attacks on my family.

What did anyone want from us anyway? Prentice had been a raging asshole, but the rest of us hadn't done anything worth killing over.

"I miss the quiet," I admitted. "I miss not needing the cameras. But you're right. If you guys can add them, I think it's not the worst idea. And if you have an extra one of those sat phones," I added grudgingly, "I'll carry one with me when I come out here in the future."

Hawk nodded. "I think that's smart."

"Okay," I agreed, not liking the idea of being under surveillance in my beloved forest.

But I knew if Hawk hadn't been coming after me—

I didn't want to think about it, but the way the snow had been coming down, all signs of our fight, all of the tracks in the woods, would have been long gone by the time anyone realized I was missing.

If they'd had cameras, they could have at least figured out how far I'd gotten on the trail before I went missing. They might have even caught the guy on camera. Without Hawk's good timing, I would have just disappeared. The thought sent a bone-chilling stab of fear through me. I wanted to pretend it didn't matter because I was safe, but I was lying to myself. If Hawk hadn't come along, I'd probably be dead.

I sighed again as Hawk slid two plates of food on the table. "More coffee?" he asked.

I shook my head. "Later. I can't handle more than two cups, and I want to savor it. You make good coffee."

He nodded, the tiniest smile touching his lips before they pressed together in a thin line. "We're leaving as soon as the snow stops," he announced as I was biting into a crisp piece of bacon.

I chewed slowly and shook my head. I'd known this was coming, and since I had no intention of us both dying because we left before it was safe to do so with the snow, I thought about the best way to get through to him. Emotional pleas about my not wanting to cut my vacation short wouldn't work. And besides, until that guy was caught, I didn't love the idea of being here on my own.

"No, I'm not doing that."

"Quinn, this isn't a negotiation." His jaw was set, jutting forward, his dark eyes steely.

I didn't know where I got the balls to argue with him. He was objectively scary when he looked like this. But it was Hawk. He'd never hurt me. And, in my experience, it wasn't men like him who hurt. It was the ones that looked harmless who were dangerous. "It is a negotiation," I said, "unless you're planning on knocking me unconscious and carrying me back over your shoulder."

His eyes went squinty. "I will if I have to," he said in a low voice.

"No, you won't," I said, "and we're not leaving the second the snow stops. First of all—"

Hawk opened his mouth, but before he could get a word out, I held up a finger to stop him. To my shock, it worked.

Chapter Thirteen

QUINN

"You saw that trail in light snow," I reminded him. "The first half isn't too bad. You can practically drive a golf cart on that thing. But the second half after the split—" I dropped my hand and picked up my fork, shaking my head in dismissal at his crazy idea. "The second half after the trail splits is treacherous in this kind of weather. If the snow hasn't melted, you won't be able to see anything. You can't carry me out with uncertain footing. We could both go down in a ravine if you slip at the wrong moment."

"I won't slip."

"Hawk, if there's anybody who could handle it, it would be you. But it's too dangerous. You know it's too dangerous. You're being reckless."

He sat back and crossed his arms over his chest. "I am not reckless. I'm the one who knows security. I know what's safe and what's not. I can't believe you think I'd put you in danger."

"You don't know these mountains like I do. And I just said if I trusted anyone, it would be you." I put down my fork and sat back, crossing my arms over my chest in a mirror of his obstinate position. "I know you don't like this situation we're in. I know you really don't like it, because otherwise you'd admit that if we sit tight and wait for the snow to melt a little, the hike back will be a lot safer."

Silence fell over the table as we stared at each other. Neither of us wanted to say it. That we'd woken up with me draped over his body, his very hard cock pressing into my hip. I liked the situation just fine, but I knew he didn't.

"I know you want us back at the house," I said. "I know you don't like being here."

"It's not that I don't like being here," he ground out, which was more of a concession than I expected.

"It's not safe to leave the second the snow stops," I pressed. "You know it, and I know it. And in any case, it hasn't stopped yet. It has to eventually. We're not in the Arctic. And if history is any indication, not long after it stops, it'll all be gone. The weather shifts fast here. Once the storm has blown through, the snow won't hang around."

"We don't have that kind of time," Hawk said.

"You don't know that," I argued, though I didn't really believe my own words. "Maybe that was just some rando in the woods."

Hawk shook his head. "It wasn't."

"How do you know?" I wanted to think his determination to leave was all about getting away from me. I didn't love that motivation, but it was better than the alternative, which was that we were in actual danger from a psycho. Bears and cougars and surviving in the woods I was comfortable with. This I was not.

Hawk looked up at the ceiling as if gathering patience. When he looked back at me, his expression was gentler than I expected. My stomach tightened, bracing for what came next.

"The zip ties," he said, his voice slow but clear. "Those weren't hardware store zip ties, Quinn. They were the kind law enforcement uses. And his camo. Most people who have camo don't have winter camo. Not in North Carolina. And the way he moved was—" Hawk shook his head. "It wasn't some random guy who wandered onto your land from the national forest. Whoever it was, they were looking for you. And now here we are, isolated and alone. We're sitting ducks."

I couldn't pretend that didn't scare the shit out of me. "But that doesn't make sense. If it's about the necklace—" I closed my eyes, trying to think. "If this wasn't some random guy, it doesn't make sense. I left a few hours after I saw Harvey. There wasn't enough time to get some professional bad guy and send him after me."

Hawk's eyes crinkled at the corners, I think at my terminology. I was pretty sure whoever it was who attacked me in the woods, his business card didn't say *Professional Bad Guy*.

"I agree, that seems unlikely. But most of the shit surrounding your family is unlikely. I'm not ignoring the danger just because we don't know why it's there. I have to go on what we know. We know a man attacked you with the intention of kidnapping you, and that's the best possible outcome he had planned. We know he was armed and prepared. And we know he's out there somewhere."

I swallowed hard, staring into the dregs of coffee at the bottom of the blue-speckled camp mug. I'd been more focused on being alone with Hawk than the threat out there in the woods. I didn't want to be scared. I'd spent enough of my life living in fear, of having to be constantly on watch to keep myself safe. I wasn't going to live like that again. And thanks to the man in the woods, I wasn't sure I had a choice. Denial could be nice, but I wasn't stupid. I wouldn't endanger our lives because I didn't want to face reality. We still couldn't hike out though. So we'd have to figure out how to be safer here.

As if he was reading my mind, Hawk asked, "Did your dad leave any weapons in the cabin?"

I nodded, then shook my head. "He did, but they're not here now. I'm not much of a hunter. Not a hunter at all, actually. I don't have a problem with it, but I like the deer too much to pull a trigger on them."

"Don't like venison?" Hawk asked, that glint of humor I loved sparking in his eyes.

I grinned back. "Love it. You can call me a hypocrite because I'll chow down on some venison, but I don't want to be the one who killed Bambi." I set my empty coffee cup on the table with a shrug. "I brought all the weapons back to the house. I don't know what Griffen did with them. I only carry the gun you saw and a hunting knife in my pack." I glanced at the firewood stacked by the woodstove. "I have an ax too. And you have your gun."

He nodded. "Two weapons and two clips between us, plus a few knives and an ax. Not a lot of firepower. We're too vulnerable. I won't risk you."

I let out a breath. I didn't know what to say to that. I didn't want to risk me either. And I liked that he wanted to protect me. Was I imagining heat in his voice when he said that? The intent in his eyes? Was I seeing something I wanted to see? I didn't think so. But this was about more than me and Hawk and what I hoped could be. This was about keeping us both alive.

He didn't want to risk me.

I didn't want to risk him.

I'd been blocking out what happened yesterday in the woods. That gunshot. The long minutes when I didn't know who fired it. If Hawk had been hit saving me—if anything happened to him—there was more going on than the two of us stranded in this cozy cabin in the snow.

"Can we stop arguing about this?" I asked. "It's pointless until the snow stops and we can see what we're dealing with."

Hawk gave a jerk of his head that looked like a nod. "Agreed." He picked up his empty plate, grabbed mine, and set them both in the sink. "I have to go check the area again, see if there's any sign of him. I'll wash these when I get back."

"Okay. Be careful out there. Visibility is down to nothing, and you don't know the territory," I said.

Hawk shook his head. "I do know it. I'll be careful, but I know the terrain."

"How?" I asked. Heartstone Manor sat on thousands of acres of private land. He couldn't know every inch of it.

"Quinn, you're out here twice a week. Of course I scouted it."

I didn't know what to say to that.

I looked down into my empty coffee mug, my throat tight. Maybe I was reading way too much into everything. His job was keeping us safe. Of course he'd scouted it. I knew that, but it left me feeling cared for. It was a little scary how much I needed that. How much I wanted it from Hawk.

I was getting myself in way over my head, and he was going to leave me brokenhearted. I could see it coming, and I couldn't turn away.

He moved to stand beside my chair. "Let's get you to the couch."

I nodded, not wanting my voice to give away the swirl of emotions rushing through me.

He scooped me up as if I didn't weigh anything, carrying me to the couch. "We'll ice that ankle again when I get back. Do you want a book or something?"

"Please. It's in my pack, front pocket." I pulled the wool blanket over me, settling back into the cushioned arm of the couch, positioned to face the door and front windows.

Hawk returned with my book and my gun, setting both in my lap. "Stay put while I'm gone."

"Cross my heart," I said, swiping my fingers over my chest.

I watched him in silence as he bundled into his

winter gear with an efficiency born of long experience. "Like last night, I'll knock three times when I come back so you know it's me."

I nodded and he was gone, the lock turning behind him. My gut tightened again. All the talk about the man in the woods made every second Hawk was gone stretch into an eternity. The snow was thick beyond the windows, the wind driving it at an angle, the sky heavy and gray. Hawk said he knew his way around, but it was dangerous out there.

I wasn't just trying to delay Hawk so we could be alone in the cabin. Being alone with Hawk was a side benefit, the silver lining to the very real situation we were in. Even without the threat of the man in the woods, the forest wasn't safe in this kind of weather. Hawk wouldn't be able to see where he was walking, and gullies and ravines were everywhere in this part of the woods.

He could slip, hit his head. He could break something. He could—

I closed my eyes, trying to breathe, to find calm. Despite my earlier accusation, Hawk wasn't reckless. He knew the territory. He knew what he was doing. He'd be back soon, and I'd see for myself that he was fine.

My spiraling emotions under control, I opened my eyes. My book lay on my lap beneath my gun, both untouched. I knew Hawk would be fine, but I wouldn't relax until he walked back through that door. Sitting there, alone in the cabin, my injured ankle throbbing and the snow coming down in sheets, I finally admitted to myself the danger we were in. I could only hope the snow was enough to keep the man in the woods pinned down wherever he'd run after Hawk's shot grazed him.

Because Hawk was right. We were sitting ducks in this cabin, playing a waiting game with the weather. The second it was clear, we'd have to get moving. And as much as I wanted to be alone with Hawk, I didn't want either of us here when the man in the woods came back.

Chapter Fourteen
QUINN

I waited, the minutes stretching so long they felt like hours. When I checked my watch, it had been just shy of a half hour when Hawk's return was heralded with the three-tap knock I'd come to recognize, the key turning smoothly in the lock.

Hawk shut the door firmly behind him, every inch of his body covered in snow. "Cold out there," he said, hanging his jacket by the door and loosening the laces on his boots with quick, efficient tugs, setting them in the tray before brushing the snow off his waterproof, insulated pants. Moving to stand in front of the woodstove, he let the heat dry him off.

"Any sign of anything?" I asked, studying him for any indication we had a problem.

If he'd seen anything that worried him, he was hiding it well. "No. I think we're good for now. Visibility is crap, like you said."

Unspoken was that when it cleared, we'd have some decisions to make.

"Another pot of coffee?" Hawk asked. "Or some of that cocoa?"

"Cocoa would be great," I said. "Unless you want coffee."

"Cocoa is good." Hawk scanned me, looking for…I wasn't sure what. His eyes landed on my ankle, his dark brows pulling together. "How's that wrap feel? Too loose?"

I wiggled my toes. "It feels better than it did yesterday. I think the bandage is tight enough."

"I'm going to pack some snow around it again. Then I'll make that cocoa."

In minutes, Hawk had my ankle set up and milk steaming on the stove, the chocolate bars I'd brought for cocoa filling the cabin with alluring scents. Hawk made a mean cup of cocoa. I had a feeling there wasn't much Hawk couldn't do.

The day passed too quickly. Far more quickly than I would have thought, given that we were stuck in the cabin without much to do. Hawk was easy company. I had my book and my cocoa. He dug an old Western novel off the shelves by the fireplace and sank into a leather armchair. We read in companionable silence until lunch, when Hawk put together a meal out of the canned and freeze-dried stuff I'd brought along.

I liked good food, hence the steaks we'd eaten the night before, along with the ice cream and cocoa. But when I was camping, convenience and overall weight were more important than my taste buds. Camping meals in a pouch were easy to carry and easy to prepare in a basic kitchen like this one. Add in some canned veggies and we had a feast.

After lunch, we went back to our books until Hawk closed his slimmer volume and got up to return it to the bookcase. He returned with an ancient deck of Uno cards, and I marked my place in my book, setting it aside. I was always up for some Uno. He pulled his armchair over to the couch, and we had an Uno tournament, using the seat of a chair as a tabletop.

Hawk might be inclined to baby my injured ankle, but he was no pushover when it came to Uno. He was sly and sneaky, dealing reverses and draw fours just when they'd do the most damage. I didn't win a single game, cards stacking in my hand until I could barely hold them while his diminished one by one. He destroyed me. I loved it. Not that I liked losing, but the sheer impossibility of beating him, combined with seeing him like this—relaxed, having fun—meant I didn't care about winning. I just liked making him smile.

Hawk didn't gloat, but the crinkle at the corners of his eyes as he called "Uno" on the last game was enough. I threw my handful of cards at his face.

"I'm never playing Uno with you again," I said, with a glare that was mostly pretend.

For that, I got a full-on grin, his unhidden delight in kicking my ass filling my heart with warmth. I liked making this man smile. I liked it far more than I should, and I did not care. He could beat me at Uno every day if he'd grin at me like this, his dark eyes bright with humor, his lips turned up in genuine amusement.

We ate again as the light dimmed, the wind outside

still whipping through the trees. Dinner was canned beef stew, followed by ice cream and more cocoa. By nine thirty, my eyes were drooping.

"I don't know why I'm so tired," I said. "I haven't done anything but lie around all day."

"Your body is trying to heal," Hawk replied. "And lying around makes you sluggish. When we get back, we'll get you set up with some crutches."

"That'll be better." I nodded, letting out a dissatisfied grunt. "I'm going to have to reschedule my clients. My ankle is better than yesterday, but it's not going to be up to fishing next week. I'll call some other guides and see if they have openings. I hate to ruin anyone's vacation."

I didn't want to think about how long it would be before I could go back to work. It wasn't just losing the income. I loved the beginning of trout season, loved being outside in March, the dance between winter and spring in full steam. Today it was whipping wind and sheets of snow. Next week it could be a sunny sixty-five, not a flake of snow in sight. And I would be missing it.

At least I'd made it to the cabin for a day or two. I'd come around to the idea that we were going home the second it was safe. I wanted to be out of here if the man in the woods came back.

I *should* wish I'd never left Heartstone Manor. But watching Hawk approach, his arm out to help me to my feet, I couldn't do that.

In just over twenty-four hours, I'd gotten to know Hawk far better than I had in the year since we'd met. And the more I knew, the more I wanted to know. And now, even knowing we had a greater threat than the weather, I still couldn't bring myself to be sorry. When this was over, Hawk would probably go back to one-syllable responses and quick exits. But for now, I had him all to myself.

I stood, leaning into Hawk's side, letting him lead me to the small bathroom. I could have hopped along with the help of my trekking pole, but I wasn't ashamed to take what I could get if it was coming from Hawk.

Like we had the night before, Hawk helped me to the bathroom, then to the bed. Unlike the night before, this time he didn't argue over taking the other side of the bed. Instead, he tucked me in on my side, said he'd be back, and disappeared down the hall. I settled into my pillows to the sound of dishes clanking against the sink. I had to admire his forethought. I'd bet his plan was to get me tucked in, then kill time cleaning the kitchen while he waited for me to fall asleep, thus avoiding the awkwardness of lying silent beside me, both of us pretending we didn't know what had happened last night.

I thought about how quickly he'd escaped the bed this morning. It was clear he didn't want anything to happen between us. Fair enough. I wasn't going to force him into anything, not that I could. But as much as his rejection burned, Hawk must've had his reasons. I'd take what I could get from him, but not more. This time I'd stay on my side of the bed.

I meant that.

I really did.

I fell asleep facing the edge of the mattress, my back to Hawk's empty place beside me, sending a clear signal that I'd respect his personal space. And conscious me was on board. Really.

Sleeping Quinn had a different plan.

I woke deep in the night, warmth all along the front of my body, my cheek on a firm pillow. *Hawk*. Too cozy to think straight, I lifted my head and found myself looking straight into the gleam of Hawk's eyes, barely visible in the dark room.

I should have moved. I didn't.

Hawk's fingers closed around my bicep. Not pushing me away. Not pulling me closer. Holding me where I was.

"Quinn," he breathed.

His low voice drawing me in, I began to close the distance between us. Hawk didn't move.

He didn't slide out from under me and disappear down the hall. He didn't push me away. He didn't gently roll me onto my back and retreat to his side of the bed.

Still, I stopped, my lips a breath from his. "I'm going to kiss you."

His only response was an indrawn breath, his fingers tightening reflexively on my arms. Tightening, but not pushing me away.

"Do you want me to kiss you?" I asked. "Because I really, really want to kiss you. I've been thinking about it—"

Before I could finish that thought, he shifted, closing the distance between our mouths. His lips stroked mine, barely a touch. Almost nothing.

This time, I was the one who drew in a breath.

He kissed me again. His mouth took mine, possessive

and demanding. I straddled him, ignoring the throb in my ankle as I moved. I didn't care how much it hurt. I'd been dreaming of kissing Hawk Bristol since I laid eyes on him. And this—his lips moving on mine, his tongue tasting me, his hands closing over my hips, the harsh breath in his throat—all of it was so much better than anything I'd dreamed.

He kissed me and kissed me, long, deep, wet kisses that went on and on, his fingers digging into my hips, my breath catching in my lungs. I wanted this, I wanted him, I wanted all of it. Everything. With a gasp, I jerked back, sitting up to pull my silk long underwear shirt over my head. I tossed it on the floor, my tank top following, baring my upper body.

"Quinn," Hawk said on a groan, his hands leaving my hips to cup my breasts, squeezing and shaping, pinching my nipples with the perfect pressure. Enough to send a spike of pained pleasure down my spine, straight between my legs. "Quinn." My name was followed by a sharp exhale before he pulled me down, his mouth closing over one hard nipple, sucking and licking.

At first, his mouth was tender. Reverent. Just as I was ready to beg, his teeth closed over the tip in a bite hard enough to leave me gasping, squirming against him. He soothed with a gentle suck, followed by another sharp bite.

My head spun, my nerves firing, bliss spearing through my brain. Hawk tipped his head back, his hands turning me, bringing my other breast to his mouth. I shivered in anticipation, the cold air hitting my skin before his warm palm closed over it, soothing my tortured nipple as he turned his attention to the other. I couldn't process this much sensation. It had been a while since I'd been mostly naked with a man, and never with a man like Hawk.

Something in me must have sensed something in him, must have known on some level that he had exactly the right combination of patience and rough, raw need to give me what I wanted. His hot, wet, sucking mouth, his hands molding my breasts, the low sounds in his throat—I was closer to coming than I'd ever been with so many clothes on. I rocked on top of him, the hard length of cock against my clit almost enough to push me over the edge.

Almost. I was still wearing my yoga pants, and I wanted more. The brush of his stubbled cheek on the side of my breast, his hard hands holding me—all that skin on my skin felt so good. I wanted more. I wanted all of it.

My head spun from pleasure and need. Hawk pulled back, his hands shifting to my shoulders to push me gently away from him. The flicker of firelight from the woodstove wasn't much, but I could see when his eyes locked on mine.

His voice was rough as if the words had been torn from his throat. "Quinn, I can't. We can't."

Through the need burning inside me, I managed to process his words. "We can if we want to," I said. "Do you want to?"

I knew Hawk had his reasons for staying away from me, but the only question that mattered was the one I'd asked.

"Do you want to?" I asked again.

Chapter Fifteen
QUINN

He let out a groan, rolling, turning me to my back. Pushing up on his knees, he stripped off my yoga pants until I lay naked, spread out on the bed before him. His hand pressed flat to my chest, below my collarbone, sliding down between my breasts, over my abdomen, to land on my pussy, his palm pressing into my clit.

His fingertips curved in the smallest gesture of possession, one that sent a bolt of pure lust straight up my spine.

"I'm on the pill," I said, breathless. "It's been a while, and I was all clear at my last checkup."

Hawk shook his head. "Quinn, that's too much."

"Too much what?" I asked, my head foggy with desire. Hawk's hands left my body as he stripped off his shirt, and all grasp of logic went straight out of my head. *Damn. That body.* Did he spend half the day in the gym?

Broad shoulders, corded with lean muscle. Even in the faint light, I could see the ridges of his abdomen, the curves of his biceps. I wanted to get my hands, my mouth, all over him. I wanted to touch, to stroke, to taste every inch.

"Too much trust," he said, and I squinted at him in the dark.

What? What was he talking about? He wanted to have a conversation? Now? "If you want to talk to me," I said, "you're going to have to put your shirt back on."

Hawk went still, and I would have bet every penny I had that if the light had been on, he would have been blushing. He shook his head. "You have too much trust in me."

"Have you been tested?" I asked.

"Yeah."

"Would you risk hurting me?"

"Fuck no." He sounded offended that I'd asked.

"I have good instincts," I said. "And it's not too much trust. Not when it's well placed." I lifted my hands, pressing them flat on his abdomen, feeling the warmth of him sinking into my palms. My fingers flexed. "I want this. I want you." Lifting my eyes, I caught his gaze. "Do you want me?"

He didn't answer. Not in words. Instead, he swept the tangled covers to the side, clearing the space around my injured ankle so if I moved, I wouldn't hurt myself. And this man asked if I could trust him? My chest squeezed at the thought that he would doubt himself so much. I didn't doubt him. I knew I was safe with Hawk.

I reached for him, and he came down on top of me, the heat of his chest delicious against my breasts as his mouth closed over mine. He kissed me. More of those endless, deep kisses, his lips moving on mine, his hands stroking. Hawk was in charge, but I touched him everywhere I could reach. His skin was like silk, so soft and sleek over ridged muscle. I couldn't stop, my fingertips memorizing every inch of him.

He slid down my body, his mouth drawing a path to that spot on my collarbone that always made me shiver. He found it almost immediately, torturing me with licks and sucks and nips until I was squirming and begging. And then his mouth was between my legs, his tongue warm and wet and curious, sending sparks shooting everywhere he touched.

"I want— I want—" I couldn't get the words to come out.

I want you to fuck me. I want to come, I want more, I want—

I couldn't say anything coherent. I rocked my hips up into his mouth, into that perfect tongue, making noises I barely recognized as my own. I'd had sex before. Not a ton of sex, but enough. I'd had good sex before. But no one had ever reduced me to begging. I closed my fingers around one steely wrist.

"Hawk. Hawk, please," I managed.

He pulled his wrist out of my grip, his fingers trailing down my side, over my hip to dip down and circle my clit. My hips jerked and I moaned, the sound a plea. One big finger slid down to press inside, testing, stretching me, filling me just enough to have my hips jerking up to take his finger deeper. It wasn't enough.

If my ankle had been healthy, if my brain had been functioning, I might have wiggled out from under him and tried to flip him over. Not that I could overpower him. Maybe I could take him by surprise, but I wasn't functioning on that level.

A second finger joined the first. The pad of his thumb pressed into my clit, and he thrust his thick fingers in, once, twice. On the third thrust, I exploded. My pussy clenched his fingers, his mouth sucking my nipple, my head spinning, the pleasure easing then building again until I was drowning in it.

Hawk shifted back, his hands hooking under my knees, gentle as he moved my right leg, thinking of my sprained ankle even now. Tears pricked my eyes, my senses overwhelmed, my body and my heart spinning, lost in this man. So fierce and so sweet. I couldn't keep up.

He pushed my legs wide, opening me, his eyes sharp, and I imagined he saw everything despite the dark room. I was too far gone to be shy. Too desperate. I lifted my arms as he came down over me, my hands sliding over his shoulders, pulling him close, eager as the head of his cock nudged me, pressing inside.

Slowly, he filled me, and it was so fucking good. I rocked my hips to take more of him, my fingers curled into his shoulders. I held on, needing, wanting all of him. And then I had him to the hilt, his pubic bone grinding into my clit, his cock filling me so perfectly I wanted to weep with the beauty of it. I curled up, holding on tight as he began to move, the bliss of it so sharp and strong it hurt.

I pressed my mouth to his shoulder, my teeth sinking

in as his hips pounded, his breath ragged, his rough voice chanting my name. "Quinn. Quinn."

That was all. Just my name, over and over, his body overwhelming mine, the orgasm hitting me out of nowhere. I wasn't expecting to come again so fast. This one made the first orgasm look like a blip on the radar.

The waves of sharp pleasure went on forever, the thrust of his hips bruising me in the best way as his control spun away and his own orgasm took him under. All I heard was my name on a rough groan. "Quinn. Oh, God. Quinn."

I held on to him, my thighs clamped to his hips, my fingernails digging into his arms, my mouth on his shoulder, teeth still sunk into his warm skin, my breath ragged in my chest. I didn't want to let go. I didn't want to move.

Eventually, Hawk's breath evened out. Warm lips grazed my cheeks, my eyelids, my mouth.

"I'll be right back," he said.

He disappeared into the bathroom and returned with something wet and cold. A paper towel or one of my face wipes, maybe. It didn't matter. Nudging my thighs apart, he cleaned me with lingering strokes. When he was done, he disappeared again, and I had a moment to wonder. Was that it? Would he put on his T-shirt and boxer briefs, slide under the covers, and turn his back to me?

I hadn't minded him running that morning, but not now. Not after that. I didn't have words for what we'd done, but it was a lot more than just sex. Being with Hawk was something I hadn't known before. Something I'd wanted and never had. More than sex, more than intimacy, it was—

I didn't think I could take it if he turned his back on me. Tomorrow, in the light of day, maybe. But not now, so soon after we'd—

He didn't. He slid in beside me, one arm pulling me close, careful of my injured ankle, tucking me into his side and drawing up the covers. His free hand stroked my hair, the backs of his fingers grazing my cheeks, sending tiny shivers down my spine.

He didn't say a word. I didn't either. I didn't have any words. I didn't need them. I smiled into his chest and soaked in every stroke, every touch.

I would have bet there was no way I'd fall asleep, finally naked and tangled up with Hawk. But I did, waking in the middle of the night to find myself draped over him, strong hands stroking up and down my spine, coming around to trace the sides of my breasts pillowed against his chest, his hard cock warm between my legs.

The second I realized I was awake and not in a deliciously erotic dream, I pushed myself up just enough to kiss him, to shift my knees wider and line myself up, ignoring the bolt of pain in my ankle. I slid back, taking him deep in a slow, teasing glide. Hawk pushed himself up on his elbows and closed his mouth around the tip of my breast, sucking hard and long.

This time it was slow, building with every rock of my hips, every pull of his mouth, until I came, squeezing his cock inside me, taking him with me. I was half asleep before he came back to clean me up, reaching for him when he returned to bed, curling into him, a smile on my face. Contented sleep dragged me under.

I woke hours later to streams of sunlight illuminating

the blanket hung over the window. The glittering, bright sunlight of a spring morning in the mountains. I registered the arms surrounding me, the silky skin and hard muscle of his shoulder. His breath in my hair. I was exactly where I wanted to be. Finally. I never wanted to move.

I smiled, and the clarity of the morning light penetrated my bliss-filled brain.

Daylight.

Clear, bright daylight.

The storm had passed. And just that quickly, the ending to my bliss reared its ugly head.

Chapter Sixteen

HAWK

Warm. I was so warm.

And content. Such a bland word. *Content.* But it was something I rarely felt. Contentment wasn't in the emotional arsenal for a man like me. My work was dangerous, and I was rarely in a place I wanted to be. I did what I had to do and moved on to the next mission.

But I felt it now. And I fucking liked it. A lot.

I wasn't fully awake, but I already knew moving on was the last thing I wanted. For the first time in years, I wanted to stay exactly where I was. *Content.*

My eyes opened, the wood beams of the ceiling coming into focus, my brain registering the warm, soft weight draped over me, the smell of Quinn's hair, the silk of it tangled in my fingers. There was the answer for my rare state of contentment. Quinn.

I stayed where I was, completely still, not ready to surrender this feeling. Not yet. I wanted a few more seconds of knowing I was exactly where I wanted to be, wanted to hold on to all of it. The cabin, this bed. This woman.

When we left here, this would be over. I shouldn't have touched her in the first place. Back at Heartstone, back in the world—this couldn't ever happen again. But for now, I had her here, in my arms. For just a little longer I could pretend she was mine.

Bright light illuminated the edges of the blanket I'd hung over the window. I knew what it meant. The snow had passed, and I had to find a way to get Quinn out of here.

She was right. The trail would be treacherous in this much snow. But not as treacherous as staying here and waiting for a bullet to the brain.

I would never risk Quinn like that. With visibility no longer an issue, I'd call my team, have them meet us at the cabin and get her to the Manor, where we could keep her safe. My gut twisted. She was going to hate being trapped indoors, under guard. By the time we figured out who was after her, she'd probably hate me for it. I could live with that. I couldn't live with Quinn being hurt. Not again.

I'd sworn to myself that this wasn't going to happen. Never. I would never dishonor my friendship with Griffen by laying a finger on his baby sister. I would never mix business with pleasure. Never. So many fucking *nevers*. But here I was, bare-ass naked with Quinn draped over me, every inch of her soft and smooth and perfect.

She looked like a delicate fairy, and while she didn't weigh much compared to me, her slight frame hid unexpected strength. Beneath that soft skin was dense muscle. She was strong. Capable. She was smart and funny and damn good company.

If we were in another life... If I was another man; if there wasn't an asshole out there with zip ties who wanted to take her—

I could have stayed with her forever. For just a second I let myself picture it. The cabin, with Quinn. Hiking, fishing, playing cards in front of the fire, taking her to bed at night, waking with her in the morning.

It was impossible. All of it was impossible. Not just because of Griffen or the man with the zip ties. What I had inside me wasn't for Quinn. She deserved the light. Love. I couldn't give her that. I was stained with darkness, with death, with a thousand wrong choices I could never take back.

My fingers tightened on her shoulder. I had seconds left. Seconds before I'd have to admit it was time to get up. To end all of this. This cozy bed, the down comforter pulled up to Quinn's shoulders, her soft breath on my skin. It would all end. The thing I wanted most, I'd have to give up.

I'd gotten used to not wanting things. I didn't deserve anything this good. I didn't deserve Quinn. I never should have touched her, but I couldn't lie to her when she asked. I did want her, badly. Even when she gave me an out. I could have said no. *No, I don't want you to kiss me.* I could have gotten up and slept on the couch, Quinn out of reach. A simple shake of my head and she would have stopped. I knew it, and I hadn't been able to bring myself to turn her away.

As much as I should have, I couldn't do it. I'd taken something that shouldn't be mine, and now I was going to have to give her up. A flash of agony hit me, and I wondered where I was going to find the strength to let her go. It was one thing to imagine, but now that I knew the reality of Quinn, how was I going to walk away and pretend this was nothing?

I'd had sex before, good sex. But with Quinn— That had been something different. I'd never fit with a woman like I did with Quinn. One night wasn't enough. Could never be enough. But it had to be. One night was all we could have.

I felt her head move, the shift of her shoulders, and knew she was awake. It was too soon. I wasn't ready. As I registered that she was awake, I knew where I'd find the motivation to leave her. I wanted her safe more than anything else. More than I wanted her with me, I needed her to be safe. I couldn't give her more, but I could give her that.

I squeezed my eyes closed, trying to force my brain in line. It didn't feel comfortable in my own head these days. I was used to being focused, everything moving on a single track. The job at hand was what mattered. That had been easier at the Manor, where the job was keeping Griffen's family safe.

Nothing was more important than family. I'd lost my own long ago, but the Sinclairs and Griffen were my family now. For years, I'd been able to stay on that single track, doing what I had to do, getting the job done. And now here was Quinn, slicing me in half. Part of me focused on the mission. And the other part of me, the core of me, didn't give a fuck about anything but the woman in my arms.

Opening my eyes, I lifted my hand from her shoulder, stroking it down the dark silk of her hair, drawing in the scent of her shampoo, savoring every sensation of holding her. Her toenails against my shin. The slight prickle of her unshaven legs. Puffs of her breath on my shoulder. The memory of her straddling my hips, rising over me, taking me inside her. My cock swelled, and I wanted.

With a wrench in my gut that felt like grief, I ignored my cock and turned my back on what I needed. The time for that had passed.

It had to have passed because if I gave in now—if I shifted her over my hips, touched her, found her wet, and slid deep inside—if I did it now, I'd never fucking stop. And that couldn't be.

Even if it wasn't for Griffen. I had nothing to bring to a woman like Quinn. The best I could do was keep safe the people who mattered. That was the only good I had to bring to the world, and it wasn't enough to deserve Quinn.

I let out the breath I'd been holding and shifted slowly beneath Quinn's body, not wanting to jolt her and risk hurting her ankle.

"Stay here," I said. "I'm going to take a look around. Do you need to get to the bathroom right now?"

Her eyes sleepy and a little dazed, Quinn sat up, the sheet pooling around her waist, her sweet, beautiful breasts bare. *That's done*, I reminded myself.

"Can you walk me to the bathroom after I get some

clean clothes out of my pack? I'll be quick. Then you can go scout around outside." Her eyes flicked to the light leaking in around the blanket, and I knew she knew our time was up.

I nodded. Something in my gut told me I had to get outside. I didn't like being blind to our surroundings now that the storm had moved on, but Quinn wasn't mobile. I wouldn't leave until she was settled.

Quinn slid to the edge of the bed and rustled around in her bag, grabbing a few things. Instead of helping her hop her way to the bathroom, I scooped her up, holding her against my chest, savoring how she felt in my arms.

The walk across the hall was too short. I set her down on her good foot in front of the sink and shut the door. By the time I was dressed in my winter gear, my boots laced, Quinn was calling my name from the bathroom door. I returned to find her hair neatly braided, her familiar fleece dwarfing most of her body over another pair of yoga pants and fluffy socks. Some men liked lacy lingerie, but I'd take this Quinn any day. Knowing what she hid under her practical clothes made my blood burn and my fingers itch to touch.

One taste and I couldn't stop thinking about her. I needed to focus, to get my head on straight. This wasn't about sex, this was about keeping her alive. I gave in to the temptation to touch her, lifting her into my arms again for the short trip to the couch.

"I'll make coffee when I get back," I said, settling the wool blanket over her. The cabin was cool, verging on outright cold, but we weren't adding wood to the almost dead fire. It was time to go, my nerves crawling up and down my spine, urging me to get outside, to check for tracks.

I opened the door of the cabin to see that Quinn had been right. The storm was gone, and the forest was a fairyland. Sunlight sparkled on the snowy ground. Icy leaves glittered against the vibrant blue sky. In the trees, I caught the rustle of squirrels and birds, the forest coming back to life as quickly as it always did once bad weather had passed.

The snow was unblemished but for the tiny tracks of small creatures, not even a deer print to mar the perfection of it all. I thought about crossing the clearing and checking the woods. The cabin first, I decided. The snow was almost two feet deep. A hell of a storm for this part of the country, especially these days.

The air was cold, the light breeze icy enough to bite, but the sky was clear, the sun strong. The snow might hang around for a few days, or it could start melting as soon as the sun had a chance to warm the air. Either way, it wasn't going to melt in the next few hours. And now that the storm had abated, I had no doubt that Quinn's attacker would be coming out of whatever hole he'd crawled into. The snow was deep but navigable. If he was going to come back, it would be today.

We needed to get moving.

I walked around the side of the cabin. Everything looked as it should. No tracks in the snow. Nothing disturbed in the woods. The window by the kitchen was the same. Through it, I saw Quinn on the couch reading her book, everything inside the cabin at peace. *Maybe*, a voice whispered in my head. *Maybe*. All was quiet. Maybe we could stay. Maybe—

And then I saw them beneath the bedroom window. Not the tracks of squirrels and chipmunks. Human tracks. Boots. I moved closer, not wanting to disturb anything until I got a good look. Pulling out my phone, I took pictures, zooming in, getting as many angles as I could.

He'd come straight from the trees to stand in front of the window. Crouching, I looked closer and took another photograph. The boot tread wasn't remarkable. It looked like that of a hundred other boots I'd seen. I stood just behind the tracks and found myself positioned perfectly to see through the narrow gap between the edge of the blanket I'd hung and the window frame.

My gut went tight. In the sliver of space between the blanket and the window, I had a perfect view of the bed. Had he stood here in the dead of night, watching us together? Had he seen her? The violation of it, the idea that he'd watched us—

I didn't care much for my own sake. It was Quinn. She would hate this. I knew it instinctively. She was so private, so independent and self-sufficient. The idea that this man who'd attacked her had watched us—

I straightened away from the window. This wasn't about how she felt. It was about getting Quinn to safety. This situation called for cold reason, logic, and all the skills I'd amassed over my long career. The man who'd made love to her in the dark of night had no place here.

Business, not pleasure, remember?

And by the way, that little voice in my head whispered, *this is why you don't fuck the client. Because it's nearly impossible to keep her safe once she's more than the job. Keeping Quinn safe is more important than fucking her. It's more important than anything.*

I did what I would have done if Quinn had been any other job. I tracked his footprints, seeing where he'd hiked in, leaving along the same path, his footprints in and out overlapping. He was long gone from the cabin.

That didn't mean he hadn't circled around to try to catch us on the trail back to the Manor.

As I made my way back to the cabin, I ran over strategies. Sit tight and wait for my team to get here, then bring Quinn back with the team to protect her? Call for a helicopter to get us down quickly, before her attacker had a chance to get settled in to ambush us? He wouldn't expect us to be moving this early and we needed every advantage we could get.

Chapter Seventeen

HAWK

Quinn looked up as I entered, and smiled. "Everything good?"

She didn't have to wait for my answer. The second the words were out of her mouth, she registered the look on my face. Her eyes turned hard, her chin jutting up.

"Hawk," she started.

I walked right past her. I couldn't do this with her. Not now. I needed to think. I wanted the team—one to help her walk, three to guard. But they'd be too slow. Our best advantage in this moment was time. He wouldn't expect us to hit the trail this early. Not with so much snow. And while the terrain was dangerous in this weather, I'd hiked that trail a hundred times since I'd come to Sawyers Bend. I could keep us from tumbling into a ravine better than I could stop a sniper's bullet. All the guards in the world wouldn't help if the man after Quinn had time to get into a tree and wait for us to pass below him.

Going to the bedroom, I dug into her pack and pulled out her winter pants. Coming back to the couch. I dropped them on top of her legs, saying abruptly, "Put these on. He was out there last night, watching us through the window. I know the trail is dangerous, but we have to go. Get those pants on while I call my team."

My chest ached as the blood drained from her face, fear invading her beautiful blue eyes. She swallowed hard and gave a jerk of a nod. Quinn would fight me like a wildcat to get what she wanted, but the second she understood how serious things were, she did what she had to do. She was headstrong and independent, but she was also smart. This would be a hell of a lot easier if she wasn't any of those things. But if she wasn't all of those things, I wouldn't have wanted her.

I grabbed my sat phone and dialed in, the line crackling.

"You good out there?" came the voice of my second-in-command.

"We're headed back," I said. "I need you to get a team on the trail headed for us."

"If you can sit tight, we can be there in just over an hour. The snow is deep, but—"

"No." I cut him off. "Someone was here last night looking through the windows, not trying to hide their tracks. They're not here now."

Kane understood immediately. "They could be waiting to ambush you on the trail."

"It's a possibility," I said. "Or they could be headed back this way. If they know Quinn is injured, they may think we won't try to leave yet. We need to get her back to Heartstone Manor. That's the priority. We'll be on the move in less than ten minutes. Meet us on the trail. And have someone arrange a pair of crutches at Heartstone. Quinn is sure her ankle is sprained, not broken, but she'll need the crutches to get around."

"I'm on it. We'll see you soon. And boss? Be careful."

"I always am," I said. Quinn had already been injured on my watch. It wasn't going to happen again.

Hanging up, I turned to Quinn. "Anything in that pack you need in the next few days?" She shook her head, then shrugged a shoulder.

"I wouldn't mind my toiletries bag and this book, but otherwise, no."

I retrieved it, grabbed her toiletries from the bathroom, took the book from her hand, and packed it all inside.

"So, we're going," she said.

I nodded, busy grabbing her parka and giving it a shake. I carried it to the couch, along with her hiking boots. "You need to get these boots on. Lace the right one as tight as you can."

She reached out her hands to take the boots. "I've got it. You get the fire in the stove put out. Then I guess we're okay to go. Someone will come back later to get my pack?" she asked.

"I'll make sure of it," I promised.

Quinn nodded. I took care of the fire. I hadn't added another log since the middle of the night, our body heat enough to keep us warm. When I turned, I saw Quinn had loosened the laces on her right boot enough to wedge her foot in.

"I'm going to get you back to the Manor," I said. "Then you can see a doctor."

"I don't need a doctor. It's just a sprain," she said through gritted teeth as she pulled on her bootlaces, tightening them to support her ankle.

I nodded, wanting to argue and knowing it was a waste of breath. I paused, not sure how to get out what I needed to say. "Last night—"

Quinn looked up at me, her eyes bright, a smile curving her mouth.

"It was a mistake," I said. "It can't happen again." I waited, braced for an argument, for her face to crumple into sadness or anger or disappointment. I wasn't going to give any ground, but I didn't want to fight with her. Not about this. Not about anything.

She stared at me, her face frozen. Then she shrugged and went back to tightening the laces. "Okay," she said, her voice muffled but steady.

"I mean it," I said. "It was a one-time thing. It shouldn't have happened, and it's over."

Quinn straightened, her boots laced and ready to go. Tossing her head to flip a loose strand of hair off her face, she said, "I heard you. One-time thing. Not happening again. I got it."

"Okay," I agreed, suddenly off-balance. She wasn't going to argue. She wasn't disappointed.

Wasn't that what I wanted? For Quinn to be okay with it? For us to never, ever do that again. No more naked Quinn, right? I'd said it was over. She was fine with it.

Good, right? *Right.*

I couldn't believe how much I wanted to dig my heels in and argue with her about— About what? There was nothing to argue about since we were apparently in agreement. But how could it be that easy? I'd been twisting myself in knots, and she was fine with it.

Get your head in the fucking game, asshole, I told myself. *This is exactly what you wanted. The best-case scenario for how that could go. The only thing that matters right now is getting Quinn home safely.*

I handed her the parka and the gloves I'd found stuffed in the pocket. "All right, gear up."

She did as she was told without protest. I did the same. When we were ready, I crouched in front of her and she climbed on my back, the straps of her daypack looped over her shoulders.

As we left the cabin, Quinn let out a mournful sigh. "So much for my vacation. It's so beautiful out here. I can't believe we have to leave because of some fuckhead with his zip ties and whatever the hell is wrong with him."

She sounded genuinely sad, almost like she was fighting back tears. For the cabin. Not for me. If I had feelings, that would fucking hurt. But I didn't. I was a machine. I had a job to do. I couldn't afford feelings.

I put one foot in front of the other as I went down the narrow, uneven trail, the footing hidden by the snow. I needed my full attention on what I was doing or I'd fall and take Quinn down with me. And still, I couldn't stop hearing the mournful tone of her voice over her lost vacation and leaving the cabin. She'd been just fine with me telling her we were over.

Not that we'd even been anything. It was one night. She hadn't cared about that, but she didn't want to leave the cabin. The cabin that didn't even have running water or electricity. And still, it rated higher than sex with me.

Fuck. Stop thinking about it. Focus on the trail and getting Quinn to safety.

It took all my discipline to keep my attention on the trail and our surroundings. I had both of our weapons easily at hand, but they wouldn't do me much good if I was so far up my own ass I didn't hear him coming.

I listened and watched, but the forest was quiet around us. Not the creepy quiet that comes with a predator, just the normal stillness after a storm. I caught the sounds of birds and the occasional crack of a branch as something small passed, but nothing else. The rustle and thump of my boots in the soft snow was the loudest sound in the quiet. I moved slowly, testing my footing before transferring my weight, glad of my caution when I encountered rocks and downed branches hidden by the snow.

It was slow going, but so far the only threat was the uneven footing. When my internal clock told me we'd been on the move for almost an hour, we came to the place where the trail split. From here, we could move faster. I couldn't see my team, but they'd reach us any minute. I had one more thing I needed to say to Quinn, and I knew it would be easier to say while we were alone.

Or maybe I wanted one more private conversation, even if it was a fight.

"Quinn," I began carefully, "when we get back, I need you to stay in the Manor. No more sleeping in the woods. Not until we find this guy."

Every muscle in her body went stiff, her fingers clenching on my shoulders, her grip hard, even through my parka.

"I can't." Her voice was strained, so tight I thought it would break.

Not expecting her response, I thought about what she'd said. Not *I won't*, but *I can't*. I didn't understand, but I wanted to.

"You have to," I said as gently as I could. "He was going to hurt you, Quinn. We can't keep you safe if you're out in the woods. And I can't risk security at the Manor to put enough of my team on you to keep you safe in the hammock. I need you to stay in the Manor with everyone else."

"Okay," she said, and this time her voice did break. But that was all she said.

Okay. So different from the "Okay" she'd given me when I told her we were over. That one hadn't exactly been cheerful, but it hadn't been this pained acceptance. "Quinn? I know—"

"You don't know." Her tone was so bleak I wasn't sure I'd have recognized it as her if she hadn't been speaking directly in my ear.

"Then tell me," I pressed, knowing this was not the time for personal confessions. Whatever kept her away from the Manor, I knew it had to be personal. Thanks to my position as the head of security, I knew everyone's secrets. But I didn't have a clue about this. What was she hiding? Why didn't I know about it?

She didn't answer, but I felt her shake her head against the back of my head.

"Quinn," I tried again, "what happened there? Was it your father?"

Another shake of her head, but no words.

"I can't help if you won't talk to me," I said.

"You can't help anyway," she whispered, her voice barely audible above the crunch of my feet in the snow.

I didn't want to accept that. We didn't have time for me to push harder. In the distance, I caught a glimpse of winter camo and a gray hat I recognized. In minutes my team would surround us. Not long after that, I'd deliver Quinn to Griffen. I was out of time.

"Promise me you'll stay in the Manor," I said.

One more nod and her strained voice in my ear. "I promise."

She didn't say another word. My team caught up, taking positions in a loose circle around us as we covered the rest of the ground back to Heartstone Manor.

In the bright sun, surrounded by unbroken snow, the Manor was straight out of a storybook. It looked as if nothing bad could ever happen there. Yet Quinn's face when I handed her into Griffen's arms told a very different story. She'd closed down completely, her face blank, her eyes on the ground, not meeting mine.

"Keep her inside," I told Griffen, wishing I had more to say, that I could give an order that would fix whatever was wrong and take that frozen expression off her face.

"The house is secure," Griffen said. "Go find this guy."

I nodded, hoping it would be that simple. Find the guy who'd jumped her in the woods and solve whatever problem had led him to think Quinn was a target. But nothing was ever that simple.

Chapter Eighteen
HAWK

We didn't find him. In the end, I wasn't surprised. We'd followed his trail back to the creek bed where I lost him. It took hours of searching to locate the place where his tracks reappeared. He was clever, leaving few signs of his passage aside from scuffed bark and fallen leaves.

The bastard had picked his way down the creek, his steps partly camouflaged by the still lightly falling snow. A half mile from where he entered the creek, he'd made a vertical jump and grabbed onto an overhanging branch thick enough to hold his weight. He must have gone hand over hand down the branch to the trunk where he'd climbed the fucking tree until he found a spot where it overlapped with another. He'd jumped from branch to branch and continued like a motherfucking monkey until he dropped back down into the snow hundreds of yards away.

This was no local boy with a grudge. This guy was something else.

The sun was almost to the ridgeline, dusk on its way, by the time we tracked his path down the mountain to an old fire road that led back to the state highway. He was long gone. One of my team came around to pick us up, saving the time it would take to hike back up the mountain.

We spent the rest of our daylight adding to the security around Heartstone Manor. Savannah and Finn's cottage already had a tight perimeter thanks to the troubles she'd had with her mother-in-law. We added a few more cameras and a second perimeter alarm surrounding the first, just in case.

The Manor itself had high security, but even there we added more cameras, inside and out, along with a wider perimeter to secure the surrounding area, covering my gatehouse and the clearing in the woods where I knew Quinn slept, along with the pool and pool house, neither of which were in use this time of year.

I watched the sun set from the control room in the lower level of the Manor, checking and double-checking every camera view. Anywhere family or staff might go, we had eyes. If anything bigger than a rabbit approached the Manor, we'd know.

Even with all that, I didn't feel like it was enough.

If this was any other client, I would have tucked myself into bed, satisfied with a job well done. But this wasn't a client. This was Griffen's family. And it was so much more. I couldn't stop seeing Quinn pinned on the snowy ground, fighting for her life. Couldn't forget her blank face as I'd handed her to Griffen.

No one was going to get to her. Not again.

By the time we finished, the sun had long since set and I was exhausted. We'd done everything we could think of to tighten security. I'd run the plans by Griffen. Consulted with the Sinclairs. We all agreed that we'd done the best we could. And still, as I trudged up the steps to the main level, something nagged at me. This guy —he would come for Quinn, I was sure of it. Given his obvious skill level, I knew I was dealing with someone with my kind of training. He wasn't going to give up. I wouldn't have. You didn't leave a job unfinished.

The house was quiet, dinner long since over. I texted Griffen.

> We're done. Got a minute?

> In my office. You eaten?

> I'm good.

Savannah had delivered a rolling cart stacked with covered dishes to the control room sometime around dinner, her gray eyes worried. "Let me know if you need anything," she'd said and disappeared back down the hall.

Savannah was worried. I was worried. Griffen was worried. We were all worried.

I walked into Griffen's office to find him already there, sitting behind his desk, the fire blazing, a steaming cup of tea beside his open laptop. Maybe reading my expression, he didn't say anything.

After years of working together, I didn't bother with a preamble. "I don't get it," I said. "Why Quinn?"

Griffen shook his head. He shoved his chair back

from his desk and strode to the sideboard. "Drink?" he asked.

I started to shake my head, then changed my mind. "A small one."

Griffen poured a splash of golden liquid into matching cut crystal glasses. Handing me my drink, he sat on the sofa by the fireplace. I sat on the sofa opposite, lifting the glass to hover beneath my nose. Whiskey. I took a sip. More of a burn than the bourbon I'd shared with Quinn. I preferred the bourbon, but tonight I needed that bite.

Griffen sat back, shaking his head again. "My best guess is that it has to do with our father's murder and whoever's been coming after us since. Nothing else makes sense."

I tended to agree, but it didn't totally track logically. Why Quinn? Of all the siblings, she was the most removed from Prentice. But then again, she was a Sawyer. And these days being a Sawyer seemed to include a target on her back.

"I didn't come across anything in her past to explain this," I said.

Sinclair Security had done background checks on everyone in Griffen's family when he'd moved home, even before he'd asked for them. At his request, we'd gone deeper. Nothing we found pointed to anyone having an issue with Quinn. No conflicts, no debts, no lovers' quarrels. Nothing that would explain the man who'd tried to take her from the trail.

"I don't think it's about Quinn. I think she's just the next target on the list." Griffen sipped his whiskey. "Or there's something else going on that we haven't figured out yet." His expression twisted as that possibility sank in.

I didn't like it any better than he did. "How was she at dinner?" I asked, haunted by the memory of Quinn's bleak voice. *You don't know.* She was right. I didn't know anything. Definitely not how Quinn could bounce back from being attacked in the woods, but completely shut down at the prospect of staying in her family home.

"She was quiet." Griffen stared into his whiskey before taking another sip. "I tried to get her to talk about it, but she closed me out. Sterling got the same."

"Where is she now?" Instinct told me she wasn't asleep in her room. Not with the way she'd reacted to staying in the Manor.

At first, thrown by the way she'd taken my ending things in stride, I hadn't fully grasped what was happening. Once my bruised ego got out of the way, I saw the whole thing with different eyes. Quinn, who was capable in so many ways, slept in the woods every night. I'd chalked it up to her being an avid outdoorswoman who preferred to be in the woods. Now I knew it was more than that.

Quinn loved sleeping in the woods, but I hadn't realized she *had* to sleep in the woods. And I didn't know why.

"She's in the sunroom," Griffen said. "She pretended to go to sleep in her rooms but came down the back stairs not long after and went to the sunroom."

"It's too cold in there," I murmured. "Too exposed."

The sunroom was down the hall from Griffen's office,

by the family gathering room. It was almost all windows, facing the woods where Quinn usually slept. Cut off from the central heating system, the sunroom wasn't used this time of year. It was as close to the outdoors as you could get while still being inside the Manor.

"She must be freezing," I said.

"She has a sleeping bag."

Of course she did. "Why—" I started, cutting off my question at Griffen's shaking head.

"I don't know," he said. "As far as I can tell, no one knows."

"And you haven't asked."

Griffen let out a long sigh and sipped the whiskey, grimacing as he swallowed. "I did ask. Once, a few months after we all came back. She said she didn't like sleeping indoors, tried to play it off like it wasn't a big deal. She avoided me for weeks after. I decided that whatever it was, it wasn't worth driving Quinn away by pushing too hard, so I let it go."

"Do you think this guy who attacked her has anything to do with why she won't sleep in the Manor?" The idea was so farfetched I shook my head at my own question.

If someone had done something to Quinn in the Manor since her father died, we'd know about it. It also begged the question of why now. She hadn't lived in the Manor since she'd gone to college. That was ten years ago. Why come back now? It didn't make sense.

"My gut reaction is to say this doesn't have anything to do with the past," Griffen said. "But at this point, I'm not ruling anything out."

"Agreed," I said, staring at the whiskey in my glass before taking another sip. "We tracked the guy all the way back to the state road, and it feels like we know less than when we started. If this is the next move from whoever's been after your family, they upgraded. This guy?" I shook my head. "This guy is good."

I walked Griffen through the details of the attack on the trail, the footprints under the bedroom window at the cabin, and the process of tracking the attacker back to the fire road. When I was finished, he took me back through it, asking questions until he was almost as up-to-date as if he'd been there with us. The whole process reminded me of our years working together, of all the reasons why I was glad to be here, having his back and keeping his family safe. And of all the reasons I never should have touched Quinn.

"He's not a local, then," Griffen said.

"Not unless there's a local with real skills."

"I don't—" Griffen began, then stopped and shook his head. "The truth is, I was away from Sawyers Bend for so long I don't know the locals anymore. And we have a lot of open land here. Enough to disappear in. It's possible he's local," he admitted. "Anything's possible."

"Quinn needs a dog," I said. The idea had been poking at me all day. She wasn't going to be easy to protect. Not long-term, once her ankle healed and tourist season cranked up. I doubted she'd tolerate full-time security, and I needed to keep my distance, for both our sakes. A guard dog wouldn't be the same as a human guard, but it was a lot better than nothing.

Griffen's eyes lit. "She'd love that. What are you thinking?"

"You remember Remy?" I asked. We'd worked with Remy a few times on behalf of clients at Sinclair Security. He trained guard dogs, and he and his dogs were some of the best out there.

"You're thinking a Belgian Malinois?"

I nodded. "They're active, but she needs a dog who can handle the trail as well as she can. They make great guard dogs. Strong, smart, hard-working, and loyal."

"You call him yet?" Griffen asked, staring into the flames, suddenly absorbed in thought.

Even though I imagined Quinn was going to be pissed at me for both making decisions behind her back and not talking to her first about this, I had indeed called Remy. "A few hours ago. Said he has an adolescent, almost fully trained. This one was meant for a family, so she's used to kids. I did him a favor a while ago, a big one, so he's willing to talk the client into waiting and send her to Quinn. I just have to talk to Quinn about it."

"Don't bother," Griffen said. "Tell Remy we'll take the dog. If Quinn refuses, we'll figure out something she can live with, and the dog can move in here."

"A dog?" I asked, raising an eyebrow. "Didn't you just have a baby? And now you want to add a dog to the mix?"

Griffen shrugged, looking a little sheepish. "I always wanted a dog. Prentice refused to let them in the house. Now that Parker and Sterling have the cat, the boys have been asking for a dog. Given everything else that's been going on, I'd prefer to get one that will keep them safe, along with giving them company. If Quinn agrees to Remy's dog, maybe I'll talk to him about a puppy."

"I'll see what he thinks when I call him tomorrow." I knocked back the rest of my whiskey and stood. "Nobody is getting anywhere near the Manor without being seen. We adjusted the team's surveillance schedule so everyone stays sharp. If this guy comes back, we'll have him."

"Thanks, Hawk." Griffen smiled at me.

"Anytime, man. You know that," I said.

"I do." He stood, clapping a hand on my shoulder. "If it was anyone else, I'd probably be up all night pacing and checking the cameras. It makes all the difference to have you here. I owe you."

"No, you don't," I said. "If anything, it's me who owes you." I'd never forget the way Griffen and the Sinclairs had saved me. I'd had enough strength to turn my back on my past but no clue where to go. They'd given me a job. Friendship. A home. A reason to keep living. I'd never be able to pay them back.

Griffen shook his head, a half smile tilting the side of his mouth. "You don't owe me anything. As far as I'm concerned, we're family." He set his glass on the sideboard and picked up a small black remote, clicking off the fire. "Get some rest. You've had a long few days."

"After I check on Quinn," I said, not meeting his eyes. I still hadn't processed the fact that I'd had sex with his baby sister.

On her own, Quinn was Quinn, an independent, adult woman who could make her own choices. But in this room, facing my friend who was as good as a brother,

I couldn't avoid what I'd done. He was thanking me for being here when I'd betrayed his trust.

I wouldn't take it back. I'd never give up a second of the time I'd spent with Quinn, but that didn't make it right. If he knew, he'd probably kill me.

"Thanks for keeping her safe," he said, sending a stab of guilt into my chest.

I nodded and followed him into the hall, watching as he jogged up to the rooms at the top of the stairs where Hope and their daughter waited. He'd never had as much to risk as he did now. And he was trusting all of it to me. His wife and daughter, his family, his home.

I wouldn't let him down.

Chapter Nineteen

HAWK

Turning left, I headed down the hall, stopping in front of the sunroom door. The light in the hallway reflected off the glass, too soft to penetrate the dark of the room.

Through the door, I heard a noise. A squeak, followed by a low, deep sound. A moan? I shoved the door open so fast it rattled, eyes scanning the moonlight room, shadows in every corner. I followed the sound, tracking a soft cry to an oversized wicker armchair. Quinn was curled up in a tight ball, wisps of dark hair peeking out at the top of her sleeping bag. Aside from Quinn, the room was empty.

Now that my eyes were adjusting, I saw the crutches on the floor beside her, next to the daypack she'd carried back from the cabin. She had a bedroom upstairs. A suite, bigger than Sterling and Braxton's rooms and smaller than Parker's, with a decent-sized bedroom and a small sitting room. I'd only seen it once, but I remembered. Unlike some of the other rooms, Quinn's was a time capsule of her in high school, as if she'd walked out of the room as a teenager and never returned.

I pulled down the top of the sleeping bag a few inches to see her face, eyes squeezed shut, a deep line between her eyebrows, her lips stiff and tight. Another whimper escaped her, the sound stabbing through me. I hated the idea of Quinn being afraid of anything.

Ignoring the voice reminding me to stay away from her, I cupped her cheek in my hand, stroking my thumb over her soft skin. I needed to wake her, but I didn't want to scare her. Her eyes popped open, locking on mine in the near dark.

"Quinn," I said, "Wake up, baby. You're having a bad dream."

She stared up at me, silent, until I wondered if she was still asleep, still caught in the nightmare.

"Quinn?"

"I can't—" The words rushed out on a breath, barely audible. "I can't sleep here. I can't. I can't, Hawk."

"Okay. Okay," I found myself saying. "Okay," I said again, maybe trying to convince myself as much as her. Because I knew at that moment I'd do anything to spare her this.

I didn't know why. I didn't understand what it was about sleeping in this house.

I would find out. I vowed that to myself. I would fucking find out what had happened to her here that had caused so much trauma she couldn't sleep under this roof.

For now, I'd do any fucking thing necessary to never hear her whimper like that again.

"Okay," I said, running over the options. I came up with one answer. It was insanity, but I thought it might be the only solution. "Where's your pack? The one with your hammock?"

"In my room. By the door." Her eyes lit with hope.

"I'll go to your room and get it. You get this sleeping bag packed up so we can bring it with us."

Quinn sat up, swinging her legs to the floor. I left her there, heading down the hall and up the stairs to her room, opening the door to see her pack just inside, propped against the wall. I loosened the straps and put it on, returning to the sunroom to find Quinn on her feet, leaning on the crutches, her daypack on her back, the sleeping bag in its stuff sack clipped to the bottom.

"Give me the pack," I said, holding out my hand. Quinn didn't argue, shrugging her shoulders out of the straps and silently handing it to me. I slung it over my shoulder. "Hold both your crutches in your right arm," I ordered.

At that, she gave me a skeptical look but still didn't argue, transferring her weight to her left foot as she set the two crutches under her right arm.

"Hold on." I scooped her up from the left so the crutches were out of the way. "It's too dark out there for crutches on the steps."

Her head relaxed against my shoulder, the smell of her shampoo drifting up to tease me.

"We're going to the gatehouse," I said.

Quinn let out a breath, the tension in her muscles easing.

It was a short walk through the courtyard and down

the drive to the gatehouse. Not far from the Manor, the gatehouse spanned the drive, matching two-story stone buildings joined by an arching stone porte cochere over the road. Once, there'd been gates there. These days, the main gates were down at the road.

On one side of the drive, the gatehouse was designed as a compact home, with an open living and kitchen space on the first level, and two small bedrooms and a shared bath on the second level. A narrow door at the top of the stairs connected to a long room built above the porte cochere, leading to the identical building on the other side of the drive. For now, the other side was closed up and used for storage, though Parker had been toying with the idea of turning it into more spacious living quarters for my team. For now, she was still focused on renovating the part I was living in.

I unlocked the door, shoving it with my foot, and flipped on the light. Quinn blinked at the sudden shift, squinting into the room. I set her on her feet, waiting for her to balance on her left foot and get the crutches organized before I stepped back.

She looked around at the space, and I wondered what she saw. I didn't think it was that bad. Basic, but basic was fine with me. Quinn's sister Parker had declared it a disaster and promised to renovate it into a rustic but luxurious dream. I wasn't sure what that meant or if I wanted it, but it didn't matter.

In the end, this was Griffen's gatehouse, not mine. I was only a tenant, and not one who wanted to complain about free room and board. To me, the gatehouse was just fine. It was clean, which was a vast improvement over its state when I first moved in. No more mice, no more cobwebs, dust, or leaking plumbing. It even had reliable electricity and hot water, which was more than I could say for the guest wing in the Manor. The gatehouse was a fuck-ton better than a lot of places I'd lived. Sure, the furniture was sparse, and none of it matched, and I only had one plate, one set of utensils, and one glass. It wasn't like I needed more than that. It was just me.

Usually I slept upstairs, but I was thinking I'd bunk on the shabby but wide, long, and incredibly comfortable couch Parker had brought over from the attics of the big house. I slept on that couch more often than not, falling asleep while watching a movie or reading.

"Bathroom's over there," I said, jerking my head toward the cramped half bath beside the small kitchen. Quinn nodded, making her way across the room, her eyes straying to me as I unpacked her bag, pulling out her hammock, under-quilt, and a small bag with an extra set of hanging straps. I connected one end of the straps to a sturdy hook in a beam overhead, securing the other strap around the handrail of the iron banister.

Hung that way, the hammock blocked the path to the kitchen, but we could work around it. It was a good thing I didn't have much furniture. Just the couch, a TV, and a folding table and chairs. Most importantly, the hammock was level and low enough for her to get in. I hoped it was close enough to her safe place that she could get some sleep. I set up the under-quilt and unrolled her sleeping bag inside the hammock, laying her pillow on top as she came out of the bathroom.

"You need help getting in?" I asked.

Quinn shook her head, eyes shimmering with tears as she stared at her hammock, set up just as it usually was in her clearing in the woods. She crossed the room in the hitching stride caused by the crutches, turning at the side of the hammock to transfer them to her right hand.

I moved to take them, laying them on the floor beneath the hammock. Her hands free, Quinn hopped up, sliding into the hammock and her sleeping bag at the same time.

"Can you sleep?" I asked as she pulled the sleeping bag up around her.

Rolling her head against her familiar pillow, Quinn's eyes came to mine, the deep blue of them swimming in tears. One, then another, rolled down the sides of her face.

"Quinn, don't do that," I said, wiping her tears with the pad of my thumb. "It's okay."

"I can't," she rasped out, squeezing her eyes shut, more tears spilling down her cheeks. "I think I have it under control, that it's over, and then I go in there, and I just— I just can't."

"It's okay. I'll be right here."

"Thanks, Hawk," she said, her voice small.

I nodded, wanting to say everything that I couldn't. Wanting to swear that anything this woman wanted from me, she could have.

Except that was a lie. The thing I thought we both might want the most was the one thing we couldn't have. She deserved better, and I didn't deserve her. Not even close.

I wiped the last tear from her cheek. "Go to sleep," I

said, following my own orders and turning out the lights before stretching out on the couch and pulling up the blanket I'd left there.

I closed my eyes, listening in the dark for Quinn's breathing to even out. When it did, I finally relaxed, following her into sleep.

Chapter Twenty
QUINN

My nose wasn't cold. That was the first thing that popped into my head when I woke up.

I was in my hammock, snuggled into my sleeping bag, swaying lightly as I stretched my legs.

My nose wasn't cold, so I wasn't outside. With that realization, my eyes flicked open, staring up at a white ceiling intersected with dark wood beams.

The gatehouse. Hawk's gatehouse.

The night before came flooding back, and my gut twisted with shame, tears prickling my eyes. I never wanted anyone to see me like that. Especially not Hawk. Humiliation didn't quite cover it.

It wasn't usually that bad. Last night wasn't the first time I'd slept in Heartstone Manor since we'd all moved home. There had been thunderstorms and snap freezes, days of rain, and high winds. I hated sleeping in that fucking house, but not enough to risk a widow-maker branch falling on my hammock. The woods and high winds were not a safe combination, especially if there had been a lot of rain and tree roots were loose in the ground.

My rooms were out of the question. I hadn't slept in that bed since I was seventeen. When I was denied my hammock in the woods, I always chose the sunroom and that wide wicker armchair. Surrounded by windows, it was almost as good as being outside. Usually, when I had to sleep in the Manor, I had an extra glass of wine at dinner, took some melatonin, and I got through the night.

No big deal. Everybody coped with their stuff in their own way. That was what I liked to tell myself. But last night—

I didn't know. I was no psychologist, but maybe between the attack on the trail and my twisted ankle, knowing my attacker had watched me in the night—

All of it mixed together was too much.

I didn't usually remember my dreams. It had been years since I had the nightmares. Last night I hadn't been able to fight them. I'd curled into a tight ball in my armchair, clutching the sleeping bag around me, closed my eyes, and I'd dreamed.

I dreamed of my dark bedroom and the big figure in the chair beside my bed. Of the electric feel of being watched, how it charged the air even in the dark. His pudgy, hot fingers stroking my bare arm. The greedy gleam of his eyes in the dark. The way he said my name. *Quinney*. Like I was a child, long after I wasn't. *Quinney*.

I never dreamed about him. I never thought about him. Not anymore. He was gone. My father was dead. No one here could hurt me anymore.

It was far easier to believe that in the gatehouse. At night, in the Manor— Just the thought of it made my skin crawl.

I sat up in the hammock and looked around at Hawk's gatehouse. Parker was right—it needed a ton of work. I didn't think the place had been updated since the fifties. But it was still beautiful. From the hammock, I could see the edges of the stonework outside around the windows, the wide-planked hardwood floor, and vintage cabinets. The ceilings were high, and the contrast of the wide, dark beams was gorgeous. When Parker was done with the place, it would be a gem.

Hawk didn't have much furniture and nothing in the way of decoration. There was a monstrosity of a velvet couch, ugly as hell, in a weird mustardy green that screamed the seventies. Parker must have found it in the attics. It was wide and long and looked soft. I felt a little less guilty about Hawk sleeping on it. He had two camp chairs sitting opposite the couch. A table and folding chairs closer to the small kitchen. That was it.

The place might have been run-down and mostly empty, but as I'd come to expect from Hawk, it was neat as a pin. An insulated carafe sat on the Formica counter in the kitchen beside a coffee mug I recognized from Heartstone's kitchens and a plate with a silver cover. I'd slept hours later than usual and my stomach was rumbling. My heart melted. He'd brought me breakfast.

The second my eyes had opened, I'd known Hawk wasn't in the gatehouse. I could feel his absence, but he'd brought me breakfast. I didn't know what to do with this man.

My current plan was to wait him out. It had stung when he told me what we'd shared in the cabin was over. Of course it stung. I liked him a lot. I was happy when I was with Hawk, and the sex had been out of this world. I didn't want to give any of that up.

But he'd made it clear it wasn't going to happen. He wasn't a relationship guy. I was his best friend's little sister. He worked for my family. All excellent reasons to keep his distance. I got it. And something told me there was more to it than his very good reasons not to have a thing with me. Stuff that wasn't about Griffen or his job. Stuff that was about Hawk and why he thought he wasn't a relationship guy.

I understood his objections. I did. But I wasn't walking away from him. There was something between us. That had been no regular one-night stand. We had something, and it was better than anything I'd imagined for myself.

I wasn't going to fight him, not head-on, but I could be patient. Hawk said he didn't want anything to do with me. Then he rescued me and brought me into his lair. He brought me breakfast. I'd learned to pay more attention to what people did than what they said. And Hawk's actions didn't say it was over. So I'd wait and see. And in the meantime...

I pulled my legs out of the sleeping bag, wincing at the tenderness in my sprained ankle. I could already tell it was better than the day before, but only fractionally. *Fuck.* This was really going to screw up all my plans.

I raised my knees and pivoted, hooking my legs over

the side of the hammock, and saw my crutches laid out perpendicular to the hammock on my right side.

I smiled to myself. There was something so hot about a man who understood the importance of details, including bringing me coffee and breakfast.

The hammock was a little higher off the ground than I was used to, but not so much that I couldn't get in and out. I hopped down on my left foot, hanging on to the hammock for balance. Letting my weight fall forward, I caught myself with my hands, successfully managing to keep my right foot from taking any weight. Getting back to my feet, crutches in hand, was a little harder, but there was coffee on the line so I made it work.

Standing mostly on my left foot at the kitchen counter, I poured a cup of coffee and looked around, spotting my pack from the cabin beside the stairs. With everything he had on his plate the day before, he'd remembered my pack. Yeah, he was worth waiting for.

My gaze shifted to the front window, and I stared across the lawn at Heartstone Manor, austere, stunning, and surrounded by unbroken snow. My heart ached. I always said I hated Heartstone, but in truth, I loved it. It was my home, and when I was very young it had been my safe place, an endless playground I shared with my brothers and sisters.

Most of all, Heartstone Manor held my memories of my mother. There had been so much love there when she was alive.

Then she died, and my father ruined everything. He and his creepy friend and their plans for me.

But my father was dead, and his creepy friend was gone. For good.

The sun sparkled on the snow around the home I'd once loved, and I sighed. Maybe it might be time to deal with my bullshit. Not today. Not tomorrow. But soon. I loved my hammock and my campsite in the woods, but... there was eccentric and outdoorsy, and then there was just being fucked up. Maybe at the grand age of twenty-seven, I was old enough to stop pretending they were the same thing.

I shivered, remembering the dream I'd had the night before, the panic that had hit me when Hawk said I had to stay in the Manor. My heart had pounded, going from zero to sixty in a blink, my lungs tight, my body frozen. I'd shut down just at the thought of sleeping in my room.

A flash of shame hit me, remembering that Hawk had seen me so weak. I wasn't weak, damn it. I was just a little fucked up about this one thing. And I would deal with it.

I would, but not today.

I finished the first cup of coffee and peeked under the lid covering the plate—one of Finn's spectacular breakfast burritos. My stomach rumbled, but it could wait. Grabbing my crutches, I crossed the room to my pack and got some clean clothes.

I made my way to the powder room beside the kitchen. It was a tight squeeze with my clothes and toiletries and crutches. And most importantly, it had no shower. I thought longingly of the last time I'd had a proper shower—the wet wipes in the cabin had been good enough when that was all I had, but nothing beat a hot shower. Crutches on stairs sucked, but I was more than a little overripe and had nothing better to do with my time. I shoved my toiletries and change of clothes in my daypack, pulled it on, and began the arduous process of climbing the stairs. It went better than I expected. I'd barely broken a sweat by the time I reached the second floor.

Chapter Twenty-One
QUINN

The upstairs needed renovation as much as the lower level, but it was functional. The layout was simple. Two bedrooms with a decent-sized bathroom between them. And again, up here everything was ruthlessly neat. One bedroom was empty. The other had a queen-sized bed, perfectly made, with a laundry hamper in the corner and a dresser on the wall opposite the bed. That was it. No artwork. No family pictures. No laundry tossed on the floor or shoes askew by the closet. The room barely looked lived-in.

I looked again, and it hit me. It was too neat. Too sparse.

This was more than military training. This was—it was like he wasn't even here. Something about that made me so sad. Hawk gave of himself so willingly. He took care of everyone. He should have a home. A nest. The only truly welcoming thing I'd seen in the gatehouse was that monstrosity of a couch, and I knew that had been a Parker addition. Everything else was utilitarian. Not that

I was one to judge, considering I slept in a hammock in the woods instead of my very nice suite of rooms in a historic manor.

I didn't think Hawk would mind my using his bathroom. It, too, was immaculate and looked barely inhabited, save for a razor and a toothbrush beside the sink, and sparse toiletries in the cabinet above the sink. I turned on the hot water in the shower, standing under the spray for as long as I could manage, with my weight almost entirely on my left leg. It was long enough to wash my hair, scrubbing my scalp and combing conditioner through before attacking my skin with a washcloth and shower gel until I felt clean again.

By the time I dried off, put on lotion, got dressed, and hobbled my way back down the stairs, I was more worn out than I wanted to be. Stupid ankle. Stupid asshole in the woods who'd attacked me.

I was most of the way through my breakfast burrito when I saw Hawk through the front window, getting out of his black SUV. A minute later, the door opened. His eyes were warm when they landed on me, a smile teasing up the side of his mouth until his gaze narrowed on my wet hair, then flicked to the stairs, then to my crutches. I understood immediately.

"I'm fine," I assured him after I swallowed a generous bite of burrito. "I was slow and careful. I didn't fall, and I really needed a shower."

He made a sound in his throat that wasn't quite agreement. I'd realized about halfway down the stairs that he wouldn't like it, but it had to be done. I'd meant to shower after dinner the night before but hadn't been able to force myself to go in my room.

"You finished with breakfast?" Hawk asked.

"Almost," I said. "Thanks for bringing it over."

Hawk gave a short nod. "We need to get going."

I raised an eyebrow and took another bite of the breakfast burrito.

"You have a doctor's appointment. You need someone to take a look at that sprain."

My eyebrow cranked up higher. My mouth was full, but I shook my head in protest.

Hawk ignored me. "Your family doctor is booked up. We're going to the urgent care by the airport. That was the only one that could take you this morning."

I chewed furiously, swallowing hard. "I don't—" I didn't get the words out.

"I'm not a doctor," Hawk said, "but my guess is they might give you a boot for that sprain instead of the crutches. You'd be able to get around a lot better."

I shut my mouth, taking another bite of the burrito as I considered his words. *Fuck.* He was right. I hated going to the doctor. I didn't mind needles, I wasn't squeamish, I just — They always reminded me of my mom dying. White coats and scrubs. That smell of antiseptic, cold and bitter.

I didn't want to go in over something as simple as a sprained ankle, but Hawk was right. They would probably give me a boot, which would be much better than the crutches. I had a boot the last time I sprained my ankle, but that had been a few years ago. I'd lent it to a friend and never bothered to get it back.

"When do we have to leave?" I asked, resigned to being poked and prodded.

"Five minutes."

"Okay," I agreed. I was stubborn but not stupid. I shoved the last bite of the burrito in my mouth, chewed, and washed it down with a final sip of coffee.

Two minutes later, we were headed out the door, Hawk following me to the passenger side of his SUV. Before I knew what was happening, he was lifting me into the seat, catching my legs and turning me, making sure my ankle didn't hit the door as I went in. He handed me my crutches, watching as I clicked the seat belt. Finally satisfied I was secure, he shut the door.

For a guy who didn't want anything to do with me, he was awfully thoughtful. I didn't hide my smile as he rounded the vehicle, only dimming it when he got in. We rode in silence down the long drive to the gates and through town, quiet at this hour of the morning.

Tourists were beginning to trickle back into Sawyers Bend, but only a few here and there. We could still drive through town in under five minutes. By May, it would take twenty. And by July, well, in July, it was better to just go around the long way because the long way was the shortcut in July, when tourists clogged the streets, drinking and eating, buying T-shirts and artwork with equal fervor. Unlike a lot of locals, I didn't mind tourist season. The tourists kept me in business.

We turned onto the state road that would take us to the airport, and Hawk finally spoke. "I don't know if Griffen told you, but we didn't find the man who attacked you."

I nodded, unsurprised. If they'd found him, they would have told me already.

"We increased security, added cameras and a second perimeter alarm in some places. But until we know more, I don't want you going anywhere alone. The gatehouse and the Manor are safe. No one's getting close to either one. Not even this guy."

None of what he'd said so far had surprised me, but his tone there made me stare at him. He wasn't telling me something. "What do you mean *not even this guy*?"

His eyes stayed fixed on the road, jaw clenching before he said, "It took us most of the day to track him from the cabin to where he picked up a fire road deep in the forest. This is not the average troublemaker or gun for hire."

"I don't understand," I said.

"So far," Hawk explained, shooting me a quick look, "whoever is after your family has been hiring local boys. A disgruntled former employee. A former vet who was a little wonky in the head. But this guy— This guy has training."

"Maybe whoever killed my father went for a higher class of assassin," I said, only half joking.

Hawk gave a rough laugh, but he didn't sound amused. "That's basically what I said to your brother. It would make sense since local talent wasn't getting the job done, but there's something off about it. I don't want to test this guy's limits. I want you to stay safe."

I nodded, holding my tongue on what I really wanted to say. There was no point. Not now. I wasn't going to stay locked up forever. I had a business to run and a life to live. But at the moment, my ankle had me constrained enough. I couldn't do anything anyway. I couldn't even drive, so my freedom wasn't worth fighting over. Not yet.

"I need to ask you for two things," Hawk said.

My eyebrows shot up in surprise. "Yeah?" I asked, curious.

"We're getting you a dog," he said.

"Really?" Delight shot through me before it dimmed. "Did Griffen—"

"I talked to him about it last night. He's all for it. I know a guy who breeds and trains Belgian Malinois. One of his dogs is almost as good as a human bodyguard."

I didn't like the sound of that. I wanted a pet, not an employee. And I wasn't crazy about a purebred dog. There were too many mutts out there who needed homes. "I don't want a dog from a breeder," I said. "We can go to the shelter and find a hundred dogs who need homes."

"You need protection, Quinn. Not some mutt who'll let anyone with a treat through the door."

"Mutts have fewer health problems," I argued, "and they can be trained just like a fancy purebred."

"A trained mutt isn't going to be as good as one of Remy's dogs," Hawk said, the side of his jaw tight. "And this dog will already be trained. You don't need one who can protect you in six months. You need protection now."

"Hawk, you can't get a trained guard dog overnight." I crossed my arms over my chest, feeling pretty sure I'd won that battle.

"Not overnight, but we're skipping the wait list. I called in a favor," Hawk said.

My cheeks warmed as I took that in, flattered by the idea that he'd call in a favor for me. But I didn't want some cold guard dog. I wanted a dog to cuddle and pet and hike with.

"Griffen said it was okay?" I asked again. Hawk nodded. "Can we at least go to the shelter and see what they have? Maybe they've got, like, a mean Rottweiler or something. Please?"

"I'll take you to the shelter," he said slowly. "After you give me the second thing I want."

"Okay. What is it?" I asked, suddenly cautious.

Hawk flicked on his blinker and turned into the parking lot of the urgent care, pulling neatly into an open spot. Cutting the engine, he shifted to look at me, his dark eyes unyielding. "I want you to tell me why you can't sleep in Heartstone Manor."

All those fizzy bubbles of joy in my chest at the idea of getting a pet went flat. My gut turned to stone. Only Ford knew why I couldn't sleep in Heartstone Manor. Ford and I planned to keep it that way. It was nobody else's business. No one needed to know. Not even Hawk.

"Quinn," Hawk prompted.

"Why?" I whispered. "Why do you need to know?"

Hawk's eyes stayed on mine, his hand lifting to cup my cheek, his skin on mine an anchor. I leaned into his hand just a little before pulling back. I didn't want to tell anyone. Not even him.

"I can't keep you safe if I don't know," he said, his voice low.

"That doesn't have anything to do with this. It was a long time ago."

"We don't know who this guy is or what he wants with you. I can't keep you safe if I don't know."

Against every instinct, I nodded. A pet for a story I didn't want to tell. I wanted the dog, but I knew enough to know this wasn't really a trade. If he felt he needed to know, Hawk would get the story out of me one way or another.

I nodded again and reached for the door handle, looking forward to seeing the doctor for the first time in forever.

I'd see the devil himself if it would delay the conversation to come.

Chapter Twenty-Two
QUINN

It was the first time in years I wasn't half panicked at being in a doctor's office. I had Hawk's last comment to thank for that. *I can't keep you safe if I don't know.*

I didn't want to talk about why I couldn't sleep in Heartstone Manor. I didn't want to think about it. I wanted to pretend it wasn't a problem at all, that it didn't matter.

Last night had reminded me that I could pretend all I wanted, but it didn't change the truth. The adult in me knew I had to face my past if I wanted to grow and mature and all that bullshit.

I didn't want to face anything. I wanted to stamp my foot and cross my arms over my chest like a child. My problems were my own fucking business. Hawk had no right to demand I tell him things I hadn't told anyone except Ford. But as I sat at the end of the exam table, gritting my teeth while the doctor probed my ankle, Hawk standing at the door glowering at both of us, I knew he was right. He couldn't keep me safe if he didn't know.

I understood Hawk's logic. I agreed with him.

And still, I didn't want to fucking talk about it.

I nodded at the doctor as he explained that I'd been mostly correct. My ankle wasn't broken. I had a grade two sprain. No hiking for at least three weeks. Any other day, finding out I was grounded for three weeks would have been crushing. I wanted to be out there leading clients on hikes through the forest, taking them fishing or rafting. I did not want to sit around with my foot up, missing all the fun. But right now I was too occupied with the upcoming conversation with Hawk to get upset about the length of my recovery.

At least I got a boot to supplement my crutches. Another few days of both, and the doctor said I could mostly ditch the crutches. He gave me some diagrams with exercises he wanted me to do, and I was done. I paid at the front desk and followed Hawk out to his SUV. As he lifted me into the seat, I fought the urge to lean forward, to rest my face against his neck and soak in his strength. Instead I pivoted in my seat, accidentally banging the big plastic boot around my right ankle into the doorframe.

"Careful," Hawk admonished, leaning in to check my seat belt. He ran a hand up my right leg, sending tingles everywhere.

I wished he'd do it again. So far, he seemed determined to stick to his *No Sex* rule. I hadn't thought about it the night before, too messed up by the nightmare I'd had to think about sex. But today... I watched him round the front of the SUV, the sun glinting on his dark hair, and wondered how long it would take until he changed his mind.

It was possible he *wouldn't* change his mind. Hawk was nothing if not strong-willed. I knew that. But he wanted me, and more than that, he cared about me. I knew that, too. Thoughts about sex could wait. Everything could wait. First, I had to get through the next twenty minutes and the story Hawk needed me to tell. I wished I could think of a good reason to keep my secrets to myself. *I can't keep you safe if I don't know.*

Fuck. I stared out the window at the parking lot, desperate for a reprieve.

Hawk got in and started the car.

"Are we going to the shelter?" I asked, looking for a diversion. And honestly, I wanted to know. I didn't want a trained guard dog, but I very much liked the idea of a dog of my own.

Hawk shook his head as he pulled out into traffic. "My friend Remy is bringing down a dog. She'll be here in a few weeks, already fully trained. He's coming with her, and he'll walk us through what we need to know to handle her."

"I don't want a trained guard dog," I said again, imagining some hulking creature with too many teeth who'd growl at me if I stepped out of line. Curiosity got the best of me. "What kind of dog did you say your friend is bringing? A German shepherd?" I didn't know much about dogs, really, except that I liked them.

"A Belgian Malinois. They're smart. Energetic. She'll take some work on your part, making sure she gets enough exercise, but she'll also be able to keep up with you on the trail."

"Mmmm," I hummed to myself, thinking about that. I'd assumed a dog was a dog. It hadn't occurred to me that some might not like hiking. I could handle an active dog. I liked that he'd picked one that would fit me, fit my life. Still, I was more interested in arguing than the conversation Hawk was waiting for.

I crossed my arms over my chest and leaned back into my seat. "I'm not buying a dog when there are so many that need homes."

"You're not buying the dog. I bought the dog," Hawk said, his voice gruff, making me think he hadn't meant to tell me that part.

I stared at him in shock. I didn't know how much a fully trained, purebred guard dog cost, but I imagined it was a lot. "You can't— Why would you— I don't—" Protests jumbled in my head.

Hawk gave a short shake of his own, never taking his eyes off the road. "It's too late. She's yours," he said.

"I still want to go to the shelter," I pushed back.

I'll admit, I was intrigued by this mysterious Belgian Malinois who would hike with me and keep me safe, and further intrigued that Hawk had bought her for me. I wasn't sure what to do with that information. Though the idea of Hawk's dog was growing on me, I had this picture in my head of a down-on-his-luck Rottweiler who just needed some love and would growl at anyone who scared me. And who said I couldn't have two dogs? How much more trouble could two dogs be?

"We're not going to the shelter," Hawk said. "You're stalling."

I didn't pretend to misunderstand. Letting out a sigh, I slumped into my seat, bracing my elbow on the car door and resting my cheek against the cold window. It was easier to do this here in the moving car where I didn't have to look at him, didn't have to watch his face. I could pretend I was talking to myself.

I drew in a short breath, bracing myself. It was like pulling off a Band-Aid. I'd just do it, and it would be over, and I wouldn't have to talk about it again. "Look, Ford is the only one who knows about this. I don't talk about it. It shouldn't be a big deal."

Words spilled out of my mouth, tumbling over each other. I could hear the desperation in my voice. I didn't want any of this to be important. I wanted it to be nothing. I just wanted it to go away.

"It happened a long time ago," I said, "And it's over. It's dumb. The whole thing is dumb. I don't know why I can't just get over it and sleep in my room. It's embarrassing."

"You've never told anyone?" Hawk asked.

"No," I said, irritated at his interruption. "No. Only Ford. I mean, my father knew. He encouraged it, but—"

I shook my head, annoyed at myself. I was getting off track and talking in circles, trying desperately to minimize this thing that had been fucking up my life for way too long. I hated everything about it.

"It's not a big deal," I said, knowing I was a liar. If it wasn't a big deal, why couldn't I sleep in my own bedroom? "It's just— Okay, so, when I was younger, my father would invite men he did business with to stay at the house. It wasn't every week, but it wasn't infrequent either. They would come, they would go. We kids didn't see them much. Griffen and Ford, sure, but not the rest of us. Then Prentice sent Griffen away—"

"You were eleven?" Hawk asked.

"Yeah. Eleven. And after Griffen left, Ford and my father were joined at the hip. Ford never disagreed with Prentice. Not back then."

I fell silent for a moment, thinking about Ford and Prentice. I'd always thought Ford lost himself to my father. He'd hidden his envy of Griffen until it had eaten him alive. Then he'd sold his soul to Prentice to get everything Griffen had: his fiancée, his place in the company, in the family. And in the end, Ford lost everything. I should hate him for what he'd done to Griffen, but Ford had paid. He was still paying. And he'd saved me when I couldn't save myself. For that alone, he had my love. My loyalty.

"Prentice had this—" I paused, searching for the right word. "Associate. I don't know what it was between them, but they—" I sat up, stretching my legs out in front of me, staring through the front window at the snow-dipped trees flashing by. "My father always had this idea of using his children to create a Sawyer dynasty. He wanted to make alliances, to choose our future spouses to acquire more wealth, and solidify his power. He loved Parker marrying into the Kingsley family."

"How did Vanessa fit into that?" Hawk asked.

Vanessa was the woman Griffen had wanted to marry. Prentice hadn't approved, though he'd allowed

Ford to marry her after he'd exiled Griffen. Ford had divorced her, though I'd never been clear if it was because he'd discovered that Vanessa was a viper or because Prentice had pressured him into getting rid of her.

"Prentice used to say Vanessa didn't bring anything to the table. I think he had other plans for Ford." I leaned my head back into my seat and mused, "I always thought that Prentice and Hope's uncle planned to marry Hope off to Ford, but then Prentice died, and Edgar figured out how to hitch her to Griffen."

"Lucky for both of them," Hawk said.

I knew what he meant. Hope had loved Griffen since they were children. I'd been a kid, but I'd had eyes. I'd known she loved him. I hadn't known he loved her back. Now that they were married, it was obvious they were meant for each other. "Yeah," I agreed. "I like seeing them so happy."

Hawk paused, and I could tell he had figured out a little of what I was about to tell him. "What was Prentice's plan for you?" he finally asked.

I appreciated the gentle way he phrased it, but my stomach twisted at his question. I pushed the words out, knowing that the sooner I told Hawk, the sooner it would be over. "One day, my father and this associate came across me and Sterling and Parker having a tea party. Miss Martha helped us set the table in the dining room with the family tea set. Very grown up. We were nibbling little cookies Chef Guérard made for us. Sterling brought her stuffed animals to the table. Just little girls being kids."

I sighed at the memory. I could still taste the cookies, smell the bergamot in the tea.

"I don't know why they were there," I said. "Maybe Prentice was showing off his family. Maybe it was just a coincidence. But Prentice's friend, he—"

I couldn't make my mouth say the words. Nothing fit. *He liked me.* That was too sweet. *He wanted me.* Disgusting, considering I was only eleven. I drew in a slow breath through my nose and let it out.

I left it alone, figuring Hawk would get it. A quick glance at his clenched jaw told me he did. "Later, Ford told me the man told Prentice he was going to marry me. Prentice told him he had to wait until I was legal. Ford said they laughed about it, and he thought they were kidding. But the next night, I woke up, and he was there."

A raw, rough growl rumbled beside me. I jerked in my seat and looked at Hawk again. His hands were tight on the steering wheel, his jaw rock hard, dark eyes blazing with rage.

"No," I said, knowing what Hawk thought was coming next. "He didn't, Hawk. He didn't—" My words caught in my throat, and I swallowed hard. "Not— It wasn't— He just sat there next to my bed, watching me sleep. I pretended not to see him, and finally, he left."

"Did you tell anyone?" Hawk ground out, his voice like sharp-edged gravel.

"No," I admitted.

"Why the fuck not?" Hawk demanded, anguish in his voice.

"I didn't think anyone would care," I said with a slow shrug. "I guess I could have talked to Miss

Martha. My mother was gone by then and Prentice never bothered to get another nanny. He just kind of folded childcare into Miss Martha's housekeeping duties. I just thought—better it was me than my sisters, and I didn't say anything. The next day the man gave me a lollipop, and I threw it in the trash. And the next night he was there again, sitting in the dark, watching me."

"He didn't touch you?" Hawk asked, his voice low.

I hated the direct question. Hated the answer. "Not then."

I paused, drawing in a breath. Heat flooded my face, nausea turning my stomach until I rolled my window down. I hated this. Hated thinking about it. Hated remembering the dark and his pale moon face and soft, pudgy hands. Hands that he'd kept to himself those first few years.

"In the beginning, he just watched me sleep. And he'd give me things. A lollipop. A doll. Then later, there was a bracelet. Earrings. He didn't visit often. Twice a year, maybe. I, uh— I developed late," I said, my cheeks flushing, this time from embarrassment. "I looked like a little kid until I was almost fourteen. And then hormones hit and—" I glanced down at myself, my frame still slight and lacking in curves.

Hawk stayed quiet, but his knuckles were white from how hard he was gripping the steering wheel. I hated going back there in my head, hated bringing it all back to life. But here with Hawk, seeing his rage—it blunted the memory. What happened wasn't dumb, and I wasn't stupid for struggling with it all these years. The whole thing was fucked and messed up, and I was right to be hurt by it. I had a right to be damaged.

I'd spent years telling myself I was weak for letting it get to me, but Hawk wasn't weak, and he looked ready to kill someone over the little bit I'd told him. A warm spark came to life in the dark, cold place inside me. There was nothing wrong with me. The wrong was with them. My father and the man in the dark. They were wrong. Not me. It was never me.

"You said not then," Hawk said, his voice tight. "When and how did he touch you?"

"When hormones hit and my body changed, when I stopped looking like a child, he got more grabby. When he ran into me in the house, he'd touch me. A hand on my lower back or my shoulder. My father would call me into his office, and the man would ask me questions."

"Give me his name," Hawk ordered.

I shook my head. "It doesn't matter." It didn't. There was nothing Hawk could do now. And I didn't like giving the man a name, as if that made him normal. A person. He didn't deserve a name. Not from me. To me he wasn't a person, he was a nightmare.

"Tell me his name." Hawk's eyes flashed to me, heavy with demand and fury.

I shook my head again. "Do you want me to finish this or not?"

Chapter Twenty-Three
QUINN

Hawk's gaze shifted back to the road, his fingers clenching on the steering wheel. After a long moment, he asked, "What kind of questions did he ask you?"

"He'd ask about school. My favorite subjects. My hobbies. He didn't listen to the answers. He didn't care. I was a prop to him and my father. I'd tell him I liked to fish, and he'd chuckle and squeeze the back of my neck and tell me to get those tomboy pursuits out of my system now so I could grow up and be a proper wife. That kind of misogynistic bullshit."

"He came into your room again," Hawk pushed.

I swallowed, my throat tight. "He did. This time he didn't keep his hands to himself." I felt Hawk go stiff beside me and rushed to say, "He didn't— It wasn't—"

I couldn't get the words out. He hadn't done the worst thing. The thing I'd been most afraid of. And still, the little he'd done had torn me apart. I still couldn't make sense of it. He'd done almost nothing. What right did I have to be so damaged from actions so small? There were people who suffered so much worse. But no amount of rationalizing could change the horror I felt when I remembered. When I went into my bedroom and couldn't erase the man in the dark.

"I moved the chair by my bed," I said, forcing myself to keep going. "I put it in the sitting room. But when he came to Heartstone Manor, it was back. He sat there in the dark and stroked my arm. After a while, he pulled the covers to my waist and stared at me lying there in my nightgown. He didn't touch me except for my arm. I pretended to be asleep, and he just— He just looked—" I choked on the word, swallowing hard again.

"You must have been fucking terrified," Hawk said.

"Yeah. I didn't know what he was going to do, and I couldn't stop myself from imagining, even once he left. That was when I started having trouble sleeping. I tried sneaking out of the house the next time he came to visit, but my father tracked me down. He was furious." I raised my hand to my cheek at the memory.

"He hit you?" Hawk demanded.

My head jerked in a nod. That was almost as shameful as his associate coming into my bedroom. What was wrong with me that I drew that deviant old man to me? That my father would strike me, over and over, for trying to avoid the nightmare he'd orchestrated for me?

"Quinn," Hawk said in a whisper. "Why didn't you tell anyone?"

I looked down into my lap, shaking my head. "You don't understand," I said, swallowing again to fight back the sob caught in my throat. "You see us now. Griffen behind Prentice's desk. Kids running through the house, laughing. That's not what it was. We weren't close. Prentice was always trying to set us against each other. What happened with Griffen and Ford didn't come out of nowhere. I was close to Parker and Sterling, and even Avery, though she was older. But not like we are now."

I pressed my cold hands to my hot cheeks, not sure I could explain to Hawk how alone we'd been in that house full of people. All of us, little islands. Isolated. Stranded.

"There was no one to turn to," I said. "Miss Martha cared for us. I know she did. But she was staff, and she had her job and Savannah to think about. Even when we were young, we knew not to look to her for too much, or Prentice would get rid of her. I didn't know who to talk to. Griffen was gone. Ford might as well have been Prentice's twin back then. And part of me was glad the man was interested in me. Because if it wasn't me, what if it was Sterling? Or Parker? What if I did something to drive him away, and he turned to my sisters?"

"You were protecting them," Hawk said. "And no one was protecting you."

"I could handle it," I said. "After my father—" I cleared my throat. "After he made his expectations clear, I didn't hide in the woods the next time the man came to Heartstone."

"He came to your room again," Hawk said, his voice grim.

I gave a single nod. "I'd dragged the chairs out of my room. I hid them in the attic. Two days before his visit, an armchair appeared in my bedroom."

"Your father was a fucking monster," Hawk said, his voice flat.

"Believe me," I said, "I'm aware. Once I left home and saw more of the world, I learned exactly how fucked up my father was. In so many ways. This is just one of them."

I shook my head. I'd never understand the man my father had been.

"To Prentice," I explained, "he wasn't doing anything wrong. He was just providing me with some private time with my future husband. Never mind that it wasn't the sixteen hundreds, and there was no fucking way I was marrying that guy. By then I was just biding my time until I could get out from under Heartstone's roof, away from my father. I didn't have a plan. But I knew once I was eighteen, I could disappear."

"I'll find out who he is," Hawk said, I thought mostly to himself.

I drew in a long breath and let it out slowly, staring out the window. Hawk's SUV ate up the miles between the doctor's office and town, and I reminded myself that I was free. The man was gone. My father was dead, and everything was okay.

Except it wasn't okay. I was all fucked up. I couldn't even sleep in my own bedroom because of what that asshole and my father had done. The man haunted me. I should be over it, but he haunted me.

"One night," I went on, "he was sitting next to my bed in the dark, stroking my arm. He told me he wasn't going to do any more than that. Not yet. It wouldn't be right. But as soon as I was eighteen, we'd get married, and then I'd be his. Except in North Carolina, you can get married at sixteen with a parent's consent," I said. "So I guess I'm lucky they let me graduate from high school."

"Why do you think he waited?" Hawk asked, his jaw unclenching the slightest bit.

I shrugged a shoulder. "I always thought it was because Prentice didn't want to explain why he let his sixteen-year-old daughter get married. That was a little too country for him, if you know what I mean." I wouldn't have thought I'd be glad my father was such a snob, but in this, I absolutely was.

"But you didn't marry him," Hawk said, waiting for my nod. "Then what happened?"

I squeezed my eyes shut for a second, but the sudden darkness only made the memory more vivid. His soft, pudgy hands all of a sudden not so soft at all. He'd been stronger than I expected, his weight holding me down, his hot, dank breath in my ear.

I'm tired of waiting.

I'd screamed. So loud. So fucking loud. For once, I wasn't thinking about sparing my sisters, or keeping quiet, or not enraging my father. I just wanted him off me. But I wasn't going to tell Hawk all of that.

Instead, I kept it simple. "When I was seventeen, he decided I was old enough. We wouldn't get married yet. That could wait another year, but I was old enough. I disagreed. He tried—" I cut off and swallowed again, looking out the window, wishing for a bottle of water. For anything. "I screamed," I said. "He didn't— He tried, but I was fighting, and I was screaming, and Ford—"

I drew in a short breath and let it out slowly.

"Ford heard," I said. "It was sheer luck. Ford had stayed up later than usual to take a call. He was heading to bed and heard me scream. He broke into my room and saw what was happening. He lost his mind."

I squeezed my eyes shut again, and this time the memory that flashed there filled my heart with a surge of vengeful gratitude.

"Ford tore the man off me and threw him on the floor. He laid into him, hitting him until his nose was flat, his mouth cut to ribbons on his teeth. I think I was in shock. My nightgown was torn, my fingernails broken, a chunk of hair pulled out at the roots."

I lifted a hand to my temple, where the hair had long since grown back. I'd been fiercely grateful to Ford, and also a little scared of him, crouching over the man, his eyes stricken and his knuckles bloody.

"Ford left the man on the floor of my room and walked me to my closet so I could change. He made sure I didn't need the doctor and then told me to go to Sterling's room and get in bed with her. I did, though I didn't sleep. The next morning, the man was gone."

"Did he ever come back?" Hawk asked.

I glanced at him, afraid of what I would see, but I couldn't read his shuttered expression. "No. I never saw him again. And Ford— I don't know what Ford said to our father, but no visitors ever stayed in Heartstone Manor again, except family. And Ford started to change. He told me he would take care of things. A year after, just before I left for college, Ford told me I didn't have to worry about the man ever again."

"What exactly did he mean by that?" Hawk said.

His words were technically a question, but I could tell he was hoping for confirmation that the bastard was dead. I couldn't give him that because I didn't know.

I shook my head. "I didn't ask. I didn't want to know."

"And you took Ford's word for it? That the man wasn't a problem anymore?" Hawk sounded disbelieving.

I knew he didn't understand, and how could he? To Hawk, who was loyal to Griffen, Ford was the villain. And Hawk wasn't entirely wrong. Ford had done some terrible things. But in this, I trusted him absolutely. "I took his word for it because I saw him after. Because that was when Ford changed. He looked out for me after that. He tried to look out for all of us."

"A little late," Hawk said.

I shrugged. I didn't blame Ford. Over the years, I'd come to understand that Ford blamed himself enough for all of us. "I was having a hard time after that night—"

"Was that when you stopped being able to sleep in your room?" Hawk interrupted.

"Yeah. I had nights when I would climb in bed with Sterling or sleep on the floor of my closet. I'd sit up all night on the sofa. After that night, every time I closed my eyes, I'd hear him breathing." My throat went tight, choking off my words.

Squeezing my eyes shut, I forced myself to swallow. To finish this, so I would never have to talk about it again.

"Ford would find me in the sunroom. Sometimes outside, under the trees. I didn't have the whole hammock thing back then, but I had a little tarp and a sleeping bag. I hid in the forest. I had plans to run away, but Ford told me if I could stick it out a little longer and apply to college, he'd get me out and I'd never have to sleep under Heartstone's roof again. And he kept his word."

Hawk sighed, and I wondered if his idea of Ford was shifting just a little. "Why did you come back?" he asked. "Why make a life here after you finally got away?"

That answer, at least, was easier. "I missed my sisters," I said. "I missed Ford. And it was never the town I hated. It was my father. And the Manor. The memories there. But still, even missing them, I wasn't going to come back here, but—"

"Your business," Hawk guessed, and I nodded.

"It was Ford's idea. I didn't come home for the breaks during college. Ford always figured out an excuse to keep me away. A trip, an internship, any excuse to distract Prentice from my absence. I told you about that kayaking trip Ford took me on to celebrate my graduation."

Hawk nodded, slowing the SUV to let a camper turn in front of us.

"At the end of the trip, I told him I wanted to be a wilderness guide. I thought he'd talk me out of it, but instead, he pitched me the idea of Sawyer Outdoor Adventures. He'd already bought the bungalow. He had a plan for me to get my wilderness certifications, take some business classes. And when I was ready, I'd have my own business."

"He didn't want you to disappear," Hawk said slowly.

My heart ached for my older brother. "I think he was very lonely," I said. "I think he had a lot of regrets. For allying himself with our father. For marrying Vanessa. For what he did to Griffen. I think he had a lot of regrets,"

I said again, "and I think he didn't want to lose any more of his family than he already had." I let my eyes slide shut and pressed my cheek against the cold window.

A warm hand closed around my fingers, squeezing tight. Eyes still closed, I squeezed back. I heard the tick-tick-tick of the blinker and opened my eyes to see Hawk turning into a parking lot. Too caught up in memories, I hadn't noticed that we weren't heading to Heartstone Manor anymore. I saw the sign and realized where we were.

Hawk pulled the SUV to a stop in the parking lot of the animal shelter. Still holding my hand, he turned to face me, his dark eyes burning with emotion, warming me from the inside. "I bought you Remy's dog," he said. "She'll be here in a few weeks, and you're keeping her." Some force in his voice compelled me to nod in agreement. "But let's go in and see what they have here."

"Okay," I agreed, wondering if that was it. Were we done with this? He wasn't going to ask more questions? It seemed like he wasn't. At least, not for now.

Hawk squeezed my hand before he let go to jump out of the SUV.

I blinked hard, brushing away sudden tears with the heels of my palms. I was okay. No more talking about my nightmares. I wasn't sure what could wash away the memories flooding my brain, but snuggling some puppies sounded like a pretty good antidote to the poison in my head.

My door opened and Hawk was there, lifting me out, my crutches in one hand. He set me on my feet, tugging me into his chest, his arms coming hard around me in a tight hold, his bristly cheek at my temple. "Fuck, Quinn. You're so fucking strong. No one is getting anywhere near you again. I promise. Never again."

I let out a breath, winding my arms around him, holding on, needing this. Needing Hawk. "I'm not strong," I said into his chest. "I'm a mess. I sleep in the woods because I'm scared of my own bedroom. That's not strong."

Hawk's arms tightened a fraction more. "No, you're wrong. You survived, Quinn. You built a life for yourself. You're smart and capable and stronger than you give yourself credit for. I know that was hard. I'm sorry I had to ask you to tell me, but I'm glad you trusted me." He rested his cheek on the top of my head for a long moment before leaning back and handing me my crutches. "Come on," he said roughly. "Let's go find you a dog."

Chapter Twenty-Four
QUINN

I recognized the redhead behind the shelter counter, Angela. A few years before, I'd taken her whole family on a canoeing trip, and I always bought her marshmallow squares when the shelter had its annual fundraiser.

Angela's welcoming smile faded when she saw my crutches. "Quinn! What happened? Are you okay?"

"I'm good," I assured her. "Just came from the doctor. It's only a sprained ankle. I'm grounded for a few weeks, but I'll be fine."

"Oh, Quinn. What a bummer." Her friendly smile returned, chasing off some of the gloom that lingered from my confession to Hawk. "What brings you in today?" she asked.

Her eyes flicked from me to Hawk, standing a few feet behind me. I glanced over my shoulder to see his arms crossed over his chest, his face set in the glower I was starting to think of as his version of a business suit.

"I'm thinking about getting a dog," I said.

"A dog!" Angela's eyebrows shot up. "That would be wonderful. Let me show you who we have right now." She walked around the counter and led us to a vestibule with a door on each side; one led to the dogs, the other to the cats.

"Definitely not a cat," I said, eyeing the door that led to the dogs, sure my future canine companion was behind it.

Angela tilted her head to the side and studied me. "You should take a look at both," she said. "We have some interesting options on both sides."

"Okay," I agreed, even though inwardly I was thinking *no way*. What would I do with a cat? I was outdoors most of the time, and while I knew plenty of cats loved the outdoors, I also knew how devastating they could be to the ecosystem. I loved the birds, chipmunks, and everything else a cat would eat if allowed to run wild.

I headed down into the dog wing, the gloom creeping back in at the sight of so many caged animals. They were in runs that gave them access to space outdoors, not in tiny little squares stacked on top of each other, but still. It was depressing to see so many without homes. Without love.

I walked down the aisle, waiting for that magic moment, for some spark to tell me this was the dog. My dog. It didn't happen. That mythical Rottweiler who just needed some love wasn't there. There were a ton of mixed-breed hounds, none of whom felt like the right dog for me. I passed by a handful of small lapdogs. A Chihuahua. A Jack Russell mix. Cute, but again, not for me. I walked up and down the dog corridor three times until Hawk laid a heavy hand on my shoulder and squeezed.

"Let's go look at the cats," he said. His tone was resigned, a sentiment I agreed with. But since we were here...

"Yeah," I sighed. "We might as well."

He slid his arm around my shoulder and pulled me into his side for the briefest moment before letting go. "Don't worry, Remy's girl will be here in a few weeks."

"I know," I said, "but I wanted—"

"I know, baby, but let's look at the cats anyway."

That was the second time he'd called me baby. Once, the night before, when he'd woken me from my nightmare. And again now. I wasn't sure he was aware the word had slipped through his lips, but I'd heard it. I let the smallest smile curve my mouth, my heart floating in my chest as we crossed from the dog side of the shelter to the cat side.

The attitude on the cat side was completely different. Where the dogs had been eager, coming as close as they could, sticking their snouts against their cages to sniff, the cats looked only vaguely interested in the humans who'd invaded their territory. Half of them were sleeping. They did look soft and cuddly, but I wasn't a cat person.

I need a dog, I reminded myself. A dog I could throw a tennis ball to and go hiking with. And yes, Hawk had a point about protection. A dog made me less of a target when I was off in the woods alone. A dog would be useful. A cat, on the other hand—the question I'd asked myself earlier popped up again: What would I do with a cat?

I turned at the end of the row of cats and started back up the other side. On this side of the shelter, the cages were stacked two high. And as I passed one, I got a little too close to the bars and a claw snagged my T-shirt. I stopped and turned, locking onto a pair of golden eyes in a majestic, furry face crowned by tufted ears.

We studied each other in silence. Huge fluffy paws. So much fur in every shade from cream to caramel to a russet brown. And it was long. So long. This thing wasn't a cat. It looked more like a miniature striped lion. I'd never seen a cat so big.

"What the hell is that?" Hawk asked. "It's fucking huge."

I tore my gaze from the cat's and looked at the index card on the cage. "A Maine Coon," I read and laughed. "His name is Leo."

"Fitting," Hawk said. "He's as big as a lion cub. Is he mixed with a bobcat? I didn't think Maine Coons got that big."

I shook my head, laughing a little. "I don't think it works like that. I'm pretty sure a bobcat would eat a regular cat. But this guy—" I stuck my fingers through the bars and scratched his chin, half sure he'd bite my fingers off and ready to jerk my hand back if necessary. Instead, he leaned in, resting his head against my hand. I liked the weight he put into it.

"That thing is too big to be a cat," Hawk said under his breath. "Look over there." He gestured to a cage near the door to the vestibule. "Kittens. Don't you want a kitten? A kitten won't eat you while you're sleeping."

I shook my head, mesmerized by the deep, rumbly

purr as my fingers dug into the cat's chin. Leo craned his neck, offering me more fur to rub. I obliged, rubbing the sides of his jaw with my thumbs, soaking in his purr, the softness of his fur. "Aren't you a handsome boy," I said in a singsong voice I'd never heard from myself before. Leo took my worship as his due, his purr even deeper, filling his long, tall body. He pulled back to butt his head against the cage door, rattling it on its hinges as if to say, *Let me out already. You're here. We can go now.*

"Stay here," Hawk said, sounding resigned and a little amused. "I'll go get your friend and see if she can unlock this crate so you can hold him."

"Uh-huh," I agreed, mesmerized by the creature before me. This wasn't what I'd had in mind when I thought, *cat*. In my mind, cats were sleek, aloof, and a shit-ton smaller. Leo wasn't part bobcat, but he wasn't much smaller than one. I wondered if he would hike with me. He was big enough. Did cats hike? I rejected the thought as soon as I had it. Even if I could somehow train him to hike with me, I could picture exactly what he would do to every bird, squirrel, and hell—raccoon—we came across. Leo would have to be an indoor cat, if he would accept that.

The door opened a minute later, Angela following Hawk. "Leo! He's been with us for a while."

"What's wrong with him?" Hawk asked, eyeing Leo with suspicion.

Angela laughed. "Nothing's wrong with him, except he's a lot of cat, and he can be moody." She watched us for a long moment, taking in Leo's rumbling purr. "I've never seen him take to anyone like that. Usually he sits in the back of his crate and glares when anyone comes in. Do you want to hold him?"

"Yes, please," I said, stepping back. Leo let out an annoyed chirp, followed by a long trilling sound.

Angela laughed again. "Hold tight, cranky pants. I'm going to let you out."

She unlocked the door, swinging it wide. Leo pounced, leaping from the crate into my arms, the impact enough to rock me back. Hawk was behind me, taking my weight, catching the crutches as my arms came around Leo. He flopped half over my shoulder and pushed his head into my neck, his purr a deep, resonating rumble. I tilted my face into his thick fur and sighed.

"I think Leo's found his person," Angela said.

Hawk let out a low sound that might have been a laugh. "You cuddle your cat," he said. "I'll go start the paperwork."

All I could do was nod. "I've got you, buddy," I said, hugging the cat overflowing my arms. He was no lightweight. Before they could leave for the front desk, I asked, "Angela, is he okay being indoors? This guy could take down every bird and chipmunk for miles around Heartstone."

She nodded. "As far as we know, he's always been an indoor cat. His former owners had to surrender him when they moved, but they said he loves to play. He's active, but definitely an indoor cat." She hesitated. "I can't— The adoption process takes more than a day. You can't just bring him home," she said, shaking her head.

"I can't leave him here," I said, my arms tightening

around Leo at the idea of putting him back in that cage and walking away. "He'll think I abandoned him."

Ten minutes ago, I'd said I wasn't a cat person. I was here for a dog; one I didn't even need because Hawk had already gotten me a dog. But that was before I saw this guy. And now—

"I can't leave him here," I said again.

"Quinn," Angela said, still shaking her head, "there's a procedure, and I need the forms and— Well, he's been fixed already, and he's up to date on his shots, but you can't—"

"Let's go to the front office and we'll work this out," Hawk said, his hand closing over Angela's elbow, turning her, propelling her back to the front desk. "Don't go anywhere," he said as he passed.

I shook my head. Leo had settled in and I leaned against the concrete wall by the door, murmuring, whispering, telling him how handsome he was. How majestic. How perfect. Leo rumbled back in agreement.

He was a cat, not a guard dog, but this guy was no pushover. I knew it instinctively. And he wanted to come home with me. Who was I to say no?

Minutes later, Hawk and Angela returned.

"All right," Angela said. "Put Leo down long enough to hit the store and get what you need to bring him home. I'll have the paperwork ready when you come back. We'll make an exception this one time, but don't tell anyone." Angela eyed my boot, the crutches I'd leaned against the wall, considering. "You've got a tough break with that ankle, and Leo's been in that cage long enough. We're a no-kill shelter, but if we weren't, he would have passed his expiration date a while ago. I want him in a good home."

"I'm a good home," I said, burying my face in Leo's neck as I hobbled the few steps back to his cage and shifted him to put him back inside. His claws curved, sinking into my shirt. "It's okay, buddy," I said. "I'll be back, I promise. I'll be back, and we'll take you home."

Never mind that I wasn't precisely sure where home was. I'd slept in the gatehouse last night. After spilling everything to Hawk, the past was too fresh and there was no way I was going to sleep in Heartstone Manor. I'd bail on my inheritance and move to Guam with Leo before I did that.

Hawk stepped forward, detaching the Velcro cat from my T-shirt. Leo chirped in what I'd swear was indignation. "We'll be back, little lion," Hawk said. "I promise."

Leo tilted his head to the side, studied Hawk for a long moment, and allowed Hawk to put him back in the cage.

I followed Hawk out of the shelter, calling to Angela over my shoulder. "We'll be back."

"Give me at least an hour," Angela called back.

Hawk helped me into the SUV and stopped, looking down at me, my crutches in his hand. "I'm not taking you back to Heartstone. You and Leo can stay in the gatehouse for the time being. When we've neutralized whoever came after you in the woods, we'll figure out what to do next. Okay?"

"Okay," I agreed, kitty bubbles fizzing through my chest, chasing off the dregs of sadness left from spilling my guts to Hawk on the way here. I didn't have to go back to Heartstone, and I was bringing home a new friend. I thought of that rumbly purr, those sharp gold eyes. The way Angela said he didn't like anybody, but he liked me. I liked him too. And he'd liked Hawk.

I smiled. For once, I'd gotten exactly what I wanted. And I was going to appreciate every second of it before things went to hell again.

Chapter Twenty-Five
HAWK

Quinn's friend at the shelter hadn't wanted to let us take the cat, but a hefty donation had changed her mind. I didn't care. By the time we'd found Leo, I felt bad for all the animals waiting for new homes. And it was only money. I'd spent years earning a ton, risking my life, and hadn't spent much. I had more in the bank than I knew what to do with.

I thought of the dog I'd bought for Quinn. From the outside looking in, I was nuts. Between Leo and Remy's dog, I'd spent upward of fifteen thousand on animals for Quinn. I should be kicking myself. That much cash on a woman I wasn't even sleeping with? Wasn't sleeping with *anymore*, I corrected myself. It didn't matter. It felt good to take care of Quinn. And after seeing her face relax into peace when she cuddled the oversized cat, I'd have done anything to make sure we were bringing Leo home with us.

Besides, I'd taken a good look at the claws on that cat.

He wasn't a protection-trained Belgian Malinois, but I'd bet he'd slice the hell out of anyone who got in between him and his Quinn cuddles. I knew the feeling.

The big box store outside town had a decent pet section. Quinn filled our cart with everything she thought she might need. Two cat beds, a pile of toys. All natural, gourmet cat food. I stood in the middle of the aisle, staring at the top shelf, debating litter boxes.

I had to acknowledge I hadn't thought this through. Until this recent threat, Quinn had essentially lived outside. What the hell was she going to do with an indoor cat? She had the guide business in town, but I already knew she wouldn't leave Leo there to spend half his life alone. She wasn't moving back into Heartstone Manor. No fucking way. Not unless she worked through the past and was ready for it. I didn't see that happening anytime soon.

That left the gatehouse. My gatehouse. Was I moving Quinn in with me? That was insane.

There were a million reasons why we couldn't be together, much less why I couldn't move her in with me. A million reasons why it wasn't fucking happening. And yet here I was, looking at fucking litter boxes. *Fuck me.* I didn't know what I was thinking. I didn't know what I wanted. This was temporary. And yet—

I reached up to the top shelf, grabbing the expensive automatic litter box. What did I care? It was only money, and I wasn't scooping cat shit. Not even for Quinn and Leo. I read the side, making sure it was big enough for Leo's oversized body. Satisfied, I rested the huge box on top of the cart, leaning down to snag a bag of litter from the bottom shelf, fighting a smile as Quinn debated between three different catnip mice.

"Get them all," I said. "Odds are he won't play with any of them because he's a fucking cat, and cats do what they want, but get them all anyway. He might surprise us. Angela said he likes to play."

The side of Quinn's mouth quirked up, sending a beam of light straight into my withered heart, and I knew I didn't give a fuck about how nuts this was. The cat. The litter box. Buying her an expensive dog. Moving her into my gatehouse.

Quinn wasn't mine. Couldn't ever be mine. But I'd still do anything to see that smile. I liked seeing her happy, especially after everything she'd told me earlier. I couldn't forget her haunted eyes, the way she'd touched her cheek. Her father had hit her. I wished he was still alive so I could kill him myself. Prentice Sawyer was out of my reach, but the man in the dark was still out there somewhere. Quinn didn't know how to find him, but I did. At least, I knew where to start. Today was for Quinn and Leo, but tomorrow I'd take the first step in finding the man who'd terrorized Quinn. She'd spent too many years suffering. Now it was his turn.

The paperwork was ready when we got back to the shelter. Quinn signed everything, and I paid while she wasn't looking. I knew she could buy all of this for herself if she wanted to. But with Prentice's rules about the will, Quinn's current income was based on the guide business. It did well, but as I handed over my credit card for the third time today, I realized that even if she'd noticed I was paying and had fought me for it, I would have done it anyway. I liked taking care of Quinn. Not just protecting her—that I was used to. It was my job, and I was damn good at it. But care, that was something else. Helping her with her crutches, making her a doctor's appointment—I had no business doing shit like that, but it felt so good I didn't give a fuck.

With coos and ear scratches, she half coaxed, half forced the oversized feline into the travel crate we'd bought. Leo looked absurd, jammed into a crate designed for a much less fluffy cat. Caramel and cream streaks of fur burst out the wire windows, his chirps and trills piteous.

"What's with the sounds?" I asked, daring to stick a finger in the crate. He glared at me through the bars but allowed me to rub his head.

"Maine Coons don't meow," Angela said. "Not unless there's another cat in the house that teaches them. Leo has heard enough regular meows by now, but I've never heard him do it himself. I'm glad someone's finally bringing him home. I've never seen him take to somebody like he has to Quinn."

I nodded in thanks and followed Quinn out the door.

The sun was dipping in the sky by the time we got the litter box set up and Leo situated in his new, temporary home. Quinn sat on my couch, her feet up, exhausted by so much activity, Leo a fuzzy mound on her lap. She was energetic and otherwise healthy, but hobbling around on crutches still took it out of you, and she'd been through a lot in the last few days.

I texted Kane, who was on shift in the control room.

> Have Finn make us up some plates and send someone over. Quinn's not coming to the house tonight.

> On it, boss.

I opened a beer and sat on the other end of the couch, my feet up, eyes closed, listening to the giant cat purr, a little jealous. I wanted Quinn to pet and coo at me. *Not going there, remember?*

But the part of me that wanted to feel Quinn's fingertips digging into the nape of my neck didn't care.

Quiet minutes passed, then a beep on my phone, and an image flashed on the screen. Kane was at the door holding a tray. He was quick. I swung the door open, ushering him inside, ignoring the grin that spread across his face as he took in Quinn lying on the couch, the mass of cat on her lap, purring up a storm.

"Hey, Quinn," he said.

"Hey, Kane. Thanks for dinner," she said with a welcoming smile.

"Anytime," he answered, his eyes falling on Leo and narrowing. "You bring home a mountain lion cub?" he asked.

Quinn laughed, her fingers digging into the spot behind Leo's ear she'd already learned he loved. Watching Leo's gold eyes fixed on Kane, my previous thought about Leo's value as a guard animal solidified further. Leo stayed where he was on Quinn's lap, but his attention was hyper focused on Kane and he'd stopped purring. I was now sure the cat would use those sharp teeth and claws on anyone he didn't like, which only made me like him more.

I noticed Kane was studying the cat in return, a healthy respect in his eyes. Kane had always been a smart man. "I'll put this on the counter," he said and set the loaded tray down in the kitchen before turning to go. As he passed by me, he said under his breath, "Awfully domestic in here, boss."

"Fuck off," I said easily, low enough that Quinn couldn't hear over the cat's purr, which had started back up as soon as Kane moved toward the door. "And stop calling me boss."

It was a long-standing disagreement between us. Technically, I was his boss on this job, but when we'd worked together at Sinclair Security, we'd been peers. I was only his boss at Heartstone Manor because he was taking a break from his real job. Until recently, Kane had led Sinclair's hostage recovery team. He was damn good at it, but he'd lost a hostage eight months ago. A kid, and that shit was always hard to live with.

He'd gone back to work, gone to the mandated therapy, but a few months later he'd asked Cooper to lend him to me for a while. He needed a break, and I was grateful to have him, especially now that Quinn was under threat. I knew as soon as he was ready, Kane would be back in the thick of things and out of Sawyers Bend. He teased me about me being his boss, but more than anything, we were friends.

"Whatever, man," he said with a raised eyebrow. "Just saying. Looks cozy in here."

I walked him to the door, speeding up the process

with a shove in the middle of his back. "She's Griffen's little sister," I said quietly. I expected Kane to nod in agreement, but he shook his head and rolled his eyes.

"Keep telling yourself that, man, if that's the excuse you need. You and I both know Griffen wouldn't get in your way."

I didn't respond to that. I didn't know. And even if he wouldn't, staying away from Quinn wasn't just part of my job. I was looking out for my best friend. If Griffen was dumb enough to trust me with his sister, that just proved he needed me looking out for his best interests. And hers. "Whatever you think this is, you're wrong. This is temporary. I'm just keeping her safe," I said with a little more force than necessary.

"Sure. Keep her safe. Or you could just keep her." Kane grinned at my scowl, clapping a hand on my shoulder. "Give a shout if you guys need anything." Ignoring my growl, he called over his shoulder, "See you later, Quinn."

"Bye, Kane. Thanks for dinner," she called back.

Leo let out a chirp that sounded like a warning. Then again, it could have been a demand for dinner because he abandoned Quinn the second I opened a can of food, broke it into chunks with a fork, and set it on the floor.

"Hey," Quinn said, sitting up. "What did Finn send over for dinner? I didn't realize how hungry I was until now." She leaned forward as if to stand.

"Stay there," I said. "I'll bring you the tray."

I pulled the covers off the plates and organized everything, delivering Quinn's tray to her lap—meatloaf with mashed potatoes and peas. The scents drifting up from the plate had my stomach rumbling and my mouth watering.

Finn was a classically trained chef, and he could make the fancy stuff as well as any chef on TV. But in my opinion, he killed it with comfort food. Meatloaf. Chili. Fried chicken. Cornbread. Biscuits. Fresh baked bread. Lasagna. All fucking amazing. I'd happily put up with the derelict gatehouse for meals like this.

The cooks before Finn had been decent, but since he'd taken over, we'd been eating like royalty. Quinn and I dug in, not bothering to talk when we had Finn's meatloaf. He'd smoked it, stuffed it with cheese and spinach, and covered it in a savory tomato sauce. *So good.*

Stomach full, I cleared Quinn's tray and brought her dessert—homemade vanilla ice cream topped with crumbled ginger molasses cookies and a drizzle of caramel. The cookies were Savannah's favorite, and ever since Finn had perfected the recipe, he made them often.

Leo rejoined us the second Quinn's tray was gone, draping himself across her lap and nudging her free hand until she went back to rubbing his ears.

"Angela said he wasn't friendly. I think she was talking about the wrong cat," I said, leaning to stroke his side. He flopped over, giving me more cat to rub. I obliged, the full, soft fur warm and silky.

"I don't know," Quinn said, "but he seems to like both of us." She glanced out the window to the dark sky. "I can't believe I'm tired so early."

"Recovering from an injury takes it out of you," I said. "It's too early for bed, or you'll wake up in the middle of the night. I grabbed the Uno deck from the cabin when I picked up your pack."

Her eyes lit. "Really? Did your ego need a stroke or something?"

"I'm not that good," I protested, retrieving the deck from where I'd left it on the kitchen counter.

"What? So the other night was just a fluke?" Quinn laughed. "You destroyed me."

"I have a good memory," I admitted. "And I had good luck." Uno was mostly about luck, but counting cards and knowing how to play your opponent didn't hurt. So much of my work came down to memory, attention to detail, and understanding people. How to read them, how to know what they wanted, and what they'd do to get it. At this point, it was second nature, and God knew I was used to making the best of whatever good luck I had.

The memory thing was a skill, one that was double-edged. On the one hand, I probably could have made a fortune if I'd switched to professional poker or blackjack, but I'd never wanted to spend my life in a casino. On the other hand, I never forgot anything, even when I wanted to. The things I'd seen—the things I'd done—played in my mind on repeat when I closed my eyes. I couldn't leave my past behind, no matter how hard I tried. For a while, I thought the memories would drive me mad. I was close to the edge when I'd gone to the Sinclairs, to Griffen, and the work they'd given me had saved me. Helping people who needed me—that was what my skills were for, not card games. That didn't mean I couldn't have a little fun.

I dealt out the deck and we played a round. I won

after a fierce battle. Quinn had snagged almost all the draw fours, and even my memory and strategy struggled to overcome the sheer number of cards she piled in my hand. I didn't care, loving her glee every time she slapped down another draw four and made me pick up more cards.

In the middle of the third round, when Quinn could barely hold her massive stack of cards and wasn't giving Leo enough attention, he uncurled himself from her lap and stretched. I'd guess he was almost four feet from his nose to the tip of his fluffy tail. He was goddamn massive. His steps light, as if he was a kitten, he picked his way across the couch. With one contained leap, he landed in my lap, narrowly missing my balls. I winced anyway, and Quinn burst into laughter.

"You okay?" she asked.

"Barely," I said, my hand coming up automatically to stabilize Leo. He arched into it, his purr a heavy rumble, butting the top of his head against my chin. He settled in, leaning into my chest, the vibration of his purr oddly relaxing.

Quinn looked at the two of us and smiled softly. "He likes you," she said.

"Yeah," I answered, scratching his head. Because with all those teeth and claws, what was I going to do, say no? I'd expected the cat to fall in love with Quinn. Who wouldn't? I hadn't thought he'd have any interest in me. Or that I'd like him back.

"You want me to take him? Is he bothering you?"

"Nah, he's fine. Besides, I don't want to piss him off. He might eat me in my sleep." I wasn't totally kidding.

She laughed, the sound almost a giggle. I loved hearing it. I wasn't going to think about that though. Thinking about making Quinn laugh and how much I liked it would only lead me down a dangerous road.

Two more rounds of Uno later, Quinn threw the cards at me. "You're cheating. I don't know how, but you have to be cheating."

I collected the cards, not bothering to hide my grin. "I wouldn't cheat at Uno. Jeez, it's a kids' game."

"Then how do you keep winning?" she demanded.

I shrugged. "I guess I'm just that good." Her answering laugh had me smiling so wide my cheeks hurt.

Quinn yawned.

"Bedtime," I announced, standing and scooping Leo out of her lap, tossing him half over my shoulder. He rubbed the side of his head against my neck and settled in, his lower half supported by my arm, his tail dangling to swish back and forth. His sharp claws kneaded my shoulder, pricking my skin just enough to hurt but not enough for me to put him down. Not with the rumble of that deep purr against my chest. I didn't know why Leo had chosen us, but I was glad he had.

Reaching down with one hand, I pulled Quinn to her feet, scowling a little as she ignored her crutches to thump her way to the bathroom. The boot stabilized her ankle enough to give her some freedom, but I didn't want her to overuse it and set back her recovery. Not when I knew how eager she was to get back out there.

A few minutes later, she emerged from the bathroom in a T-shirt and sleep shorts, and hopped into the hammock I'd rehung. "Thanks for taking me to the shelter, Hawk. And for, you know, everything." Her jaw cracked in a wide yawn.

"Anytime," I said, and I meant it. I was a fucking moron, but I meant it. I dropped Leo on her chest, wondering how long he would stay in the hammock with her.

Leaving them to settle in, I headed upstairs to change. I was down a few minutes later. I checked the hammock, seeing that Quinn was already asleep, Leo dozing on top of her. When I passed, he lifted his head, looking at me with those golden eyes as if to say, *I've got this*. And weirdly, I knew he did. I wished for just a second that the hammock was big enough for two. Or three, counting the cat.

But this was better. Smarter. Stretching out on the couch, I scrolled on my phone, too awake for sleep.

Hours later, I was mostly out when my phone vibrated on my chest. At the same time, a flash of light illuminated the gatehouse, too long to be lightning but just as abrupt.

I was instantly awake, checking my phone first to see a message from Kane.

Chapter Twenty-Six
HAWK

> Perimeter alarm. Northwest corner of the manor grounds. Security light malfunctioned on the western corner of the manor.

Just when I thought it had been an anomaly, a second perimeter alarm went off in the woods behind Savannah and Finn's cottage. Ten seconds later, a text from Finn hit my screen. Their security lights were flashing on and off at all corners of the cottage. As far as they could see, there was nothing out there. I texted back, telling them to stay put and away from the windows.

Fuck. Unless there was an army after us, this didn't make sense. The cottage and the northwest corner of the Manor grounds were too far apart to be the same person. I shot off the couch and crossed to the folding table where I'd left my laptop, pulling up the cameras. There was no one there. *Fuck.*

I put in the earpiece I'd left by my laptop.

"Report," I said the second I was connected.

"I split the team," Kane answered. "They can't find who set off the alarms. There's no one out there."

The hammock rustled, and I glanced over to see Quinn sitting up, blinking, dark hair sliding away from her cheeks. If it was any other situation, I'd bring her to the house, stash her with everyone else, and go out with the team. But I couldn't do that to her. Not after everything she'd told me. She was too raw. Too vulnerable. I wouldn't take her there. Not now.

For a second, I thought about having someone stay with her. And again, if it had been anyone else, I would have put a guard on her and headed out to join my team. But this wasn't anyone else. It was Quinn. And I wasn't leaving her.

I didn't have time to think about why or what that meant. Another perimeter alarm went off. This time, the pool house. I flicked to the cameras; glad we'd wired everything tight. I could see almost every inch of the acres surrounding the Manor. The cameras' night vision was so clear it might have been noon, and there was nothing fucking there.

Not a chipmunk, not a deer, nothing that moved on two legs. So what was setting off the fucking alarms?

"Check for a malfunction," I said.

"Already on it," Kane said, "but I don't know how it could be. One camera or light might make sense, but not like this."

From my folding table in the gatehouse, I could see Heartstone Manor through the front windows. The security lights on the roofline flashed in a discordant pattern, lighting the surrounding lawn and blinking out over and over. Another perimeter alarm went off, this time between the gatehouse and the front gate. I knew with the number of trees between us and the gate, I wouldn't be able to see anything if I looked outside, but the proximity left me uneasy. If this was the man after Quinn, did he know she was here?

I caught the rustle of the hammock and the soft thump of Leo jumping down, the heavier thump of Quinn doing the same.

"Hawk," Quinn said from behind me. I turned to see her leaning on her crutches. "What's going on?"

"I don't know. The perimeter alarms are going off, and the lights are going nuts. But as far as we can tell, no one's out there."

"Is there a problem with the system?" Quinn asked.

I shook my head. "Don't know. Kane's checking for a malfunction, but he hasn't found anything yet."

"I'm okay if you need to go," she said.

"No," I said, eyes locked on the screen. I watched part of my team converge on the site of the last perimeter breach. Nothing there.

"Hawk, really, I can—"

"No fucking way," I said. "I'm not bringing you to the house, and I'm not fucking leaving you."

Quinn let out a huff of air that I'd swear hid relief. "Do you want a cup of coffee?" she asked. I started to say no and realized I did want coffee. And maybe she needed to get me one, to have something to do while we waited to see what was coming next.

I didn't have time to think about that as the proximity

alarm by the gate started pinging over and over as if someone was running back and forth through the invisible beam. The camera showed nothing, but the lights on the front gate were going off with each alert.

I directed my team through the woods, over the grounds, chasing down every ping on the system. The lights were going wild. The Sawyers in the Manor were on lockdown, under guard. And no matter where we looked, there was no one fucking out there.

Which meant that someone was fucking with us. What I didn't know was how.

"Drink this," Quinn said, setting a steaming cup of coffee in front of me.

"Thanks, baby." I took a sip. "We're okay," I said, mostly sure I wasn't lying.

She nodded, pulling out a folding chair to sit beside me, leaning in to stare at the screen. Calm and curious, not afraid. "Are you sure you don't need to go?"

"I'm not leaving you. We're all right, but I'm not taking any chances with you."

She nodded. I looked down to see Leo sitting beside her. He let out a strident chirp, his golden eyes demanding. I scooped him up, setting him on my lap, scratching his chin absently as I sipped my coffee and watched the security lights flashing, a microsecond delay between the lights flashing through the front windows and those in the screen.

"Is it random or a pattern?" Quinn asked.

I shook my head. "Random so far."

Kane's voice sounded in my ear. "Pool house proximity alarm and lights are going off again. Nothing there.

Collins scared the shit out of some deer in the woods. That's the only living thing we've seen."

I nodded, even though he couldn't see me. "Any luck finding a malfunction in the system?"

"So far, it's clean," he said, frustration evident in his voice. "Except it can't be because there's nothing fucking there."

"Yeah, I got you," I agreed. I considered the only conclusion, and I didn't like it. It was impossible. But given that there wasn't anyone out there, it was our only answer.

"We've been hacked," I said.

"No way," came Kane's immediate response. "No fucking way. Lucas put these programs together. No one hacks Lucas's shit."

Normally, I'd agree with Kane. Lucas Jackson was our in-house white hat hacker at Sinclair Security, and he was the best. The fucking best. Kane was right. Nobody hacked Lucas. "I hear you. But as impossible as this is, it's the only answer that makes sense." I watched the lights, ignoring Kane's muttered denial. Something shifted, the random flashes coalescing into something that wasn't at all random. A pattern.

Quinn leaned in closer, her hand closing on my arm. "Hawk, is that—"

I nodded. "It's fucking Morse code," I said.

I focused on the lights on my screen, catching the flashes, bits and pieces from different areas of the grounds coming together in a defined pattern. The front lights on Savannah and Finn's cottage went in two short flashes. The front of the Manor gave two long flashes. There was nothing for a long beat. Then a short flash at the pool house followed by two long flashes. A short, then long flash at the gates. A long flash on the front of the gatehouse.

"What does it say?" Quinn asked in a whisper, her eyes flicking from camera to camera on the screen. "My Morse code sucks."

I checked again, just to be sure.

Fuck. I was right. "It says 'I'm watching you.'"

In my ear, Kane said, "No fucking way."

"Our proof is right there," I said in answer, as the pattern started again at the beginning. "We've been hacked."

"Who the fuck could—" Kane started.

"I don't know, but we're going to find out," I said. "Have the guys check for intrusions in the system, though my guess is you won't find them. Anybody good enough to get past Lucas's security isn't going to leave any tracks."

"Lucas is going to be pissed," Kane muttered.

Pissed was putting it mildly. Lucas would go ballistic.

My eyes locked on the screen. I watched three different proximity alarms light up at the same time. The front gate. Quinn's clearing. The pool house. The sensors fired together in three short flashes. Then, three long flashes. Three final quick flashes, and everything went dark.

"Mayday," I murmured. Three short, three long, three short. The signal for Mayday.

We waited. Sixty seconds. Nothing. Another minute. Nothing. When it had been quiet for five minutes, I told Kane, "Split the team into three groups and check the front gate, the clearing, and the pool house."

We waited. Another five minutes passed, and Kane's voice sounded in my ear. "We may have been hacked, but someone was here. There's a box in the clearing."

"A box?" I asked, not expecting that. "What kind of box?"

A picture popped up on my screen of a white gift box sitting in the dirt exactly between the two trees where Quinn usually hung her hammock. The lid was decorated with a blood-red ribbon tied in a bow, resting on top of the box, slightly askew. A brown cardboard tag dangled from brown twine; *Quinn* written in dark ink.

Fuck.

At least we confirmed what we'd suspected. Quinn was the target. I glanced at her. Her eyes were riveted on the screen.

"Swab it for explosive residue," I said, knowing the team should have at least one pack of swabs on them.

We watched as one of my men approached, gingerly wiping the outside of the gift box with a white square of papery material. He held it up to the camera, still white.

"No residue," I murmured for Quinn's benefit. "Open it," I ordered.

"Switching you to local video," Kane said in my ear as a new square popped up on my screen, the gift box filling the space, the bow the color of blood, the inside of the box dark with shadows. Gloved fingers nudged the lid, knocking it to the dirt. Everything froze for a beat, but nothing happened. No explosion, no movement. Nothing. The fingers filled the screen again, reaching in and pulling out a circle of something. I couldn't see until he turned his hand, the gift inside catching the light with a silvery gleam.

"Is that—" Quinn started to ask, leaning in, squinting at the screen.

"Confirm the contents," I said, dread turning my guts to ice.

"It looks like a collar," my man in the clearing said. "Pink. The tag is personalized."

"What does it say?" I asked.

"Leo. It says, Leo."

Fuck. The implications of that spilled through my brain.

"He was watching us," Quinn whispered, sitting back, her face pale. She pulled Leo from my lap to her arms, cuddling him close.

"No one is going to hurt you," I promised, adding, "Or Leo. No one is going to hurt either of you."

Quinn nodded, her eyes locked on the screen. "What do we do now?" she asked.

"We wait and see if the show is over," I said grimly. "And if it is, we go to bed and call West in the morning."

She nodded again, her eyes still locked on the screen.

"That box is evidence," I reminded Kane. "Call West first thing tomorrow and fill him in. He can see if he can get any prints off it."

"Got you, boss," Kane said, his usual humor falling flat. "The cameras don't show anyone in the clearing. I went back over the footage, and it's blank. The box pops on the screen out of nowhere."

I sighed, by then not surprised. Whoever had done

this was good. No, better than good. Better than the best. Which was us.

We waited another half hour, but everything remained quiet. At close to three in the morning, the forest was dark and silent.

I signed off with my team. Quinn sat beside me, sipping her cold coffee. "We're assuming this is the same man from the woods, right? How could he have hacked into the system?"

I shook my head. "I don't know, but I'm going to find out. For now, it's over. We need to get some sleep."

She stood, dislodging Leo, who let out an annoyed trill. She only made it three steps toward the hammock when I stopped her.

"Not the hammock. We're sleeping upstairs, away from the windows, where we have a secondary escape route." The hallway over the drive was locked on both sides, the other wing of the gatehouse secured, and I was the only one with the key. If this side was compromised and we were upstairs, we still had a way out.

Eyes bleary, Quinn didn't argue. She thumped up the stairs, the boot on her foot, and tumbled into my bed. I carefully unstrapped the boot and eased it off her ankle, setting it on the floor before sliding into bed beside her.

Too tired and too unsettled to fight myself, I gave in to the urge to pull her into my arms and hold her close. "You're going to be okay, Quinn."

She nodded against the pillow, settling in and drifting to sleep almost immediately. Leo jumped onto the bed and curled up on top of us, letting out a contented purr.

My arm tightened around Quinn's waist, and I closed

my eyes, alert for the slightest sound. Something inside me knew whoever he was, whatever he wanted, he was done for the night. The picture of that pink collar hovered in my brain, taunting me, exactly—I suspected—as the man in the dark wanted. He'd been watching us. Why?

What was his end game? To scare Quinn? To get her alone? Had he thought I'd leave her undefended while he fucked with our systems? I didn't know. And I wasn't going to figure it out by staying awake, staring at the ceiling.

I let myself fall into a light doze.

Tomorrow would be soon enough to figure out the rest.

Chapter Twenty-Seven

QUINN

My eyes popped open at the ring of my phone in the distance. Downstairs. I'd left it downstairs. Why was my phone ringing?

It stopped abruptly. I lifted my head, only a little surprised to find myself draped over Hawk. Of course I was, because it seemed every time we ended up in bed together, I got as close to Hawk as possible the second I fell asleep.

On the other side of the bed, a second phone rang, this one Hawk's. That couldn't be good. He shifted against me.

His voice filled my ear, low, heavy with sleep but alert. "West." Silence. Then, "You're there now?" I couldn't hear West, only Hawk.

Beside us, Leo uncurled, stepping delicately to place his full twenty-five pounds on Hawk's stomach, which earned a grunt from Hawk, and then dropping his big head to butt into my forehead. I lifted a hand to rub it and was rewarded with a deep, rumbly purr.

"All right," Hawk said. Then, "Yes. You talk to Kane yet?"

Hawk took over rubbing Leo's head, the corners of his eyes crinkling in welcome to this giant, furry addition to his life. Leo switched from my rubs to Hawk's without complaint.

"Text me what we need," Hawk said into the phone. "Quinn and I will stop on the way. We'll see you soon."

I let my eyes slide closed. From Hawk's question about Kane, I deduced West's call wasn't about the craziness of the night before, which meant something else had gone wrong. Why would the police chief be calling? I didn't want to know. For just one more second, I didn't want to know.

Hawk's arm tightened around me, his hand leaving Leo to stroke down my back. "Baby. It's early, but we have to get up."

I loved that he'd called me baby again. I loved that I was waking up with him. I loved that we had this ridiculously big cat on top of us, purring and acting like he owned us. And I already knew I wasn't going to love what was coming next.

I kept my eyes closed and pressed my face into Hawk's neck, inhaling the scent of him, absorbing his heat. Finally, I whispered, "What happened?"

"There was a break-in," Hawk said carefully. "At your bungalow, at Sawyer Outdoor Adventures."

"What?" I sat up too fast, knocking Leo off-balance and jostling my ankle, sending pain stabbing up my leg. I sucked in a sharp breath as Hawk reached out to brace me, steadying Leo at the same time. Leo jumped off the bed and sauntered to the stairs, sending both of us a look of annoyance.

I let him go without comment, distracted by Hawk's news. Of all the things I'd been worried about, my business wasn't one of them, not beyond the hassle and disappointment of postponing clients because of my twisted ankle.

"It's okay," Hawk said quickly. "The structure is sound, but there's a lot of superficial damage inside, and you lost most of your inventory. All the windows are broken, and the front lock is busted."

"What about the shed out back?" I asked, my heart thudding in my chest, my head light with panic. The inventory was one thing, but my equipment was in that shed. Kayaks and canoes. Life vests and fishing poles. Tens of thousands of dollars in gear. Gear I needed to run my business.

"He didn't say." Hawk took in my panic. "Breathe, Quinn. I'll call him back." He dialed West and said, "What about the shed? The building behind the bungalow. Any damage there?" Hawk's eyes stayed on my face, his free hand reaching out to stroke down my arm and close around my hand, squeezing hard. "Good. I'll have her check when we get there. We'll be on the way in ten." He clicked off and tossed his phone at the end of the bed. "West said he can't see any damage, but he wants you to take a look when we get there."

My mind was racing with possibilities. Who? Why? To what end? *What do they want?*

Another question occurred to me. "Why didn't the alarm go off?" I asked.

Hawk shook his head. "I don't know."

"Was it the same guy as last night? The same as in the woods?"

"I don't know that either," Hawk said. "Kane sent West the security footage from the cameras at the bungalow. We can take a look later and see if we think it's the same guy as on the trail. We still don't know what happened here last night."

"It has to be the same guy," I said. Nothing else made sense. I still didn't understand why my finding a necklace my father had given to his mistress would cause this kind of reaction.

Hawk shook his head, sitting up and swinging his legs over the side of the bed. "I don't like to make assumptions."

"So what do we need to do?" I asked. "You told West we had to stop somewhere." The only way to keep my head together was to focus on practicalities.

"We need to board up the windows at your bungalow and put in a new lock on the front door. West said he'd text me the measurements for the windows. We'll head to the hardware store and get tools and some plywood."

I sighed. "I've got a pretty stocked toolbox. Electric drill, hammers, nails, screws, stuff like that."

"Plywood?" Hawk asked.

"I don't have plywood," I admitted.

"So just plywood and a lock," Hawk confirmed. "West said they've almost finished processing the scene. By the time we get there, we should be clear to go in. Maybe by then Kane will have some news on what the cameras caught."

I looked over to where my pack leaned against the wall beside the bed. I had one last pair of clean hiking pants, one pair of clean underwear, a mostly clean T-shirt, and my hoodie. I'd have to remember to go back to the main house to restock. A shiver went down my spine at the thought of going into my room to get to my closet. I pushed it aside. I needed clean clothes, and Hawk would go with me.

"Give me a second in the bathroom," Hawk said, interrupting my drifting thoughts. "You get that boot on your ankle, then I'll go down and make us coffee while you get ready."

Less than ten minutes later we were in Hawk's SUV headed into town, leaving behind an annoyed but fed Leo. I let out a gusty sigh, too sleep-deprived to really think about what was happening. I loved my little business, the cute bungalow that housed Sawyer Outdoor Adventures. Why would someone break in? Why break every window? It was destructive, and if I was being honest, felt personal. Someone intent on breaking in to steal stuff for pawning wouldn't have targeted the main building. They would have gone for the shed.

None of this made sense.

As we drove, it occurred to me that I'd better call Sterling. She'd been planning to go into the office to start calling clients about the schedule changes caused by my twisted ankle. It was still early, but I didn't want her walking into whatever mess was left from the break-in. She picked up on the second ring.

"Hey, did I wake you up?" I asked, remembering that I wasn't the only one who'd been up half the night.

"No, no, I didn't sleep well after the light show last night. I've been up for a while, was about to head into work."

"I'm glad I caught you," I said. "Look, um, don't go in to work today."

She paused, clearly confused. "Why? I have calls to make."

I found myself not wanting to tell her. Sterling had taken enough hits in life, and the last year hadn't been easy. I wanted to shield her. I'd always wanted to shield her, my baby sister, so full of love and so easily bruised. But this was life, and she'd shown all of us she was tougher than she looked. I wasn't going to lie to her like she was a child.

"West called," I said. "Someone broke into the bungalow. They smashed all the windows. Trashed the place, I guess. I don't know all the details. West is going to meet us there. We're headed to the hardware store to get plywood."

"Well, I'm coming to help clean up, then."

"Sterling, you don't have to—"

"I'm coming in, Quinn. I'll be there soon." Her voice faded out as she said, "I need more coffee for this bullshit." The phone clicked off in my ear.

That was Sterling. She looked like a princess, but when it came down to it, she was stubborn as hell.

She'd had to be. She'd spent most of her teens and early twenties drinking herself into an early grave, angry at the world. Leaving everyone who loved her to watch, helpless, as she spiraled. Nothing we said, nothing we did, made a difference. Then Prentice had died and Griffen had hit her with his own brand of tough love.

I didn't know the details. That was between Griffen and Sterling, but it must have been what she needed. After a brief period of adjustment that included a few minor tantrums, she'd gotten her shit together with the same focus she'd put into tearing her life apart. She'd stopped drinking and asked Griffen for a job. Now, despite the setbacks she'd faced along the way, she was back to being the sweet, bullheaded little sister I'd adored as a child. Emphasis on bullheaded.

"Sterling is going to meet us there," I said as we turned into the parking lot of the hardware store. "I told her not to, but..."

Hawk just nodded. "She is your sister," he said.

"What does that mean?" I asked, catching the spark of laughter in his dark eyes.

"Stubborn runs in the family," he said, the side of his mouth quirked just a fraction.

I couldn't help grinning back, despite my heavy heart. Hawk was the least funny guy I knew and possibly the stingiest with his words, but he made me laugh more than anyone, even when everything seemed too dark to bear.

We were in and out of the hardware store in less than twenty minutes, the back of the SUV loaded with sheets of plywood, a shiny new deadbolt, a box of commercial-grade trash bags, duct tape, and assorted other things Hawk thought we'd need to clean up the mess.

"You want to stop at Daisy's bakery?" he asked as we made our way through town.

I thought about it and shook my head. "I need to see how bad it is. And after, that's when I think I'm going to need some sugar. A lot of sugar."

Hawk nodded and we rode in silence, his hand wrapped around mine, his grip warm and strong. I didn't know what was happening with us. He'd said things were over. He hadn't made a move on me since the cabin. But he'd held me in his arms all night. That wasn't sex, but it wasn't nothing either.

I wasn't going to think about it. I didn't have room in my brain to process whatever was going on with Hawk. Not when I was obsessing over the state of my business. I was just glad he was with me. Glad I wasn't alone.

We turned into the small gravel parking lot of Sawyer Outdoor Adventures to see the door hanging open at an awkward angle, the window on either side smashed, glass littering the front porch. My stomach twisted, the violation of it physically painful. *Why?*

It took me a few seconds to see past the destruction. Two cars were parked in front of the bungalow. One was Sterling's. I didn't recognize the other, but I did recognize the man sitting on the front steps, his arms braced on his knees, his dark curls damp with the morning mist. Forrest Powell. The CFO of the Inn at Sawyers Bend, and Sterling's ex.

Forrest was a mystery to me. He'd shown up in Sawyers Bend not long after we'd all moved back into Heartstone Manor to satisfy the terms of Prentice's will. By all accounts, Forrest was a great CFO, but he'd been a shitty boyfriend. Sterling had been crazy about him until it came out that he'd come to town for two reasons:

revenge against the Sawyer family, and to recover an ugly little statue Prentice had stolen from his father. Sterling had just been convenient access to the Sawyers and the Manor.

In the end, Forrest had let go of revenge. Prentice and Ford had stolen Forrest's father's statue and his company. Griffen had tried to save it. Forrest got his ugly little statue back, a statue that contained the key to finding what remained of his family's fortune. He'd even kept his job at the inn.

But he'd lost Sterling.

I'd figured he'd leave town as soon as he reclaimed the statue from West. Who wouldn't? He'd gotten what he wanted. But according to Forrest, what he wanted had changed. Now that he'd lost her, what he wanted was Sterling. And Sterling wasn't having it.

She'd quit her short-lived job at the inn when the truth came out and had come to me for work. I'd been happy to have her, even happier to be working with my sister, getting to know her all over again now that we were both adults. We were closer than we'd ever been, but even I didn't know where she stood on the subject of Forrest. Not really.

I knew she'd dumped him. I knew she still refused to speak to him. She'd asked Griffen to ban him from Heartstone Manor, and he'd happily complied. But she'd also insisted Tenn and Royal not fire him. She'd said he was good at his job, and just because he was a shitty boyfriend didn't mean they should have to look for another CFO. Tenn and Royal had reluctantly kept him on, though their budding friendship with Forrest had chilled.

And Forrest had stayed. He did his job well, as far as I knew. Everyone spoke highly of him on that front. But no one in the family had anything to do with him. He didn't have any friends in town. And still, he stayed. And in the last few months, every time Sterling needed him, he was there.

I knew West had taken her aside to see if she wanted Forrest run out of town, which wasn't really a West move. Our police chief was so close to my brothers he was practically family, and still, West didn't bend the rules. But Sterling was as good as a little sister to him, and for her, he might have. She'd turned down that offer too. And here Forrest was again, exactly where Sterling needed him.

"You talk to her?" Hawk asked Forrest, stopping at the bottom of the stairs to study him.

Forrest shook his head. "Not sure she knows I'm out here. But she called West for details on the break-in, and he called me. Said he didn't want her here alone with the alarm offline and the lock busted, but he didn't have enough manpower to cover her. She's inside, cleaning."

Hawk gave a short nod. "Got it. We're going to go inside to take a look around. You busy?"

Forrest shook his head, his eyes sad but resolved. "I've got time."

"Stick around and help me board up these windows."

"No problem." Forrest stood. "You need coffee? I'll run down to Sweetheart while you check out the damage."

I'd turned down Hawk's offer a few minutes before, but now, seeing the splinters in the doorframe from the broken lock, the shards of glass scattered over the front porch, I needed that sugar sooner than expected.

"I could use something sweet," I admitted. "And maybe a metric ton of caffeine."

Forrest nodded. "I'll be back in fifteen, and then I'll help you take care of those windows."

Hawk gave him another short nod, and his warm hand came to my lower back, urging me to the door. "Come on. Let's go see what we're dealing with."

Chapter Twenty-Eight
QUINN

I swung open the door to see Sterling, broom in hand, tears streaking her cheeks. She stopped sweeping and looked up. "I don't know who made more of a mess, the guy who broke in or West's people and their fingerprint dust."

I let out the breath I'd been holding. When Hawk said there'd been a break-in, I'd envisioned the cash register emptied. Not a big deal since most people used their cards or their phones. I'd figured maybe I'd need a new laptop. West had said the shed looked untouched, and that was where the real valuables were stored, so I'd thought— I don't know what I'd pictured, but it wasn't this.

I felt like throwing up. Everything was destroyed. Everything.

The best I could say was that the building itself hadn't been burned to the ground. The structure seemed sound. That was something. But every window was smashed. The display case up front was shattered as if someone had gone after it with a baseball bat. The contents—small hunting knives, compasses, and a few GPS devices—were gone. The racks of packs hung on the wall were torn down, the packs themselves shredded. Every piece of clothing I could see was cut up to ribbons, the racks they'd been on knocked to the ground.

The antique canoe I'd found in a thrift shop in Asheville and hung high on the wall was on the floor, splintered, as if someone had stomped on it until it broke into pieces. The matching paddle was broken in half. I'd loved the way it gave my place a homey, vintage feel. I could find another. I would find another. But it wouldn't be the same. Nothing would be the same.

"Is the gear in the shed?" Hawk asked in a low voice.

Before I could answer, Sterling said, "The door was locked. I don't think he tried to get in. I didn't do an inventory, but everything looked the way it should, so that's good." She tried to smile but her voice cracked, fresh tears spilling down her cheeks. She brushed them away with the heel of her hand. "I don't know why whoever did this tore up everything in here and didn't go after the stuff in the shed. He could have loaded up a truck in five minutes and sold it all. It doesn't make sense."

"I don't think robbery was the motive."

I turned to see West in the doorway, his dark hair disheveled and his eyes tired.

"You Sawyers are really packing out my schedule, you know that? I have a whole town to take care of." His words were sarcastic, but his smile was kind. He'd been Griffen and Ford's best friend as kids, though as they got older, I'd seen him more with Griffen than anyone else. "I'm sorry, Quinn," he said, moving forward to give me a hug.

I leaned into him, squeezing back.

"We got a good print off the hammer we found by the display cases," he said after I stepped back. Turning to focus on Hawk, he added, "No prints off the box your team brought in. Or on the collar. Kane is still going over the security footage, but my guess?"

Hawk raised an eyebrow in question.

"I know logic says we're dealing with one guy," West said, "and from the timing of the alarm here going offline, it's possible."

"But you don't think so," Hawk said.

West shook his head. "I can't say definitively. Based on the security footage I've seen, and your description of the guy who jumped Quinn, it could be the same person. Same height. Same build. But based on what Kane said happened at Heartstone last night—" West shook his head. "He used the words 'surgical precision.'"

"That's how I'd describe it," Hawk agreed.

The four of us looked around the main room of the bungalow. This was rampant destruction. Everything in sight was shredded, slashed, broken, and shattered. Why? Why would someone do this? It wasn't a jewelry store, but some of this stuff was valuable enough to sell. Why destroy it?

West looked to me, then back to Hawk.

"You have a theory?" Hawk asked, his eyes narrowed on West's face.

West's head jerked in a nod. "Look, I don't have your

experience. I'm a small-town police chief. I did some time in bigger cities around the state, but I'm not on the same level as you and Griffen."

Hawk shook his head. "Forget about that. What do you see?" he pressed.

"I think this wasn't about robbery. I think he was looking for something, and the rest of this is either rage that he didn't find it or a cover for the search. Whoever hit this had some skills," West went on, his eyes coming to me. "He disabled your alarm and did a decent job avoiding the cameras. But this mess—this isn't surgical precision, even if it's a cover for something else. There's temper here. It's sloppy."

"Whoever went after Heartstone last night wasn't sloppy," I said.

West nodded. "Kane said Lucas Jackson is the best. Said he's going to lose his mind when he finds out his system was hacked. Whoever is capable of hacking a system like that— Maybe they lost their temper, but whatever was going on, the motives for Heartstone and this were not the same."

West's earlier words echoed in my brain. *I think he was looking for something.* I glanced to Hawk, then to West.

"What is it?" West asked, and Hawk gave me the tiniest of nods.

"I didn't say anything to you," I began, "because it didn't seem important. Not *police business* important. But the day I left for the cabin, the day this happened—" I glanced down at the boot on my ankle. "I stopped into Harvey's office. I'd found a necklace in the cabin, and I was curious if Harvey could figure out who it had belonged to."

West's eyes narrowed, and I imagined I could see his mind working the problem. "You think the necklace belongs to the mystery woman you've all been looking for?"

"I think it's possible," I said. "Prentice wasn't using that cabin for hunting. He was meeting someone there. A woman."

"Harvey didn't recognize the necklace?" West asked.

I shook my head. "He and Griffen went through the family jewelry, so I thought if it was a family piece, he'd recognize it. But he didn't."

"Who has it now?" West asked.

"As far as I know," I said, "Harvey still has it."

West nodded. "I'll have a word. If someone thinks you found something or thinks you know something you shouldn't know—" He turned to Hawk. "I'm assuming you're in charge of keeping her in one piece?"

"Absolutely," Hawk agreed.

West turned back to me. "I don't have to tell you to be smart, Quinn. I already know you're smart. Which means I know you're going to listen to whatever this guy tells you to do, yeah?"

"Yeah," I agreed. I looked around at what was left of the business I'd built from scratch. I thought I could feel the rage behind the destruction. I had no interest in finding myself on the other side of that rage. "I'll be careful," I promised.

"This is my fault," Hawk said, surprising me.

"How is this your fault?" I asked, turning on him,

glaring at the remorse heavy in his dark eyes. "I had an alarm system, and you guys added the cameras. And if not for the cameras, we wouldn't know anything."

Hawk glanced at West. "Up until now our parameter for security has been Heartstone Manor. I added the cameras here because Quinn's system didn't come with them, but Heartstone was the focus. Now—" He shook his head. "Kane, Griffen, and I will reassess. This can't happen again."

I couldn't fathom why someone would do *this* and then come back for round two, but I wasn't about to argue with the experts. If they wanted to add more security, I'd take it.

"I'll let you know if we get a hit on that print," West said.

We watched him go. At the thud of his cruiser door closing, Hawk let out a long breath. "My focus was on keeping you safe. I didn't think they'd go after the business."

I just shook my head, suddenly exhausted by the scale of the mess surrounding us. "No, Hawk. This sucks. I'm not going to lie. It sucks. And it's a huge mess when we're running on a few hours of sleep, but—" I looked around again, exhaustion dragging me down. "This stuff isn't my business. This is just window dressing."

Sterling stopped and looked up from where she'd been sweeping glass into a massive pile of shards and splinters of wood and scraps of fabric. "She's right, Hawk. I'm the one who checks everybody in for their trips and checks them out after they come back laughing and sunburnt. All this stuff? It's the gravy on top. It's the stuff they buy when they come back and want a memento to remember their trip. But this isn't Sawyer Outdoor Adventures. That's Quinn. She's the one who shows them the right place to fish, or the perfect waterfall hike."

"It's you, too," I said, fresh tears welling in my eyes. "The summer camps were your idea. And we ended up with a lot of happy kids."

Sterling grinned back at me, her face lighting up. "Yeah, we did. I didn't even think I liked kids. So I guess for now, we're the business. It's the experiences, not the hats and T-shirts and hiking poles. Doing inventory is going to be a bitch," she said, looking around. "But everything's insured. A month from now, when your ankle is healed and you're out with clients, this will all be a blip." She reached up and brushed her palms over her wet cheeks. "It's just stuff." Her eyes went to my right ankle and the clunky black boot. "It's just stuff," she said again.

I thumped across the room and hugged her, resting my cheek against her temple and rocking her from side to side. "I love you, Sterling."

"I love you too, Quinn." She squeezed me hard. "It's going to be okay."

"Yeah, it's going to be okay," I agreed. "We just have to get through this and—"

I caught a glimpse of Forrest through the broken front windows, a to-go tray with four coffees in one hand and a bakery box in the other. He wouldn't come in. I knew that instinctively. He was still looking out for Sterling, but he knew she wouldn't talk to him. And he wouldn't push it. I'd seen that for myself.

I'd hated him on principle because he'd broken my

sister's heart, used her for his own gain, and lied about who he was. If I felt anything other than hate for Forrest Powell, I kept my opinions to myself. It was Sterling's heart at stake, not mine. But in truth? I liked how he cared for her. When he'd begged her to forgive him the day the truth came out, I thought he was full of shit. I figured the second he got that statue back from West, he'd be gone. And all these months later, he was still here. Waiting. Hoping she'd give him another chance. He didn't push. He didn't get in her face. But he was here. I liked that for Sterling, even if she wasn't ready to accept it. Even if she might never be.

I gave her another hard squeeze. "Coffee delivery's here," I said. "Hawk is going to get these windows boarded up. I'll help in here, and we'll see how much we can get done."

The cappuccino and blueberry muffin gave me a jolt of energy, but it didn't last long. Inside the bungalow, I swept and sorted and organized. The back room, where I kept extra inventory and used to sleep when I lived here, wasn't as damaged as everything in the front. And there, I could see what West meant. While not as much had been destroyed in the back, every corner, every drawer, every cushion had been overturned or emptied.

Someone had been looking for something. Maybe I was off base, but I didn't have anything of value here. I didn't have anything of value at all. No stash of money or jewelry. The only thing new in my possession was the necklace. Not that it was valuable, but if someone was looking this hard for it, it had to be a clue. I let that idea roll around in my head as we worked.

The grinding whirr of the drill screwing the plywood into the window frames cut through any attempt at conversation as Sterling and I cleaned, the inside of the bungalow getting progressively darker as the windows were boarded up. Whoever had broken in had also smashed the overhead light in the main room, and by the time Hawk and Forrest were three-quarters finished with the windows, Sterling and I had the front door propped open for light.

A few minutes after the last window was covered, I heard a car engine start. Forrest leaving, I guessed. We'd made decent progress inside. There was still inventory to sort through, but we'd gotten up all of the glass and broken pieces of wood and metal. Between the two of us, Sterling and I had filled three contractor bags with debris.

Hawk filled the doorway, cutting off most of our light. In the sudden dark, fatigue hit me full force. My ankle throbbed like an aching tooth, and I realized the rest of me was numb with exhaustion.

"We're done here," Hawk said, his arms crossed over his chest and his badass at-work glower firmly on his face.

"We still have to go through the—"

"No," he interrupted Sterling. "You're both exhausted. Everyone was up half the night. You don't have adequate light in here. We're done."

Sterling opened her mouth to argue, and I shook my head. "He's right, Sterling. I'm so tired I could fall asleep standing up. My foot hurts like a bitch. I need a break. This is just—" I surveyed the room. "This is just depressing. And there's no rush. Technically I'm still on vacation. You can deal with rescheduling everything from home.

All the apps are online anyway." I glanced around. "I didn't see the laptop."

"I have it," Sterling said quickly. "It's in my room in the Manor. I was working on some things—" She shrugged a shoulder. "So that's one thing we didn't lose." She nudged a half-full trash bag to the side. "I just don't want to leave this unfinished."

"I know," I said. "But we need a break."

"Come on," Hawk said, crossing the room to slide an arm around my shoulders. "You first," he said to Sterling and tilted his head to the door. "We'll lock up. I don't want either of you back here until my team has better security in place. Until we figure out what the hell is going on, neither of you comes here alone. Understood?"

Sterling nodded, as did I. She didn't like taking orders any better than I did but sweeping up the destruction had been sobering. I kept thinking about the force of that hammer, smashing everything in sight, and what might have happened if one of us had been here alone. If we'd come in early or worked too late.

The man in the woods had tackled me, he'd had those zip ties, and because of his attack, I'd sprained the fuck out of my ankle. But this—he hadn't hit me or gone out of his way to hurt me. Even the night before—assuming it was the same man—he hadn't damaged anything or hurt anyone. But this mayhem, this destruction, was somehow more terrifying.

What had driven it? Rage or fear? Maybe both.

"I don't like not knowing what the hell is going on," I said as I passed through the door.

Hawk had installed a shiny new deadbolt above the

splintered section of the doorframe where the old lock had been torn out. He turned the key and said, "I know. We're going to figure it out."

"I know," I agreed.

Together, we watched Sterling get behind the wheel of her car and back out of the parking lot, heading out of town in the direction of Heartstone Manor. I leaned into Hawk, sagging from exhaustion. It was barely past noon, and I was done. I didn't know what was more tiring—the work of cleaning or trying to keep my shit together surrounded by the destruction of the business I'd built, client by client.

I tucked my face into Hawk's chest and let out a shaky sigh. "I wish I'd never found that necklace," I said. "Even if it is a clue."

And then I felt miserably guilty. What if it was a clue? What if it helped us get Ford out of jail somehow? Here I was, feeling sorry for myself that my business got trashed when my brother was locked up for a crime he didn't commit.

I let out another shaky breath. "I don't mean that," I said. "I want to find out who killed Prentice, and if it's related to this necklace somehow, to the woman Prentice was seeing— I want to get Ford out of prison. It's just— I didn't think—"

Hawk's arm tightened, pulling me close. "You can be both, baby. You can want to get your brother out, and still —this sucks. I've only been in here once when we put the cameras up. But your place was cool. You worked hard on it. It's okay to be pissed and wish it hadn't happened. Doesn't mean you don't want to help your brother."

We stood there for a minute, Hawk's cheek pressed to the top of my head, his strong arms holding me against him. "Let's get you home," he said. "We'll get some ice on that ankle. I know it's got to be hurting."

"I need a shower first," I said. "And maybe a nap."

"Whatever you want, Quinn," he said.

I wished in the deepest part of me that he meant it. Because the only thing I really wanted was him.

Chapter Twenty-Nine
HAWK

Quinn didn't make it as far as the shower. She was dragging by the time we got back to the gatehouse, emotionally and physically exhausted. She took one look at her hammock and crawled inside without even taking off her boot.

I let her be, covering her with her sleeping bag. After rubbing his long body against my leg, Leo hopped up and settled in on top of her. I got myself a cup of coffee and sacked out on the couch with my laptop, going through my messages from Kane. I'd kept an eye out through the morning, but nothing pressing had come up. No one on-site had been able to trace the intrusions to the security system.

One of Kane's messages said he'd talked to Lucas Jackson, and Lucas was headed up to Sawyers Bend to go over his system personally. I stared at my laptop screen, working through everything in my head. I couldn't make it all hang together the right way. According to Quinn, and substantiated by the zip ties, her attacker's focus had been on securing her, not engaging with her in another way.

It was that part that I couldn't stop thinking about. Whatever he'd wanted with her, he hadn't wanted to do it there on the trail, despite the appearance of isolation. Had he known I might come along? But how could he? Either way, he'd planned to take her somewhere. Carrying a resistant hostage over such uneven terrain wasn't ideal. Far more logical to do whatever he planned to do right there.

So where was he taking her? And why? No clue. The necklace was an obvious answer, but this was a lot of planning over a piece of jewelry. Either the necklace was the key to everything, or we were missing something.

I went through it again. He had started with kidnapping, then watching us through the window at the cabin. And then last night—if he'd been successful getting through the security system—he could have come right for Quinn. The shitty reality was that at the end of the day, I was only one man, and someone who wanted her badly enough could have found a way through me, or at least tried.

But whoever he was, he hadn't come close. Instead, he taunted us. Fucked with us. Left that box. He wanted us to know he was watching and that he hadn't gone away. But he hadn't made a direct attack or attempted to take Quinn again. Unless he'd expected me to leave Quinn in the gatehouse alone and then had switched his plan when I hadn't left her. But at this point, he had to know I wasn't that stupid.

So then what? He'd gotten pissed his scheme hadn't gone to plan, and he went and busted up her place? Why? Did he want us distracted?

It bugged me that I couldn't pin down the logic of what this guy was after. Did he want Quinn? The necklace? Was he the man in the dark, come back for Quinn? And what about Harvey? The Sawyers trusted him implicitly, but I couldn't forget that he was the one with the mystery necklace, and he'd been Prentice's lawyer for decades. I hadn't turned up anything suspicious on him, but everywhere I looked, he was there, in the background. Was he watching over the Sawyers as he claimed? Or was he pulling strings we couldn't see? I didn't like that I had more questions than answers.

A part of me wanted to go over to the security room and review the footage from the night before and the cameras at Sawyer Outdoor Adventures. And the rest of me—the rest of me wanted to be exactly where I was, content to be near Quinn.

Content. There was that word again. Not happiness. Happiness was bright sparks. Fireworks. Happiness wasn't a constant. Even in the past decade, my life turned inside out and steeped in darkness, I'd known moments of happiness, of joy. But not contentment. Not this peace. This knowing that when I woke in the morning, I was exactly where I wanted to be.

With her. Because Quinn didn't just bring the contentment, the peace. She brought those sparks, those fireworks of joy. When she laughed. When she cried out my name in my arms. And with her, every moment was strung together on a thread of pure contentment.

I couldn't change where I'd been. I couldn't take back all of my regrets. I held too many memories, things I'd done, things I'd seen, that made me wonder if I was a monster. But maybe I could be her monster. Like the dog Remy was bringing down—something fierce and dangerous to keep Quinn safe.

I watched her sleep, taking in the rustle of the hammock as she breathed, slow and deep, and I knew I would do anything to protect her. Do anything to make her happy. There had been women before, but none like Quinn. None who fit me. None who I could see, at my side, the future stretching out before us.

I couldn't quite picture it, couldn't see myself with a picket fence and 2.5 kids. But I could see myself with Quinn. With Leo and the dog. I could see all four of us in this gatehouse, together. For Quinn, I would stop giving Parker such a hard time about fixing it up and would let her have her way. I didn't care much about the outdated kitchen and cramped bathrooms, but Quinn deserved better.

Deep inside, a nagging voice asked me why I thought I could have her. Why I thought I deserved someone so good, someone as perfect as Quinn, after everything I'd done. Since I walked away from my old life, I'd listened to that voice telling me I was guilty. That I deserved to suffer. Now? I wasn't sure that voice was wrong, but I was finished listening to it.

I'd seen Quinn's face when she'd taken in the destruction of her business. *She* might be the heart of Sawyer Outdoor Adventures, but that didn't mean seeing everything she'd built shattered around her hadn't broken her heart. And watching her, her blue eyes dark with pain and grief, I'd wanted to hold on to her and promise we'd fix it.

I hadn't wanted violence. I hadn't wanted to answer the destruction with more of my own. I wanted to protect. To repair what was broken. To love. And maybe with Quinn that meant I wasn't the monster I thought I was. Something had changed in me. Maybe it was the passage of time. Maybe it was simply that Quinn had tamed the monster inside me. Maybe both. I felt like a different man with her. I wanted to take care of her. To keep her safe, to make her happy. And maybe, a little, to let her take care of me.

I knew she wanted me. I wasn't blind, and she hadn't been pushy, but she hadn't been hiding her feelings either. Quinn was a smart woman. She was capable and strong, and she wanted me. Who was I to tell her she was wrong?

I'd seen firsthand how short life could be. How quickly dreams could die. Whatever we could have together, however long the universe would grant us, I wasn't going to waste any more of it pushing her away.

* * *

Quinn slept a solid three hours. Long enough for me to check in with my team, with West, with Lucas, and with Griffen. I needed to stop in at the Manor and see my people, but that could wait. I wasn't leaving Quinn to sleep alone in the gatehouse, and I didn't want her to wake up to someone else on guard.

When she finally surfaced, her cheeks adorably flushed, dark hair sliding over her face, she sent me a shy smile and said, "I'm starving."

Leo let out a trill of protest as I lifted him out of the hammock, the sound morphing to that rumbly purr as I carried him into the kitchen and set him down in front of his food bowl. Behind me, I heard a thump as Quinn's boot hit the ground.

As I scooped the contents of a cat food can into Leo's bowl, I said, "I need to check in with my team. Let's head over to the Manor and raid the kitchen."

"Sounds good," Quinn said. "That muffin this morning didn't go far. While we're there, I need to grab some clean clothes."

She moved to head for the door, but I stopped her, crouching in front of her and offering her my back. "Jump on," I said. "Save that ankle. You spent way too long on your feet today. Some activity is good for healing, but if you overdo it—" I didn't have to finish. She jumped on my back, her weight always a surprise. She looked slight, but muscle wasn't light, and Quinn was compact but strong.

I loved that about her; how strong she was. I knew she saw herself as weak because of her problem sleeping in her room in the Manor. But I didn't see it that way. I saw a woman who'd lived through hell to protect the people she loved. She was strong, body and soul.

Her warm breath on the back of my ear, the heat of her draped over me—this was what I wanted. Quinn. Just Quinn.

The walk to the side door of the Manor was only a few minutes, the remnants of the snowstorm crunching under my boots. I set her down at the top of the steps, unlocking the door and letting us in.

"Let's get your clothes first," I said.

At her hesitant, "Sure," I headed for the elevator. Better to get it done so she could relax and enjoy her food. We rode up in silence, not saying anything until I set her down outside the closed door of her bedroom suite.

"Do you want me to do it?" I asked. Quinn wasn't picky about clothes. I was pretty sure I could handle restocking her wardrobe. For a second, I thought she'd take me up on it. Then her chin lifted a fraction, and that familiar Quinn stubbornness kicked in.

"I can handle it. There's a duffel bag in my closet. We'll fill it up, and I'll be good for a while."

I pushed open the door to her room and followed her into a time capsule. Pale pink walls, a white desk and matching dressing table, and in the bedroom a neatly made twin bed with a white eyelet coverlet. It was a young girl's room. Nothing in here reminded me of Quinn.

She kept her eyes straight ahead, marching as quickly as she could to the walk-in closet. "Up there."

She pointed to the top shelf closest to the door, and I pulled down a huge, navy-blue duffel bag. Setting it on the floor and unzipping it, I helped Quinn dump most of the closet inside. She didn't have a lot of clothes. Jeans, shorts, hiking pants, and a few dresses. T-shirts, long and short sleeve. A few sweaters and hoodies. I found another bag on the shelf, and we filled that with underwear, socks, and the rest. Quinn grabbed some extra toiletries from the bathroom and dropped them on top.

I carried the bags out, Quinn thumping behind me. Tossing the bags in the elevator, we joined them. I hit the button for the main level, shoved the bags into the hall for later, and pressed the button for the lower level of the Manor. A moment later, I pushed the door open to reveal the wide hall running the length of the lower level of Heartstone Manor.

I loved it down here. The upper floors of the Manor were designed to replicate the English country house William Sawyer's bride had grown up in. White walls, dark wood, shiny floors. Artwork and priceless rugs. Formal and elegant, every inch exuded wealth and power. The lower level was a different world, everything granite and exposed metal pipes. It looked hundreds of years older, though it dated to the same period as the rest of the house. There was something cave-like about it, the spaces basic and strong. There was no pretense down here.

We walked down the wide hall to the kitchens. When the house had been built, the various rooms that made up Heartstone's kitchen took up half the lower level. With the advent of better technology, both the staff and the space needed to run the kitchens had shrunk, though the kitchens still took up several rooms.

Most of the activity was focused in the main kitchen. When he took over, Finn rearranged the space, making it his own. Griffen had told me it strongly resembled the kitchen they'd grown up in when the French chef who'd taught Finn to cook had been in charge.

The table in front of the doorway was set for tea, ready for the kids to come home from school. Finn stood at the stove, stirring something that smelled like a red sauce.

He grinned when he saw his little sister. "Quinn, how's the ankle?" Before she could answer, his face fell. "Sterling said your place got hit. She said it was bad. That sucks, I'm sorry."

Quinn nodded. "Yeah, it's still standing, but that's the only thing going for it right now."

Finn's eyes flicked to me. "Same guy?"

"We're trying to determine that," I said.

Finn nodded and turned back to his sauce. We'd had our moments, Finn and I. I hadn't liked him making a move on Savannah. I saw it as family preying on the staff. Savannah's mother, Miss Martha, had been the housekeeper here for decades. Savannah had grown up in Heartstone Manor. Now she was the housekeeper, and she was damn good at her job. She was a badass and she could handle Finn, but I still didn't like the idea of anyone trying to take advantage of her. She worked hard. She was a good mom and a good friend, and Finn's reputation had been crap. I'd ordered him to leave her alone. He'd told me to back off. I did, but I kept an eye on him. Right up until I realized that Finn Sawyer was head over heels in love with Savannah and that I had nothing to worry about when it came to them. They'd been married for a month, and he showed her how much he loved her and her son, Nicky, every day.

A year ago, I wouldn't have thought Finn Sawyer would be my example for anything. He'd been angry and sullen, resentful of being home, and generally a dick to everybody. I didn't see that man now. I saw a man who was content. Happy. He'd gone from a man angry at the world to one who had everything.

I wanted that.

But I wasn't Finn Sawyer. Finn had been damaged by life and his father's cruelty. He'd hate me saying so, but Finn had been a victim. I wasn't a victim of anything. I was the nightmare in the dark. I didn't deserve Finn's brand of redemption.

I had to find my own path. I just wish I knew what it looked like.

"You two hungry?" Finn asked.

"Starving," Quinn said. "Can we raid the fridge?"

"Any interest in leftover meatloaf?" Finn asked. "I made Sterling a meatloaf sandwich she said was divine. Not bragging, just quoting."

"I can make it if you're busy," Quinn said.

The look Finn shot her almost made me laugh. "Sit at the table," he ordered. "I have hot water on for the kids when they get home. You want a cup of tea?" Quinn nodded and sank into a chair.

"I'll skip the tea," I said. "I need to go check in with Kane, but I'll be back for a meatloaf sandwich."

"Roger that," Finn said.

I left them there, knowing Quinn was safe with her brother.

Chapter Thirty

HAWK

Just a few doors down the hall from the kitchen, I opened the door to the security room. Formerly a pantry, our security room was a nice space. Savannah and her team had cleaned out the shelving and replaced it with long tables, upgrading the electricity to handle all the monitors, CPUs, and the rest of the surveillance system.

It was always a little cold in here, the only real drawback, but I liked having a base in the heart of the Manor, liked having my team close by. For now, the team rotated out of Sinclair Security's headquarters in Atlanta. While they were here, they stayed in rooms Savannah had repurposed farther down the hall. They weren't damp or dark, but still bore more resemblance to a cell than a bedroom. Savannah was working on opening up rooms in the attics above the guest wing. Back in the day, that space had held the servants' bedrooms.

William Sawyer, the Sawyer who'd designed Heartstone for his bride, had believed the key to a loyal staff was treating them well, and servants' rooms were small but comfortable, and warmer than those in the lower level. Moving the team up there would have been a great plan, except the electrical and the plumbing on that side of the house were dodgy at best. Pipes refused to drain for no apparent reason. The electricity died without warning and returned just as randomly. Until the plumber and electrician figured out the problem, Savannah didn't want any more of that wing in use.

None of my team had complained. Especially not once Finn took over the kitchens. We knew when we had it good. Griffen took after William Sawyer when it came to his views on the staff.

Kane looked up from the monitor in front of him when I came in.

"Any news?" I asked.

"Not since you last checked in," Kane said.

We'd been going back and forth with updates all day. After a few hours of sleep, the whole team had gone out to check the perimeters everywhere we'd had false alarms. They'd confirmed that except for the box left in the clearing, whatever had set off those alarms had been coming from inside the system.

As much as I wanted to fix every problem at hand, tracing the hack in the system was Lucas's area, not mine. I could set up a security system. I knew how it operated. But when it came to the code itself, I was out of my depth. As far as anyone could tell, the hack hadn't done any damage to the system. Everything was operating as it should be but remembering how completely the guy had controlled our system left me uneasy.

I caught the team up on what else I'd found out. "Lucas is bringing some extra people down with him," I said. "So we'll have more boots on the ground around the clock without spreading everyone too thin. Also, West confirmed that the lawyer, Harvey, still has the necklace. Turns out he'd brought it home. Harvey mentioned to West that both he and his receptionist thought things were out of place at the office the other day when they got in. Nothing they wanted to bother West about, just a few things where they shouldn't be. But the secretary swears the back door was unlocked when she got there."

"Huh," Kane said, considering the new information. "So the guy goes looking for the necklace at Harvey's office, doesn't find it, and then assumes Quinn still has it and searches the bungalow?"

"That's my guess," I said. Although it didn't explain the rage. Harvey's office had barely been touched. Quinn's space had been destroyed. "I'm going to get something to eat in the kitchen. Lucas will be here the day after tomorrow. Maybe he can find something that'll lead us to this guy."

I left Kane and headed back to the kitchen to find Finn sliding plates on the table. The meatloaf had been good on its own, but on lightly toasted bread, with cheese melted on top, it was amazing. I watched Quinn as she bit in, her groan of pleasure giving me ideas that had nothing to do with food. She caught my eyes and her cheeks flushed pink.

It took everything I had not to scoop her up and take her back to the gatehouse. But we needed food, and I wasn't abandoning this sandwich. Not even for sex with

Quinn. I ate, ignoring Finn's eyes on us, the smirk curving the side of his mouth. If Quinn hadn't been sitting across from me, I was sure I'd get a ton of crap about mixing business with pleasure, and family staying apart from the staff, and everything else I'd shoveled at him when he'd been falling in love with Savannah.

And he wouldn't be wrong. It turned out I was the one who'd been wrong, and I deserved a little shit for it. I was sure Finn would get around to me later. But Finn wasn't the asshole I'd thought he'd been, and he wouldn't give me a hard time in front of his sister. She'd taken enough knocks for the day. Anyway, I'd learned that feeding people made Finn happy, and when Finn was happy, he wasn't as much of a dick.

Stomachs full, we leaned back in our chairs.

"Chocolate cake for dessert tonight," Finn said out of nowhere.

Quinn smiled. "I can't imagine eating another bite of anything, but I will definitely be ready for chocolate cake after dinner."

"I'll send a tray over. Unless you want to come in and eat in the dining room?"

Quinn shook her head. Finn grinned at me, already knowing I'd rather eat in the gatehouse, or the kitchens—anywhere but in the formal dining room with the family.

Quinn's eyes moved to me. She looked a little sheepish when she said, "Are you ready to go back? Now that I'm not starving anymore, I really need a shower."

I had plans for her shower. But first— "Stay here for a minute while I bring over your stuff," I said. "I'll be right back."

WILD HEART

Quinn settled into her seat, and I left, jogging up the stairs to snag her duffel bags. I dropped them beside the closet in the empty bedroom of the gatehouse. She was sleeping with me, but she could take over the extra room and make it her own. At the least, she could use the closet rather than sharing with me. I didn't have a ton of clothes, but the gatehouse closets were tiny.

Quinn was sipping another cup of tea when I got back. As soon as she saw me, she put down her teacup and stood.

When she got to me, I put up a hand and stopped her, turning and dropping into a crouch. "Climb on, I'll give you a ride."

Her eyes lit at the idea of another piggyback. I didn't even mind Finn's smirk. I doubted he could resist a dig, but to my surprise, he just smiled and shook his head.

"Never thought I'd see you reduced to a pack animal," he said, but the words had no sting. "The things we do, right?"

A jolt of understanding hit me. Not only did Finn know I was totally fucking gone for his sister, but he also liked it, and he wasn't going to give me a hard time.

Fucking hell. Who would have thought Finn Sawyer would be more mature than me?

I nodded, not ready to put my swirling thoughts into words. I carried Quinn back to the gatehouse and up the stairs to the second level, setting her on her feet in front of the bathroom door.

I hesitated. I knew what I wanted. Knew all the things I'd been imagining doing with Quinn since the moment I swore I'd never touch her again. But I hadn't said fuck all to her about any of it. Maybe she'd changed her mind. Maybe—

She stood there staring up at me. Her teeth sank into her lower lip, and she looked shy and uncertain. In a blink, the uncertainty vanished. Quinn's fingers curled over the hem of her shirt, and she whipped it over her head, leaving her standing there in dusty pants and a plain white bra.

One dark eyebrow lifted, a dare sparking in her bright blue eyes.

I took her dare happily, pulling my own shirt over my head and throwing it across the room. The grin that spread across her face filled my heart. We didn't have to talk. Not yet. Not as long as we were on the same page here.

Her hands went to the button on her pants, and I took over, unsnapping them and sliding them down. Pressing my cheek to her hip, I stroked my tongue over the juncture of her thighs, loving her gasp of surprise and delight.

"Gotta get this boot off you," I muttered, tearing at the Velcro and gently sliding her foot up and out of the protective boot.

I stood, taking her with me and carrying her to the shower, cranking the water hot while I took care of the rest of my clothes. She stood there smiling up at me, her cheeks pink, her eyes bright, and said, "You changed your mind."

I cupped her cheek in my palm and kissed her. "I changed my mind," I murmured in agreement.

There wasn't enough room in the shower to do what I

wanted to do with her. Another reason I was going to stop being a pain in the ass and let Parker do whatever she wanted to do in the gatehouse, including a much bigger shower, with that tile bench she'd talked about. Things I thought I didn't need. I hadn't until now.

I took Quinn's weight as she balanced on one foot, her right ankle still too weak without the boot on to take much weight. She tipped her head back, wetting her hair, and I let myself look, taking in every inch of her. The delicate curve of her breasts, her pink nipples furled into tight points despite the heat of the water. My hard cock pressed against her belly, but I could wait. I had Quinn in my arms, naked. We'd get to the bed eventually.

She washed her hair and combed conditioner through before turning her attention to me, squeezing shower gel into her palms and stroking the foamy suds over my skin with long, slow sweeps of her hands. I closed my eyes and let the water run over my face, drinking in her touch. I washed my hair, helped her rinse her own, and shut off the water.

Lifting Quinn out of the shower, I set her on the edge of the counter. She leaned back against the sink, her eyes alive, scanning me from head to toe. I was already hard, but if I hadn't been, the greedy look in her eyes would have been enough to get me there.

I could be patient just a little bit longer. I needed to do this, to take care of her, to show her what I didn't have the words to say. I squeezed her hair with the towel and combed it back from her face. Quinn watched me, her eyes still sparkling but serious and maybe a little confused. I'd been gentle with her before. Always. I was always gentle with Quinn, except maybe in bed. But not like this.

I picked up a bottle of lotion from the counter where she left it after her last shower. "This one?" I asked.

She nodded. Squeezing some into my hand, I stroked it over her damp skin, lingering over her small, round breasts that filled my hand exactly the way I wanted them to, her nipples hard and begging for my mouth. They'd have to wait. I smoothed lotion on her shoulders, down her arms to her elbows, and over every individual finger. When I got to her legs, I was tempted to bury my face between her thighs, to feel her come like that, against my mouth.

But she was getting cold, and the countertop wasn't big enough. Another reason we needed a new bathroom. If we had a wider bathroom counter, I could lay her out, spread her thighs—

I didn't need a counter. The bed was only steps away. Every inch of her skin moisturized, I stood, picking her up and carrying her to my bed. Quinn lay back, her wet hair spread around her.

"You really changed your mind," she said.

I didn't answer. We could talk later. I was going to do what I'd been thinking of since I'd peeled off her clothes earlier. Sliding my hands around her hips, I dragged her to the edge of the bed, lifting her legs to drape over my shoulders as I sank to my knees. I knew exactly what I wanted. My mouth on that sweet, perfect pussy.

Quinn let out a cry at the touch of my tongue to her clit. At the sound, I knew I loved this woman. I was done lying to myself about her. She was everything, and I could do more for her than just keep her safe. I could give her this, too. She tasted like heaven, like Quinn, and I lingered over her, licking and sucking her clit, rubbing my tongue against it. I traced her damp flesh with my fingertip until her hips rocked up, begging me to slide it inside and fill her. I fucked her with one finger, then two, dragging her to the edge of orgasm and then moving back, leaving her pussy to press kisses up the insides of her thighs until she was begging.

"Hawk, please, Hawk." And then finally, with a snap of temper, "Stop teasing me and let me come!"

I liked her demand so much, I gave her what she wanted, loving the way she unraveled against my mouth, around my fingers. Loving the way she screamed as her pussy clamped down on my fingers, her tight grip almost dragging me over the edge along with her. I rose over her, pulling her up the bed and spreading her legs wide, pressing inside her through the last pulses of her orgasm.

I managed to hold back, needing to feel her body relax around me. Buried inside her, I looked down into her beautiful eyes and kissed her, murmuring her name against her lips between tender kisses. "Quinn, my Quinn."

After a minute, I started to move, pushing her knees back, filling her completely, grinding into her swollen clit until her head tipped back and she cried my name.

"Oh, God, Hawk."

This time when her pussy clamped tight around me and her words dissolved into breathless moans, I gave in to her pull and came with her.

When I could move again, I got up, wetting a washcloth in the bathroom. Her cheeks flushed a shade of pink that was fucking adorable, but she let me take care of her as she had before. I liked cleaning her up, liked seeing a part of me inside her so intimately. More, I loved knowing she trusted me that much.

When I was done, I tossed the washcloth back toward the bathroom and slid beneath the sheets, drawing up the covers. I started to pull her into my arms, but her hand came up and hit me flat on my chest, holding me back.

Chapter Thirty-One
HAWK

"What changed?" she asked.

Because of course Quinn wasn't going to let me get away with not talking about it.

"Before, you said this couldn't happen, and now— What changed?"

I didn't want to talk about it. It was enough for me to make the decision. Talking about it was— I didn't like the way it made me feel, raw and exposed. I'd spent so long making sure no one could hurt me, no one could make me feel the shit I was running from. But this was Quinn, and I couldn't deny her what she needed.

If she was going to be in this with me, she had a right to know. "I'm not good enough for you," I said.

Her eyes narrowed, and a line grooved between her brows. "What do you mean you're not good enough for me? Is it because I'm a Sawyer?"

"No," I said. "I mean, yeah, probably that too. But no, not because you're a Sawyer. Because you're Quinn.

Because you're goodness and light and beauty. And I'm everything you're not."

"That's bullshit," she said, her eyes sparking blue fire.

"It's not bullshit." I leaned back, looking down at her. "Listen, you think you know who I am. You see me at Heartstone, working with your brother, watching out for your family, and you think you understand who I am. But you don't know."

"I know what I need to know," she shot back. "But fine, tell me who you are."

I paused, the enormity of what I was about to admit hitting me. Even Griffen didn't know all the details, just the gist. I reminded myself that this had to be done. Quinn had to know, so she could make her own decision. And if she chose to never speak to me again, if she ran away in terror? Well, that would be what it would be. But we couldn't go further until she knew the truth.

"When I left the military, when I joined Sinclair Security, I was barely human anymore. I was thinking about ending my life because I couldn't imagine I deserved to live after the things I'd done."

Quinn's fiery eyes softened, her brows still pulled together. This time, I thought, in worry instead of annoyance. "What could you have done that's so bad?" she asked. "I know you, Hawk—"

I cut her off. "You don't." I shook my head at the hurt in her eyes and searched for the right words. "In some ways," I said, "you know me better than anyone on this planet." I took her hand in mine and pressed it back to my chest, over my heart. "You know me here. But you don't know— You don't know the things I've done, Quinn. I was a stupid fucking kid. I was in the Rangers with your brother and Evers Sinclair. We were young, but we busted our asses, and we made Ranger, and we thought we were the kings of the universe. And then—"

I hated putting it into words, hated remembering getting that call. My entire life had shattered in an instant. I let it out in a rush.

"And then my mom and dad died in a car accident. I was twenty-three. We were close. They were the best parents. I had a fucking great childhood and then it was all gone. I was an only child. They were only children. There weren't grandparents or aunts and uncles to step in. It was just the three of us, and then I was alone, and I — I didn't—"

I swallowed, hating the prickle of heat in the back of my eyes, hating the hollow pain in my chest when I remembered. Quinn pressed her hand to the side of my neck, squeezing gently, her eyes soft.

"I lost it a little bit," I said. "No, I lost it a lot. I think I didn't— I didn't know what to do. Everything I thought I understood about my life was gone. And then being a Ranger wasn't enough anymore. I wanted the danger, to feel something, anything. And when I was offered a transfer, I took it. I thought I could lose myself in work I was good at. I thought I could just— I don't know, at the time, I told myself it was a good career move, that I was building my future. But—"

"You were running," she said, and I nodded.

"I was running, and I—" I drew in a slow breath and let it out, trying to sort through everything in my head, trying to figure out how to explain. "I worked with a team. We were off the books. I was still technically army, but not really. There was a lot of gray area. And our CO, our commanding officer—"

I stopped, searching for words to explain. Quinn waited patiently. I couldn't look at the compassion in her eyes. I knew she was ready to forgive me anything. I didn't deserve that. I'd never deserve that. Forgiveness was off the table because some crimes went too far for that.

"I didn't ask questions. And Quinn, I did things—" My throat tight, I forced myself to say, "I took a lot of lives. Lives that, looking back, I think were innocent. The army trained me well. Hand to hand, explosives, sabotage. I'm not a sniper, but I'm a better than good shot. I learned a lot of ways to kill, and I used them all. I didn't ask enough questions," I said again, not knowing how to explain the confusion of that time. "I let myself trust my commanding officer, and it took me way too long to realize my trust was badly placed. And the people who paid for my mistakes—" I shook my head again. "I didn't pay. Innocent people paid, Quinn. And I— I can't fix any of that. I can't take it back. I can't make it right. I don't have that power. The things I did were monstrous."

"Did they feel monstrous when you were doing them?" she asked, and I saw more curiosity in her eyes than condemnation.

I shook my head. "He always had a good explanation. Reasons why, even when things sounded dodgy. There was a school, or it was a residential neighborhood, but there was always a reason why. And I didn't ask enough questions."

"I thought you were in the army," Quinn said, propping herself up on her elbow. "I thought you military types weren't supposed to ask questions."

I let out a sigh. "That's not an excuse. Yeah, you follow orders. But the stuff I was doing— Quinn, I wasn't a child. I couldn't have done that kind of work if I was stupid. I can't use protocol or ignorance as an excuse. At some point, I should have stopped and asked what the fuck we were doing. But I didn't. And it wasn't just innocent civilians who paid the price."

"Well, obviously not," she said. "Because you paid. You're still paying. How long ago was all of this?"

I shrugged. "Doesn't matter. It was recent enough, and I wasn't a kid."

"Have you killed anyone since you left? Since you've been with Sinclair or here?" she pressed.

It was a valid question, and I got where she was going with it, but I could tell she didn't get it. Not yet. I had to make her understand, so she could make her own decisions about me. "That's not the point, Quinn. In the right circumstances, I'll do what has to be done. I know better now. I won't make those mistakes again, but being sorry doesn't erase what I did."

She nodded, paused. Finally, she asked, "What did you mean it wasn't just civilians?"

This one I really wasn't ready to talk about, but I already knew Quinn wouldn't let it go. I shuffled through memories I'd been avoiding for close to a decade, trying to figure out a way to appease her curiosity without spilling my guts. I couldn't. She'd told me everything when I asked for her secrets. She deserved the same honesty in return, even if it was the last thing I wanted to do.

"For all the wrong I did," I said, "the thing that pushed me over the edge, the thing that drove me to walk away, was pulling the trigger on a friend."

"A friend? Or a bad guy?" Quinn asked slowly, her eyes thoughtful, not afraid or repulsed.

I was surprised. I would be afraid of me. Sometimes I *was* afraid of me.

"Both, I guess. Someone who had been a friend. It was one of the few times my CO told the straight truth. She was a friend. More than a friend to one of my buddies. She was also a double agent. She led our team into a trap, and we lost seven men. I had a plan to take her in alive, but it didn't work out. I killed her. I fucked up. I should have found another way. I did the right thing for the right reasons, and it was the one death I couldn't live with. So, I walked."

I closed my eyes, feeling the pulse of hot blood on my hands when she died, my desperate attempts to save her, even though I'd pulled the trigger, knowing the agony her loss would bring, the ripple effects already spreading. The team had disbanded, my friends dead, my CO on to other schemes. I'd walked away but it hadn't ended the nightmare. I relived it every time I closed my eyes.

Quinn reached up and cupped my cheek in her hand. I leaned into her palm. "Hawk," she said gently. "The things you did, they're not a stain you have to carry with you. Everyone fucks up. Everyone makes mistakes."

"Not like this," I said, my eyes still closed, my entire being anchored by the heat of her hand on my face.

"No," she agreed. "Not like this. Most of us are never in the kinds of situations you lived through. At that age, having just lost your parents—"

"You don't need to make excuses for me," I forced out, my voice rough and low.

"They're not excuses, Hawk, but they are reasons. It's not that you shouldn't feel the weight of the things you did. We all have to live with our mistakes. But your past doesn't have to erase your future. And you've done a lot of good since you left. You've saved lives. Doesn't that count for anything?"

Her words sank in, but they felt uncomfortable, like an ill-fitting jacket that pulls on your elbows. "I'm not sure I can let myself see it that way," I admitted. "It feels too much like letting myself off the hook."

"I'm not saying you shouldn't take responsibility, or that I have the right to absolve you of anything. I'm just saying it doesn't mean you can't have a life. It doesn't mean that you don't deserve to be loved."

"I don't know if I can go there yet, Quinn," I said, opening my eyes and falling into hers. "But I'll tell you what I did figure out."

She raised an eyebrow, a slight smile curving her pink lips. "Tell me what you figured out."

"I figured out that I'm a monster." She opened her mouth, probably to argue. I laid my thumb across her lips. "Let me finish."

In answer, she nipped the tip of my thumb, and my cock jerked in appreciation. *Later.* I had to say this first.

"I figured out that I'm a monster," I said. "But maybe you need a monster to keep you safe. You're a light in this world, and maybe I'm here to make sure you get to shine. I don't deserve you. I'll never deserve you. But if you want me, I'm yours."

Quinn's eyes filled with tears. Alarm spiked in my chest, and she raised her hands, cupping my face, she pulled me closer and kissed me.

"I want you," she said against my mouth. "I want all of you, Hawk. Whatever you've done, whatever you carry with you, I don't care. I want all of you to be mine."

"Then I'm yours," I said and kissed her back, knowing that of all the things I'd done, all the choices I'd made, this was the one I'd never regret.

Chapter Thirty-Two
HAWK

The next three weeks were probably the best of my life. Quinn and I settled in as if we'd always been two halves of a pair. It was so seamless it might have been scary, but I'd faced far scarier things than the woman I loved fitting me like a puzzle piece. I was done running from Quinn. I was done running from my feelings. I was just flat-out done with running.

For so long, I'd only been surviving, putting one foot in front of the other, focused on my work without any plan for a life outside of that. Now there was Quinn and Leo and a dog to come. I had my own little family. A home. For the first time in years, I woke up in the morning exactly where I wanted to be.

It would have been perfect, except for that fucking stranger out there who was after Quinn. I'd waited my entire life for Quinn Sawyer. I wasn't going to let anyone hurt her. She'd been hurt enough as it was. I couldn't stop thinking of that man from her childhood, the way he'd essentially stalked her in her own home, and with her father's permission. Now, all these years later, it was happening again. Someone out there was after her, and he'd come for her in the two places she felt safe: the woods and her business. I wanted to say we were close to catching him, but it would be a lie. We had nothing solid, although it wasn't for lack of trying.

Lucas Jackson had showed up from Atlanta two days after his system had been hacked, with four extra people to supplement our team. He went through the system, cursing most of the time, and left after assuring us he'd added some safeguards and that no one was fucking getting in. He'd also commented that when we found the guy who got through his code, we should send him Lucas's way. He had some questions. I figured that once he'd grilled the guy, Lucas would try to put him to work. Since he'd been with Sinclair Security, Lucas had been collecting hackers for his team. He wasn't getting this one. The second I knew who we were after, I was taking them straight to West and jail.

Since Lucas's visit, we'd been in stasis, waiting for something to break. Someone had tried to get back into the guide business, but the added security we'd put in scared them off. All we got was video of someone in dark pants, a dark hoodie, and a balaclava. Not much to go on. Based on size and weight, we were fairly confident the perpetrator was male. He was a match for the man Quinn had described in the woods, but that was all we knew.

Two days after Quinn's business was hit, Harvey's

house was broken into and searched. Fortunately, he'd turned the necklace over to West and it was securely locked in the property room, in an area only West had access to. A week after Harvey's house was hit, someone broke into his office again, this time not as quietly or carefully as the first search.

After the second break-in at Harvey's office, I brought my team over with some extra equipment, and we added Harvey's office to our surveillance along with Quinn's guide business. Since then, things had been quiet. I wasn't fooled. None of this was over, and as the peace and quiet stretched out, the itch under my skin got worse. I was missing something. I had to be.

I wasn't the only one who was getting increasingly restless. Quinn's ankle was almost healed. She and Sterling had rebooked a few of her canceled trips, those that wouldn't be too much strain on her barely healed ankle. I hated the idea of her out there, living her normal life, when we didn't know who was after her, or why. Everything pointed to the necklace, but...that didn't feel like the answer.

The man from her past, the one she said Ford had taken care of—I couldn't find any evidence that he was connected to Prentice's murder, or the mystery woman Quinn thought the necklace had belonged to. No one currently at Heartstone Manor knew much about Prentice's movements right before he'd died. But there was one person who knew everything I needed to know: Ford. He was the one who'd dealt with the man from Quinn's past. He'd know if there was any way that man was back, or if he'd been involved with Prentice in the past few years.

I already knew without asking that Quinn wouldn't want me to question Ford about any of this. The one time I'd suggested it, she'd pushed back hard. She was fiercely protective of her older brother. She didn't want him to know she'd been in danger and didn't want me bothering him. She'd said he was under enough stress as it was.

I didn't give a shit about Ford Sawyer's stress levels. I was worried about Quinn's safety. If there was a connection between her attacker back then and the man who was after her now, I needed to know.

I didn't want to poke at her, didn't want to aggravate what I knew was a raw and tender wound, but I had to know. As I'd told her the day I prodded her into telling me the truth, I couldn't keep her safe if I didn't know.

Almost three weeks after her business was broken into, I tried again. We were lying on the couch in front of the fire, facing each other, Leo sprawled on Quinn's stomach, purring as Quinn rubbed his ears.

"Quinn," I prompted, "we're running into too many dead ends with this guy. I need to look into everything, even when it seems unrelated."

It was like she could see straight into my brain. She knew immediately what I was getting at. Her jaw lifted, her eyes narrowed, and she said, "Ford took care of it. He said the man wouldn't be a problem, and he hasn't been."

"And you never asked for more detail than that?" I pushed.

She shook her head, our eye contact breaking, her eyes cutting away, focusing on Leo in her lap as she stroked and rubbed. "He told me not to ask," she said. Then, her chin jutting up again, she looked back at me. "Leave Ford out of this. There isn't anything he can do to help."

"He can help by telling me what he knows," I said as gently as I could. I thought I understood Quinn's loyalty to her brother, but it was making my investigation complicated.

"Hawk, someone tried to kill him in there," she said, her blue eyes bright with pain. "He needs to keep his attention on staying safe, not whatever's going on with me. I don't want him distracted."

I nodded but didn't say anything. I wasn't going to lie to Quinn. Not outright. But I wasn't going to let this go. I couldn't, not when her safety was at stake. I penciled a new to-do item on my list for the next day: visit the state prison and ask Ford Sawyer a few questions.

The next morning, we woke early. Quinn and Sterling had plans to spend the day putting the final touches on their cleanup at the guide business in preparation for reopening the following week. I had Kane and two other guys on watch while they worked. I left her on the front porch with a kiss and told her I'd be back in a few hours.

I'd never met Ford Sawyer in person, and I wasn't sure what to expect. Everyone said when they were younger, Ford and Griffen were like twins, different only in their hair color. I'd seen pictures around the Manor that backed this up, but the man sitting at the table across from me held only echoes of Griffen in his face. The sea-green eyes and sharp cheekbones were familiar, but that was it. For a second, I felt a pang of sympathy. He'd done some shitty things, but he didn't deserve to be in prison for a murder I was almost positive he didn't commit.

I understood why Ford had forbidden Quinn from coming to see him. I knew without asking that this man was not the brother she remembered. Ford's hair was short and dark, his face too thin. Where Griffen radiated energy, Ford was faded, and almost frail, although no less a Sawyer. That said, despite his gaunt face, the shiny shackles on his wrists, and the orange prison jumpsuit, he gave the impression he was in charge of the room and not the prison guard in the corner.

Ford sat across from me at the table in the empty visitors' room, hands folded, expression reserved.

"Hawk Bristol," he said with a slow nod, as if he'd called this meeting and not me. "My brother's head of security." He raised an eyebrow. "Everything all right at the Manor?"

"Everyone's in one piece," I said, matching his tone. "But Quinn was attacked three weeks ago."

Ford nodded. "I heard about that. I was informed that you're on the case and that she couldn't be in safer hands."

"Who?" I asked. "Griffen?"

Ford shook his head. "Haywood. My lawyer."

That made sense. In the fall, the DA who'd pushed Ford into his guilty plea had left the job, replaced by a new DA who Haywood thought might be open to new evidence, if they could find any. Since then, I knew

Haywood had been going over every detail of the case, hoping to shake something loose.

"He making any headway?" I asked.

Ford's head angled to the side, and he studied me in a way that suddenly reminded me of Griffen, sharp and assessing. Finally, he said, "His investigator found the camera."

My eyebrows shot up in surprise. "The missing doorbell camera from across the street?"

Ford nodded in confirmation. "The judge is reviewing the footage," he said, his tone so neutral he might have been talking about someone else's case and not the chance that he could be out of prison in a matter of days. I wondered immediately if he'd told anyone else. I wouldn't have, in his position. I'd wait until it was a sure thing.

"Does Griffen know?" I asked.

Ford shrugged a shoulder. "Not unless Haywood told him. Nothing is solid yet. Cole said the time stamp and the footage are what we were looking for, but one thing I've learned since this started is that there aren't any guarantees. Even if that camera proves I was at the inn when Prentice was shot, it doesn't necessarily mean I'll be out of here any time soon. Or that I won't get killed before the judge makes his decision."

I nodded, knowing Ford was right. Even if the camera had the footage they needed, there was no guarantee the judge would accept it as new evidence, or that whoever was pulling the strings to make sure Ford took the fall for Prentice's murder would allow this new evidence to stand. "Where did the investigator find it?"

"A pawn shop by the airport."

"Had it been there the whole time?" I asked.

Ford shook his head. "It showed up a few months ago."

Prentice had been dead for over a year. The camera had been stolen the day of his murder. So where had it been between the day it was stolen and when it turned up at the pawn shop? And why was the memory card with the footage still inside?

"You'd think whoever stole the camera in the first place would have deleted the footage that gives you an alibi," I said and saw that Ford was already there.

"You'd think," he agreed, dryly. "And the judge isn't a fool. He's taking his time deciding if this new evidence is as clean as it looks."

I understood why Ford wasn't jumping for joy at this new development, and why he hadn't said anything to Griffen or the rest of his family. Getting his plea overturned was still a long shot, even with camera footage showing he was home at the time of the murder.

According to my own investigations, back then Ford had been living in a suite at the inn. While there were cameras all over the property, Ford's suite had been built for his grandfather and had a private entrance that wasn't covered by the inn's security. Great for his privacy once he started living there. Not so great for proving his innocence in his father's murder.

But there was a small bungalow opposite the private parking area Ford used, and that bungalow had a video doorbell. The doorbell had happened to catch Ford's car, as well as the side door he used to enter and exit the inn.

It would have been perfect to support Ford's alibi, except it had been stolen the day Prentice was murdered. Tough luck for Ford.

I sat back, crossing my arms over my chest, thinking. "What did Haywood say was on the camera?"

Ford leaned in, bracing his forearms on the metal table. "Me coming back to the inn that morning, driving too fast into the parking lot. The time stamp was two hours earlier than the witness who saw me speeding away from the Manor, but it lines up with the statement I gave when I was arrested. The doorbell camera also caught a delivery truck that shows up on the inn's cameras, corroborating the doorbell's time stamp and proving that the witness's estimated time was off. Then it shows me going into the inn and not leaving again for the rest of the day."

I turned that information over in my head. It was the perfect alibi, stolen on the day of the murder, and now it conveniently turned up in a pawn shop a few weeks after someone tried to assassinate Ford in prison. I didn't trust convenience when it came to most things, but especially not murder. "I wonder if whoever tried to have you killed in here wants you let out so they have an easier target."

A slight smile twisted Ford's mouth as he sat back, propping his ankle on his knee, the chains rattling as he moved. "The thought had occurred to me. This place isn't the Ritz, but the guards are decent. It's not as easy as you'd think to get away with shit. If someone wants me out of the picture, I'd be a much easier target out there than I am in here."

I nodded in agreement. Ford wasn't a part of his father's will or its conditions. Prentice had cut him off completely. If he got out, he could go anywhere and do anything he wanted. He'd have his freedom but at a cost. Unlike Griffen, Ford didn't have the skills to watch his back. Once he was out, he'd be a sitting duck. Unless he came home. Assuming Griffen would let him.

Chapter Thirty-Three
HAWK

"So, what is my brother's security chief doing here?" Ford asked, interrupting my train of thought. "I know you didn't come for an update on my case."

"No, I didn't," I said, pushing aside the problem of Ford and his eventual release. "I need to know about the man who attacked Quinn in her room when she was a teenager."

"She told you about that?" Ford asked, leaning forward a fraction.

"Did you know she still can't sleep in her room?"

Ford gave a curt nod. "It wasn't as bad as it could have been," he said, "but it was bad."

"And the man who attacked her?" I pressed.

Ford raised an eyebrow. "What did Quinn say?"

"Quinn said you told her it was taken care of, that she doesn't have to be afraid. She told me to leave it alone."

"But you're not leaving it alone," Ford said.

"I'm not," I agreed. "I can't. For one thing, we haven't been able to find the guy who attacked her. Her ankle is almost better, and by next week she'll be out there, back to work, and a lot harder to protect. At this point I can't leave any stone unturned. We're talking about a man who has a grudge against Quinn, someone who tried to hurt her once, and he's out there somewhere. I need to know—"

"He's dead," Ford cut in.

"Does Quinn know that he's dead?" I asked, sure she didn't.

Ford shook his head. "No." He straightened and looked down at his hands, examining the cuffs on his wrists as if he'd never seen them before. Finally dropping his hands into his lap, he sat back and said, "Seeing Quinn hurt woke me up. I was—"

He paused, but kept his eyes locked on mine.

"I was lost for a long time," he said. "Chasing what I thought I wanted, what I thought would make me happy. I got rid of Griffen. I let my father use Finn and almost got him killed for a deal. For money. And then I saw my little sister, my father's fucking friend, our business partner, holding her down, hurting her. And everything changed." He leaned forward, bracing his arms on the table, his face less than a foot from my own. "You ever have that happen, Hawk? You ever have your whole life change in a blink?"

I gave a curt nod. I knew what it was like to get lost in pain, get lost chasing something you thought would make you happy, only to find out you'd destroyed everything good in your life in the process. And I knew how one act, one moment in time, could suddenly make you see it all with crystalline clarity, every fuckup, every mistake laid bare. Yeah, I knew what that was like.

"I pulled him off her," Ford said, "beat the shit out of him and kicked him out of the Manor. When he was gone, I made sure Quinn was okay, and told my father that was it with having his skeevy business associates under the same roof as my siblings. Especially the kids. Especially the girls. He didn't like it, but he went along."

"And the man who attacked Quinn? What was his name?" I asked. "What happened to him? I'm assuming you didn't kill him."

A ghost of a smile flicked across Ford's face. "I didn't kill him. Like I said, after I beat him up, I let him go."

"And?" I asked, sure Ford hadn't left it at that.

"And then I spent the next year systematically dismantling his financial empire. I went behind my father's back and bought up loans and shares in his companies. In the end, once Prentice found out, he let it go because the destruction of his friend's empire turned out to be profitable for us. I wasn't in it for the money. The day I called in the final debts, I threatened to tell his wife and daughters what he'd done. He killed himself. And before you can ask," Ford said with a lift of his chin, "I'm not sorry. I'd do it again if I could."

Another man might have chastised him. Another man might have told him that justice was for God or the legal system to mete out. But I wasn't that man. This was Quinn we were talking about, and she deserved that kind of vengeance. The man who'd hurt her deserved everything he got.

"Did it occur to you that it might make Quinn feel better to know that he's dead?" I asked.

"I didn't want to— I didn't want her to—" For the first time, Ford stumbled over his words.

"You didn't want it to change the way she sees you," I said.

Ford gave a curt nod.

"She thinks you're her hero," I said, bluntly. "The man who attacked her has been a blight on her life since she was seventeen. Trust me, she wouldn't fault you."

Ford didn't react to that statement.

"Name?" I asked. "I want to do some checking of my own."

"Robert Sydney," Ford said immediately.

"And did Robert Sydney have anyone in his life who might be looking for revenge? Who might go after Quinn now that you're out of reach?"

Ford's already pale face went sheet white at that question. After a long moment, he shook his head. "His wife had her own money, and she remarried a few years after he died. The daughters are married now, with young kids of their own. I had an investigator keep an eye on them. He said after the shock faded, they all seemed better off. From what he could find out, Sydney was a Grade A asshole. The world is a happier place without him in it."

I'd call Sinclair and ask someone to look into Robert Sydney and make sure Ford's info was all there was to know. But I doubted we'd find anything. From what Ford said, Robert Sydney was another dead end.

"Are you going to tell her that he's dead?" Ford asked.

I nodded.

"How much are you going to tell her?"

"I don't like keeping things from Quinn," I said, telling half the truth. There was a lot I was keeping from Quinn, but nothing like this. Nothing that was about her life. When it came to the attack, she was still trying to recover from it all these years later— "She has a right to know, don't you think?"

Ford's face flashed with pain.

I knew all about hiding the truth from the people you cared for, afraid it would show them how little you deserved their love. Hadn't I tried to push Quinn away for the same reason?

In a moment of sympathy, I said, "I'll tell her he's dead, and I'll tell her we talked, but I won't tell her the details. You can do that when you get out of here."

Ford cleared his throat. "Thanks."

It was funny how much I understood Ford. I didn't like him on principle. Griffen was the closest thing I had to family, and this man had gotten him exiled from his home out of greed and selfishness. But the thing was, I thought Ford and I weren't that different. We'd both done things we'd lived to regret and seen ourselves become people we didn't recognize. And I had a feeling that, like me, Ford Sawyer was looking for redemption. He just didn't know on what path he'd find it. He waited here in purgatory for a chance he was afraid to hope for.

I'd gotten my chance in Quinn, who'd shown me that while I'd never be an angel, there was good still in me somewhere. Maybe Ford would get his chance. Assuming he could stay alive long enough for redemption to find him.

I stood. "I got what I needed," I said. "Maybe the next time I see you, you'll be on the outside."

Ford stood. "We'll see. That video might get me out of prison, but that's not the same as figuring out who killed my father."

"One step at a time," I said, nodding to the guard in the corner.

I left Ford there and drove home in the early spring sunshine, a little off-kilter. I hadn't thought I'd feel anything but contempt for Ford Sawyer. I wasn't sure I liked him, but he wasn't the villain I'd expected.

He'd given me a lot to think about. I wasn't surprised he'd driven Quinn's attacker to his death. Ford was smart enough not to kill the guy straight out, and vengeful enough to make sure he ended up dead. Maybe I should condemn him for that, but I wouldn't. Couldn't. Not when I would have done the same.

Before I got back to the Manor, I called Evers Sinclair and gave him Robert Sydney's name. I'd know soon enough if Ford's story lined up, and, more importantly, if there was someone lurking in Sydney's past who might be taking vengeance on Quinn. Then, on a whim, I stopped in town and visited Sweetheart Bakery. Maybe a treat from Daisy and her grandmother would sweeten up Quinn after I told her where I'd been all afternoon.

* * *

Quinn was home from the guide shop when I got back, reading on the couch with a purring Leo. Seeing her there, at peace, her mouth curved in a smile of welcome, the guilt hit me. I'd done what I needed to do, but I hated going behind her back. I was done hiding shit, mostly, and I wouldn't hide this. This was very much her business.

"What's wrong?" she asked immediately.

"You're going to be pissed," I said.

Quinn narrowed her eyes and sat up, dislodging Leo, who let out an annoyed trill and jumped to the back of the couch. "What did you do?" she asked, her brows pulled together.

"I went to go see Ford."

"Hawk! Why?" Her eyes were spitting blue fire.

I sat on the other end of the couch, pulling her legs into my lap. "I know you asked me not to talk to him. I waited longer than I should have, hoping something would turn up, but I needed answers, and he had them." I squeezed her thigh gently, prompting her to meet my eyes. "I'm sorry I went to see him when you asked me not to. I wouldn't have done it if I had another option. You know Ford would want to know you're in danger. You're not doing him any favors by leaving him out of your life. He loves you."

She let out a long sigh. "I told you he took care of it," she said mulishly.

"I know what you told me," I said. "But I needed to know what that meant. I needed to cross this guy off my list. You understand? I can't waste resources investigating somebody who's not a problem. But I needed to hear from Ford what *took care of it* meant."

"And?" Quinn asked, after a long silence.

"The man who attacked you is dead," I said.

Quinn relaxed back on the couch for a second before she stiffened and sat up. "Did Ford kill him?"

"No," I answered quickly. "He died a year after Ford threw him out of Heartstone."

Quinn reached for Leo, who let her gather him to her chest. Leo tucked his head under Quinn's chin, rubbing against her as she stroked down his back. After another long silence, she said, "But Ford had something to do with it."

I shook my head. "Not the way you mean, but in a way. He didn't kill him. Robert Sydney killed himself."

Quinn let out a long breath. "Why won't you tell me more?"

"Because the story is your brother's to tell," I said, "And I promised him I wouldn't. He didn't murder anybody. But he did make sure you'd be safe. When he gets out, you can ask him."

Quinn started to sit up again, but Leo curved his claws into her leg at the sudden movement and she settled back into the couch. Her eyes bright, she asked, "When he gets out?"

I told her about the camera and that the judge was reviewing the evidence to decide if it was enough to overturn Ford's guilty plea.

"Of course it is," Quinn said, eyes burning with indignation. "It backs up his alibi and shows he was telling the truth. Why is it taking so long to just let him out? How long has the judge had the camera?"

I wondered for a second if she was going to jump off the couch and go hunt down the judge to demand he let her brother out of prison. "Hold your horses, baby, it's not that simple."

"Why isn't it simple?"

I wanted to kiss her, to hold all that fire close. Quinn was fierce in defense of those she loved. I wasn't jealous. I just wanted to be on the list. "There's some question of where the camera has been all this time, and how it ended up in the pawn shop where Haywood found it. This is a high-profile case. The judge isn't going to rush. And even if Ford gets out, it's complicated."

I wasn't going to mention that Ford might be in more danger outside prison than inside. And I didn't want to remind her that even if Ford was released, Heartstone Manor was Griffen's house now, and he might not welcome home the brother who'd had him exiled. If Griffen let him through the doors, and if Ford was willing to sequester himself in Heartstone Manor until we found his father's killer... But that was a lot of *ifs*.

"When will the judge decide?" she asked.

"No idea. We just have to be patient." Quinn gave an adorable grunt of annoyance. Hoping it would distract her, I said, "I stopped in town on the way home. Sweetheart Bakery was doing one of their pop-up things."

"Quiche?" Quinn asked, raising an eyebrow and licking her lips.

My eyes landed on her wet lower lip, and I wasn't thinking of food anymore, but I answered her question.

"Quiche. Daisy said you like the ham and Swiss the best. And she talked me into these pretzel s'mores things she said we should stick in the microwave for a few seconds before we eat them."

Quinn licked her lips again, sending my brain and my body in one direction and it had nothing to do with food. I was off the couch a second later.

"Where are you going?" Quinn asked.

I hit a few buttons on the oven and shoved the quiches in to warm up. The box said twenty minutes. Just enough time for round one. Striding back to the couch, I scooped up Quinn, ignoring Leo's yowl of annoyance. He'd get his princess back soon enough.

For now, she was all mine, and I was going to make the next twenty minutes count.

Chapter Thirty-Four
QUINN

It was my nose that woke me. Not a smell, but rather that the tip of my nose felt like a block of ice. I was buried beneath the covers, draped over Hawk, his body warm and solid beneath mine.

It took a minute for my brain to get in gear—too many winter mornings waking up in my hammock. It felt so familiar I didn't immediately put together that I was not in a hammock in the woods. I was in the gatehouse, and therefore my nose should not be an ice cube.

My eyes flicked open. I sat up, dislodging Leo, who let out a trill of annoyance and curled up on top of Hawk, glaring down at me. Frigid air invaded our warm cocoon under the blankets, and I immediately regretted moving. *What the hell?*

I lay back down, clutching the blankets close, and looked up to see Hawk's eyes open, watching me with a glint of amusement in their dark depths.

"Heat must have gone out," he said. "I'll go down and check it out."

I didn't argue. It was seriously cold now that I was awake enough to feel the room around me, and unlike when I slept outside in the winter, I was naked under these covers and unprepared for braving the elements. Moments ago I'd been blissfully, comfortably, deliciously naked with Hawk. Now I was trying to figure out how much of the freezing air I'd have to endure before I could pull on some clothes.

Hawk slid out of his side of the bed, and I stayed where I was long enough to watch his gorgeous, tight ass, his broad shoulders, and messy dark hair as he disappeared down the stairs. Hawk was a lot of wonderful things—kind, patient, strong, smart—but on top of all of that, he was one beautifully made man. The second he was out of sight, I dove for the closet, yanking on clean underwear and a camisole, then a set of long underwear. I was reaching for my jeans when I heard Hawk's voice, steady and serious.

"Quinn, we have a problem." He was back up to the bedroom seconds later.

"What?" I asked, my mind going straight to security. Had someone broken in? Was there some threat, a message— "What happened?"

"A pipe under the kitchen sink burst," Hawk said.

I looked down to see his feet were wet. They weren't the first thing I noticed since he was still distractingly naked.

"Wait," I said, pulling my jeans on over my long underwear and wincing at the frigid temperature of the denim. "A pipe burst under the kitchen sink? Why are your feet wet?"

"The whole first floor is under an inch of water." Hawk's tone was so matter-of-fact that the gravity of the situation took a second to sink in.

A burst pipe was one thing. The whole first floor under an inch of water? That was something entirely different. The next steps cascaded through my head. It would take time to repair and clean up. And if the weather was bad enough to burst our pipes, we weren't the only ones, which meant it might take even longer.

Billy Bob, Savannah's cousins Billy and Bob, had become the Sawyers' de facto handymen. There was always so much to do around Heartstone Manor that we kept them busy full-time. Billy Bob could do a little bit of everything, but they weren't plumbers. Unless this was a simple fix—unlikely with an inch of water covering the first floor—we were going to have to wait for the real deal.

I pulled a sweater over my head, the next problem clicking into place. Depending on how long that water had been sitting on the floor, there would likely be more damage than just the busted pipe. We weren't going to be able to stay in the gatehouse. Not for a few days at least, maybe more like a week. Or longer.

I looked up to see Hawk pulling out the duffel bag we'd brought from my room at Heartstone weeks ago and knew he'd already put together the same pieces that I had.

"I'll get dressed," Hawk said. "Throw your stuff in there, and we'll head over to the Manor to figure out what to do."

"Okay," I said, trying not to think about the water covering the floor below and what it meant. I took a minute to brush my teeth, a flutter of anxiety in my chest. I didn't want to leave the gatehouse. I was happy here. I was safe here. I had Hawk and our little nest together, and everything was perfect.

We had Leo— At that thought I turned to Hawk, toothbrush in hand. Taking a second to spit out toothpaste, I said, "Leo— The litter box— He hasn't been able to get to it."

Leo, for his part, didn't look at all concerned. Curled in the middle of our abandoned comforter, he groomed his front paws with deliberate attention, unconcerned that half his home was underwater.

Hawk looked up from where he was shoving clothes into an olive-green rucksack. "I unplugged it when I was downstairs. Looks like the electronics didn't get wet. We'll bring it over to the Manor."

"But—" That flutter of anxiety bloomed, crowding my lungs until my breath caught and my voice died. I wanted to say I wasn't staying in the Manor. *I can't— I won't—*

I couldn't get the words out, but I didn't need to. Hawk's eyes warmed. "We'll figure it out, baby. Okay? We'll figure it out."

"Okay," I said quickly, that flutter in my chest refusing to ease as I thought of my room in the Manor, of staying there with Hawk. Maybe with him I would be able to... *No.*

My stomach turned as my mind filled with the idea of Hawk surrounded by those tainted memories. Hawk, sleeping in that bed. No. Just— *No.*

I finished brushing my teeth, packed my toiletries bag, and filled my duffel bag with my things, my heart growing heavier, my chest tighter as I understood that wherever I was going after this, it would be a while before I came back to the gatehouse. It was Hawk's gatehouse, but I was starting to think of it as my gatehouse too. Ours.

And what if...

I yanked together the sides of my duffel and tugged on the zipper. I needed to chill. This didn't have to be a big deal. I didn't have to stay in the Manor, in that room. I had options.

My father's will forced us to live at Heartstone Manor if we wanted to inherit whatever he'd left for us. Harvey had been generous enough to interpret this as meaning *on Manor grounds* versus *underneath the Manor's roof*, which had given me some leeway for sleeping in the woods and at the hunting cabin. The will also allowed us to be absent from the Manor for fourteen days every quarter.

For those of my siblings who traveled for work, the two-week limit could get a little difficult, but for me, it had never been a problem. My work was here. My friends and family were here. I liked to travel, but I could easily get in a few trips without pushing the limits of the will. I still had the full fourteen days this quarter. We could stay at the inn for the next two weeks. We'd be close enough to the Manor and Sawyer Outdoor Adventures for both of us to work. It was the perfect solution. No big deal. I gave a final tug to the zipper of the duffel and started to lift it.

"Leave it," Hawk said. "I'll get it later." I looked up to see him at the top of the stairs, carrying the enormous electronic litter box.

"Why did you bring that up here?" I asked. "Aren't we taking Leo with us?"

"We have to figure out what we're going to do before we drag Leo out of here, but he needs his litter box. I figured I'd plug it in up here and bring his food and water bowl. He'll be safe and dry while we work out a plan."

"It's too cold," I protested, hating the idea of leaving Leo behind.

Hawk glanced over at Leo, snuggled into our pillows, partly under the comforter. Somehow the big cat managed to take up half of a queen-sized bed, and he looked smugly comfortable. "He's already wearing a fur coat," Hawk said. "We won't leave him here forever. I'll get his food and water while you get your boots on." With a wry smile, he added, "Your regular trail shoes are soaked. You'll have to wear your hiking boots."

I sat on the edge of the bed and pulled on the boots, glad for the extra support for my newly healed ankle. Hawk returned with Leo's food bowl and water. At the dry rustle of his food in the bowl, Leo's head popped up. The second the bowl touched the floor, he stood, gave a luxuriant stretch, and leaped off the bed in the direction of his breakfast.

"See? He's fine," Hawk said. "Once we know what we're going to do, we'll come back and get him."

I followed Hawk down the stairs, noticing for the first time that he wasn't wearing his normal boots. These were dark brown, well-worn, and looked waterproof. At the bottom of the steps, he grabbed my parka off the hook by the door and handed it to me. When I had it on and zipped, he reached for me.

"I'm carrying you over," he said. "It's wet in here and icy out there. I don't want to risk your ankle now that it's finally better."

I nodded, struck momentarily silent by the sight of the first floor, covered in a layer of icy water. It was soaking into the cabinets and the flooring, just touching the bottom of the couch. We'd been so warm upstairs under the comforter that I had no idea when this had happened, but from the look of things it had been hours ago. Hours for icy water to soak into everything, to freeze — I couldn't calculate the amount of damage we might be looking at.

Hawk let out a short huff of breath, almost amused. "Well, Parker's going to be happy. She finally has her excuse to get her hands on the gatehouse." He wrapped an arm around my back. "Look at it this way—by the time we move back to this place, Parker will have brought it into the current century. At the least, we'll have a decent kitchen and a bigger bathroom."

I was still processing the "when we move back in" as Hawk swung me into his arms. My cheek pressed to his shoulder, my thoughts racing.

Hawk pulled open the front door and water spilled down the steps. So much water. We stood there, watching it run out in a flood, until it had mostly drained away and we could shut the door behind us.

In theory, I absolutely wanted Parker to get her hands on the gatehouse. I'd seen what she'd done with

Savannah and Finn's cottage. It had been all peeling linoleum and chipped paint, with ancient appliances and a stained ceiling. Parker had stayed on time and under budget and still managed to give Savannah a jewel of a cottage.

She had marble countertops and a gas fireplace in the bedroom upstairs. There was plenty of room for Savannah and Finn, and Nicky had his own bedroom and bathroom on the first floor. The place was beautiful. And Parker wasn't just good at renovations. She was great at decorating. Every little piece in the cottage had been a perfect fit for Savannah, and for Finn when he'd moved in after their wedding.

I knew Parker would do the same to the gatehouse, and I knew I'd love it when she was done. The gatehouse needed the work, and Hawk deserved better than a shabby, out-of-date place to call home. I wanted all of that, and apparently Hawk did too. It sounded like he wanted it for us. Together. I loved that idea, that the gatehouse would officially be *our* gatehouse. And yet—

Repairing the water damage and renovating the gatehouse was going to take time. The terms of the will only gave me fourteen days. *Maybe*— I thought of the cabin. *Maybe*— I closed my eyes to block the sight of Heartstone Manor looming closer and closer, listened to the crunch of Hawk's feet on cold stone as he carried me up the path to the house, my nose stinging from the damp, freezing air.

There must have been sleet in the night. The grass and trees were glazed with a layer of sparkling ice. The sky was still overcast, but the sleet and rain had thinned.

It wasn't so much coming down as hanging in the air like an icy fog. Despite Hawk's warmth and my winter parka, it was cold. The heat of the Manor was more than welcome by the time Hawk carefully navigated the slick front steps, set me down, and unlocked the front door.

Chapter Thirty-Five
QUINN

We found the family assembled in the dining room. Usually, both Royal and Tenn were long gone at this hour. I didn't see Royal, Daisy, or Avery—Royal would have braved the roads to get Daisy to Sweetheart Bakery, and Avery would have hitched a ride, wanting to check on her brewery. But Tenn was still working his way through a pile of pancakes beside Scarlett, August, Thatcher, and Nicky.

Griffen and Hope were at the head of the table, Hope holding baby Stella, with Parker and Nash beside her. Aunt Ophelia and Nash's mother, Claudia, were probably still in bed, but Sterling was there, sipping her coffee with an empty plate in front of her.

Clearly, we weren't the only ones for whom the weather had turned everything upside down. "No school?" Hawk asked, setting me on my feet.

"No school!" Nicky and August shouted. Teenage Thatcher didn't join them in their cheer, but a smug smile curved his mouth.

Scarlett shook her head at the kids. "The roads are still icy everywhere, and it doesn't look like it's going to warm up any time soon, so they canceled school."

Tenn leaned back, sliding his arm around Scarlett's shoulders, and said, "Royal managed to make it in with Daisy and Avery, but they all may end up staying with Daisy's Grams tonight if the roads don't improve." He gave us a long look, studying Hawk's arm around my waist. "What brings you two here so early?"

"Heat went out in the middle of the night," Hawk said, his eyes moving from Tenn to Griffen. "A pipe under the kitchen sink burst. The whole first floor flooded." Hawk looked to Parker. "Looks like you're up. I don't think this will be a quick fix."

A gleeful grin spread across Parker's face and she clapped her hands. "Finally! Once Quinn moved in, I figured I'd never get you two out of there long enough to get any real work done."

"I think there's a lot of damage," I said, my chest aching with the wrongness of it all. I wanted to be happy for Parker. I loved seeing her smile like that, but all I wanted was to go back to how things were yesterday. I wanted to go home, but home was soaking wet and slowly freezing.

Not knowing I had reason to be upset, Parker just shrugged. "It needed a new floor and a new kitchen anyway. I'll go over a little later and check it out, talk to Billy Bob and the plumbers to see where we need to start."

Nash nudged Parker's side with an affectionate smile.

"I've never seen anybody so happy to hear about a burst pipe and extensive water damage."

Parker laughed and rubbed her hands together. "I have a whole notebook of plans for the gatehouse. Detailed plans. Half of the stuff has been ordered and is sitting in storage, waiting."

Hawk snorted in amusement at this, and I smiled out of habit, but my mind was elsewhere. I didn't want to be in the Manor any longer than I had to, and that was just fucking depressing.

Oblivious, Parker went on. "We'll need to talk colors and furniture, but you two can just move into Quinn's room and I'll get started."

I didn't hear anything after that. I saw Parker's mouth moving and felt Hawk's arm tighten around my waist, but everything inside me went numb.

No, no, no, no, no.

I didn't realize I was saying it out loud. Hawk's arm tightened even more, and he gave me a little shake, turning me to face him. "Quinn. Quinn."

I snapped out of it and stared up at him, my lips pressed together tightly so another sound wouldn't escape. I caught a low whimper and realized it was me.

"Quinn," Hawk repeated, "it's okay."

"Hawk," I whispered, ignoring the curious eyes in the room, focused only on him. "I can't." My chest was tight, and I couldn't think.

Since the day I'd had to move back to Heartstone, I'd been dealing with this, dreading being in my room and doing anything I could to be anywhere else. But now— I didn't know if it was being attacked in the woods or knowing someone was out there waiting for another chance at me, watching me. Or maybe it was finally talking about the past with Hawk, or Hawk going to see Ford. Maybe it was falling in love with Hawk, being vulnerable and open with him in a way I hadn't been with anyone else. Or it was that all of it was happening at the same time. Whatever it was, lately I'd tilted straight from *handling it* into *no fucking way*, and I had no idea how to tilt myself back.

All of a sudden, it was too much. I wasn't going in that room. I couldn't let the past taint me and this new life I was living.

"Hawk, what's the problem?" Griffen asked from across the room.

Hawk pulled me in close, whispering, "We'll figure this out, Quinn. I promise."

I felt my body shaking against him. I fucking hated every second of this. I wasn't weak. I didn't want my family to see, to know, but— I shook harder, the pressure of their eyes too much. I couldn't—

"Quinn can't stay in her room," Hawk said flatly.

I heard Scarlett cut in, saying in a soft voice, "Boys, you done with breakfast?" A pause I imagined was filled with nods. "Why don't you three leave the table and go get into some trouble? And Thatcher? Please ask Savannah to come up. I think we need her organizational skills." Chairs pushed back from the table.

I lifted my head to look at Griffen. I was a grown woman. I didn't need Hawk to speak for me. My voice tight, I forced out the words. "I can't, Griffen. I won't stay there. We'll go stay at the inn for two weeks, and when my two weeks is up—"

"No," Hawk said. "That's not an option."

I pulled back enough to look up at him. "Why not? I haven't used any of my days for the will. Why can't we just—"

"It's not secure," Griffen said, answering for Hawk. "Just because there hasn't been a direct attack in the last few weeks doesn't mean you're out of danger, and it's impossible to secure the inn as well as we can the Manor. It's not safe."

I bit my lip hard to keep myself from shouting out my frustration. Squeezing my eyes shut, I tried to tell myself I was okay. Everything was okay. I could handle this.

I could tell myself that all day, but my brain and my body weren't buying it. My heart was racing. I could feel myself shaking, and I thought I was about to throw up. Everyone in the dining room was quiet. So quiet. And I knew they didn't understand. No one understood. They probably thought I was crazy.

I raised my eyes a fraction and looked across the table to see Sterling, her gaze heavy with pain. Her eyes flicked to Parker's and then back to mine. "Quinn," she breathed, her voice barely audible, "it was him, wasn't it? Dad's creepy friend." A tear welled and dripped over her eyelid to streak down her cheek. "Is that why? Did he—?"

I shook my head violently, squeezing my eyes shut. I couldn't bear the agony on her face, her tears. None of this was Sterling's fault. She'd been a child. More of a child than me.

"What are you two talking about?" Tenn asked, his voice gruff.

Parker answered, her words coming slowly as if she was reluctant to speak them aloud. "Dad had a friend. A business partner. He would come to stay here. And he had—" She stopped, searching for words. "He had an interest in Quinn. There was talk of him marrying her when she was of age, but I didn't think it was serious. I didn't think—"

I couldn't stand the desperate expression in her eyes, the guilt on her face. I shook my head, but she kept going.

"Quinn?" Parker said, my name a plea. "You never said— I didn't know. How didn't I know?" Nash reached out to take her hand, and I looked away.

I wanted to run. I wanted to rip myself out of Hawk's arms and just fucking run until I couldn't run anymore. It happened. I survived. I didn't want to fucking revisit it. I didn't want to explain it to anybody. I didn't want to talk about my fucking feelings. My frightened, bitter, repulsive feelings. I just wanted it to fucking go away. Why couldn't it just go away?

"Quinn?" Griffen prompted, his green eyes shattered.

Of all things, I couldn't stand the fear I saw in his eyes. I knew what he must be imagining. It had been bad, but it could have been worse, and I couldn't let my family imagine things that hadn't happened. Squeezing my eyes shut tight, I lifted a hand and brushed away my tears, straightening and stepping the smallest bit away from Hawk. I needed to stand on my own two feet for this.

"He would come into my room at night," I said, my

eyes on Griffen because I couldn't bear to look at anyone else. I paused, trying to gather my thoughts. I needed to tell them, but saying the words out loud was torturous. I didn't want them to see me differently, to see me as a victim, but I was so fucking tired of letting the past control me, no matter how impossible it felt to break free.

I kept going, my words coming in hesitant jerks, tangling in my mouth as I told them about the man in the dark. I couldn't reassure them fast enough. I just wanted everyone to stop looking at me with those guilty, pitying faces.

"I'm fine," I said again, loud enough to fill the thick silence. "I'm fine now. I'm past it," I said, "but I'm not sleeping in that room."

Chapter Thirty-Six
QUINN

"Are you okay with being in the Manor?" Hope asked gently. "As long as you don't have to go in your room?"

I tried to think about that. "I can handle being in the Manor," I said. "When I'm not in my room, I can forget, mostly. I don't think about it. When I'm in my room, it's all I can—" I stopped short. I didn't want to keep talking about this. I'd never wanted all of them to know, and now that they did, I was done.

"You can't stay at the inn," Griffen said. "And the hunting cabin—" He shook his head. "Aside from it being too far out to be practical to live in, it's also too hard to secure. But you don't have to go in that room again, Quinn. Not ever. This is a fucking forty-thousand-square-foot house. We'll find another option."

"What if you take my room?" Finn asked. I shifted to see Finn and Savannah standing in the doorway to the butler's pantry. They must have come straight up when Thatcher got to the kitchen.

"What do you mean?" I asked.

"I moved into the cottage with Savannah and Nicky," Finn said. "I took all the stuff I wanted out of the room. It's just sitting there. It's a totally different layout than your room, different colors, and it's on the opposite side of the hall, so it has a different view. And it's closer to the head of the stairs, so you wouldn't even have to go past your old room. It would need new furniture, but—" He looked at Savannah. "There's stuff in the attics, right?"

"Plenty," she said. "We could probably furnish this house another time over with everything that's in the attics." Savannah tilted her head to the side, thinking. "Finn's room has those dark blue walls with white trim, and that pretty rug with the vines woven in it. More Quinn's style than Finn's anyway." She looked to Parker. "There's that sofa we've been trying to figure out what to do with." She looked at me. "It's a twin to the one in the gatehouse, in the same lovely mustard green." She rolled her eyes.

"Do you think that would work?" Hope asked, and the understanding in her eyes nearly broke me.

"I don't know," I said as honestly as I could. "But I think I should try."

Tenn pushed back his chair and stood. "None of us has anything to do for the next few hours. I bet we can get everything switched out while you two pack your stuff."

"It's already packed," Hawk said. "But let's go upstairs and take a look. Then maybe you," he said, looking down at me, "can go with Parker to the attics and see what you like." Quietly, too low for anyone to overhear, Hawk said, "Do you want this? If you don't, we'll figure out something else."

Truthfully, I wasn't sure this would work. Could it really be as simple as moving down the hall into another room? But there were two very good reasons I had to try. First, Heartstone Manor was my home. I didn't want that creepy asshole, that nightmare from my childhood, to scare me away for the rest of my life. This was my house, not his. My family was here, and I didn't want to be afraid anymore. I wanted a place under this roof, and my family was ready to give it to me. I had to try.

And second, Griffen and Hawk were right. Heartstone Manor was the safest place in Sawyers Bend. Safer than the gatehouse. Far safer than the cabin or the inn. This wasn't over. It wouldn't be over until we caught the man who'd attacked me. And I had a lot to live for. I'd always had a lot to live for, but now I had Hawk. We had a cat. We had a life. I was in love with him. I was pretty sure he was in love with me. He definitely seemed happy to keep me around. I wasn't going to risk any of it by getting myself killed. Not out of fear.

"I don't know if I can do it," I said in a whisper. "But I can try. I want to try."

Hawk wrapped his arms around me, tucking me into his chest, my forehead against his warm neck. "We'll try," he said in my ear. "And if it doesn't work, we'll figure out something else. Okay?"

"Okay," I whispered.

Hawk's arms tightened around me before he let me go. "All right," he said to the room. "Let's go do some decorating."

I let out a surprised laugh at words I never thought I'd hear out of Hawk's mouth.

Parker stood and sprung into action. She'd always been organized, smart, and had great taste, even when we were kids. But until Griffen put her in charge of renovations around the estate, I'd never seen her bossy side. Not like this. She was a pint-sized general.

To Savannah, she said, "Why don't you direct traffic upstairs while I take Quinn to go through the furniture options."

"I'm on it," Savannah said, heading for the stairs.

Parker rounded the table, stopping in front of me and Hawk. "I'll get the gatehouse done as quickly as I can," she said to me, her eyes brimming with fresh tears.

I leaned in to hug her tight. "I know you will. Don't cry, Parker. Please. You weren't even here."

"Not at the end," she said quietly, "but I was here when it started. I should have seen it was more. I should have—"

"Please, don't take this on, Parker. It's not your fault. The only ones to blame are Prentice and his asshole friend."

She shook her head, wiping away her tears. "I'm going to make you a sanctuary in Finn's room. In your new room. It's bigger than yours, and the bathroom is in decent shape." She wiped at her face again and looked at Hawk. "I have a few beds upstairs, but they're all queens, and I don't have a decent queen mattress available, or extra bedding. Can you and Griffen bring that stuff over from the gatehouse? Quinn and I will go to the attic and pick what she likes."

"We're on it," Hawk said after giving me a long look to make sure I was all right.

I wasn't sure if I was, but I was willing to follow Parker to the attics and see how it went. I nodded, and he left, meeting Griffen in the front hall.

Parker turned to Nash, Tenn, and Finn. "You three can empty Finn's room. Savannah will show you where to store his things." Her eyes swept up Sterling, Hope, Scarlett, and me. "Let's go help Quinn pick a bed. And I think the armoire. Or maybe the bookshelf—"

We followed her up to the attics, listening to her mumble furniture options as she climbed the stairs. Before I knew it, we were in front of a stack of disassembled beds leaning against a wall in one of the attic storage rooms.

"These are all queens," Parker said. "I think the black iron would look good, but—" She pulled on the black iron frame, leaning it away from a wooden frame behind it. "I think this might be more your style."

She revealed a bed that looked like it was made of tree limbs. The headboard was tall, framed in bark-covered logs about three inches in diameter and filled with narrower, peeled limbs crisscrossing to fill the space. I reached out to touch, expecting to find the wood delicate, but it was strong under my fingers.

"It has a low footboard, so there's plenty of room to stretch out. And there's a matching desk, armoire, and bookcase. When I found it, I thought of you," Parker said.

"It's beautiful," Sterling said, reaching out to run a finger over the lacquered bark. "Why is it up here?"

Parker shrugged. "I don't know. I guess someone decided it's too rustic for the house, but—"

"I love it," I said. Whoever had banished it to the attics was right, it was too rustic for Heartstone. But so was I. And I knew Hawk would love it, too.

"Perfect. Then let's go look at some artwork. Finn still has all those posters on the walls." Parker wrinkled her nose. There was no world in which Parker thought posters tacked up on the walls was appropriate decor. "Hope and I found some beautiful landscapes of the mountains. And one of a fox I think you'll love."

By the time we were done selecting the paintings, a few end tables and a desk chair, Finn, Tenn, and Nash had the room empty of everything but the rug. Savannah was running the vacuum when we came in, our arms filled with everything we could carry down on the first trip. I only flinched a little as I turned down the hall, my eyes skipping to my old bedroom door, barely seeing it from Finn's room. No, not Finn's room. *My* room.

I stopped beside Savannah. When she turned off the vacuum, I said, quietly enough that no one heard under Parker giving orders, "Later, can you have someone empty my room? I want it erased. A blank slate. Can you—?"

Savannah gave me a quick hug. "Absolutely. I won't throw any of your things away. I'll pack those up in case you want them someday. But I'll get rid of the furniture, the rug, and the drapes, and paint the walls. Is that good?"

I nodded. The idea of it lightened the weight on my

heart. I wanted that furniture, that bed, out of the house, somewhere far, far away. "Thank you," I said.

In answer, Savanah just gave me another hug.

Parker stood beside the doorway, pointing and calling out orders as Finn, Tenn, Griffen, and Hawk carried, arranged, and assembled. It wasn't long before they had the bed set up with our mattress and bedding from the gatehouse. The couch was, in fact, identical to the one we'd left behind, just as Parker and Savannah had said. The mustardy green velvet was as ugly as its twin, but it felt like home.

The room was more than big enough, with plenty of space for the bed, the couch, and a coffee table, along with an area for the desk and bookcase and an armoire for extra storage. Not that we'd need it. The closet was huge in comparison to the gatehouse, and the bathroom was three times the size.

I unpacked our things while my sisters and the guys hung the paintings. Someone found a small flat-screen television somewhere and set it up where we could watch it from the couch. I emerged from organizing our toiletries in the bathroom to find Griffen carrying in the huge litter box, Hawk just behind him, Leo's travel crate in one hand and his food bowls in the other. Tenn brought up the rear, his arms overflowing with bags of litter and cat food.

"Close the door," Hawk said, setting Leo's crate on the floor. "Leo's going to have to stay in here until we introduce him to Shadow and make sure they'll be friends."

"Why?" Sterling asked. Her Shadow wasn't quite a kitten anymore, but she wasn't a fully grown cat.

In answer, once the bedroom door was closed, Hawk let Leo out. He stuck his head out and swung it from side to side, glaring at so much company. Spotting me, he let out an annoyed trill. Seeing Leo here in this new place, I took a deep breath, the tightness in my chest gone, at least for the moment.

"Come here, Leo," I said, spreading my arms and leaning down. "Let me show you your new home."

He picked his way across the rug and sprang into my arms, sending me back half a step.

"I thought you said you got a cat, not a mountain lion," Finn said, barely holding back laughter. "He could eat Shadow in one bite."

Leo leaned into me, purring, butting my chin with the top of his head before squirming to jump down and explore. He followed Hawk to where he'd set up his litter box by the bathroom, his food and water on the opposite side of the room.

"He seems bigger over here," Sterling murmured, giving Leo a cautious look. They'd met, but Sterling was right. The high ceilings and open spaces of the gatehouse fit Leo's size. Heartstone had high ceilings, but not like the gatehouse. In here, Leo looked more like his namesake. "We'll introduce the cats slowly," she said.

I wanted to promise her Leo wouldn't munch on Shadow, but the truth was I had no idea how Leo would react to the smaller cat. Better to keep them apart for now.

I spotted Savannah talking to Parker. The next thing

I knew, Parker was clapping her hands for silence. "What do you think?" she asked me.

"I love it," I said honestly. I wasn't sure how I'd feel come bedtime, but so far so good. "Thank you, guys."

"We love you, and that's what we're here for," Parker said. "Now, I need some more muscle before I call Billy Bob and start talking about the gatehouse." Her eyes came to me and Hawk. "You two stay in here for at least a half hour. Make yourselves at home in your new place. We have a little more work to do. Let's go, everybody."

We watched them all file out behind her. "Your sister is seriously bossy," Hawk said. "Makes me want to hire her. She gets shit done."

"I know. But I don't think she'd work for you. She's so good at this." We looked around the room, taking in the rustic hickory bedroom set, the familiar couch, the view of our gatehouse. "I think this is going to work," I said, and I almost believed it. I wanted to believe it. Everything felt different. I felt different. Free. Whole. New.

"Where did they go?" Hawk asked. "And why can't we leave?"

"They're clearing out my old room," I said. It would take time to repaint, to pack my childhood things, but I knew in my gut that the furniture, that hated bed, would be gone before the thirty minutes was up. "Savannah knows I don't want to watch. I just want it all gone."

"Your family loves you," Hawk said.

"I know." We watched Leo sniff around the couch before jumping up and stretching out on the velvet as if it was his throne.

"You think they'll really leave us alone for a half

hour?" Hawk asked, closing the small distance between us.

"I think so," I said, tilting my head back to meet his eyes, my chest warming at the heat I saw there.

"Good," Hawk said, dropping his head to brush his lips across mine. "Because I had plans for this morning, and that busted pipe got in the way."

"Really?" I asked, reaching up to wind my arms around his neck. "What kind of plans?"

"Naked plans," he said, taking my mouth in a kiss that spun my head, his hands sliding under my camisole and up my back.

"I like naked plans," I said when his mouth moved to my jaw and lower, to suck at that tender spot where my neck met my shoulder. Reaching down, I grabbed the hem of my sweater, catching all my layers at once. I leaned away from Hawk and whipped my clothes over my head. "Do you think you guys tightened all the screws on that bed frame well enough?" I asked with a teasing grin.

"Let's find out." Hawk lifted me off my feet, carrying me to the bed.

He tossed me on top of the comforter, and I bounced, but the bed didn't move an inch. Pausing to lock the door, Hawk came back, tearing off his clothes as he crossed to the bed. His shirt gone, he unsnapped my jeans and stripped me naked, his face lighting in a wide smile.

"I love you," he said, his words quiet and filled with truth.

My heart burst with joy. I didn't know what I'd done to deserve this man, but I wasn't letting him go. I reached for him, but he was already coming down on top of me, his strong body surrounding me in safety and setting me on fire. I pulled him closer until our eyes were only inches apart. "I love you too, Hawk."

He kissed me, giving me his heart with every touch, every breath. After, we dozed, the feel of the bed familiar even in this new place. This time, we woke with warm noses to Leo standing on top of us, demanding his dinner.

Later, after a meal with my family, where Hawk was quiet and everyone else acted mostly normal, we went to bed early. I lay awake for a while, waiting for the fear, the heavy dread to drag me down, but it didn't come. There was a flash of nerves as we turned down the hall and I caught sight of my old door, but then we were in our new room, and it was nothing like the past. Tired, I turned into Hawk's arms, my cheek on his shoulder.

"You okay?" he asked, stroking his hand down my hair.

"I think I am," I said. Sliding my arm across his chest, I held him tight before relaxing against him and letting out a long breath. "I think I've never been better."

Chapter Thirty-Seven
HAWK

Five minutes before my alarm was set to go off, my eyes opened. I was used to waking up before my alarm. I still wasn't used to waking up with Quinn. She lay draped over me, her silky hair teasing my chin, her legs tangled with mine. We'd been sleeping in her new room in Heartstone Manor for a little over a week. So far, it was working out.

Quinn still flinched at the top of the stairs whenever she caught sight of the door that had been hers. But after the first few days, the flinch was almost unnoticeable, and once she was in her new room she mostly seemed to forget there was anything to be afraid of. Twice since we'd moved back into the Manor, she'd woken in the night with a jerk, her breath coming fast, heart pounding against her ribs. Both times she shook off the nightmare, turning to me in the dark, her body warm and welcoming, her mouth seeking mine.

I loved touching Quinn whenever I had the chance. Touching her, making her come. Feeling her slick, tight heat around my cock. Hearing her soft moans in my ear. I loved all of it. But beyond the physical, it was this. Her trust. That she knew I was her safety. I was the big bad thing that scared off her nightmares. And she was mine. I'd give everything just to have her as she was now, at peace in my arms.

Peace never lasted long. Now that her ankle was healed enough to go back to work, she'd booked a handful of light hikes and easy fishing trips. Nothing on technical terrain, and so far, nothing longer than a half day. She was easing back into things, wary of overtaxing her ankle and slowing her recovery. Plus, until we caught the guy who'd attacked her, messed with our security system, and broke into Sawyer Outdoor Adventures, Quinn was on board with my decree that she wasn't going anywhere by herself.

I'd been at her side since she'd been back to work, tagging along for a waterfall hike and picnic and a few fly-fishing trips. Watching her work had been an education. Quinn could answer any question about her mountains, and she loved sharing her knowledge with her clients, loved watching them laugh and have fun. She'd found her calling, and she was amazing at it.

I glanced at the clock. It was almost time for her to get out there and be amazing. I rolled to my side, taking Quinn with me, smoothing her hair back from her face as she resettled on her back.

"Time to get up, baby," I murmured against her lips.

I loved the look in her eyes as her lids fluttered open and sleep cleared from the blue depths. In those first moments, she was completely unguarded, and the warmth that flooded her eyes when they met mine made me feel like I could conquer the world.

Quinn's smile was sleepy, her hand coming up to cup my cheek. "It's still dark," she said like she always did.

I felt my lips curve as I smiled down at her. "It'll be light soon enough." I thought about kissing her, but I knew better.

In an hour and a half, she'd have a line of clients outside Sawyer Outdoor Adventures expecting a half-day waterfall hike and picnic. She and Sterling had prepped the picnic supplies the day before, but they still had to pack the food, get releases signed, and take care of all of the various things they did to deliver a top-notch experience.

I took a risk and dipped my head to stroke my lips over hers, loving the way she arched into me.

"Later," she whispered, a wicked glint in her blue eyes. "After the hike. We'll need a shower. And maybe a nap. A long, naked nap." She reached up to press a quick kiss to my chin before she rolled out of the bed.

I stayed where I was, watching her walk to the bathroom, the camisole she'd slept in just barely grazing the top of her sweetly curved ass. I looked my fill before sliding out of bed and straightening the covers. Soon enough we'd be back from the hike, and I could strip her naked and talk her into a long, lazy bath instead of that shower. It turned out that the claw-foot, cast-iron tub in her bathroom was more than big enough for two, a fact we'd taken advantage of a few days before. I was ready for a repeat.

The tub would have to wait for now. It was time to get moving.

The long table in the dining room was sparsely occupied at just past seven in the morning. Griffen sat at the head, chewing on a piece of toast, his infant daughter at his chest in a baby carrier, fast asleep. I guessed Hope was also asleep upstairs in their bed. Tenn sat beside August, Thatcher, and Nicky. From the empty plate beside Tenn, I guessed Scarlett had shoved some food in her mouth and headed down to her glass workshop on the lower level to get an early start. Sterling was in her place at the far end, staring into her coffee cup, her eyes half closed. In the last week, I'd learned that Sterling was never fully awake until after her second cup of coffee.

Griffen looked up as we entered, his free hand coming up to rub the sleeping baby's back through the carrier. "You have a hike today?" he asked, keeping his voice low.

"The waterfall again," Quinn said. "Another picnic. I've got some repeats on this one. It should be a good group."

That was all anyone said, aside from the kids bickering on the other side of the table about some game they'd played with their classmates. Quinn and I filled our plates at the buffet and ate. I still wasn't used to sitting at the long, formal table in the family dining room. I wasn't family—I was help. Griffen wouldn't have liked the distinction, but he was the boss, and he could afford to blur those lines. A few months ago, it was my hill to die on. There was family, and there was help. No one crossed the line. Full stop.

Then Finn had married Savannah, smashing through any line that might keep them apart. And I'd fallen fully, completely, and helplessly in love with Quinn. And somehow, she seemed to think she loved me back. There was no way I was going to ask her to hide away in the kitchens to eat when she wanted to be with her family. And I knew without asking that if I tried to leave her in the formal dining room and take my place belowstairs, she'd march down and drag me back to her side. Since *at her side* was exactly where I wanted to be, my only choice was to let it go.

Apparently, family and help could mix without the world imploding. Prentice Sawyer was probably rolling over in his grave, but that wouldn't bother anyone here.

Quinn was sipping the last of her coffee when my phone beeped, the distinctive ping of the Heartstone security system. I straightened, looking down at the screen and tapping the still frame from one of the cameras. It was a shot of the trail to the hunting cabin, one of the new cameras we'd installed after the attack. I wasn't sure what I expected to see. A bear, or maybe a buck. It had to be something big to set off the camera's alert. There was nothing there but an empty trail.

Before I could call Kane to check it out, my phone pinged a second time, this one in Quinn's clearing. Another of the new cameras. And again, it showed nothing.

"Everything okay?" Griffen asked, his voice still pitched low enough not to disturb the sleeping baby in his arms.

"I don't know," I said slowly, tapping yet another alert, this one a tamper alarm at the gate.

My screen flashed a message from Kane.

> Are you seeing this? Looks like the same as before.

I didn't have a chance to answer before my phone rang with a call from Lucas Jackson.

"Jackson," I said.

"I left him an opening," Lucas said, "and he waltzed right in."

"Same guy?" I asked.

"Looks like it," Lucas confirmed. "Same method of entry into the system. This time we were ready for him."

"Who is it?" I asked, more than ready to end this for good.

"Don't know," Lucas said, "but I do know where he is. I traced the IP address. Does 752 Main Street mean anything to you? Why have I heard that address before?"

Holy shit. "That's Harvey Benson's office. The Sawyer family lawyer."

"Didn't you add coverage to his office?" Lucas asked.

"Office and home, yeah. But I didn't get an alert coming from either place. Only within the boundaries of the estate. You sure it's coming from Harvey's office?"

"I'm sure," Lucas confirmed.

"One second." I pulled up the cameras on Harvey's home and office. Nothing. Nothing on the cameras, nothing tripping the sensors. I lifted the phone back to my ear. "I'm not showing anything unusual," I said. "Could he be spoofing the IP address?"

"It's possible," Lucas admitted. "Whoever he is, this guy is good. But still, I doubt it. I'd get that police chief of yours over to Harvey's office. My guess is our guy is there. Or he was."

"I'll keep you posted," I said before I hung up. I immediately called West, looking up to meet Griffen's eyes and raising a finger. He nodded, by all appearances relaxed as he sipped his coffee. I'd known him long enough to spot the tension in his shoulders.

"Yeah," West answered with a grunt. I caught the rustle of wind against the phone mic and guessed he was either out for a run or on his way into the station. I was hoping it was option number two. I filled him in.

West huffed out a breath, clearly like me, equal parts excited to catch this fucker and confused about the end game. "I'll be there in less than ten," West said. "I'll call Harvey on my way and make sure he's not planning on coming in early. Where are you?"

"At Heartstone with Quinn," I said. "We're about to head into town. She has a hike this morning with clients. We need to get moving. Keep me posted."

"I will. Don't leave town without hearing from me," West said.

"I won't." I hung up again, looking up to see every eye on me, all of them filled with a combination of worry and curiosity, except Griffen. He looked like he was ready to tear off someone's head with his bare hands. I knew that look. Griffen had been fierce in defense of our clients when we'd worked together. That was nothing compared to the way he felt about keeping his family safe. He'd lost them for years. The idea that he might lose any of them again, that someone might threaten his wife or his daughter, was untenable.

And suddenly it occurred to me exactly how much Griffen trusted me. Like Quinn's, his trust humbled me. It was everything. When I'd been at my lowest, Griffen had been there. We weren't blood, but he was my family all the same, which made the Sawyers mine. Nothing was going to happen to this family. One way or another, this had to end.

"Is Chief West going to get the bad guy?" August asked, his eyes wide.

"Chief West always gets the bad guy," Sterling said, sending August a wink. "That's why he's the police chief."

"He's on it," I assured the kids. "If the bad guy is there, Chief West will get him."

"Do you think this is him?" Quinn asked.

"We don't know yet." I glanced at Griffen, then back to Quinn. "We need to head into town. You have a hike in less than an hour." I leaned forward to catch Sterling's eye. "You'll ride with us. Gives me less to keep track of." She nodded, standing to push back her chair.

Quinn did the same. "Let's get moving. Maybe West will call with good news."

"Keep your eyes open out there," Griffen said.

Quinn gave him a grin and a salute. "I always do," she said.

She did. I'd been impressed by how at ease and comfortable Quinn was in the woods. But even with that, she was always alert, always careful. She respected the environment as much as she loved it.

We rode to town in silence, Quinn's eyes bouncing between the dark screen of my phone and the trees flashing by the windows. We were pulling in to park behind the bungalow that housed Sawyer Outdoor Adventures when West called back.

"We got him," West said, a note of relief in his voice. "The deputy's putting on the cuffs now. Guy fits your description, right down to how he's dressed. Brown camo versus white, but that makes sense since the snow is gone."

"What was he doing when you caught him?" I asked.

"The back door was open and he was tearing Harvey's desk apart. Not like before. This was messy in the extreme. He was yanking out drawers and tossing them, tore the cushions off the sofa. The laptop on the desk was open. I'm sending you a pic of the screen. I can't interpret it, but maybe Jackson can."

My phone chimed with a text, and the picture filled the screen. The background was a generic field of grass under blue sky, but open in the center was a black window filled with white text. Lines of what looked like code. I wasn't a hacker any more than West was. I knew the basics, enough to handle the security systems we designed and monitored at Sinclair Security, but as I zoomed in on the picture, I knew this was far above my pay grade.

"I'm forwarding it to Jackson," I said.

Thirty seconds later, I got a text in return.

> I can follow it right up to where I booted his ass out. I don't know why he set up in the lawyer's office to do it, but whoever broke into the system was using that laptop.

I relayed Lucas's message to West, who said, "We've got him on breaking and entering at a minimum. I'm going to bring him in and see if we can get him to talk. Where are you now?"

"I'm at Sawyer Outdoor Adventures." I looked up to see Quinn striding forward, her hand out to shake that of a middle-aged man. A woman around his age stood beside him, the pair flanked by two kids, a boy and a girl who looked like they might be twins. "Quinn's first set of clients is here."

"Look," West said, "can you put some of your team on Quinn for this hike? You two are the only ones who've seen this guy face-to-face. You've heard his voice. Fought with him. I need to question him, and since Quinn is otherwise occupied, I want you observing."

I'd been focused on Quinn for so long my knee-jerk reaction was to tell him no, that I wasn't leaving her side. But I had to use my brain. All signs pointed to this being our guy. Only Quinn and I could ID him, and I wasn't going to ask her to cancel her trip and come into the station to look this man in the eye. She'd been through enough at his hands already. I had extra people on the team since Lucas's visit. We could spare two people to guard her, and I wanted to see this guy myself. It wasn't that I didn't trust West—he was smart and damn good at his job. But as he'd said, I'd fought this guy. If we had him, I needed see him with my own eyes.

"I'll be there in twenty minutes," I said. "As soon as I get things settled here."

"Meet me at the station," West said and hung up.

Sterling stood behind me, her platinum hair back in a utilitarian braid, her eyes bright with curiosity. "Did West get him?"

"It looks like it," I said. "Hold on a second." I called Kane. "West has the guy. It looks like he's a match, but we want to make sure. Can you send Holly and James?" They'd come in with Lucas, and they were top-notch. Moving to the back of the building, out of sight of the arriving clients, I continued, "I want them to join the hike like they're just another pair of tourists so they can keep an eye on Quinn and Sterling."

"You don't think West has our man?" Kane asked.

I thought it was highly likely, but I'd been burned before. Badly. "He checks all the boxes, especially when we add in the code Lucas recognized on the laptop on Harvey's desk. But—"

"You don't want to count your chickens," Kane finished.

"Not when Quinn is at stake," I said.

"I'll have them there in fifteen. Keep me posted."

"Will do," I said. I shoved the phone in my pocket and glanced around for Quinn.

She was smiling at two older men wearing hiking pants and carrying trekking poles. I caught her eye and she excused herself, heading to the back of the shop.

"Everybody's here," she said. "I think we're almost ready to go. Did you hear from West? Was it the guy?"

I didn't want to crush the light in her eyes, but I couldn't bring myself to shade the truth and give her the *yes* she wanted. I wasn't going to lie to Quinn. "We think so," I said. "He looks good for it, but West needs me to come in. I'm the only one other than you who's seen the guy in person."

"Do I need to go with you?" Quinn asked, her eyes dimming as they flicked to the clients clustered in the front of the shop, some of them rifling through the goods she'd restocked. "I don't want to cancel, but if West needs me—"

"I'll go now so I can observe while West questions the guy. There'll be plenty of time for you to come in after the hike if he needs you. Holly and James are headed in. You remember them?"

Quinn smiled. "Yeah, they're great. Are they going to pretend to be clients?"

"Yes. I wouldn't leave you if I didn't think it was safe. I just need to be sure." I ran my hand down her arm.

"I know you wouldn't."

There was that trust again. The best gift of my life, aside from her love.

I could taste freedom on our horizon. If West had the guy, it was over. And once the threat was eliminated, we could settle into life. Into being together. I wanted that, wanted our life to be ours.

I hadn't felt like this since my first few years in the army, this sense of anticipation, of eagerness for adventure. I wanted that feeling again, this time with Quinn. She was a woman to adventure with. Wrapped in each other under the covers, we'd talked about trips we wanted to take. Hiking a glacier and sleeping in a tent hung from the side of a cliff. Kayaking out West and tackling the Appalachian Trail. I wanted all of it, as long as she was there. It was so close I could feel it.

I stayed long enough for Holly and James to get there. They walked in holding hands, Holly's hair in a low ponytail and James wearing a ball cap, both of them dressed for a spring hike in the mountains. Holly looked twenty-five but was in her early thirties. Her husband was currently deployed, so she hadn't minded the temporary shift from Atlanta to Sawyers Bend. James was in his late twenties but looked older thanks to the gray at his temples. He smiled at Holly with the indulgent affection of an adoring spouse, though he was currently fighting with his boyfriend in Atlanta, who did not like that his man was in the boonies so he could guard the one percent.

Looking at the two of them, you'd never guess they weren't madly in love. They caught my eye and we exchanged nods. "I'm headed to the station," I told Quinn in a low voice. "Stick close to Holly and James and keep your eyes open."

"I always do." Quinn didn't do PDA in front of clients, but she caught my hand in a tight squeeze and lifted to her toes to kiss my cheek. "You too," she said. "I mean, keep your eyes open."

I felt my lips curve at the thought that she was

cautioning me to be safe. I wasn't the one heading out into the woods. I was going to the safest place in town, the police station.

Chapter Thirty-Eight

HAWK

I found West in his office. He looked up from the paperwork spread out in front of him. "He's in processing. We got a name. Wayne Randell."

"Is he local?" I asked.

West shook his head. "Not exactly. Permanent address is in Seneca, in the upstate of South Carolina. He's a former Marine. Honorable discharge, but since then racked up a few charges of petty theft. Some assault charges. Minor possession charges. No felonies, but from what I'm seeing, that's probably because he hasn't been caught. According to the permits—back when we still needed them—the guy likes his guns."

West's desk phone rang, and he picked it up. "Yeah, yeah, I'm on my way." He hung up. "They're bringing him into the interview room. I'm going to go talk to him. You good to observe?"

I nodded, intensely curious about this guy. What did he want with Quinn? West followed me into the small observation room on the other side of the two-way glass.

We watched the deputy bring in Wayne Randell. He strolled into the room in a confident, long-limbed stride. West and I watched him in silence. Randell was the right height. A little taller than me, leaner, but fit and strong. Brown eyes. He wore faded gray/brown camo. Not the winter camo of before, but as West had pointed out, it wasn't snowing anymore. Randell looked annoyed, but not overly worried.

He fit, but everything about him made me itch. I studied him, looking for something that would rule him out as a suspect. It wasn't there. He was a fit. And yet—

This wasn't the first time I'd had to identify someone I'd only seen once and under extreme circumstances. I wouldn't make a positive ID unless I was sure. And I wasn't fucking sure. I'd expected to be. There'd been something about the guy while I was fighting him. A feeling that I'd know him anywhere, that I'd find him and we'd finish things. But this guy, Wayne Randell— I wanted him to be a puzzle piece, snapping into place, but the best I could say was that he fit.

"I'm going in," West said. "I'll see if I can get him talking before he lawyers up."

"Ask him about the laptop and the necklace," I said. "And how he got around the security system."

West nodded. He closed the door to the observation room behind him. A few seconds later, the door to the interview room opened, and West entered. His voice through the speakers was distant and formal, as I rarely heard it.

"I'm Chief Garfield," he said, pulling out the chair opposite Randell and sitting.

He went on with the standard intro, informing Randell he was being recorded, that he had a right to call an attorney, and the rest. When he was done, he slouched back in the chair and crossed his arms over his chest, all formality gone. If he'd tipped his head back, closed his eyes, and taken a nap, I wouldn't have been surprised.

"So, Randell, you want to tell me what you were doing in Harvey Benson's office this morning?" West looked across at Randell with half-closed eyes, as if barely interested in the answer.

Wayne Randell sat back and crossed his arms over his chest, mimicking West's posture. He leveled dark eyes on West and said, "Not doin' your job for you."

"Fair enough," West said easily. "So far we've got you on breaking and entering. I can charge you with that, but a little conversation might help your case."

Randell set his jaw and stayed silent. Questioning people wasn't my specialty. I liked to do my work behind the scenes. But West had told me once he loved it. Thrived on it.

Undeterred by Randell's silence, he went on. "You're from Seneca? I haven't been down that way since I caught a Tigers game with my uncle last year. Done some fishing down there. Davidson River's got some good fishing, but I caught a trout on the Chattooga last year—"

West droned on about his trout for so long that I thought Randell and I were both going to fall asleep. Lulled by West's loving description of a twelve-inch rainbow trout, Randell finally shook his head and said, "Y'all get the tourists up here with your breweries, but the fishin' is better in the upstate. I got a pool on the

Chattooga that always gets me at least a sixteen incher. So far, nothin' as good up here. Just a lot of overpriced rooms, fancy food, and small fish."

"Why are you still here, then?" West asked, letting his eyes seem to drift shut.

Randell slouched back farther, kicking out a foot and resting it on his knee. He jerked one shoulder up in a shrug. "Hopin' things would take a turn."

If I was West, I would have launched over the table to get Randell to talk. Instead, West raised an eyebrow, as if this was a normal, everyday conversation.

"Yeah? Did they?" West asked. "Take a turn?"

"Turned fuckin' down is what." He jutted his chin out, looking sullen and defiant, but he didn't say more.

West appeared unbothered. "It happens. You planning to stick around?"

"Guess I have to now," Randell sneered, shaking his cuffed hands so they rattled.

West sat up straighter, opening his eyes all the way and meeting Randell's belligerent gaze dead-on. "About that." He lifted his chin in the direction of Randell's cuffed hands. "I've been short-staffed around here. And I don't like paperwork."

"Yeah?" Randell asked, leaning forward a fraction.

"I could talk Harvey out of pressing charges if you could fill in a few blanks for me." West let that sit between them for a minute.

After long consideration, Randell shook his head. "Put it in writing. Immunity or whatever it is. Or I'm not talking."

"You haven't said anything worth making a deal

over," West said. "What brought you to Sawyers Bend? I know it wasn't the fishing."

"Had a job offer," Randell said, grudgingly.

"Yeah?" West sounded mildly curious. "What kind of job?"

Randell clammed up with a shake of his head.

West nodded. "I'm curious," he said. "Any chance that job had something to do with a necklace?"

At this, Wayne Randell stiffened, his arms still crossed over his chest, but they tightened as if he were pulling closed an invisible barrier. His chin went hard and jerked up.

Direct hit. This guy wasn't as smooth as he thought he was.

"I don't know anything about a necklace," he said.

West nodded slowly, as if he'd bought Randell's obvious lie. "I'm just curious," he said. "See, I'm guessing that's not what we'd call a truthful answer. Not a lot of good reasons to ransack a lawyer's office. If you needed a little spare cash, there's plenty of businesses on Main Street with some money in the till and light security. I keep telling them to get better locks, more cameras, but you know how small-town people can be." West shrugged as if helpless to reason with his citizens.

Randell sneered. "They're idiots. It's way too easy to bust open a regular lock."

"I agree," West said, nodding. "I noticed that there weren't any busted locks at Harvey's."

Randell shook his head.

"So how'd you get in?" West asked.

"Do I look stupid?" Randell demanded, suddenly

sitting up and lurching forward, his eyes hard. "You want to ask questions? Get me a lawyer."

West shrugged. "You want me to call a lawyer? I can do that, no problem. We can stop talking right now and I'll call a lawyer. Then we'll pick this up later. After charges have been filed."

Randell leaned forward, bracing his arms on the table. "What charges are you filing?"

"Breaking and entering, to start. Add on felony theft. That fountain pen you slipped in your pocket was worth at least two grand. Harvey likes his fountain pens," West said with a note of apology at Randell's appalled expression. "Or—" He stopped and shrugged. Propping a foot on his knee, mimicking Randell's earlier position, West waited.

Randell asked, "Or?"

West shrugged again. "Or you could tell me what you were doing in Harvey's office. See, I've got a curious situation going on around here. Break-ins we can't explain. Looks like somebody's looking for something. If I could get that figured out, if we knew what that someone was looking for and why, if we knew they were going to stop and leave town... Maybe I wouldn't feel the need to press charges on the breaking and entering this morning. Maybe I could let it go and save myself some paperwork."

Randell sat back in his chair, the cuffs on his wrists jangling with the sudden movement. "Take these off," he said, thrusting his wrists at West.

West let out a sigh and leaned forward, key in hand. "You don't keep those hands to yourself, you'll find yourself in a world of pain. Understood?"

A shadow of fear flashed in Randell's eyes. He nodded. "Understood," he said, his voice so low I almost missed it.

West didn't. He unlocked one of the cuffs, leaving the other on Randell's wrist. Randell curled his lip at West but didn't protest.

"You gonna drop those charges, then?" Randell asked.

West gave another of those languid shrugs, as if he didn't care all that much about any of this. "I really can't say. Not at this point, when I don't have any useful information."

"Are you telling me that if I talk, you're not going to charge me?" Randell asked again.

I couldn't see West's face, but I saw the shift in his shoulders, the tilt of his head. He'd hooked his catch. Now he just had to reel him in.

"I can't make any promises until I hear what you know. But I can promise that if it turns out you can fill in some blanks, I'm not that interested in the breaking and entering. Nothing was damaged, and Harvey will get his pen back. I'm more interested in why you were there in the first place."

Randell sat back in his chair, tipping his head to stare up at the ceiling. A long moment later, he sat up, the belligerence drained from his expression. This was a man ready to do business. "Yeah," he said, "I know about the necklace." He crossed his arms over his chest again and gave a defensive shrug of one shoulder. "It's known around my parts that I'm available to help people out with certain problems. Usually retrieving lost items."

"Lost items?" West asked with a raised eyebrow.

Randell ignored his question. "I got a call from a friend of a friend sayin' that somebody had some work for me. He brought me a burner phone. Told me to answer when it rang. Weird shit. I mean, who does that?" Randell shook his head slowly. "Said he'd pay well and I've been thinking about going down, doing some fishing in Mexico. I could use the cash. So I took the phone, and later that day it rang. The guy on the other end sent me a picture of a necklace. A gold oak leaf on a chain. Told me to find it, but he had shit for intel. Said the pretty little guide had it. Said she might have hidden it somewhere in that big-ass compound the Sawyers have. Or maybe she gave it to the lawyer. Or maybe she was carrying it around with her, or she brought it to work."

Randell raised his hands in exasperation, the loose handcuff slamming into the metal chair, letting out a clang that echoed in the small room.

"Did you find the necklace?" West asked, knowing the answer, considering the necklace was locked in his office safe.

"No!" Randell spat out. "Fuckin' no, I did not. I fuckin' looked everywhere I could get to."

"So this is all about the necklace? Is that why you jumped Quinn in the woods? You thought she had it with her?"

Randell's eyes clouded. "The pretty guide? I didn't fuckin' touch her. Wasn't paid to rough up a woman."

West's eyes flicked to the camera. I didn't need the silent message. I was already dialing Holly's phone.

Quinn wasn't alone out there, but if Randell wasn't the man in the woods, she wasn't as safe as I wanted her.

"Why the necklace?" West asked. "Why not cash? As far as I can tell, a small gold oak leaf on a chain isn't exactly valuable. Why does your client want it so badly?"

"Fucked if I know," Randell said with disgust. "He was willing to pay me ten grand if I found it, but so far all I'm doing is burning cash in this fuckin' town and I've got nothin' to show for it. I just want to get paid."

He shook his head, raising his eyebrows as if expecting West to commiserate.

"The client's pissed because he wants me to find the necklace, sayin' I got two more days and then he's pulling the plug. Then he called last night. Said the necklace was definitely at the lawyer's office. Said it was in his desk, and I could get in without worrying about the new alarm, but I had to get there—" Randell shook his head as if in disbelief. "He gave me a window. Fuckin' weird. Said I had to be there between seven thirty-five and seven fifty in the morning. I'd have fifteen minutes to get in, search the desk, and get back out. I figured I'd take one last shot at it before I left town."

"And how did you get in?" West asked.

Randell shrugged. "Just like he said on the phone, I walked right in the back door. It was unlocked."

"And the alarm didn't go off when you opened it?" West asked.

"No, man, I told you it was unlocked. I walked right in."

"And the man who called last night, he was the same man who called before?"

At that question, Randell went still. "I— Yeah— He —" Randell fell silent for a long moment before shaking his head. "He sounded the same, but the guy talked low and kind of rough. Like he was disguising his voice. The guy last night did the same. He sounded the same, but—" Randell shook his head once more. "I can't swear it was the same person."

West nodded slowly as my gut went cold. None of this was adding up. Holly didn't answer her phone. I tried James.

"So what did you do when you got inside?" West went on as if the issue of the caller wasn't important.

Randell relaxed back into the chair. "I started going through the desk. Only got through three fucking drawers when you showed up."

His words stopped the breath in my lungs, and I realized what was wrong.

The timing didn't line up.

Up until he got to the phone call, there was a chance this was our guy, despite his protest about not hurting Quinn. The way he talked and his attitude didn't match the efficient, highly skilled man I'd fought on the snowy trail, but enough matched up that it could have been him.

But the time frame was wrong.

The hits on the system at Heartstone had come in at seven twenty-five a.m. The caller had told Randell he had to enter no earlier than seven thirty-five. And he hadn't said anything about touching the laptop.

West had followed the same train of thought. "Why'd you go for the laptop?"

"What laptop?" Randell asked, looking truly confused for the first time.

"The laptop on Harvey's desk," West said, his voice sharp, all pretense gone. "What did you want with the laptop?"

"Nothing! I wasn't sent after a fucking laptop. I've got a laptop. Jesus. I was looking for the necklace, which wasn't there. So now I'm not going to get paid." Randell slapped his cuffed wrist on the arm of his chair, seemingly soothed by the loud clang.

West ignored his tantrum. "So you didn't touch the laptop."

"No. I fucking told you. It was open when I got there. It was loud, like—" He waved his hands in circles. "Like the fans were on or something. But I didn't touch it. I was there for the necklace."

West went completely still for a beat before smoothly coming to his feet. "Hold that thought," he said.

I was at the door when he opened it, closing it quickly behind him. "He's not the guy from the woods."

"No," I agreed. "He's our guy for the break-ins, but he didn't have anything to do with Heartstone's system. He isn't the guy who attacked Quinn."

"He was set up," West said grimly, looking through the mirror at Randell tugging at the cuff on his wrist. "Whoever took Quinn set him up so you'd feel safe enough to leave her. Fucking hell."

I tapped Quinn's contact on my phone. No answer. "Fuck."

"You know where she is?" West asked.

I was already out the door, sprinting for my SUV. My

phone rang in my hand before I could wrench open the door. My heart lurched to see Sterling's name on the screen.

"Sterling, what is it?" I said, breath tight in my lungs.

"Hawk," she sobbed. "Hawk, Quinn's gone."

No. Fear flooded me, dragging me down. Terror was a roar in my ears, drowning out logic, drowning out everything. *Gone.* Quinn was gone, and I was no closer to finding the man who had her than I had been weeks ago.

No. I had to let go of the fear and embrace the ice. I had to be ice-cold. A machine. I couldn't let the horror of Sterling's words penetrate or I wouldn't be able to think.

"Sterling," I said, reaching for calm. "Take a breath. Get it together and tell me what happened. Where are Holly and James?"

"They're here. They're here. They're looking for Quinn. But we can't find her. She's gone. We—"

I listened to her rough breaths. She went silent, and there was a slow inhale followed by a slow exhale.

When she spoke again, her voice was steadier. "We weren't far in. We were just at the bridge, you know?"

"I know the bridge," I said. I'd taken the same hike with them earlier in the week. The bridge was a little more than a quarter mile from the trailhead.

"One of the twins," Sterling said. "The girl, she's a goof. She likes to joke around. She was messing around on the railing and she fell over the side. We all stopped, looking over the railing, and James jumped down to get to her. She was screaming, she was scared, and she cut her leg pretty badly. It looked like there was a lot of blood.

When we turned back around, Quinn and Jay were gone."

"Quinn and Jay? Who's Jay?" I asked. There hadn't been a Jay in their group when I left for the station.

"Jay," Sterling said. "He's a repeat. A client from the fall. Quinn took him hiking in September and then fishing in October and again in November. We know him. He showed up late, said he was in town to visit friends, and— But he can't be— We know him!"

"What's his last name, Sterling?" I asked, my mind racing through the possibilities. From the bridge, they were close enough to the parking lot at the trailhead that he could have carried Quinn right to his car. If he'd knocked her out, she'd barely have slowed him down.

"His name?" Sterling asked, her voice shaking. "It's Jay. Jay...something with an R. Jay Ra— Jay Ro—"

Sterling tried to jog her memory, but as she spoke, the sounds in my ear twisted and reformed into a name that sent a wave of dread through me. "Sterling, was it Jay Reynolds?"

"That's it," Sterling shouted, relieved for only a second. "How did you know?"

I didn't answer her question. I couldn't. I didn't know how to tell her that this was my fault.

Jay Reynolds wasn't here for Quinn. He was here for me. He always had been.

From the beginning, this hadn't been about the Sawyers or the necklace. It was me. It was my past. It was the evil I thought I'd left behind, reaching out its oily tentacles to drag me back to hell and bring Quinn down with me.

I couldn't think about Quinn in his hands. I'd seen what Reynolds was capable of. As my CO, he'd given me orders I never should have followed. He'd wallowed in the dark, using his team for profit, for vengeance, without thought for the value of human life. When I'd left him, I'd dismantled his operation. Now he wanted payback. He was a monster, and he had Quinn.

"Tell Holly and James to get everybody back to Sawyer Outdoor Adventures," I barked into the phone. "No stopping. If the girl has to go to the hospital, let her parents take her. You stay under guard. Do you hear me?"

"I hear you," Sterling said. "What are you going to do?"

"I'm going after Quinn."

I just hoped I wasn't too late.

Chapter Thirty-Nine
QUINN

I came to with a smack of metal to my temple. My body bounced but didn't move much. Something was holding me in place. Another bounce. Another smack of my head to cold metal. A rumble in my ears.

I was in a vehicle.

I'd been on the trail. How had I gotten in a vehicle?

Light stabbed into my eyes, and I slammed them shut, clarity pushing through the haze in my head and the chemical taste in my mouth. There were zip ties around my wrists, pulled tight, cutting into my skin. I wasn't tied down; I was wearing a seat belt, my body slouching to the side, shoulder and head leaning against the door, smacking into the metal frame every time we hit a bump.

I strained my ears, listening for other cars, trying to gauge how fast we were going. I caught the rough grind of gravel under tires. Light flickering as if filtered through trees. I let my eyes drift open the tiniest sliver. Looking through my lashes, dense trees flashed by. A fire road or a long, private driveway. I didn't dare glance over at the driver. Not yet, not while I was still figuring out what was going on.

How had I gotten here, wherever *here* was? We'd been walking up the trail, Sterling taking the lead, followed by the couple with the twins, then me and Jay, a repeat hiker who'd shown up at the last minute. Holly and James had stuck close to me, no more than an arm's reach away. The air was cold, the sun shining, my ankle twinging only the tiniest bit.

And then a scream. The girl. A wail of agony from below and her mother's cry of alarm as she rushed to the bridge. And that was it. That was all I remembered.

"I know you're awake."

The flat, cold voice grated on my ears. I knew his voice, but I'd never heard it like this. He was fun. Friendly. Always laughing or cracking a joke.

My eyes open, I forced myself upright, off the doorframe, though it was hard to maneuver with my hands secured in front of me. Dragging my eyes from the road, I looked over at Jay, trying to make sense of what the hell was going on. I didn't recognize him as anything other than Jay Reynolds, my repeat client who liked to hike and fish.

I shifted in the passenger seat, testing my wrists against the zip ties. A glance down told me I was out of luck on that front. Hawk had shown me the difference between hardware store zip ties and those used for restraints. These were the latter. Thin bands of metal ran through the plastic around my wrists, and there was no give when I strained my arms.

We were driving too fast to jump out of the truck, and I was too high up. If I could get my hands free—

As if he was reading my mind, Jay said, "I wouldn't try it. I'll just have to put you out again. That was my mistake the first time. I didn't want to knock you out. Didn't realize you'd fight like a demon." His smirk was almost approving.

I stared out the window and slowly recognized the fire road we were on. Fire roads like this were all over the place, narrow gravel roads that gave access to the deeper parts of the mountains. This one led to Sawyer land after a short hike through the national forest. If you weren't coming from Heartstone Manor, this was the fastest way to get to the hunting cabin. My cabin. This fire road was how Jay had escaped Hawk the first time. And now it seemed we were heading back.

"Who are you, really?" I asked. "You're clearly not who you said you were, so what do you want with me?"

He flicked a glance at me, his eyes a pale sky-blue. Not the eyes of the man who'd attacked me in the woods.

"Your eyes were brown," I said.

"Contacts," he answered succinctly.

"Which ones are contacts?" I asked, not sure it mattered, but letting my instincts to find out more information take over. I didn't know what mattered and what didn't, because I had no fucking clue what was going on.

"These," he said, rolling his pale blue eyes. "The brown is real. My version of a disguise."

"Why did you need a disguise?" I pressed.

"I didn't want Hawk to spot me before I was ready,"

he said as if it was obvious. He clearly assumed we'd both had a good look at him the first time he'd come after me.

"Why were you looking for the necklace?" I didn't know how much time I had to get information from him or if I'd get a chance to use it. But I had to try.

Jay, my mystery kidnapper, let out a low chuckle, his icy eyes flicking to me again, then back to the road. "Not everything is about you Sawyers. You're so self-centered. I don't give a shit about the necklace or your poor brother rotting in jail. None of this is about you. You're just a convenient tool."

"A tool for what?" I asked, confused.

Jay shook his head again. Not in disagreement, but in commiseration. Or sympathy.

"You don't know what you let in through your door, do you? Your brother does. Griffen Sawyer might be playing captain of industry these days, but he knows. Instead of hiring Hawk Bristol, he should have put him down like the animal he is."

My heart chilled at his words. We'd been so wrong. What the hell was going on? "Is that what you're here to do?" I asked.

Jay ignored me.

No one was putting Hawk down. He wasn't an animal. I knew that. He was a man who'd made mistakes, mistakes he regretted deeply. But he was also a man who loved. Who cared and protected. He was kind. Patient. And I loved him more than I'd known I could love. No one was going to hurt him. Not while I was alive to stop them.

My eyes fell to my zip-tied hands. Big words for a

woman with her hands bound. How the hell was I supposed to save Hawk when I couldn't even save myself?

"What do you want with Hawk?" I asked. I couldn't do anything physically, but if I could keep him talking, maybe I'd learn something I could use.

"I'm here to remind him."

"Remind him of what?" I asked, more confused with every word this man spoke.

He didn't answer, his fingers tightening on the wheel as the truck skidded to a stop. The man I knew as Jay Reynolds turned to look at me, his pale eyes cold and hard. No pity. No compassion. It hit me that I wasn't sure he saw me as human. As soon as I wasn't useful—

"What are you going to do with me?" I asked, not sure I wanted to hear the answer.

"That depends on how much trouble you give me," he said, his tone close to friendly as if we were talking about the weather. "We're going to hike up to the cabin. Bristol is going to come rescue you. Then he and I are going to have a conversation."

Fuck. I was bait. And Hawk would come, I had no doubt.

"What if he doesn't come to the cabin? What if he looks somewhere else?" I asked.

"He'll come. I know him. He's already figured out this is where I was taking you the first time. He'll be here."

"And when you're done with your conversation?" I asked. "What happens then?"

Jay stared at me for a long moment, studying my face

as if he saw something there I couldn't decipher. He was a stranger, but he looked at me like he knew me. He gave a short nod as if deciding something. "After," he said, "I'll let you go."

After Hawk was dead. I couldn't let that happen.

"What if I don't hike up there?" I asked. "What if I run?"

"Then I'll knock you out again," he said in that same almost friendly tone.

I think I preferred it when he sounded scary.

"I can carry you up if I have to. It's your choice. One way or another, you're going to end up in that cabin. You can hike in, or if you're comfortable being unconscious in my arms—" His gaze skated over me, lingering on my breasts, sliding down my legs. "You're not my usual type. I like my women tall and curvy, but I could make do. Bristol always had good taste."

Well, that answered that question. On one hand, I didn't like going along with anything this asshole wanted, but he made a valid point. I didn't quite believe his leer, but I'd pick conscious over unconscious any day.

"Are you going to undo my wrists?"

He let out a chuckle that sounded like he was having fun. "Not a chance in hell," he said. "You're enough trouble like this. It's not a difficult hike when it's not iced over, something you know well. You can handle it." He put the truck in park and unsnapped his seat belt. "Stay put."

He jumped out of the truck, circling around the front to collect me from the passenger seat. In the few seconds I had alone, I scanned the front seat of the truck, frantically looking for anything I could use as a weapon. A screwdriver, spare keys, a flashlight. Anything. The truck was weirdly empty. Not a napkin or soda can in sight. No fast food bags littering the floor or dust on the dashboard. And nothing I could use as a weapon.

Then the door was opening, and he was there. The truck was so high I looked him dead in the eye as he leaned in to unsnap my seat belt. Without thinking, I jerked my bound wrists up, aiming for his Adam's apple. I didn't get close. He was fast, so fucking fast. My bound hands moved only inches before his were there, his fingers wrapping around my fists, wrenching my hands back down to my lap.

Like when we fought on the trail, he didn't hurt me, but he controlled me with barely any effort. "Option number two is still on the table," he reminded me. "Easier to get you up there under your own power." He gave me another one of those assessing glances, this one more calculating than sexual. "You don't weigh much."

He didn't have to convince me. I didn't want his hands on me. Especially if I was unconscious. Just the thought of him touching me while I was out, of not knowing what he was doing, what he'd done—I shivered.

"I'll walk," I said. I let him pull me from the car and set me on my feet.

"This way." He tugged on my shoulder and aimed me at the hillside. There wasn't a trail from this side. Anyone hiking here would stick to the fire road if they were smart. Wandering off the trail was a fool's game, especially this time of year. I knew how easy it was to get turned around in the forest. A few years before, we'd lost an experienced pair of hikers to exposure. They'd stepped off the trail to take a picture, wandered a little farther than they meant to, and never found the trail again.

At the moment, getting lost was the least of my worries. I'd have to hope Jay knew where he was going. He reached up to swipe at his eyes, and when he looked back, they were their familiar brown.

"Let's go."

I followed him up the mountain, trying desperately to figure out how I was going to warn Hawk before Jay could hurt him.

The first really steep section we hit, my ankle twinged as I dug my boot into the earth. The hikes I'd taken over the past week had been more like walks, chosen to let me get back into shape gradually. This was more like hiking with some climbing added in. The terrain was steep and uneven once we got away from the fire road. I had to concentrate just to keep myself from slipping and tumbling down the mountainside.

At a particularly sharp twinge, I felt a new flutter of fear in my chest. If my ankle gave, I was fucked. I didn't want him to knock me out again, which he certainly would if I was unable to walk. And if I somehow managed to get away from him, I had to be able to move. I needed my hands free. I needed my trekking poles. Neither were options.

"What do you have against Hawk?" I asked, trying to distract myself from the ache in my ankle.

"You don't need to know. I told you; this isn't about you. If you keep your mouth shut and do what I tell you,

I'll let you walk away, and you'll never have to think about any of this again."

I wanted to call him a liar, but instead I kept my mouth shut. Antagonizing him wasn't going to help. I knew he wasn't going to let me go. I'd heard this story before. *Do what I say, and then I'll let you go.* That was what bad guys said to get what they wanted without resistance. Then they killed their victims anyway. I'd seen his face. Been in his truck. This had all gone too far for him to just let me go. Especially if he planned to hurt Hawk.

Which meant I had to stay focused.

"Are you going to kill him?" I asked, not sure he'd tell me the truth but needing to hear his answer, hoping his tone or his expression would tell me something I could rely on more than the lies coming from his mouth.

He gave me a considering look as we hauled ourselves over the crest of a ravine and trudged through the underbrush at the top. "I don't know," he said, and something in his voice told me this was the truth. "I haven't decided yet."

"Are you going to kill me?" I found myself asking.

His voice was flat when he said, "No. Unlike Bristol, I don't kill women. Everyone has a line. Women and children are mine. Not something Hawk can say. Did he tell you about that? Did he tell you about all the times he committed cold-blooded murder? The innocents he killed?"

I shook my head, dropping my eyes to the uneven terrain beneath my hiking boots. Hawk hadn't told me specifics, but he'd told me enough. I hadn't asked for more. I knew he regretted so many of the things he'd done. He was torturing himself enough. He didn't need me to pry and make his pain worse.

"You never killed an innocent? You didn't make mistakes?" I asked.

Jay kept his eyes on the forest. After a long silence, broken only by the crunch of our boots in the dead branches and leaves, he gave a short nod. "Maybe. But I figured it out before he did."

"Figured what out?" I pushed.

"The lies," Jay spat out. "I figured out what was a lie and what was the truth. I figured out who I couldn't trust. I learned what you don't know yet."

He slowed, waiting for me to catch up, his hand closing over my braid at the base of my neck, jerking me to a stop. Pain stabbed through my ankle at the unexpected change of direction, and I let out a squeak of surprise.

His face shoved into mine, his breath hot on my cheek. Fire burned in his brown eyes. "You haven't learned yet. Hawk Bristol is a fucking killer. You think I'm the problem? Did you ever consider that I'm the one coming to the rescue?"

"I don't need you to rescue me from Hawk," I said, knowing I should keep my mouth shut. *Don't argue with crazy people, Quinn.* But it was too late.

"He took what I loved." Jay let go of my braid and stepped back, fury blazing off him. This man wasn't cold or flat. He was aflame with rage. "He took what I loved and left me alone. You think he's a man? He's a killer. Worse than me. Worse than anyone. And now I'm going to take what he loves. And that's just the beginning."

This time I kept my mouth firmly closed. I couldn't have spoken if I'd wanted to. Emotionless Jay had scared me, but this man, alight with vengeance—he was terrifying. I put one foot in front of the other, following the man who held my life in his hands. Probably letting him lead me to my death.

I didn't know what else to do.

I had no doubt that Hawk would find me, no doubt that he was headed to the cabin. And when he got there? How was I going to warn him? How was I going to tell him to run? To run, and not look back.

Jay prodded me and I picked up the pace. I knew if I slowed him down, he'd knock me out again. If I was unconscious, I couldn't fight for my life. If I was unconscious, I couldn't warn Hawk.

One foot in front of the other, again and again. It took me a minute to realize we were on familiar terrain, and sooner than I'd expected. By the time the cabin came in sight, I was limping. Dragging myself up half the mountain had been far too much for my newly healed ankle. But that was the least of my problems.

Jay shoved me ahead of him into the dark, cold interior of the cabin. Memories of Hawk spilled over me. The dinner he'd cooked. The night we'd spent in that bed. This cabin was the beginning of the best time of my life. I didn't want it to be the scene of the end.

Jay grabbed one of the chairs at the table and swung it around to face the door. Turning me by my shoulders, he shoved me down. My butt hit the seat hard, and I tilted to the side, my bound wrists and weak ankle throwing me off-balance. I was still getting my bearings when the first loop of duct tape tightened around me. Another loop and another, securing my body to the chair.

When he was done, he tore off a six-inch strip of tape and slapped it over my mouth.

"Just in case you feel like getting chatty," he said. "Your part in this is done. You just sit there and look terrified. I'll take care of the rest."

I raised my eyes and looked through the open front door of the cabin into the bright sunshine of a spring morning.

I'll take care of the rest.

The rest was exactly what I was afraid of.

Chapter Forty
HAWK

It took too long to get to the cabin. I knew he was taking her there, to the place where this had started weeks ago. My team was following any leads in town, in case I was wrong. My gut drove me, screaming that I wasn't wrong, that time was slipping away, and with it, my chance to save Quinn. I pushed my SUV to the limit on the mountain roads and covered most of the trail at a dead run. Still, it took too long. I slowed on the last quarter mile, leaving the trail to loop around the west side of the cabin so I could approach from the back.

I'd never been afraid like this. Even as the words crossed my mind, I realized they were inadequate. This wasn't fear. This was a bone-deep terror. I could handle fear, knew how to set it aside and get the job done. But this—this was beyond anything I'd felt before. This was Quinn. He had Quinn.

How had we missed Jay Reynolds? I'd looked through her client records. There could have been a Reynolds. There definitely wasn't a Jay Reynolds. That I would have remembered, no question. Memories flashed through my head as I moved through the trees. Reynolds was a sociopath, completely without empathy. People were game pieces to him, their only purpose a means to an end. Jay Reynolds would kill Quinn without hesitation if it served his purpose. I needed to get her away from him.

I stopped in the trees behind the cabin, taking measure of the situation. Smoke twined up from the chimney, filling the crisp winter air with its comforting scent. It was cold, but not cold enough that they needed a fire for safety. He was making a point, marking territory he saw as mine. But it wasn't mine. It was Quinn's. Which made it all that much worse. He'd touched her. Taken her. They'd been alone for almost two hours. What could he have done to her in that much time? Was she still alive? Had he—

I forced myself to lock down my spiraling terror, the urgency to get in there, to free her at whatever cost.

I needed to think. I had years of missions behind me, but none as important as this one. This was the one I had to get right. Nothing was going to happen to Quinn. I couldn't let it.

I scanned the back of the cabin, but Reynolds was ready for me. He'd covered both the bedroom and the kitchen windows. There was nothing to see from back here. Moving around to the east side, I saw he'd done the same there as well. He was herding me, forcing me to come in through the front.

If I'd had more time, I could have worked out a better approach, but every second Quinn was in his hands, the danger increased. I didn't have time. I had to move. I had to get her away from him.

The front door of the cabin was wide open. Keeping low, I made my way around the corner, easing closer to the door. From my vantage point, I caught the flicker of flame in the woodstove. I thought about trying to devise a way to see inside without exposing my position, but everything took too much time.

Hand on my weapon, I unsnapped the holster and stepped into the open doorway.

The first thing I saw was Quinn, duct taped to one of the kitchen chairs, a strip of tape over her mouth. Her eyes were wide with fear, but alert. The second she saw me, she shook her head frantically, her eyes sliding to something off to her left.

I got the message. She wasn't alone. He was there, to the left. And I knew without words that she wanted me to leave, to run, to save myself.

Like that was going to happen. If only one of us was leaving this cabin, it was going to be her.

I stepped inside, ready when a dark shape moved in from the left to stand behind Quinn. He wore faded brown and green camo with matching gloves and dirt-smeared boots. A deep green winter hat was pulled low over his forehead, shading his eyes. He'd wrapped a dark brown scarf around his neck and mouth, leaving me to guess at the rest of his face.

I got an impression of dark eyes, of contained rage burning in the shadows. That was it.

I thought of Randell, the paid thief, and those phone calls. How he thought he knew who he was talking to but couldn't be sure. Was this Reynolds? Maybe not. I didn't know. Whoever he was, I needed to get Quinn away from him.

His hand came into view, fingers wrapped around the hilt of a hunting knife. I took a step closer and the knife went to Quinn's throat. I froze, feet glued to the floor. I was afraid to breathe. Afraid to blink.

It had been years since I'd been in the same room with my former CO. He'd been a monster then. I had no clue how far he'd go now. Not when I didn't know why he was here.

"Drop the knife, Reynolds," I said. "She's not a part of this."

He didn't react except to press the knife against Quinn's pale skin. He hadn't drawn blood. Not yet.

I stayed where I was. I couldn't spook him. A jerk of his arm and Quinn would be dead.

"Drop your weapon," he said, his voice low and hoarse. Not a natural speaking voice.

"I'll put my weapon down," I countered, "after you let her go."

The knife shifted and Quinn whimpered, her blue eyes swimming with angry tears, begging me to run. Begging me to leave her. That wasn't going to happen. I was going to get us both out of here. Alive. It would be a hell of a lot easier if I had a fucking plan and I wasn't dealing with a sociopath.

I could give up my weapon if it would buy me time. The weapon in my hand wasn't my only defense, just the most visible. Raising my left hand in the air, palm out, placating, I said, "I'll put my weapon on the couch, okay?

Move that knife away from her throat, and I'll put it down."

I got the sense of his eyes narrowing. The knife eased back. Not far enough, but it wasn't pressing into her skin. Slowly, I pulled my weapon from the holster and laid it on the couch, closer to me than to Reynolds.

I put both hands up and stepped back. "Let her go. She doesn't have anything to do with this."

"She has everything to do with this," he growled. In a flash, his hand came up, and the knife was flying through the air directly at my face.

I didn't think. I moved. My hand closed around the hilt, the blade slicing into the side of my finger. I stared at the knife in my hand and back at Reynolds in confusion. I wasn't naive enough to think he was unarmed now that he'd lost his knife. His cmo jacket probably hid a sidearm. But why give up the weapon he'd been using to keep Quinn under control?

"Drive that through your heart," he said, "and I'll let her go."

Quinn shook her head, muffled pleas smothered by the duct tape. I knew what she was saying. *No. Hawk. No.*

I raised the knife, aiming the tip at my heart.

"This is what you want? For me to kill myself? And then I'm just supposed to trust you to let her go? You just said she has everything to do with this. You can't think I'd be that stupid."

His hand closed over the back of Quinn's neck, fingers tightening. She let out a scream behind her gag, the sound part terror and part pain.

I got the message. He didn't need the knife to kill Quinn. She was duct taped to that chair, and he had two good hands. He could snap her neck in a heartbeat, long before I could close the distance between us.

I could have thrown the knife back at him. I could take a chance and dive for him. But that would risk the woman I loved.

I stayed exactly where I was, bringing the knife closer until the tip dug in, slicing easily through the fabric of my sweater and shirt beneath. It was so sharp I barely felt the burn as the tip cut into the skin above my heart.

Quinn sobbed, tears streaming down her cheeks. I wanted to comfort her, to tell her to trust me. But I wouldn't lie. I didn't have a plan. The best I could do was play along until I figured out what the bastard wanted. My death seemed to be at the top of his list. Only a few months ago, I might have made it easy on him, the weight of guilt clouding my desire to live. But things had changed. Quinn had changed me, had shown me I deserved life, deserved love. That I had something to offer the world that might make up for the wrongs I'd done.

Better to atone than to give up. I wasn't going to let Reynolds take my future. He'd taken too much from me already.

"More," he demanded.

"Step away from Quinn and I'll give you more."

He shook his head. "You owe me pain."

That didn't make any sense. None of this made sense. "I don't owe you anything," I said. "You landed on your feet after I got out."

And he had, as far as I knew. I'd fucked with Reynolds's operation once I figured out what he was really using my team for. But he'd never faced charges, and he had contacts everywhere. He'd been better off than he deserved to be. Diminished, maybe, but not out of the game.

His fingers tightened on the back of Quinn's neck, then slid around to rest on the front of her throat, her chin lifting to ease the pressure. A second ago, she'd been begging me to leave with her eyes, the fire I loved very clear. Now they were wide with terror, no plea left. Only fear.

"Did he tell you?" he asked Quinn, looking down into her raised eyes. "Did he tell you the things he did? The people he killed?" His fingers tightened, cutting off her air supply.

"I'll do whatever you want if you let her go," I said. I wasn't playing this game. I wasn't letting him use me to torture Quinn with fear until he killed us both. I had to get Quinn out, whatever the cost.

Even if that meant I had to hurt myself to do it.

"Did you tell her about Neva?" he asked.

Hearing that name, I went cold inside. *Neva.* My last official kill working for Reynolds. The death that pushed me over the edge. The loss that woke me up. And of all the missions Reynolds sent me on, the one I knew was actually justified.

"Yes," I answered truthfully, my voice hoarse with guilt and well-worn pain. I'd done the right thing when it came to Neva, but that didn't ease the agony of killing a friend.

He dropped his hand from Quinn's throat, her breath drawn in a gasp. Reaching up, he unwound the scarf from his neck, dropping it to the floor. With a jerk of his hand, he pulled off his hat.

The face he revealed was not that of Jay Reynolds, my former CO. I stared into the brown eyes of the man who'd been my friend. Almost a brother. The man I'd thought I'd lost along with Neva.

"You're dead," I said stupidly.

Obviously, Emmett Blake was not dead. Emmett Blake was standing in front of me, very much alive. He dropped his hat to the floor and slid his hand back around Quinn's neck, his long fingers squeezing until she squirmed.

"Let her breathe," I said, and his fingers relaxed the tiniest fraction.

"You killed Neva," he accused. "I let you live because you were a brother. I was so close to taking your life in exchange, but I let you live. You were suffering. For a while, I thought the guilt would kill you and do the job for me. But you found the Sinclairs and Griffen Sawyer, and you let them convince you to live. I watched you. All these years, you were alone. You worked. You helped people. And you suffered. Alone. Exactly like you deserve to."

Quinn whimpered, jerking her head to the side when his fingers tightened again on her chin, pulling her head back to look up at him.

Leaning down, his mouth by her ear, he said, "He put a bullet in her heart. My love. His friend. And he murdered her." Standing, he dropped his hand from Quinn and stared at me. "Didn't you?"

"I did," I said.

There was no point in saying anything else. We'd both been there. He'd seen me pull the trigger. Moments later, Emmett Blake had disappeared. I'd never imagined he'd been out there, watching me. Shouldn't I have felt him? Shouldn't I have known? But then Emmett had always been one of the best. He was a shadow in the night, capable of getting in almost anywhere, of disappearing into a crowd. Of hacking almost any system, even back then.

I should have known, and I hadn't. Hadn't seen this coming at all.

"So many times," he said, "I had you in the sights of my rifle. So many times, I almost pulled the trigger. But I let you live because you suffered. Because you paid more alive than dead. Death would be a release that neither of us deserves. Then you came here, and I followed. I watched you living in that run-down gatehouse. Getting scraps from the Sawyers' table. You were alone, and you suffered like you deserve to suffer. But then you weren't suffering anymore, were you?"

Emmett reached up with his free hand to stroke Quinn's hair back from her face, the gesture tender. Gentle. And terrifying.

"I saw the way you looked at her," he said. "The way you changed your morning rounds to check on her while she slept. She was different, wasn't she? Long before you ended up in this cabin, long before you touched her. She was different."

My throat tight, I nodded with a jerk of my head.

"That morning the bear cubs played under her hammock, I knew." He tucked a strand of Quinn's sleek hair behind her ear. "I knew you weren't suffering anymore. Not the way you had."

He dropped his hand away from Quinn and stepped back, all his focus on me.

"You don't get to live a full life, Hawk. You don't get her. You don't get a home and a family. You don't get any of it. You took all of that from me, and you only get to live if I let you live. You only get to live if your life is a punishment."

I dropped my hands to my side, the knife clattering to the floor. I wasn't going to stab myself in the heart. That wasn't going to save Quinn. I wasn't sure what would save us now. Emmett was right. I had taken his love away from him. And now that I had Quinn, I could imagine all too well how far he'd go to exact his revenge.

All I had was the truth. I hoped it would be enough.

Chapter Forty-One
HAWK

"Emmett," I said, using the first name I rarely voiced. It was always Blake for him, Bristol for me, Reynolds for our CO. Last names or nicknames. Always. Except for Neva. We always called Neva by her first name. She'd been a contractor who worked with our team when Reynolds needed her. Not local, not American. Her origins were murky. My best guess was that she came from somewhere in Eastern Europe. She'd told Blake she was Russian. In the end, it didn't matter. Neva was who she was paid to be.

Blake hadn't seen that part. He'd fallen head over heels in love, and he'd stopped asking the right questions.

"I killed Neva," I said, steeling myself against Quinn's flinch. "But there are things you don't know. You were gone after it happened. I needed to explain, but you disappeared. All this time, I thought you were dead."

"Don't try to sell me some bullshit story," he said, his hand curling into a fist at his side. "You were jealous, and you fucking killed her."

I shook my head slowly. "No, Emmett. I knew you loved her. I never would have—" I shook my head again, my heart aching with pain as my memories flooded back, dragging me to that moment I'd never been able to let go of. I'd pulled the trigger. I'd killed her, killed my friend.

"Fucking lies," Blake spat out. "Stop with your fucking lies. You shot her. I saw you shoot her."

I nodded. "I did. I didn't want to, but I did."

"You shot her," he screamed, pulling his sidearm and pointing it at me. "You put a fucking bullet in her heart, and I'm going to do the same to you."

I stood there, the inevitability of it rooting me in place, the past rushing into the present at light speed, catching up with me at last.

"You're not wrong, Emmett. I shot Neva. She was my friend. She was your love. And I killed her. I watched her fall to the sand, dead, and I walked away. I've regretted it, and what it did to you, every day. I regretted it as I pulled the trigger. And in the same situation, I'd do it again. She was working both sides, Emmett. She turned on us."

Emmett's hand was rock-solid on his gun as he stared at me over the barrel.

"Let Quinn go," I said. "You can do what you want with me. This isn't Quinn's fault. She had nothing to do with Neva. She's not responsible. Make me pay. Not Quinn."

He didn't even look at Quinn, his eyes locked on me. "The second she's out of the picture, I won't be able to control you. You'll just have to trust that I won't hurt her after you're dead."

"And how am I supposed to trust you, Emmett?" I asked.

"Stop fucking calling me that," he shouted.

"Fine, Blake," I corrected. "I can't trust you. You attacked her in the woods. You kidnapped her."

"I haven't hurt her. Scared her a little, but your girl is tough. She'll survive. And maybe she deserves to suffer a little for letting a monster like you into her bed."

"You don't get to play judge and jury, Blake. There's too much you don't know."

"I know enough. I know Reynolds sent you after Neva with an execution order. Ever wonder where that bastard has been all these years? Nowhere. I took care of him just like I'm going to take care of you."

I wasn't surprised. I'd thought about doing the same.

"You know I went after her on Reynolds's orders, but did he tell you why?" I asked, sure Blake was in the dark.

I'd meant to explain back then, to tell him the painful truth. But by the time I'd dealt with Neva's body, Emmett had been gone. Officially, he'd deserted, but we were mostly off the books, erased from official records. So in reality, Emmett Blake had simply ceased to exist.

"Do you know why?" I asked again.

He sneered at me. "Because she was interrupting Reynolds's supply line. Eating into his profits. It's why you killed her."

"Maybe she was," I said. "But I didn't give a fuck about that. If it had been about money, about his business, I would have let her go. You remember—back then, we were only just figuring out what Reynolds was really up to. The backroom deals using us as muscle to protect his bottom line. Using national security and terrorism and all that patriotic bullshit he was selling to get us to stop asking questions."

"Maybe you were only just figuring it out," Blake spat out. "I fucking knew! I told you what was happening and you said I was paranoid."

I nodded. Dark, sticky guilt was heavy in my chest. He was right. I'd been clinging to patriotism, clinging to the belief that I was the good guy. Even then. Even when the evidence had been in front of me. "You think I would kill Neva over money?" I asked. "Over fucking orders? She was my friend."

"I loved her." The words were torn from Emmett's throat, his agony slicing through me.

I absorbed his pain. I deserved it. Because I knew. I knew what it was to love in a way I hadn't then. I'd thought it was mostly about sex. And some of it had been. But now I knew that with the right person, sex *was* love. Laughing together, falling asleep together. It was all love. And I'd taken that from him. But he hadn't known the truth.

"You didn't know who she was," I said. "You can't stand there and tell me that you knew she was working with the cell that set those IEDs. She gave them our route, the timing. Everything. And they spared our vehicle, didn't they? Shot out our tire at exactly the right moment and slowed us down just enough. Didn't you ever wonder how they took out seven of us, and we came out untouched?" I paused, remembering the horror and betrayal I'd felt at her actions once I realized. I looked at him.

"That's a lie!" Finally, Blake's composure broke. His voice cracked, his hand stabbing his weapon in the air at me, his finger too tight on the trigger. "That's a goddamn lie."

"Not a lie," I said, keeping my voice as calm as I could while staring into the barrel of his weapon. "Did you ever, in all these years, ask yourself what would have driven me to kill Neva?"

"You did it to line your fucking pockets, just like the rest of them," he said.

"Fuck you," I shot out, my calm dissolving in an instant. I'd never sold out my team or my friends. Never.

I had to get my temper under control. I couldn't risk Quinn, but God damn it—

"Fuck you," I said again. "You're right. We were as good as brothers. So you should have known that I never would have hurt her. I fucking tried to take her in without any damage. It wouldn't have gone well for her. She would have spent years in a cell unless she'd had the intel to make a good deal. I honestly don't know what would have happened to her, but she could have lived. She didn't give me a choice."

"She never would have betrayed me," Blake said. "Never. You're a liar."

I shook my head. "She—"

I sucked in a long breath, trying to force my tight lungs to expand. I had to get him to see the truth through his pain. It was our only chance of getting out of here alive. And beyond that, Blake deserved to know the truth. I exhaled in a rush of breath, knowing I was going to hurt him again, and spit out the words.

"Blake, she didn't see it as betraying you. She saw it as ensuring your future together. She diverted the team with bad intel, sending us straight into the path of those IEDs, and she got paid a fuck-ton for it. She was going to use the money for you. For the two of you."

Blake's eyes slid shut, his face contorting in pure misery. I knew what he saw behind his closed eyes, knew the visions that haunted him. We'd lost seven men that day. I still had nightmares. The concussive boom. The flash of light, the dust, then the silence. Body parts everywhere. My friends, my brothers, gone in an instant.

Something about it had always felt off. The timing, the last-minute route change. I'd known from the second I came to on that dusty road, that it hadn't been a random attack. And I'd started to dig. I'd been coming around to the idea that Reynolds was dirty. After that day, I started to investigate as fully as I could and still stay under the radar. I'd uncovered so much more than I'd wanted to know. I'd only scratched the surface of everything Reynolds was up to, and in the process I'd uncovered Neva's duplicity.

"I confronted her," I said. "Before you saw me kill her. Before you came into the room, I confronted her. I'm sorry, man. I know you loved her. She loved you. She did. She swore it was all for you. It was enough so you could both get out."

"No. No, no, no." Blake's head rocked from side to side as if he was trying to shake off the truth settling into his heart. "I don't believe you."

Although the gun was still pointed at me, I no longer

saw an enemy. I saw my broken friend, a man I'd loved like a brother, having his heart broken all over again.

"I'm sorry," I said. "There's nothing I've done that I regret more. I wish I'd known what she would do. I wish I'd planned it differently. But a part of me didn't believe what I'd discovered. A part of me still thought she might have an explanation. But she admitted it. Then you walked in, and she—"

I let out a breath, my throat locking up, heat prickling the backs of my eyes at the memory. I hated remembering the moment her eyes had shifted, and I'd seen her change, seen her calculating how her future would play out.

"She didn't want you to know. And if she'd let me take her in, everything would have come out. She knew I didn't want to hurt her, even if she deserved it, but I wasn't going to let her go either. Not after what she'd done."

For a minute, I'd thought I had her. Then the door had opened, Emmett had walked in, and her face— The grief. The remorse. Neva had pulled her weapon, pointed it at me, and I'd pulled my trigger first. I still didn't know if I'd been faster or if she'd let me get the shot off.

"You want me to pay?" I demanded. "Fine. You can make me pay. I killed her. I didn't have a choice, but that doesn't absolve me. But let Quinn go. She's not a part of this."

"She makes you happy," Blake said, the words both an accusation and a plea.

"She does," I said. "For the first time, maybe since my parents died. Yeah. She makes me happy. She makes me glad to be alive. You want to take that from me? Then take me out. But let her go."

Blake's hand came down on the top of Quinn's head, his fingers draped over her forehead like a fleshy spider, tightening over her skull. My gut tightened with them. Blake's head dropped, his eyes fixed on Quinn.

With a slow exhale, his hands fell to his sides. He slid his sidearm back in the holster, snapping it closed. "Why didn't you tell me? Why wouldn't you have told me?" he asked, sounding lost.

"There wasn't time," I said. "She was getting ready to run when I figured it out. I was looking for you, looking for her, and I found her first. When it was all over, you were gone. I thought you were dead. I looked for you. After I got out, I went after Reynolds, fucked with his operation so he had to walk away, and I looked for you."

"I didn't want to be found," Blake said, shaking his head, his eyes still on the floor.

I knew the feeling. "And I stopped looking. I couldn't live with it," I said.

I hated thinking about those days. I'd been lost, on the edge of giving up completely. Every time I closed my eyes, I saw the light fading from Neva's, her blood spilling from her chest. I saw all the deaths I'd caused, and questioned every single one. It was too much for one man to carry.

"I'm sorry I couldn't bring her in alive," I said. "I'm sorry I found her first. I'm sorry about fucking all of it."

Blake sagged, still on his feet but diminished. He lifted a hand to dig in his pocket and I tensed, looking to the couch, gauging how fast I could get to my weapon.

Before I made a move, a blade flashed, and Quinn slouched forward. She lurched to her feet. The knife flashed again, freeing her hands. She reached up to pull the duct tape from her mouth.

"Hawk," she said the second she could speak.

I shook my head. I still had to get her out of here. "Go!" I said. "Run back to the house and find Kane."

"I'm not leaving you here." She looked at me, incredulous, and my heart ached.

My Quinn. Brave. Loyal. Strong and smart. It was that last part I was depending on the most.

"Go back to the house, Quinn," I said.

"I'm not leaving you here, Hawk." She scooped up my weapon from the couch and slid it into my holster, taking a position just behind me.

"At least yours is loyal," Blake said, his voice thick with bitterness.

I shook my head. "Neva was loyal to you in her own way. She just wasn't loyal to your cause."

"Turns out I wasn't loyal to my cause either," Blake said with a defeated shrug of one shoulder. "Considering that our cause wasn't patriotism, it was actually Reynolds's bank account."

"We didn't know," I said, voicing the excuse I rarely accepted myself. I was only just able to accept the idea of absolution for me. How could I give it to Blake?

Quinn's arm slid around my waist. She leaned into me, watching Emmett Blake with sharp eyes.

"So," she asked, "what do we do now?"

Chapter Forty-Two
QUINN

Emmett Blake looked from me to Hawk. His hands hung loose at his sides, and his whole manner had shifted. When he'd grabbed me, when he'd been fighting with Hawk, Blake had been in command. Of himself, of the situation. And now, for the first time, he was off-balance. Uncertain.

All his fight had drained away. He shoved his hands in his pockets and rolled his shoulders back as if preparing to face opposition.

"You should call that police chief of yours," Emmett said. "He's probably got a list of the laws I've broken."

Hawk stared at Blake for a long moment before looking to me, silently asking my opinion. I thought about it. Calling West was the logical response. But it didn't feel like the right one. Blake had been Hawk's friend, as close as a brother, according to both of them. And they'd both experienced a horrible loss. Now that I knew the truth, that Hawk had taken a life he'd wanted to save, that Blake had lived all these years thinking his best friend had betrayed him—

I believed in law and order, but law and order didn't feel like the answer to our problem. So, what did we do next?

I glanced across the room at the kitchen, and I knew at once what I wanted to do. "I think I could use a drink," I said, my eyes on the bottle of bourbon Hawk and I had shared during the snowstorm.

Both men looked at me in surprise.

To Hawk, I said, "Do you want to call Kane and let everybody know we're okay?" I shifted my eyes to Blake and raised a brow. "Are we okay?" I asked.

"You're not in any danger from me, if that's what you're asking," he said. His voice conveyed a touch of curiosity, and if I wasn't mistaken, respect.

Hawk nodded. "I think we could all use a drink." Pulling out his phone as he strode across the cabin to the kitchen, he dialed and said, "Kane, we're good. Quinn is safe, and we're both uninjured. Everyone from the hiking party okay? Sterling? The girl?" He snagged the bottle of bourbon off the shelf and three of my blue-speckled camping mugs. His eyes skipped to Blake, and he fell silent for a moment, then said slowly, "Still looking. No. I don't need backup. I'll call when we're headed back." He hung up.

I hadn't heard Kane's side of the conversation, but I had a feeling Hawk had dodged any explanation of what had happened to my kidnapper. It looked like we were all undecided about what to do with Emmett Blake. I sank into a chair at the table, the same chair I'd been duct-taped to.

Hawk took the seat opposite me, reaching down to lift my right leg and resting my ankle on his knee. "The girl got a few stitches and a lesson in not goofing around in the forest. Everyone else is fine." He rubbed at my tender ankle gently. "How's the ankle?"

I shrugged, knowing I'd be annoyed about it later. "Not great. I was up for an easy stroll in the woods, not a scramble up the side of the mountain."

Blake shook his head. "I'm sorry. My plan was never to hurt you." He let out a gusty exhale. "I was so blinded by vengeance, by punishing Hawk for being happy, that I didn't—" He shook his head again. "I should have taken more care. Hawk was right. This wasn't about you. This was between Hawk and me. I never should have involved you."

"No, you shouldn't have," I agreed.

Hawk poured a finger of bourbon into one of the mugs and slid it across the table to me, doing the same with the other two. Hawk raised his in a toast. Blake and I joined suit, and we clicked our mugs together.

"To happy endings," Hawk said before taking a sip.

I drained most of my bourbon in one swallow, blinking at the smoky burn.

Blake, I noted, took a spare sip before pausing and staring into his mug. "Is it a happy ending?" he asked.

Hawk smiled, mostly with his eyes, the faintest curl to his mouth. "Are you going to kill me?"

"No," Blake said, and looked up at Hawk with caution.

"Are you going to kill anybody else?"

Blake shook his head.

"Do you believe me?" Hawk asked. "About Neva?"

Blake gave a single, slow nod. "I believe you. I wish I didn't. I wish it had all gone differently. I wish a lot of things. But I believe you."

"Then, yes," Hawk said, his eyes coming back to me, filling with warmth. He reached a hand across the table, his fingers closing over mine. "I'd say it's a happy ending. Maybe if you can stay out of trouble, one of these days you'll dance at our wedding."

Our wedding.

Blake barked out a rough laugh and drained the rest of his bourbon. "Hawk Bristol, the romantic. I never thought I'd see it." A grin curved his mouth, and he shook his head, looking at me. "You should have heard him when I was falling for Neva. *No woman will ever come between me and the mission,*" he intoned, lifting his chin and looking suddenly both pompous and self-righteous.

I couldn't stop the giggle. I didn't know that version of Hawk, but I could picture him perfectly. A hint of pink touched Hawk's cheeks and he shook his head, hiding his smile with the camping mug as he sipped his bourbon.

"Live and learn, right?" He squeezed my fingers.

I was still stuck on his casual mention of our wedding. I knew we were in love, knew it was serious. He'd as good as asked me to move into the gatehouse with him. He was living with me in Heartstone Manor. But a wedding was a whole other thing. A wedding was forever.

A goofy smile stretched my mouth. Hawk and I were

getting married. Not today or tomorrow, but eventually. Eventually was good enough for me. More than good enough. Eventually marrying Hawk Bristol was a dream come true.

"So," Hawk said, pouring everyone a little more bourbon, "what have you been doing since we got out? Other than skulking around seeking vengeance."

Blake let out a laugh. "Vengeance was mainly a side gig once I dealt with Reynolds." He tipped his head back, studying the rough logs of the slanted ceiling before looking to Hawk. "Freelance hacking is the easiest way to describe it. I got out of wet work. I don't have a taste for it. Never really did."

"White, black, or gray?" Hawk asked, his eyes narrowed with interest.

I wasn't sure I understood his question, but Blake did.

"Mostly white with a little gray here and there. I got dirty enough working for Reynolds. Not going there again."

Hawk sat back in his chair, his fingers sliding from mine as he crossed his arms over his chest, studying Emmett Blake. I imagined I could see the wheels turning in Hawk's brain.

Finally, Hawk said, "Lucas Jackson wants a word with you."

Blake raised an eyebrow. "Lucas Jackson?"

"Sinclair Security's head of digital security, or whatever the fuck they're calling his department these days. He leads a team of white hat hackers who mostly work behind their keyboards but can handle being in the field if the job calls for it. Jackson designed that system you broke into so easily."

"Fuck easy," Blake said with a laugh, followed by another sip of bourbon. "That system is a thing of beauty. I haven't had a challenge like that in a while."

"But you still got in," Hawk said.

Blake shrugged a shoulder. "There aren't many systems I can't break into. It's a gift."

"One you've honed to a sharp blade," Hawk commented.

Blake nodded in agreement. "What does Jackson want with me?"

Hawk shook his head. "I don't know for sure. My guess? He wants to offer you a job."

Blake shook his head immediately. "The Sinclairs aren't going to hire me, and I'm not sure I want that kind of work."

"What do you mean, *that kind of work*?" Hawk asked. "You couldn't do better than working for the Sinclairs."

"It's corporate," Blake said, his eyebrows drawn together in clear disgust. "It's showing up every day in a suit with a fucking briefcase. That's not me."

At that, Hawk burst into a rare laugh, his eyes lighting with humor. "Clearly you haven't met the Sinclairs. Axel likes his suits because that's Axel. And I'm not going to say everyone else doesn't wear a suit when the job calls for it, but that's rarely anyone on Jackson's team. If you're ready to rejoin the world, you should let me bring you to Atlanta and introduce you. If it isn't a fit, you don't have to stay."

Blake didn't look like he was sold on that idea. He

brought the mug to his lips and took another sip, then set it on the table with a clank. "I don't know," he said. "It's been a long time since I've been part of a team."

I watched Hawk take this in, consider it. I didn't think he was ready to say goodbye to his friend, to have him disappear as he had so many years before.

"You should go to the Sinclairs," Hawk finally said. "They can give you work you'll like, and—"

"I can find my own work. It's not about the money."

Hawk leaned forward, locking eyes with his friend. "You can't keep running from the past. You deserve to have a life too. And you can relax there. They get it. They'll get you."

Again, I wasn't sure I fully understood the subtext, but Blake did. He thought about it for a minute.

"You'd vouch for me?" Blake asked.

Hawk answered with a nod.

"Why? Especially after all of this? I hurt your woman. I didn't mean to, but that doesn't change what I did. I hurt her, and I scared her." Blake squeezed his eyes shut tight, opening them slowly to land on me, so heavy with guilt they reminded me of Hawk for a moment. "I'm sorry."

"I know. I'll survive." Now that the adrenaline surge had begun to fade, I was a little giddy, a lot exhausted, and not inclined to hold a grudge, even if I couldn't quite bring myself to accept his apology. Now that I understood why Emmett Blake had come after Hawk in the first place, I could live with what he'd done. If I'd watched someone murder Hawk, I'd want vengeance, too.

Hawk looked at his watch. "It's still early. If you're up for meeting with Jackson and talking to the Sinclairs, I think we should get you out of Sawyers Bend before West starts asking questions."

Blake drew in a slow breath and let it out. "Yeah. If you're okay with vouching for me, then yeah." He ran a hand through his short, dark hair. "I'm not sure I'll stay, but I want to talk to Lucas Jackson as much as he wants to talk to me."

"All right." Hawk picked up his phone and sent a text. A few seconds later, his phone chimed with an answer. A second after that, it began to ring. "Jackson," he said when he answered. "You got Cooper there? I'm going to bring you a present." His eyes flicked up to land on Blake. "The guy who hacked your system. If you three can come to terms, he might be looking for a job." A pause. "One minute." Hawk dropped his phone to his side and looked at me. "You feel up for a ride?"

"To Atlanta? With you?" I asked. Hawk nodded. "Absolutely," I said with a grin.

"We'll be there in four hours," Hawk said. "Is the safe house free? I'm bringing Quinn, and we'll need a place to stay. Blake too." After another minute of listening, he said, "Got it. See you soon." Hawk hung up the phone. To Blake, he asked, "Where'd you leave your truck?"

"On the fire road," Blake said. "I don't need it. You can leave it there. I'll deal with it later."

"Somebody might steal it," I said.

Blake shrugged. "Then Merry Christmas to them." He rolled his shoulders back and lifted his chin. "How do we do this?"

"I need to bring Quinn back to the house," Hawk said. He looked to me. "Your family is going to need to see you before we head to Atlanta. It scared the hell out of all of us when you went missing."

Hawk rose and scooped up our empty camp mugs, bringing them to the sink and giving them a quick rinse from the water jug, saying, "I'll wash them later."

My heart brightened at the simple throwaway comment. He'd wash them later. Because we'd be back. Not because there was a crisis or a storm, but because we loved it here. Together.

The cabin I loved hadn't been the scene of our end, but of another beginning.

Hawk came back to stand in front of me. I heard Blake murmur something and pass us on his way outside. I wasn't paying attention. My eyes were glued to Hawk. He was smiling, his dark eyes warm as he lifted his hands to close over my shoulders, pulling me close enough for me to sink into his eyes.

"You're really okay? I'll call West if you want me to."

"And have your friend arrested?" I asked, lifting my hands to slide around the back of his neck, pulling his face down to mine.

"You're the one he kidnapped," Hawk said, a smile in his eyes, despite the serious subject matter. His lips brushed mine as he said, "You get final say."

I answered with a kiss, falling into Hawk, letting him take my weight as I licked at his lower lip and nipped lightly. I tilted my head to the side, fitting my mouth to his, every part of me alive at the way he kissed me back. Like he'd never get enough. Like I was all he wanted.

"I love you," he said, his lips at my ear.

Before I could say anything, he straightened and turned, dropping into a crouch. I didn't hesitate to climb on. My ankle wasn't in great shape, and we needed to get back to the Manor quickly. But mostly I didn't hesitate because there was no place I'd rather be than tangled up with Hawk. I leaned in and kissed the side of his neck.

"I love you too," I said. "So much I'm almost glad your friend tried to kidnap me. Otherwise, we'd be in the old folks' home before you worked up the nerve to kiss me."

Hawk grunted out a laugh and headed to the door. "I would have made a move," he argued. "I was kidding myself about staying away from you. You were meant to be mine from the beginning."

I didn't argue. Not when he was right. I'd been put on this earth to be with Hawk, and he was born to be mine. We had the rest of our lives in front of us, the adventures to come drawing closer with every beat of our hearts.

Epilogue
QUINN

Hawk got us in and out of Heartstone Manor in less than thirty minutes, dragging Griffen off with Blake for explanations while I took the elevator up to our room to pack our things and shower as fast as humanly possible. When I made my way back downstairs, I half expected to find West waiting with his deputies. Griffen was open-minded, but he was also my big brother.

The front hall was empty when I got there, carrying a backpack stuffed with enough clothes for both of us for a few days. Despite the craziness of the day so far, I still felt a little giddy, like I was skipping school. The picnic hike had been my last of the week, and my ankle needed a break. It was the perfect time to play hooky, and I was dying to meet the Sinclairs and get a glimpse of the life Hawk had lived before he came to Heartstone Manor.

Griffen, Hawk, and Blake emerged into the hall, Blake and Griffen with serious expressions, Hawk wearing a smile in his dark eyes. He spotted the backpack.

"Is that for both of us?"

"Yep." Before he could ask, I shrugged off the pack and handed it to him.

He slung it over his shoulder, turning to Griffen. "We'll be back in a day or two. I don't think you'll have any trouble here while we're gone."

We still didn't know who had hired the guy who'd broken into Harvey's office to get the necklace, or who the necklace belonged to, but I didn't care. That was a tomorrow problem.

"We're covered if we do. You and Quinn have fun. We'll take turns keeping an eye on your monster cat." He gave Blake a nod and followed us all to the door.

While I'd been upstairs, someone had brought Hawk's big SUV around to the front of the house. Hawk opened the passenger door and lifted me in, leaning across me to fasten my seat belt. I knew he knew I could do it myself, but then he wouldn't have an excuse to press a quick kiss to my lips as he snapped my belt in place. Blake took the back seat.

I fell asleep in the car, probably from the hike up the side of the mountain on a bum ankle. More likely from the adrenaline letdown. Three hours later, I opened my eyes as we pulled to a stop in Atlanta's congested afternoon traffic. Squinting out the window into the bright sun at a sea of glass, metal, and exhaust, I mumbled, "So many cars," and let my eyes drift shut.

I opened them again as we pulled into a parking garage, the gate raising automatically at our approach.

We drove down, pulling into a spot by the elevators marked *Guest*. A door opened, and a tall, dark-haired man emerged, his ice-blue eyes bright, a smile beaming from his handsome face.

"Cooper Sinclair," Hawk said before getting out of the car and rounding the front, meeting Cooper for a back-slapping hug.

Blake, Hawk, and I were sucked into a whirlwind of Sinclairs, all tall, dark, and broad-shouldered like Cooper. They accepted Blake into their midst with little comment, and couldn't stop beaming at me beside Hawk. It was impossible to miss their joy for their friend, or his at showing me off. I'd never thought of myself as a woman that a man would want to show off. I wasn't what society considered particularly beautiful or glamorous. I was just Quinn. But to Hawk, just Quinn was more than enough.

I expected the Sinclairs to drag Blake off to a conference room or something, but instead we went upstairs for drinks and an early dinner. Takeout arrived, and we ate at the long dining table in the penthouse apartment Cooper shared with his wife Alice, who also served as the office manager at Sinclair Security. I had a feeling there was very little that went on here that Alice didn't know. Knox's wife, Lily, had stayed home with all the kids, and Evers's wife, Summer, was out of town with a celebrity client, but I met the infamous Lucas Jackson and his wife, Charlie Winters.

Lucas was a little scary, taller and broader than every other man in the room, with dark hair and intense green eyes. At his side, Charlie was a bright spark, beautiful and funny, and more than enough to keep up with him.

Other than my sisters, I didn't know many women who came from families like mine. Charlie was a Winters, her family even more influential and notorious than my own. One complaint about overbearing brothers and we'd bonded. The second Griffen decided Heartstone was secure, I was determined to invite her for a visit.

In the end, we stayed two nights, the trip to Atlanta a revelation. I'd seen Hawk relax with Griffen a few times. I thought I knew what he was like when he loosened up. But not like this. These people were his family, like Griffen was his family, and now we were surrounded by them, all so happy to see him, happy he was with me. I was hugged and gently teased, welcomed thoroughly, leaving me with no doubt how much Hawk was loved. His wide smile told me he knew it, too.

That first night, after dinner, we went back downstairs to the safe house apartment the Sinclairs had given us for our visit. Blake was in a similar apartment across the hall. It was early, but we were both exhausted. After watching Blake's door close and lock behind him, Hawk turned to me with a gleam in his dark eyes.

"Finally alone," he said, backing me into our apartment and crowding me through the living room and into the bedroom.

I decided to make it easy on him and jumped, throwing my arms around his neck and wrapping my legs around his waist. Hawk caught me with a laugh, his arms tightening, his head dipping to rub his scruffy cheek against my neck.

"I loved meeting your family," I said, my breath

catching as his teeth closed over my jaw in a claiming bite.

"They loved meeting you. Alice was starting to think I made you up."

"Why did she think that?" I asked on a gasp, my head falling back as Hawk kissed down my neck, nuzzling my collarbone.

"Because I told her you were a fairy who sleeps with the bears and other woodland creatures, and rescued a mountain lion from the pound. And I told her you were the perfect woman."

"Not perfect," I said on a sharp exhale as I bounced on the mattress.

Hawk came down on top of me, his clever fingers going straight to the button of my jeans, stripping me naked before I could get my breath. "Perfect for me. The most perfect woman on the planet, and the only one for me."

I didn't get the chance to respond. Hawk's mouth closed over mine as I pulled at his shirt and unzipped his pants, desperate for him to be as naked as I was. After being kidnapped, forced to hike on my bum ankle, and then driving to a completely different state, I wouldn't have thought I had the energy for more than slow, lazy sex. Maybe after a nap.

Hawk proved me wrong. The second I felt his warm, naked skin against mine, the length of his cock nudging me, I went wild. I couldn't get him inside me fast enough. I needed him filling me; needed to claim him as mine now that the danger was gone and we were just us. Hawk and Quinn, two people in love. Two people meant for each other.

He must have felt the same way. He pushed forward, his cock filling me, the stretch, as always, at once almost too much and exactly enough. When he was seated to the hilt, he stopped for a heartbeat, his forehead pressed to mine. He was completely silent, except for the rasp of his breath, but I heard him anyway.

I love you.

I sank my fingers into his shoulders and held on for the ride, my own words spilling from my lips with every thrust.

I love you.

I love you.

I love you.

Until I couldn't speak at all and screamed out my orgasm instead, my heart so full I thought it might burst in my chest. After, Hawk brought me a warm, wet washcloth and cleaned me up, peppering kisses along my collarbone and whispering, "Good thing Coop had the safe houses soundproofed."

I was still giggling when he slipped into bed and pulled me into his arms.

"We have to talk," he said, his words serious but his eyes still laughing.

"About what?" I asked.

"About my plan."

"You have a plan?" I reached up to rub my palm along his cheek, loving the rasp of his end-of-the-day beard. "If you grow this out, you'd look like a real mountain man."

"You want me to grow it out?" he asked, letting me rub his cheek like I was petting Leo. I could almost feel his purr.

"Definitely," I said. "Now tell me about your plan. Does it involve moving into the cabin for two weeks and having nonstop sex? Because I'm on board for that."

"Kind of," Hawk admitted, looking a shade bashful for a second.

"Really?" I pushed up on my elbows and stared at him, enthusiastic and intrigued. "Tell me more."

"It involves me marrying you in the clearing where you used to hang your hammock after I have a chance to plant some flowers and build an arbor. And then a two-week honeymoon in the cabin."

I loved the picture he was painting in my mind. "Is this a proposal?" I asked, not seeing a ring and not caring in the least.

"No, not yet," he said, shaking his head. "I have to find your ring first. That might take a while. And you need a little time to make sure."

I captured his face between my palms to stop his shaking head. "I don't need time, and I don't need a ring."

"Maybe not," Hawk said, pressing a slow kiss to my lips. "But ever since I realized I didn't just want you, that I love you, and I want to spend the rest of my life with you, I've had a picture in my head of the ring I want to put on your finger. You don't have to wear it if you don't want to wear a ring. I know you don't wear much jewelry. But I need to give it to you."

"Then I'll wear it for the rest of my life," I said, punctuating my vow with a kiss. "As long as I get to keep you with me until we get engaged, you can take all the time you need."

"I'm not going anywhere," he said, stroking his hand down my hair. "I know how lucky I am. And I know I don't deserve you. But I don't care. I'm keeping you anyway."

I didn't argue. I was planning to spend the rest of my life proving to Hawk exactly how much he did deserve me. Because, like him, I knew exactly how lucky I was. I'd had a crush on him since the day he'd shown up at Heartstone Manor. A crush based on the gut instinct that Hawk Bristol was something special. But that crush, as powerful as it had been, was nothing next to what I felt now: a love so deep I knew it would last for the rest of my life.

We spent the next day packing in all the family time we could before we had to go back to Sawyers Bend. I spent some of the day hanging at Alice's desk, watching the comings and goings at Sinclair Security. The professional environment was mysterious and intimidating at first, then more than a little stifling. I couldn't stop thinking about all the people out there in the city, and the cars and the concrete, and the way the air smelled. As wonderful as everyone was, I could only take the city for so long. I missed my trees.

Hawk woke me the second day with a long, slow kiss. "Ready to go home?" he asked.

"I love your people, and we should come back soon, but yes," I said. Remembering the message I'd gotten late the night before, I continued. "And Sterling texted to say that Leo won't stop yowling at the door to our rooms. She said every time she opens it, and he sees it's not us, Leo glares at her and goes back to sulk on the sofa. If we don't get home soon, he might shred the room in protest. Even Griffen hasn't had luck calming him down. I don't know what he's going to do when the dog shows up."

Hawk had laughed and carried me to the shower. It took only a few minutes to pack. We swung by the office on our way out.

I wasn't surprised to find Lucas Jackson and Blake side by side, staring at lines of code on a monitor, deep in a discussion I couldn't hope to understand.

Blake swung his chair around, reaching out a hand to shake mine. "I owe you, Quinn Sawyer," he said. I started to demur, but he shook his head, squeezing my hand a little harder before letting go. "No. You extended me the grace of a forgiveness I didn't earn," he said, his formal words striking me silent. "I owe you," he repeated. "But even if I didn't, I would tell you—" He glanced up to Hawk. "It's going to take some digging to find out who hired that jackass, Randell, and sent him after the necklace. I'm going to find him for you."

"It's not like we haven't looked," Lucas said wryly, standing to give Hawk a one-armed hug in farewell.

"You looked," Blake said, lifting his chin at Lucas. "But I haven't looked."

"Arrogant," Lucas said under his breath, but it was with a smile. I had a feeling Emmet Blake was going to stick around Sinclair Security for a while.

Evers came around the corner, a wide grin on his face that I thought hid a little sadness at saying goodbye so quickly after Hawk's return.

"You sure you aren't coming back to Atlanta?" Evers asked.

"Hell no," Hawk said, his arm around my waist. "Once things calm down a little more at Heartstone, I'll have time to get the grounds in shape. And Quinn doesn't like the traffic in Atlanta."

I shook my head. I definitely did not like the traffic. "I'll take bears over cars any day," I said with a laugh. "But we'll be back for more visits. And once we get the Manor in better shape, you can all come visit whenever you want. It's not that far. Griffen would love it. We all would."

Evers gave me a tight hug, leaning down to whisper, "Take care of him. He's one of the best men I know."

"I will," I promised. It was an easy promise to make.

The ride back to Sawyers Bend was quiet. It was one of the things I loved most about Hawk—he wasn't a big talker. He didn't mind listening to me talk, but he also liked the quiet. Most people chattered just to fill the quiet as if silence was a threat. Not Hawk. He drove, his fingers twined with mine, both of us watching as the flat land rolled upward into the mountains, the wet spring landscape flashing by, a hint of green on the trees.

I let my mind wander, thinking of the work Parker was doing on our gatehouse, and the dog—our dog—on her way in only a few short weeks. I still wasn't sure I needed a guard dog, but Hawk had shown me the videos his friend Remy had sent of her following his commands, and I'd fallen headfirst in love. She was fierce and smart, and she was going to be mine. *Ours.*

My thoughts drifted to the hikes I wanted to take

Hawk on after my ankle was fully healed. He'd mentioned he liked fishing. I had a few secret spots I rarely shared with clients but couldn't wait to share with Hawk.

I was still half in my daydreams when we walked into the Manor, only a little late for dinner. Thanks to a last-minute text, our places at the table were set and waiting for us. I wasn't expecting the raised voices that greeted us, arguments shooting back and forth across the packed table. Most of the family was here, and it seemed like they were all yelling.

"What's going on?" I asked in confusion.

Griffen was the only one who looked remotely calm. "Cole Haywood called," he said, his voice grave. "Ford is being released on Monday."

Relief hit me like a joyous sledgehammer, tears springing into my eyes as I leaned into Hawk's side, my knees a little weak.

Ford was coming home. Where he belonged.

Then it hit me. Why was everyone arguing? I looked to Griffen. "Is he coming *home* home? Back to Heartstone?" It occurred to me that he didn't have to. He'd been cut from the will. He could only stay if Griffen let him. "Are you—"

I didn't have to finish the question. Griffen gave a sharp nod. "He doesn't belong in prison, and despite everything, this is his home. I already made it clear to Haywood that he should come straight here."

"Then why—" I looked at the rest of the family in confusion. Tenn was arguing with Royal, Parker glaring at Sterling.

Griffen shook his head. "I think they're just in shock. And—" Griffen shrugged. "Ford getting out of prison doesn't erase the past." He gave me a gentle smile. "I know you have reason to be grateful to Ford, but I'm not the only one in this house he hurt. This is his home, but he might not find it a welcoming one. Not at first."

"Is that why you don't look happy?" I asked, still confused.

Griffen shook his head, his eyes flashing to Hawk's before they came back to mine. "I'm willing to give Ford a chance. And I'm glad he's getting out." He shook his head slowly. "But I don't like the circumstances."

Hawk nodded knowingly. I didn't get it. What circumstances? Ford shouldn't have been in prison in the first place. Now he'd be getting out. That was a good thing.

"The camera," Hawk said, looking down at me. "It's been missing since your father's murder. After the failed attempt to kill Ford in prison, the camera with evidence of Ford's alibi just happens to turn up in a pawn shop? The judge didn't like the timing either. That's why he took so long to make his decision."

"He allowed Ford to withdraw his guilty plea," Griffen said, raising his voice to be heard over Avery's shout at Royal. "And based on the new evidence, the DA has dropped the charges against Ford, but—"

"I still don't get it," I said. "How is that not good news? The charges are dropped and now they can find the real killer. Ford is coming home."

"It's not that it isn't good news," Hawk said. "But it's harder to get rid of someone in prison than you'd think.

It's not the Wild West in there like on TV. Someone wants to eliminate Ford. And now he won't be in prison anymore. He'll be out here."

Understanding hit me. "You think whoever had that camera is the one who made sure Ford ended up in prison in the first place, and now they're using it to get him out so they can kill him?" My question ended in a squeak of anxiety.

Griffen and Hawk looked at each other, exchanging a silent communication I couldn't decipher. Neither of them answered my question.

Hawk pulled me into his arms and pressed a kiss to the top of my head. "Don't worry," he promised. "I'll keep your brother safe."

I melted into him. "I know you will," I said, drawing strength from Hawk even as I saw his promise hadn't erased the worry in Griffen's eyes.

Ford was coming home.

It was up to us to make sure he lived long enough to enjoy his freedom.

TURN THE PAGE FOR A SNEAK PEEK OF BROKEN HEART, BOOK SEVEN OF THE HEARTS OF SAWYERS BEND

Broken Heart
SNEEK PEAK

CHAPTER ONE
STERLING

"Give me the statue."

Forrest stared at me, his green eyes surprised, then carefully blank. "Sterling, hi." He paused.

"You heard me," I said.

"What?" he asked, shaking his head.

Of course, he was confused. After refusing to speak to him for over a year, I was standing on his doorstep just before midnight, demanding he hand over a priceless family heirloom.

"I need to see the statue," I clarified, impatient. "Let me in."

Forrest still wasn't getting it. Why would he?

He didn't know that the statue had been haunting me. Teasing me. Demanding I come here and see if I knew what I thought I knew.

For most of the last year, that ugly little statue of Emperor Vitellius had meant nothing to me. Nothing and everything. The statue was the reason for my broken heart. It was the reason Forrest Powell had come to Sawyers Bend and taken a job at my family's Inn. The reason he'd pursued me and made me think he loved me. The statue was the cause of all my heartbreak.

Except that it wasn't. Forrest Powell was the cause. He was the one who'd chosen to lie. He was the one who'd used me for his own ends. The statue of Vitellius was innocent. And while Forrest's secrets had broken me, the statue of Vitellius held its own secrets. Secrets that might have the power to set me free.

Even after a year, the sting of his betrayal hadn't faded. I couldn't bring myself to look him in the eye. I stared carefully at his left ear and insisted, "I need to see the statue. Just let me in."

Without another word, Forrest stepped back to allow me through the door of his house. I'd never been here. He bought the place after I dumped him, putting down roots when I'd expected him to walk away. He had what he'd come for, after all.

It had been weird, not knowing where Forrest lived. Too many nights, I woke, dreaming of the statue of Vitellius, until I'd hunted down Hawk, our head of security, and asked him for Forrest's address.

Hawk knew all. He had a file on Forrest. He gave it to me, grudgingly, and only after asking, "You sure you know what you're doing?"

"Nope," I'd answered. "But I need it anyway." Feeling

the weight of his brotherly concern, I'd added, "It's about the statue. It's not personal. I promise."

He'd grunted and given me the address, saying only, "Be careful."

At the moment, I didn't care about being careful. I just wanted to see the statue. Following Forrest into the house, I had an impression of high ceilings, wood beams, and glass, but that was it. I didn't bother to look around. We came to a stop in his modern chrome and concrete kitchen, and I turned to face him, my eyes on the frayed collar of his t-shirt.

"Why do you need to see the statue?" he asked, his voice low. He sounded cautious. Good. He should be. And maybe if he felt cautious, he'd give me what I wanted without an argument.

"I can't explain until I look at it. I know it's late, but this is important." I could have waited for a better time. I could have come to see him in his office. But after months of that fucking statue teasing me, the night before, the answer had come to life like a puzzle piece snapping into place. I'd gone back and forth over it all day, until I realized I couldn't wait a second longer, no matter how much it hurt to be this close to him.

I could feel Forrest's eyes on my face, assessing me. "I'll get it," he finally agreed, turning to head for a hallway off the kitchen.

"Get a pad of paper and a pen, too. I forgot to grab one on the way out of the house," I said, yanking out a chair and sitting at the kitchen table, then popping back up, prowling around the room for the switch that would turn on the light above the table. "I need a light. Do you have a magnifying glass?" I called after Forrest.

I sat back down, tapping my fingers on the table. I was so close to finding out if I was right. I needed to know, needed it enough to put myself through this pain. I'd lied when I said the sting hadn't faded. This wasn't a sting. Being this close to Forrest was fucking agony.

People say time heals all wounds, but it wasn't doing a damn thing for this one. It was all my own fault, too. Not the breakup—that was one hundred percent Forrest's fault. His lies and his stupid attempts to convince me that he'd made a mistake, that he cared about me. I wasn't falling for that bullshit again. Losing him the first time was bad enough; the ache in my chest a raw thing that never went away. Not that I could admit that. Like the perverse creature I could be, I'd convinced my brothers not to fire Forrest, setting myself up for the torture that was sharing the small town of Sawyers Bend with the man I never wanted to see again.

I took after my father, arrogance my failing. I was too proud to admit it was killing me, having Forrest this close. I could have changed my mind and asked my brothers to fire him. They would have done it gladly. I could have asked West, our police chief, to run Forrest out of town. West was notoriously by the book, but he might have done it for me if I'd asked.

But I wouldn't ask, couldn't ask. Everyone I loved had seen me at my worst. The whole goddamn town had seen me at my worst. Over and over. Now, I was clawing my way to my best, and I wasn't going to let a single person see my broken, bleeding heart. Especially not Forrest Powell.

I waited for him to come back with the statue, my heart speeding up in my chest. I needed to see it. I needed to know.

I hadn't thought about the statue at first. The shock of Forrest's lies had clouded everything. It had been hard enough just getting out of bed in the morning. I didn't have any room for wondering about the statue that had brought Forrest to me in the first place.

Later, after the worst of it became bearable, the statue began to invade my dreams. A rock crystal bust of Emperor Vitellius on a white marble base embellished with bronze medallions. The whole thing was only six inches tall. As a piece of art, it wasn't particularly valuable. More than that, the bust of Emperor Vitellius was straight-up ugly. The rock crystal carving was mostly transparent, giving him a ghostly look that wasn't enough to hide the petulant, whiny expression on his face.

As a child, Vitellius had reminded me of my father, Prentice. So much so, that after my father had stolen the bust from Forrest's father, I'd imagined he took it because the Vitellius reminded him of himself. Forrest's father had a kind smile, unlike Prentice. Back then, I didn't know that my father hadn't just stolen the statue from Forrest's father, he'd taken his company as well. And Forrest's father, distraught at the loss of everything he'd worked for, had taken his own life.

As a child, I hadn't known any of that. I'd only known that the Vitellius fascinated me. It was ugly. Graceless. But something about it had tugged at me. The Vitellius statue had secrets. I'd hide behind the thick velvet drapes in my father's office to poke and prod at the statue, asking it in whispers to tell me its secrets.

It hadn't. Until one day, the Vitellius whispered back.

I didn't tell anyone what I'd learned. I knew what a secret was. And then, the statue had disappeared, and, in the way of children, I'd forgotten about it. A year ago, the Vitellius reappeared, the linchpin of my failed romance.

Forrest had come to Sawyers Bend to find the statue and steal it back. He'd come to get revenge on the Sawyers for ruining his father's life. In the end, he hadn't done either. It hadn't taken Forrest long to figure out that my siblings and I were nothing like our father. And Forrest had ended up buying the little statue at auction, erasing the need to steal it back from my father. The Vitellius was his again.

And I'd been the fallout.

Forrest returned, setting the statue of Vitellius on the table in front of me, followed by a spiral-bound notebook open to a blank page. He placed a pen and a small magnifying glass beside it. "Are you going to tell me what you're doing here?" he asked.

I ignored him, picking up the Vitellius and turning it over so I could get a better look at the bottom of the marble base. I still couldn't see it, though Forrest had told us it was there. Picking up the small magnifying glass and turning on my phone's flashlight, I leaned in, squinting, willing my eyes to focus.

There they were: numbers and letters in a long string, engraved by laser. Neat, precise, and so tiny I'd never seen them before. The few people who knew about the string of numbers and letters thought it was an account number, but no one had been able to find the source of the accounts. According to Forrest, those accounts were supposed to be stuffed full of cash. The promise of all that cash was the reason my father had stolen the Vitellius in the first place. And that cash was the reason I'd knocked on Forrest's door after all this time.

It was Forrest's money, but he couldn't find it without me. Because I knew something no one else did. It wasn't an account number engraved on the bottom of the statue. It was a code. And I was the only one who knew how to break it.

Or at least I hoped I did. I could be completely off base. It's not like I was an expert. More like a closet math geek who had always loved the lore of secret codes. In high school, they'd fascinated me. By the time I was old enough to do something useful with that fascination, I'd been neck deep in rebellion, wasting my time drinking and chasing boys, my budding intellectual curiosity extinguished.

It had taken me years to come back to myself. So much time wasted, leaving me in my mid-twenties with a college degree and a roof over my head, but not much else. I was getting my shit together, piece by piece. I had a job. I thought I might have a plan for a career. But I was still pretty much a mess. And then I started dreaming of the Vitellius. I didn't know what it meant, thought it might be my broken heart dreaming of Forrest the only way it could bear.

It turned out the dreams weren't about Forrest at all. They were my brain trying to remind me of the past and those stolen moments behind the heavy velvet curtains. The dreams were the Vitellius whispering his secrets to me one more time.

A few days ago, I woke in the middle of the night, my eyes flying open to stare at my ceiling, seeing everything at once. The numbers were a code, and I would have bet the little I had that I was the only one who knew the key.

Taking a deep breath, I let it out slowly, my mind racing. I'd needed to see those laser-engraved numbers and letters to know. And now that I had, I had a decision to make. A part of me wanted to trust Forrest, but I wasn't a fool. I'd done a lot of foolish things in my short life, far too many to count, but I wasn't a fool, and I wouldn't be one now.

Setting the Vitellius on its base, I leaned back in the chair and crossed my arms over my chest. "I know how to find the money," I said, steeling myself to meet his eyes. I expected to see greed or triumph, or perhaps even disdain.

I didn't expect blank confusion. He looked like he hadn't even heard me.

"Forrest," I said, my tone sharp, snapping awareness back into his eyes. "I said, I can find the money."

This time, he heard me. I expected him to laugh. Smarter people than myself had tried to find Alan Buckley's lost fortune. My own father had spent years trying to figure it out. An annoyingly familiar voice in my head demanded, *What makes you so special?*

Instead, Forrest said, "I don't care about the money."

"Yeah?" I asked, raising an eyebrow. That had been his story when we found out why he was really in

Sawyers Bend. He didn't care about the money, he just wanted me, blah blah blah. I hadn't bought it then, and I wasn't buying it now.

He'd already proven he was a liar. Forrest's father had hundreds of millions of dollars after he sold his first company, and he'd hidden it all. It could be over a billion by now.

That was too much money to not care about, no matter who you were. I'd grown up in a house that was practically a castle. These days, I was mostly broke, but after the way I grew up, I knew better than anyone; money can't buy happiness, not even close, but it sure as hell doesn't hurt.

Forrest leveled his dark green eyes on me, no trace of humor in his expression. "Chasing the money cost me enough. I don't care about it anymore."

"Well, I do," I snapped.

No change in his expression.

I tried a different tack. "I'll find it for you. For a cut."

At that, he straightened, frozen for a second before the side of his mouth curled up, and he crossed his arms over his chest. "How big a cut?"

And there was the CFO my brothers had hired. After his dumb assertion that he didn't care about the money, I couldn't resist poking at him. "Well, if you don't care about the money, how about I get all of it?"

The side of his mouth quirked higher, light sparking in his green eyes. "I don't think so. You can't get the money without my statue, and technically, it's my inheritance."

"Well," I said, "since I'm pretty sure the inheritance

my father left me is a big fat nothing, maybe the finder's fee on yours will make a nice nest egg. Fifty percent."

The grin disappeared from Forrest's face. "Ten." So much for not caring about the money.

"Forty-five," I countered.

"Fifteen."

I looked down at the Vitellius, then steeled myself for the impact and looked Forrest dead in the eyes. My chest ached, a raw wound that stole my breath. Deep inside, I silently screamed, *Why? Why did you have to fuck everything up by being such an asshole?* And beneath that, the question I couldn't stop asking. *Why couldn't you love me?*

Fucking hell, it hurt to look at him. It took everything I had to hide my heart.

Maybe Forrest was right. Maybe the money wasn't worth what I'd lose chasing it. My heart. My self-respect. My sanity. I'd let this man bring me to my knees. I'd crawled out of a bottle after my father died and my oldest brother came home. I'd spent the last year getting my life together. Was I going to risk all that hard work just to fill my bank account?

The problem was, it was only partly about the money. I had room and board covered, but not much more. I was working for my sister during the day and studying when I could, but my potential new career would take time to pay off.

I was sure the trust my father had left me was empty. It would be five years before I'd find out, but knowing Prentice Sawyer, I couldn't believe he'd left me a single penny. I wanted a nest egg. Security. I never wanted to ask anyone for anything ever again.

More than the money, I wanted to solve the puzzle. I needed to solve it. For months, the Vitellius had been haunting me until I finally figured out what the little statue was trying to tell me. I could do this. I wanted to figure out what no one else had, to prove to myself and everyone else that I could do it. I wanted to beat my father and walk away laughing, my bank account stuffed full.

Would it be worth it? To be this close to Forrest, to feel this stabbing agony every time I was stupid enough to look him in the eyes? Definitely not for fifteen percent. But maybe...

I shoved my chair back from the kitchen table and stood. "Twenty-five. I have better things to do with my time than negotiate with you. Twenty-five percent, or I'm walking out the door."

ARE YOU READY FOR STERLING & FORREST'S STORY?

Visit IvyLayne.com/BrokenHeart
to see what happens next!

Never Miss a New Release:

Join Ivy's Reader's Group

@ ivylayne.com/readers
&
Get two books for free!

About Ivy Layne

Ivy Layne has had her nose stuck in a book since she first learned to decipher the English language. Sometime in her early teens, she stumbled across her first Romance, and the die was cast. Though she pretended to pay attention to her creative writing professors, she dreamed of writing steamy romance instead of literary fiction. These days, she's neck deep in alpha heroes and the smart, sexy women who love them.

Married to her very own alpha hero (who rubs her back after a long day of typing, but also leaves his socks on the floor). Ivy lives in the mountains of North Carolina where she and her other half are having a blast raising two energetic little boys. Aside from her family, Ivy's greatest loves are coffee and chocolate, preferably together.

For More Information:
www.ivylayne.com
books@ivylayne.com
Facebook.com/AuthorIvyLayne
Instagram.com/authorivylayne/

Also by Ivy Layne

Don't Miss Out on New Releases, Exclusive Giveaways, and More!!

Join Ivy's Readers Group @ ivylayne.com/readers

THE HEARTS OF SAWYERS BEND

Stolen Heart

Sweet Heart

Scheming Heart

Rebel Heart

Wicked Heart

Wild Heart

Broken Heart

THE UNTANGLED SERIES

Unraveled

Undone

Uncovered

THE WINTERS SAGA

The Billionaire's Secret Heart (Novella)

The Billionaire's Secret Love (Novella)

The Billionaire's Pet

The Billionaire's Promise

The Rebel Billionaire

The Billionaire's Secret Kiss (Novella)

The Billionaire's Angel

Engaging the Billionaire

Compromising the Billionaire

The Counterfeit Billionaire

THE BILLIONAIRE CLUB

The Wedding Rescue

The Courtship Maneuver

The Temptation Trap

Made in the USA
Las Vegas, NV
14 May 2024